Dottie Rexford

Cora Pooler

CORA RETURNS

info@barringerpublishing.com
Copyright © 2020
All rights reserved.

Barringer Publishing, Naples, Florida
www.barringerpublishing.com

Cover, graphics, layout design by Linda S. Duider

ISBN: 978-1-7339837-8-5

Library of Congress Cataloging-in-Publication Data

Printed in U.S.A.

Cora Returns
Dottie Rexford

This Book is Dedicated to:

My Sisters
Kathy 'Midge' Schickler
Sandy Cliver
and
in memory of
Jeanne Dailey

Appreciation

When I reflect on the birth and growth of *Cora Returns,* I realize how many have been a part of its journey. The critical, encouraging thoughts and suggestions offered in my Avon Park, Lake Placid, and Sinclairville writing groups have made this book better than it would have been without them. I thank them with an appreciative heart. I am also beholden to Jeff Schlesinger and all those at Barringer Publishing who took my words and encapsulated them into a fine work. Even more, I am grateful for their patience and kindness when I was, perhaps, a little more stubborn than I should have been. There have been so many who have encouraged me during the writing of *Cora Returns.* I thank you all.

Chapter One

It was October. The cattails were bursting their brown, furry skins, spreading tiny pieces of fluff in the ditches and marshes. Orange, fat pumpkins waited to be plucked and cut into scary faces. Mums spread in brilliant masses, and the leaves on trees, so rich in color and thick on limbs were beginning to drop, to slowly blanket the earth with a crunchy, copper cover. It was an unusually warm October. Reluctant to share their brilliant bits of color, trees and vines held onto their leaves as long as they could. A delicious, pungent odor erupted from the vineyards. Ripe, plump grapes burst with sweet juices, as they hung in bunches and were picked from the vines. The air had lost the heaviness of summer. Instead, there was a fresh, invigorating crispness marbleizing the warm air. It pleasured the lungs as it mingled with the acrid scent of ripe fruits, vegetables and flowers, penetrating the nose with an agreeable bitterness.

Late in that month, Daniel and I drove through the country savoring the rich colors and the musky, odorous mist of fall skimming through our open windows. It was the month of our anniversary, and each year, we celebrated the whole of it, with remembrance and gratitude for all the days of our love.

That night as I lay sleeping beside Daniel, he died—my husband, my completion. He died. I have few clear memories of the year that followed; yet even now, when I relive the discovery of his death, the pain pierces as bright and sharp as before. It is the aftermath that fades. As the sadness shadowed and a tenuous cover of acceptance eroded the unbearable aftertaste of death, my mind began to leave that place and wander to the days that were to come. The assumption of full responsibility for the company Daniel had established was mine. I was well-versed in the expertise demanded by that charge, but I didn't want it. I tried. Though my body and mind were weary, depleted of desire and aspiration, I tried. I failed. But in the wisdom that pushed forward to the front of commitment, I realized there was someone who could do what I could not.

Someone, who held as purposeful, as did Daniel and I, the need for fuller, productive crops, throughout the undeveloped nations—Daniel's dream. And mine. Marie Zelinski. Trained by me and by Daniel, she knew the complete works and goals of his vision. She comprehended and valued its worth. The challenge was offered. She accepted. I was free.

Before I left, I penned a letter to Daniel, took it to the cemetery, and read it to him.

Dear Daniel,

I miss you. When you left, you took all that was beautiful to me, all that was precious. But you didn't leave me empty. Every fragment inside my skin was filled with sorrow. The pain infused all thought, all action. Yet the spirit is a mighty thing, Daniel, and slowly, stealthily, it dispels the piercing sting and renders it bearable. I was able to walk through the forest of the unfinished business you'd left.

I'm going back to Wander Lane. Perhaps, I'll live again in the Amish community. Perhaps, not. Though the simple loveliness, the clearly defined mind and body boundaries appeal to my weary soul, I don't know if they always will. Beneath my drying tears, I fear the old need for thinking my own thoughts, deciding my own actions, is growing, and I don't know if I can temper my soul to adjust to 'The Way.'

There are so many gifts you have given me—Love. Happiness. Kindness. Knowledge. Acceptance. God. It was you who told me to take the love He has given, the love for another, to put it in my heart in a special place and treasure it. Nourish it. Keep it clean, pure and loving, without lustful thought or deed for another. Let it bring joy. Let it give warmth to the other. And that's how you loved me. I will not forget you. You will stay in that special place and be treasured forever.

I pray one day I will be with you again.

Love always, Cora

I buried the letter in the soil that held Daniel's body.

Chapter Two

I traveled through the hours of sunshine and into the night. I passed through cities, villages, spreading fields, wooded lands, rolling hills, leaving my English home behind me. I was going back to an old and dearly loved place, never forgotten, from which I had been banished—self-banished, banished by my own deeds, my own choices. The Amish world. It was dark when I came upon Wander Lane. The only light a whispering glow of seeping, swirling radiance emanating from old, ornate streetlamps. There were no figures walking the dimly lit sidewalks. No one to be seen in the flickering light dancing over storefront glass, offering a glimpse of shelves and wares within. It was too late. All was closed. I slowed the car to a sideling pace, and my eyes, wandering over the empty shops, halted when they saw the words, precious words, painted on Harriet's eatery window . . . Harriet's Homemade Soups and Hearty Sandwiches. I stopped and gripping the steering wheel with both hands, bent my head and closed my eyes. A scant spread of tears flowed and wet my cheeks. The image of Harriet filled my mind, not dead, but worse, a breathing body. Nothing else. Mind gone, she would neither remember me, nor would she remember any of our secrets. My friend, Dianna, my only sporadic source of information, had written and told me of Harriet's decline. Without her letter, I would not have known. I would have thought Harriet was still there to share what could not be told to anyone else, to love me without judgement, to console the sorrows of my heart.

Biting my lip hard, changing heart pain to physical hurt, I pressed my foot on the accelerator and turned the car to make its way up the hill to home, my home, my Amish home. The home that *had* been mine . . . until I left. Shunned once more. Ten years ago.

The night was dark, dense. There was no earth light. No stars shining through the clouds. No house lamps burning oil saved for wakened bodies. The only lights to lead me home were car beams and the soft glow of memories rising from heart to brain, their faded edges sharpening as they rose. They were all I needed.

I came to the place on the road where it leveled for a space, and I stopped the car, got out, stood there, turned, looked down the hill to the village, saw the dim glow of streetlights, remembered standing there thirty years ago, the baby in my arms. I carried her down that hill, in the dark, and I left her in Olivia's house, on a chair when Olivia left the room. Laid her on the chair, looked at her a long moment and then walked out of the house. Left the baby. Not mine. My sister Lily's. Though they didn't know then. My community. The Amish. They thought the wee one was mine. And so, they shunned me. I could not tell them truth. Even though thirty years gone, as I looked down the road I'd trod that night, and pictured Olivia's house in my mind, the pain of leaving that small body was sharp.

I could hear the wind murmuring softly through the trees, the gentle rustle of leaves touching, sliding against those near, retreating, connecting again, so briefly . . . a teasing, tender song. Feeling the wonder of it, sensing the passage to a time long ago, wanting to change that time, relive it, make it better, and thinking to send my plea to God, I raised my eyes to the sky. And, as if in answer, the clouds broke apart and revealed the stars they'd been hiding. And I wondered, does my secret, my guilt, ride on those stars? One star? Many stars? Is there a star for every secret held within our world, or is each of us allotted a single star? And if I had but one, would my star be the biggest?

A child. Left on a chair. Robbed of her heritage. Annabelle, renamed Talitha, a child reborn. My niece. Still Annabelle in my heart. And now, no one to know or to tell of her whereabouts. With memory gone, not even Harriet to know or to tell. Just me. Unless the midwife and the mother who took her were still alive, and if they had told. But I thought not. The mother had sworn the midwife to secrecy, and turning from the stillborn child, the grieving mother replaced her baby with another's living child. Annabelle. Talitha. She took her back to the home of her unsuspecting, unquestioning husband. She took her back to her unsuspecting, unquestioning Amish community. My Annabelle, her Talitha.

The clouds drifted and joined. Covered the whole of the sky. The earth was dark again; the stars with their secrets, gone. I got in my car and went back down the hill, hoping to find the motel I'd slept in so many years before when I tried to return to my former life, my Amish life, as I was doing once more.

The motel was there. Same place. Same facade. I checked in. Different owner. No smile.

"Name?" she said crisply, eyes on the paper before her.

"No computer?" I looked across the counter, saw no evidence

of current technology.

"Don't need one." Eyes still trained on the paper, her words fell sharp from her mouth. "Name?"

"Cora Pooler."

She looked up and studied me, rubbed her eyes. "You Amish?"

I smiled. She knew the name. "Maybe."

"Humph." She took my money, handed me my key card. "Room's around the back. Check out at 11:00."

"I might need the room longer."

"Well, if you do, make up your mind soon." She sniffed. "Can't save a room lessen it's paid in advance."

"I'll take my chances."

"Don't have to act hoity-toity."

I shrugged. "Didn't think I was."

Frowning, her faced furrowed in deep, ditched lines, she leaned forward and peered at me. "You don't act like no Amish woman to me."

"Didn't say I was. Just said *maybe*."

"Humph."

"See you in the morning." I reached and patted her hand.

"Not me, you won't. I ain't working no twenty-four-hour days," she said, pulling her hand away, tapping her fingers on the counter.

"We'll see," I said.

I could feel her eyes watching me as I walked out the door. I smiled and fumbled through the dark to my car. I got in and drove around the building. I reckoned the old lady was on the phone and talking even before I slipped the key in its slot and pushed open the door to my room.

Chapter Three

I woke late. I'd slept well. If there had been dreams, I didn't remember them. Burrowing into the comfort of pillow and rumpled sheets, I smiled. It was the first morning a soft cover of peace blanketed my waking thoughts of Daniel's death and dissolved the tears that waited behind my lids.

The bed was too comfortable to leave. It was good to lie and think, to put Daniel away for awhile and plan my day. With eyes closed, I envisioned my choices. The farm. I could go to the farm. Drive by. Hope to see, even briefly, a glimmer of *Maem* and *Da,* or the boys, their families, my sister Violet. But I was reluctant to make that choice. Not yet. I wasn't sure I was strong enough to tackle probable shunning . . . even knowing the quickest glimpse of family would bring immeasurable joy. Should I seek out Aaron—old and good friend, Aaron? Could he maybe be married now? To Violet? Lose one sister, take another. I didn't know. Dianna, my Wander Lane informant, had sold the little, Amish, village house that Olivia, appreciating the hospice service Dianna had bestowed upon her, had willed to her, and wonder of wonders, Dianna had married Oliva's old lawyer, the husband of Diana's ill, now deceased, sister, and the man who, while her sister was bed-ridden, partook of an affair with Olivia. Life is filled with extraordinary and baffling twists and turns. And Dianna and said lawyer, Mr. Sweete, had *flown the coop*. My gossip reporter was gone.

There was Harriet, but she with her diminishing awareness, though I loved her dearly, was probably not a good source for trustworthy news. Harriet's niece, Bailey, on the other hand, would have a take on every happening in Wander Lane. Trustworthy? Not a chance. I searched my mind for a knowing, principled and truthful person who knew the history of Wander Lane's prior ten years and came up with one person. The sheriff. Lowell Parker. Cantankerous. Rigid. Sarcastic Lowell. Not the most loveable man in the world, but he was honest.

The bed was no longer comfortable. It had bred a decision inspiring irritation of great magnitude. I would go to the sheriff's office, and he would tell me all I wanted to know . . . if it suited to do so. I didn't like him, and he didn't like me. But it was the best choice . . . for the moment. And I still had unanswered questions.

There weren't many changes in the sheriff's entry room. Tilly was still there, older, yet preserving a youthful prettiness. The area around her desk, and the desk itself, was clean, orderly, correct. Across the way, the waiting section's puzzles, coloring books, and magazines, precisely, shared space with a box of tissues and a box of crayons.

There was a difference. A change. On either side of the door leading to Lowell's office were new posters. Van Gogh was gone. On one side of the door was an enlarged picture of an open-mouthed women armed with banners grasped tight and placards raised high. My head could hear their cries for justice, the need that outweighed decorum. And on the other side of the door were two men standing in a ring, armored with puffed-out gloves, ridiculously punching each other, proving the strength of their manhood. I smiled. Tilly knew how to retaliate.

Turning from my perusal, I saw her, sitting at her desk, smiling, looking at me.

"You're back," she said.

"Uh-huh," I nodded.

"Cora Pooler." She shook her head. "Won't Sheriff Lowell be pleased." And she laughed. "I don't think so."

I shrugged my shoulders. "Is he in?"

"I'll buzz."

"No, don't. I'll just go in."

It was her turn to shrug. "I'll say I was in the little girl's room if he yells . . . but I don't think he will. I have a feeling his anger will outweigh words and he'll just sit and smolder awhile."

He did. I walked in his office. He looked up and saw me, his lips tightened and his face masked empty. But I knew the anger behind it.

"Your office is still a mess," I said. "Have you not found time in the last ten years to file a few sheets of paper, or even, maybe, throw some away?"

Not taking his eyes from my face, he lifted the phone and growled into it, *"Next time buzz."*

"She wasn't at her desk," I lied.

He stared at me, silent. I waited. I could sense his teeth clenched tight.

"Isn't it just a little petty to be so angry just because

someone walks unannounced into your office?" I said, lifting my eyebrows.

He glared at me.

"If you want, I'll go back out and push the buzzer myself. If that will make you happy."

He grunted, half-smiled. "Cora Pooler. My nemesis. And I'd be happy to see you, if I didn't know there was a bushel of questions overflowing in that head of yours. Of which, I probably have no answers. At least none I want to give you."

"There are," I said quietly.

I watched the tiny bit of smile leave his lips. He looked older. Older than the damage ten years should have laid upon his face. Too many wrinkles. Sunken cheeks. My eyes lowered, gazed upon his hands clasped together on a clump of messy papers. Veined hands. Darkly purpled, plump with blood. Heavy veins ribboned across his aging hands, rivaling the hands that lay strong, ready to tackle, to rescue, sitting in my bank of ten-year-old memories.

I sighed. "We grow old." I looked back up into his face. "Yet, you're still here. Not yet retired. Have you thought of it?"

"No."

I smiled. His answer was vehement.

"You're no spring chicken yourself, Cora Pooler."

"That I'm not. Fifty-eight. It's been thirty years since I walked that baby down the hill. Twenty-five since that baby's mother, Lily, died, drowned in that damn creek."

His eyebrows lifted. "Damn?" he said. "Your Amish blood all used up?"

"It's a frequently used Amish word," I said, smiled. "But not quite in the same context."

"You're here to ask about Lily, aren't you?" Lips pressed

together, he shook his head with weary motion. "You think I've got answers."

"Do you?"

"Yes, and I told you ten years ago." He leaned across the desk. Eyes squinted. Forehead furrowed. "Suicide. But you didn't listen. Thought I was teasing. I wasn't."

"I didn't believe you then, and I don't now. You can be a non-humorous jokester."

"You think she was murdered."

I heard his words as a statement. "It could be so."

"An Amish boy?" He leaned back in his chair, lifted his eyebrows, and grinned.

"Yes."

"The father?"

"*Yes.*" And I looked at his face, so sure, so smug.

"Jacob Lapp." He cocked his head. "Good old Amish boy. Now a good old Amish man. Twenty-five years gone, and you would still condemn him. You're forgetting, Cora, the Amish don't kill." He straightened in his chair. The words clipped stern from his mouth. "You're talking murder, Cora. And I repeat, *Amish men don't kill.*"

"Nor do Amish women. And by your reasoning, Lily couldn't have committed suicide, couldn't have murdered her own flesh. Your words, not mine. *The Amish don't kill.* Even themselves."

"Have you been to the cemetery, Cora?"

"No." A trembling started in my hands. I clutched them together to stop it, could feel it stretching into my torso, a shaking I could not control.

"Maybe you should."

"I can't," I whispered.

"Why not?"

"Because I would see the marker, and the pain, the guilt, would come back, so great again. So great." My clenched hands rose to rest on my chin, and I pressed my arms tight against my chest to keep my body from rocking my shame.

"Guilt?"

"I took her baby from her."

He bit his lip.

"I left her baby on a chair. I walked away. *I left her baby on a chair and walked away.*" I could barely say the words, but I did, and yet they stayed within, repeating themselves over and over across the unforgiving memories in my head.

"I think you need to see the grave."

I heard his words fall gently, and I knew I should listen. I didn't want to. The underlying kindness of them stilled me with a frightening foreboding.

"Will you go?" he asked quietly.

"I'll try." I covered my face with my hands and nodded.

"I'll send Tilly with you."

"No." I shook my head, then kneaded my hands over my forehead, drew them down, pressed tight, along the sides of my face, rubbed my cheeks hard, and regained control. "I'll go alone."

Forcing my eyes to stay focused on the road, not straying to sneak longing glances at the fields, the pastures and barns, the homes on either side, I drove to the dirt path that would take me up the hill that housed the dead Amish. At the bottom of the hill, I parked the car, got out and looked at the sky. The clouds, weighted by their heavy, gray, water-filled underbellies, moved slow and laboriously, and were pushed by a wind that promised, by the very nature of spring, a drift to greater velocity. I encouraged my feet to walk quickly over the hard, packed, soil, to reach the green patch of carpeted graves, before the rain fell.

I stopped at the fence that guarded the graves, pushed the gate open and went through it, and stood on the ground of the dead. Once there, I could not move. I looked upon the rows of stone slabs, the markers all alike, plain and simple. Like those who lay beneath them. One of them was engraved *Lily Pooler.* I lifted my hands and dropped my face into them, pushed my fingers against my closed eyes to keep my tears in, protecting the images and the thoughts behind them. Lily pulled from the creek, carried home, washed, taken to the village for embalming. Lily returned home, dressed in white and laid out in a simple wooden casket. Someone sitting beside Lily all the while, day and night—three days, silently viewed. Women conquering tears. Stolid men shaking hands. The line of buggies, horses groomed to shining, trailing the buggy taking Lily, embraced within the darkness of a closed wooden box, to the place her body, its spirit gone, would rest forever.

I dropped my hands and shook my head; I looked for Lily's grave marker.

I couldn't find it.

There was a tree outside the far side of the cemetery. The rain was starting. Not yet fierce. Hoping it wouldn't reach that magnitude, I climbed over the fence and sought refuge beneath the tree's limbs and young leaves. Leaning against the bark, I closed my eyes and listened to the peaceful patter of raindrops falling on the leaves. I smiled and stayed there awhile. When the tapping of rain diminished, and I knew the impending storm had decided to move elsewhere, I opened my eyes and took in the beauty of a clean-washed, bright-colored earth. Hugging myself, I shivered with pleasure; my eyes taking it all in. And then, I saw a small stone resting a short distance from the tree. Pleasure left me. I knew what it was. Without going to it, without reading the words engraved upon it, I knew what it was.

They had buried Lily outside the fence.

Chapter Four

Memories of that time, that morning, the cemetery, cause my heart to tremble. They were smashed together like a mass of hurling pain. *My Lily. My Lily. Swallowed by the ground unsanctioned. Shunned even in death.*

I remember rushing down the pathway to my car . . . running, slipping and sliding on the rain-slicked dirt. I remember jerking the car door open, flinging my body inside, dropping my head against the steering wheel, and pounding its hard, unforgiving substance with my fists. Wanting it to be every Amish soul that had labeled Lily unfit and had dropped her into unholy ground. My anger was so solid, I felt I could gather it together, hold it in my hands, shape it into a hard-balled missile and hurl it over the whole Amish community, dropping shards of destruction on them all.

It should have been a beautiful drive to my parents' house. It was spring—May—tulip, daffodil and tree-blossoming time. I should have seen cows released from stanchions to pasture, freed from the daily spread of silage and stiff, dried hay. Once dropped before their restricted, reaching heads, they were freed to dip their heads into the new growth of sweet baby grass, free to feast unencumbered. I should have seen black-clad men, coats discarded, sleeves rolled up, repairing fences, raking fields, anticipating and pondering the schedule for planting and seeding. Women's wash hanging firm from the sweep of spring-happy fingers no longer fearing frostbite. Children rolling on grass, running through puddles, laughing as they went about their chores. But I didn't. I didn't see any of that. The outside of my eyes saw only the road and behind those eyes, the vision of a single grave under a tree.

I reached the turn at the top of the hill that took me to my old home—my Amish home. I stopped the car at the end of the driveway and made myself look. It was there. Just as it had always been. Bright and white and windows gleaming. And I knew without seeing, the porch was swept, the doorknob wiped clean, and the frame around the door clear of spiders and bugs. I turned my eyes and saw two young boys playing in the yard. Barefoot in grass that still would be damp from the recent rain, laughing and sliding on slick ground, they tossed a ball back and forth. Surprise cut through my anger. I had not expected children. I had repressed the years I wasn't there and kept the memory of what was. And now, I wanted everything to be the same as I'd last seen it. And it wasn't. And, in my heart, I knew it couldn't be so. Trees grow. Trees die. Brothers marry. Children are born. Some things change. Some things remain the same. I could hold on to those things—a barrier, a cushion against the pain of loss, a way to rejoice in that which stayed the same and welcomed my heart home.

Beyond the children, I could see a new building. A small

house. And I knew immediately what it was. A *dawdi haus*. A house for parents grown old ... home, authority, and responsibility relinquished, the house they had ruled for so many years surrendered to their children. Now, it would be my siblings steering the shape of daily duties. I didn't like that. I wanted it to still be my father and mother. As they were—*Maem and Da*, strong and accountable.

How could I be angry at an old man and woman shed of their strength and deserving rest, peace? How could I be angry with an old man and woman who couldn't protect their daughter? I swallowed and felt my lips tighten, my cheeks draw in. Of course, I could be angry. They were still parents. And they had been so much younger when she'd died. How could they let their child be treated like trash that was thrown into a hole dug for garbage? I squeezed my eyes shut, tented my fingers over my mouth and nose, and breathed heavy against them. Yes, it was right to be angry.

Through a haze of growing ire, I sensed, saw, the movement of children running across their yard. My yard. The same young boys. And yes, they would be going to the house to fetch a knowing or, if needed, protecting parent. It wouldn't stop me. This raging anger was justified, and I would confront the makers of it. Parents or not. It mattered not who they were. They had done wrong—serious wrong.

I got out of the car and started toward the little house. I saw my sister, Violet, come out the big house's back door. She stood on the stoop and looked at me. She had aged. Even through my rage, I saw her as old, and a fleeting hurt swept sharply through my being. She made as if to step forward and stop me. I held out my arm, hand out, palm facing her.

"No," I said. "No."

She stopped, said nothing and let me go by. I saw pain in her face. She knew me, and the depth of my anger would be matched by her own trepidation. It didn't stop me.

My father opened the *dawdi haus* door. *Da*. His stare was short, but not so short I couldn't see his questioning face turn cold. He would not let the knowing of my shunning allow him to welcome me. His hand rose swiftly to close the door against me. My hand was quicker, and I held it open.

"Let me in."

He didn't say anything just pushed hard at the door.

"Oh no," I said, and I saw my anger scowl his face, just for a moment. And then, it was cold nothing again. "No. No. No. Not this time!" I looked straight into his eyes. "You shut the door against me ten years ago, and I walked away. Not this time. Not this time!"

He turned and walked away from me. He stopped at the back of the room. His back to me, he stood still and quiet.

Maem was at the stove. For a fleeting instant, I was aware of the mixed scent of meat and vegetables simmering on the stove—warmth, comfort, youth. And then it was gone. All my senses concentrated on *Maem*. Her face, still loving, revealed joy mixed with sad, a terrible and intense yearning. Fear. She had lifted her arms, and her hands, clenched firmly together, pressed tight against her chest. *Maem*. I ached to go to her. But I was afraid. If I were to touch her, would she turn away? If she did, what would I do? Can you be alive and dead at the same time?

I heard my father's cough. I looked at him. He had turned and was looking at me. "Go!"

His voice was sharp enough to cut through love, to stop the

want to quiet temper, to kill a starting fall into forgiveness.

I lifted my head. I felt the cords in my neck grow taut. The words spit from my mouth.

"You let her lie buried outside the place of peace and remembrance."

He was not moved by the force of the words. He did not reply. He stood—a silent statue. When he did not stir, and his body seemed to be an impenetrable fortress, I stepped so close to him, I could feel the heat of his breath on my face.

"You will answer me!" I wondered if he heard the strength of my rage. As I remember this moment, I don't think he did. He never wavered in his stance. Never a tremble. Never could I discern a doubt. His face stayed close to mine. His words were few. Sharp and final.

"I will say this once. You are shunned. You're not welcome into this house."

"Will I go to Hell if I stay? Will you push me out? And if my heart stops beating, and I fall right here, right now, before you dead, will you bury me next to Lily? Yet, how could you do that? How can *you* determine I am in a state of sin, if I tell you now that I have confessed my sins to God, and He has forgiven me?"

I saw him struggle, knew he did not want to speak even one word to me, but he did.

"You have not confessed your sin before God and the brethren."

"And so, I am shunned?"

He was done. He turned his back to me. But before I lost the sight his face, I saw tears slip over his tightly stretched cheeks, and I ached to touch them, wipe them away. *Da.*

I looked at *Maem,* still standing by the stove, wooden spoon in her hand, it stained red from the many stirrings of thick, rich sauces and soups. Her cheeks were flushed, and her eyes were swollen with tears she would not let fall.

"It was so long ago," she said. "I go to the tree and stand by her grave. And I say the hymns to her. And I pray she can hear them. And if she cannot, I pray God does. It was so long ago." She paused. "But I remember . . . my lovely young girl. I remember."

I could barely hear her words; they were so soft . . . and full of love. And I looked at my father's steely, unbending strength. And I thought, how deep were his tears that he could let *Maem* suffer so? And my anger was back—sudden and intense.

"Where are you, old man, standing so far from the one whom you married, the one who gave birth to your child. Your daughter is dead, and your wife is still grieving. Can you not go and hold her? And do you ever go to Lily's grave? Where were you when Lily lay dead in your house? Did someone sit the three nights with her? My brothers, did they? Did anyone come to see her on the day before she was buried? Did you pull the sheet from her face? Did they look at the girl they condemned?" My voice rose higher. My arm lifted itself and pounded his back. He didn't flinch. It hit again. And again. Then stopped. It changed nothing. "How can you know she killed herself? Because the bishop said so? Who is he to know? He's just a man like you. Right now, I hate you. You should have defended your wife!"

I sensed *Maem* come beside me. I felt her hand on my arm. Gentle.

"Go, Child. He hurts as much as we do, and he knows I go to sit by her. He doesn't stop me." Her hand moved up and down my arm. Soothing. "He's a good man, better than me.

He obeys."

"The *Ordnung*," I stated.

"Yes," she agreed. "The *Ordnung*. He can't go and talk to her. Your heart still knows the Amish Ways. All that could be done for and by Lily was done, *is* done, when she took her last breath."

"You go to the grave. *Da* doesn't stop you?"

"No, like I told you." She smiled. "But he makes me confess before the assembly each and every time I visit your sister."

"Or you'll be shunned."

"It's the rule of the *Ordnung*. You know that, Cora. It's how we live, and so, at one time, did you."

"It's not always right." I set my lips tight. "Sometimes it forgets there is a better guide. I should send the bishop a Bible. Several Bibles. English Bibles. He can spread them around."

"You should go." My mother's whisper reached my ears.

"I'll take flowers to her grave," I said, sadness slipping over anger, tendering it.

"And say hymns."

Her words were sweetened with tears, and I nodded.

"Go, now, your *Da* needs peace."

I looked at him. He had not moved, and I thought his aging body must be aching. I wanted to not feel the sorrow for him that came unbidden to my heart, the need to go to him, put arms around him and hold him. But I didn't go to him. I knew a hug would break him.

I squeezed *Maem* close to me, a quick moment, and left.

There was a little girl in the yard. She watched me get in the car. A strange feeling crept through me. I shrugged it off and drove away. My mind was full; there was no room for speculation.

Chapter Five

I was depleted. Yet empty as I was, my foot on the pedal, my hands on the steering wheel, I knew, without thought, the lay of the road, the turns, the pastures, the trees and the fields on either side. It was old in my heart, seared there, but memories broke out of hiding to take me down that road I'd walked and run and laughed, stumbled over broken pieces of blacktop, skidded across winter frozen surface, and stamped, splashed and slid on rain-muddied edges of dirt . . . so many years ago.

Bile rose in my throat. I needed to stop. I pulled to the side of the road, and as I got out of the car and stood by it, leaned against it, steadied my trembling body, I realized I was at the spot where I'd stopped and held Annabelle. I looked down at Wander Lane, tucked so firmly and quietly in the valley, where I'd already known I would leave her. I lowered my face into cupped hands, pressed them tight against skin, wanting them to push memory away. It helped. The feel of that pressure strengthened the need to return to the Cora I'd become.

There is a peace that lives within the forest, a soothing sweetness that drifts from the sway of thickly leaved limbs—a gentleness. Feeling its pull, I stepped away from the car and walked across grass towards the trees. I felt my body calm; my trembling ceased.

There was a patch of Lily-of-the-valley at the edge of the woods. Stirred by a delicate breeze, their tiny white bells nodded a silent song to the ground, and I inhaled the soft scent of their petals. A forest is a magic place. There is a sense of permanence, power and beauty that creeps from it into the one who leaves self and absorbs it.

And there was an old tree trunk, lying on the grass, near but apart from the flowers, close to a tree grown large from many years of soaking in nature's nourishing soil and water. I sat on it and shadowed by the dense coat of leaf upon limb, I felt hidden and safe.

I closed my eyes and bent my head.

Father, thank you for bringing me to this place. It is lovely. There is sometimes a soothing pressure that you lay upon my heart. It stirs within me and slips like a flower unfolding and smoothing a fragrant balm of silken petals everywhere on the inside boundaries of my skin. I feel this now, and I am grateful. This day has been hard. The years have been many since I've seen Lily, touched her, laughed with her . . . tried to teach her little bits of wisdom that would make her life fuller. But You took her. You reached into the creek and silenced the beat of her heart. I don't know how she got in that creek, but I know she didn't leave the water alive. You took her unto Yourself. And You let them bury her body outside their cherished ground. Why? And why did You not allow, guide, make my maem and da obstruct that indecent, unwarranted burial?

I stopped my words. Anger was seeping into my soul and with it, guilt. The English world had taught me I could be honest in voicing my fears, my sins, my ugly thoughts to God, and He would still love me, guide me, forgive me. There was still too much Amish in me, and I shuddered at voicing words that would not please Him . . . or might question His ways.

I sat on the log, fingers pressed against my eyes, hoping to push away unwanted images and I heard a noise—a rustle in the woods, neither loud nor frightening. But close.

Dropping my hands onto my lap, I turned my eyes to the sound, and I saw a woman, Amish, large, lumber from the trees, step into the patch of lilies and grab at them, pull them, roughly, out of the soil. She didn't look my way and as if her time was short, she grabbed the flowers, dropped them without sorting into the pocket she'd formed with her apron, then turned, without looking my way, and scuffled back into the trees. I didn't recognize her. I thought, though my years with the Amish had been sporadic, I knew the subtle appearances and mannerisms, the unique consistencies of the Amish Wander Lane families, and I should be able to recognize individuals. And this woman was as aged as I. I should have known her. But I didn't.

Grateful the unexpected Amish lady had interrupted the direction anger and guilt were taking me, I thought it prudent to cease talking to God. In its depths, my heart knew I could say anything to Him, but at that moment, my sensibility and Amish blood weren't able to reach that place.

I sat on the log for awhile, wrapped in the scents of tree, flower and soil, hugging myself in the pleasure of them. Then I got up, walked to my car, and drove away.

I stopped at the motel to change my shoes, wet from the rained roadside grass, and reflected I should feed my body. I'd eaten nothing that day and was hungry. The rich scent of beef chunks and vegetables simmering on *Maem's* stove stirred real in my nose, and I thought if I'd just held tongue and temper, I could be eating it now, with them. I should have eaten first; yelled, later. But I didn't, so I grabbed sweater and purse and set out to find food.

Of course, my feet would take me to Harriet's Homemade Soup and Sandwich Shop, where, ten years ago, I'd found a heart, Harriet's, overflowing with love, perception and wisdom. However, my feet didn't know what my mind did. They were anxious to get me to be the same woman that they had known, but my mind knew that woman had changed. Grown old. Memories caged in a hoarding brain that would not let them loose.

I hesitated at the door. My head held a picture of the dining room, a room behind the door I'd not seen for several years, and I wanted my eyes to see that picture become real. I opened the door, stepped in, and it was. Like the fields and the woods and the straw-hatted, suspendered men I'd seen working the land that day, it was the same. Except Harriet wasn't there.

I breathed in the smell of it. Smiled at the messy array of bulletins and notices tacked on the board behind the welcoming counter, that wide space still littered with jars of root beer barrels, red and white striped candies, pennies, paperclips, pens and a jumbled mass of menus. And the walls still held the framed Stoll, Miller, and Eicher quilts. The same as when I'd left, were the Amish tables and chairs, fashioned by hands strong and capable— hands with a simple, inborn beauty flowing through their fingers into the wood. The floor gleamed. The room was Amish clean.

It was early dinner time. There were a few diners scattered about. Mostly *Englishers,* as was the man sitting at the far end of the room—Lowell Parker.

He was looking at me. I couldn't read his face. I wondered if he could read mine. If he could, he saw anger.

I walked with firm step to his table.

"You should have told me."

"Sit," he said, but I heard no welcome in his voice.

"It would have been easier if I could have been, at least a little, prepared."

"No, it wouldn't have been." He pushed his foot against the chair across from him. It slid from beneath the table. "Sit."

I did.

He looked at me for a moment. Hard. Then he bent forward and spoke across the table. "I don't want you causing trouble. It's over and done with. Accept it or get out of town."

"I don't want my parents thinking Lily is in Hell."

"It's been a long time, Cora. And maybe they do think about her, and probably it does hurt when they do, but I doubt they sit all day long twiddling their thumbs and wishing they could change what they can't."

"But it can change. You can find out what really happened and get Lily buried back where she belongs . . . inside, not out, inside the cemetery, with her people."

He shook his head; his sigh was loud. I didn't budge.

"You know Bishop Herrfort," I said, glaring at him. "You could get him to look with favor on an investigation."

"Herrfort's on his way out. The man's *old*. Let it go, Cora. Let it go!"

"He'd listen to you."

"No, Cora, he wouldn't."

"You married his sister. He's family."

"She left the brethren 'cause of me. And then Wander Lake. You think he'd do anything for me?"

"You watch over Aaron and Jacob. His nephews. And yours. They're blood."

"How 'bout making a little sense. Aaron and Jacob are adults. Middle-aged adults. They don't need any 'watching over.' The bishop and I get along pretty good. We work together on most things. And I want to keep it that way with him . . . and who comes after."

"You won't talk to Herrfort because Jacob's the one who was seeing my sister and, in all likelihood, knows more about Lily's death than anybody else."

"Leave it alone, Cora. You're stirring up trouble where there isn't any."

"I can't," I said. "I'm the one who took her baby from her and caused the string of circumstances that led to her death." I drew in a deep breath and willed myself to keep the growing swell of tears from falling from my eyes. "It's my job to take care of her, even in death, and to get her buried where she belongs. Don't you see? She's in that grave because of me. *I need to know what happened.* And I *will* find answers."

"They've already been found, Cora. Leave it alone. There's nothing to be found."

"We'll see," I said and left.

Chapter Six

The first thing I heard when I woke the next morning was the pound of rain above the ceiling, and the first thing I saw were the hands on the clock pointing to numbers too high for my day's plans. I could dress for the weather, but the hours could not be restored. The logical thing was to expunge my stomach's urge to be filled, but if I showered fast, threw clothes on quickly, and stashed a couple candy bars into my purse, I could drive up the hill to my Amish home, before *Da* and the brothers came in for lunch . . . dinner . . . there was no lunch in an Amish house, only breakfast, dinner and supper.

So that's what I did . . . clothed my body with dark fabrics, skirt below my knee, blouse buttoned to the throat, shoes flat and black. No make-up, hair in a bun. My mirror reflected me plain. I hoped plain enough. Then I shoved one whole, smashed, chocolate bar into my mouth and headed out the door.

Once out the door, the first thing I did was step in a puddle. The next thing I did was lift my arm and shake my fist. It felt good and alleviated a bit of justified anger. Certainly, if a motel required their exit doors to immediately place a guest in the midst of nature, it would be expedient to provide waterproof awnings. Especially on days the clouds spewed water shot from their heavy, black bellies. It was time to find better lodging.

Fortunately, by the time I reached my car, driving rain had dwindled to drizzle. Unfortunately, my mind wasn't quite ready to totally let go of a pitiful want for nature's perfection, thereby causing temper to overcome caution, and I backed my car too fast and too far. It hit a three-foot-high, thick, yellow, cement post. I got out and kicked the culprit. Hurt my toe. But my bumper looked fine. Sometimes, foolish washes all over you, and sometimes, it brings with it, funny. And funny brings ridiculous. Which turns into laughter. And it did. I laughed and I laughed. Fortunately, as I blew a kiss to the post and patted my bumper, there was no one to see and wonder at my atypical movements. I got in my car, a better tempered, albeit a bit frazzled woman, and drove up the hill that would take me to the Poolers.

I pulled into the driveway of my "growing-up house," got out of my car, and stepped gingerly over the damp grass to the stone paved pathway leading to the porch. The earth had been turned on either side of the path, the rich soil waiting to be planted with *Maem's* pink impatiens. And I wanted that to be so. Sighing, I hoped George or Harry, Sampson or Willie—whichever brother was living in the main house, or Sister Violet, would remember and honor *Maem's* love for those flowers. It seemed it might be so. The borders were ready for planting.

I stopped at the bottom of the porch steps. Bowing my head, I pressed my palms against my cheekbones and covered my eyes with my fingers. *Father, give me the words I should say when they open the door and I see behind them the home that was mine. I'm not even sure who lives there anymore. But they're mine. Please let them remember, know me. I'm still a Pooler, theirs. I belong to them. Shunning doesn't dilute or revamp blood. I pray they don't turn me away. But whatever happens, I thank You for bringing me here. I need them. I need to be here. I need to quell the despairing doubts in my heart. I pray in the name of my Savior, Jesus Christ, Amen.*

I put my hand on the railing and looked up above the steps and across the porch to the front door. It seemed so far from the place where I stood. The door had no window. There was no way to prepare before I knocked on it. No way to peek and see who might come to open it.

I felt the cold wet from the railing under my hand, and I lifted my hand, and I looked at the sheen of fallen drops spread across my palm. I rubbed my other hand against it, then wiped them on my skirt. After a moment of emptiness, I moved my eyes to travel, again, up the steps, across the porch, and to stop at the door. There was no way to be done with walking that path and knocking at that door. I couldn't reverse my steps. I could not turn from the aching emptiness of my heart to be filled. It was time. I placed my foot on the first step and started up.

I knocked. Waited. I knocked again. My knuckles had barely dropped from the door, when it opened part way, small fingers holding it still from opening farther. A little face peeked around its surface. A girl. Her prayer *kapp* was a bit tilted and curling, stray tendrils lay captured on her flushed cheeks. I guessed her age to be about seven. She bit her lower lip, perhaps to quiet its tremble, but she looked directly at me.

I bent my head to speak to her, but before I could get my words out, she lifted a finger to her lips and shushed me.

"Shh. You can't come in. *Maem's* sleeping. She's sick."

31

"Are you alone?" I asked, putting my hand on the door, hoping to see behind it.

"I can't tell you."

"Can I see her?"

"If you're hungry, you can go to Uncle Aaron's house. They're all eating there, and *Maem* needs rest. Aunt Violet told me to sit by *Maem* and not to let anybody in, and if anybody comes and needs dinner or anything else, they should go to her house. So, you better go."

"It's a big job you have." Hearing the tremor in her words, and troubled that such a young child should have so much responsibility, I kept my voice soft. "Maybe I can help you."

"I can take care of *Maem*. You need to go."

Though there was a tremor in her voice, I heard strength in her words. "You're sure? I'm a friend of your Aunt Violet's. She would happy if I would keep you company."

"Please go away."

I sighed and shook my head. "Okay. And I think I will stop and see your Aunt Violet." And, I thought to myself, *give her a few choice words.* "You're a *gut* girl. I'll tell her you're doing a really good job."

"*Denki.*"

I moved and started down the steps.

"Lady?"

If words could hold tears, that word did. I turned back and looked at the child. She'd pushed the door to fully open, and she stood beside it, her fist clutching the knob, her lips quivering, her eyes full."

"Lady, I think my *maem* is hurting." She bit her lip, paused. "A lot."

"Show me," I said.

"I can't."

"Just a quick peek."

"*Da* would be mad." She put her fingers in her mouth, looked downward, and spoke softly to the floor "She's not really sleeping. Just kind of sleeping." She looked up at me. "And making funny noises."

"You know, sweetie, I think your *da* would be really proud of you if you saw your *maem* needed grown-up help, and you let a grown-up, me, help you make her better." She looked up at me. I hurt for the fear I saw on her face, the want to fix what she could not. "You're so brave, and I think, together, we can make your *maem* better."

"I can take of her." She pressed her lips together and swallowed, "But maybe I could let you help me. Would you tell *Da,* I did a *gut* job?"

"Yes. A very *gut* job."

"Okay," she said, and she took my hand, pulled me into the house and we walked, together, across the floor to her mother's bedroom. She stood a moment at the threshold, then grasped the fabric of my skirt, clutched it tight. "He won't be mad?" The words stumbled from her mouth.

"I promise."

"Okay," she whispered.

We went into the room. Her mother was lying on her side, her legs cradled to hold her swollen stomach, her chin pressed tight against her neck. Low moans, raspy, tortured, seemed to rise from a deep and dark place. I couldn't see her face. Her *kapp* had fallen and loose strands of hair shielded her forehead and cheeks.

"What is your *maem's* name?" I asked the child. I wanted to say it. Quietly. To let her know there was adult help in the room.

"Talitha. My *maem* is Talitha. Talitha Pooler."

"What?"

I think I frightened her. She let go of my skirt and stepped away from me.

"Talitha," she said again, her voice so low, I could scarcely hear it. Startled, I asked "What's your *da's* name?"

"Willie. Willie Pooler. Sometimes William."

Her words wavered through the air into my ears. My heart stopped.

Oh, my God. Oh, God, help me.

"Are you going to help her?"

I looked down at her. I saw no sign of Lily in her. I turned my face to the mother. Her straggling strands were blond. That's all I could see that would tell what I feared . . . what I knew in my heart was so.

"Are you going to help her!"

I detected a smidgen of anger in the child's voice, strength. It would help us. I stooped and gripped her arms. "Listen carefully, little one, and do exactly what I say. Can you do that?" Her body, so little, baby-soft under my palms, stiffened, and her eyes reflected a returning trepidation. I needed her to trust me. I smiled. "We can help her, both of us. Together. Will you help me?"

She nodded.

"It will be all right. I promise. *Gut* girl. Now tell me, can you run fast?"

She nodded; her eyes locked into mine.

"*Gut.* Now I want you to run to your Uncle's house. Just as fast as you can." Her head bobbed up and down.

"When you get there, go straight to your *da* and tell him

your *maem* needs him. And tell him Cora is with her. Can you do that?" She nodded again.

"*Maem* needs help and Cora is with her," I repeated. "Okay?"

She swallowed and whispered, "Okay."

"*Gut* girl. Sweetie, I promise she'll be all right. I promise." A quick, fervent prayer ran through my mind. *Please let it be so.* I gave her a hug and kissed her cheek. "We'll do this together. We're a team."

She nodded.

"Now run!"

Chapter Seven

I didn't watch her run down the road. She was an Amish girl. She would do as told. Instead, I went to the bed and looked down at her mother. Except for her mouth expelling short, quick breaths, she lay still. I reached and smoothed my hand over her cheek, sliding the clinging wisps of hair adhering to her skin to rest on her head. She neither moved nor opened her eyes at my touch. She was an Amish woman. Stoic in pain. Accepting.

There was a stool near the bed. I drew it closer and sat, bent and whispered "Lily" in her ear. She stirred, moved her face to show clearer, raised her lids half-way.

I could see. I could tell. Lily. I saw Lily.

She closed her eyes again. Her cheek sank back into the pillow. I rested my hand on her shoulder. "It will be all right."

I couldn't help her. Talitha. Lily's child. I remembered nothing about birthing. I was there when Annabelle, Talitha, was born. But I couldn't remember her separating from Lily's body. In my mind, I remembered it seemed to take too long. And I did remember our sister, Violet, grabbing my hand, squeezing, crying. And *fear.* I remembered fear. I remember so clearly what I felt, but dimly what I saw. I couldn't help her. Lily then. Talitha now.

There was a moan from the bed. Louder than the others. Talitha labored onto her back, lifted her hands to the sides of her face, pressed hard, opened her mouth and let loose an agonizing rush of air.

I froze.

When it was done, Talitha lay limp. I sat helpless, hands clasped, and looked hard at her face. It was pale, lined with pain, yet even so, a clear reflection of Lily. But different. Older. Creases that Lily had never grown into sat upon her face. Sinking lines at the sides her mouth, her nose, her eyes. Talitha was older now than Lily was on the day Lily birthed her. She was only five years old when Lily died, and just a newborn baby when I gave her away. She was older now than Lily was on the day Lily stood beside me and watched me receive the judgement of Bishop Herrfort. Watched me placed under The Ban. Shunned. Separated from the brethren.

I watched in silence. Talitha seemed to be near sleep. I hoped this reprieve would last till Willie, or someone, came.

But the quiet didn't last long. The pains returned, each one sooner than the last. I didn't know what to do. I got a pan of water and a rag from the kitchen and wiped the sweat from Talitha's face. As she lay on her back, she lifted her head to look at me. The weight of it seemed too heavy for her to hold up, and her head dropped, sank deep into the pillow. She looked so small. So helpless.

"I don't know you," she whispered, turning her face enough for me to see it. She half-smiled. "You've never done this before, have you?"

"A long time ago. I barely remember."

"It's okay. I've done it before. Three times. I know what to do." Her smile grew full. "I hurt. You wait. And it will happen." She stopped, stiffened, her face taut, showing pain. When the spasm was done, she blew a gentle stream of air through her lips. "And it will be all right." She closed her eyes, pressed her lips together and murmured, "And the prize is worth the playing."

Another pain, and her smile was gone. It was hard to watch. It seemed the child should have reached Aaron's house. I glanced through the open bedroom and great room doors and hoped I would see buggy and horse pulling into the driveway.

Nothing.

"Where's Katy?"

Her words, weak and faltering, stumbled through her lips, and I wasn't sure how to answer. I thought it might upset her to know I was so frightened and unsure of my abilities that I'd sent the child, Katy, for help. So, I lied. "She's a little tired, so I sent her to rest for a bit. She was reluctant to leave you, but I told her I'd watch over you."

"She's a *gut* girl, my Katy is." Talitha closed her eyes and smiled. It seemed she'd drifted to a quiet place.

I put my hand on her arm and waited.

"Cora?"

I lifted my eyes and saw Violet looking down at me. She smiled and patted my head.

"I think I was near sleep." There was a bit of moisture at the corner of my lip. I wiped it away with the heel of my palm.

"More than near," she laughed, "more like totally there."

I had slipped to the floor and rested my head on Talitha's mattress. My hand was still on her arm. I looked at Talitha's face for a moment. It was tranquil, pale. She seemed to be at peace, without pain. I wondered how long this see-sawing attack on her body could last.

"I'm glad you're here," I said to Violet as I smoothed my hand over the crumpled sheet where my head dropped, then I rose to sit back on the stool.

"Why don't we go into the parlor and talk?" Violet offered her hand to help me from the stool. "I think Talitha will rest for awhile."

"I don't like to leave her."

"She'll be all right." And she led me into the big room.

I stopped outside the closed, bedroom door and scanned the efficiently divided sections of the great room—living, dining and kitchen areas. There was no one in them.

"Where's Katy?" I asked.

"She stayed with the family at Aaron's house."

"Your house now, too." I heard the taint of resentment in the tenor of my voice. She ignored it. "And Willie?"

"He's gone to get the midwife."

"Will it take long?"

"Long enough for us to talk. You know buggies are slower than cars." She motioned me to sit. "You've ridden in both. And don't look at me that way. I've been to many birthings. I can assure you, Talitha's not ready to drop the wee one yet."

I scowled at the coldness in her tone. I'd been a second mother to her, and our relationship had been warm, close. We'd shared laughter, tears, and secrets. And I was here when little Kate was put in a position where her young years were too few for the task, and I'd taken the sole responsibility to care for the child's pregnant mother, obviously in the last throes of labor, from her shudders. There should be at least a minimum of thankful welcome emanating from Violet.

"Okay," I said, a matching anger projecting towards her. "Why don't you just tell me what's bothering you."

"You upset *Maem* and *Da*." She set her face firmly and glared at me. "They're old, and they lost a daughter, and you're blaming them for what *she* did."

"What who did, Violet?"

"What she did. *Lily*."

"What did she do, Violet?"

"She killed herself."

"Do you really believe that?"

"I don't want to."

We sat quietly, facing each other, Violet in an old, stuffed chair, soft and worn by years of holding tired men fresh from the fields or barns, hungry, waiting for supper to be put on the table. And after repast, returning and napping in that same chair, me in the rocker, sat in by mothers and grandmothers rocking their babies to sleep, crooning soft lullabies, reading toddlers bedtime stories, listening to teenage woes, and watching them all with loving eyes.

"Why do you believe it? Why do you believe Lily killed herself?" I asked.

"I have to." She sank her chin into her neck, lifted her hands, and rubbed her eyes. Then she lowered her hands, leaned her body toward me, and repeated with firm voice. "I have to. The bishop said it was so. He said Lily ended her life, sinned against God."

"Oh, Violet, dear little sister, the bishop isn't always right."

"I live here, Cora. It's peaceful here. I want it to stay that way." She looked straight at me. "The bishop is always right."

I knew she meant her words to be strong, but I could hear the tremble behind them.

"Right now, Violet, your face reflects no peace."

"Once, I had a sister who listened to me; she even heard the words hiding beneath those spoken. She left, shunned, and I had to find a new place of wisdom and acceptance. A place of strength and certainty. And Bishop Herrfort was always strong and certain." Violet paused, looked down at her lap, and then back at me. "I was only sixteen when you left the first time. And what a time of quiet misery that was. No one yelled or screamed. No one even spoke of the situation. A baby born. A baby given away. An Amish baby. And no one spoke of the shunning. Not one word. Your name was erased from every lip, even from those who loved you most." She bit her lip, sighed. "I did go to Bishop Herrfort. He listened, and he told me what a great sinner you were. I couldn't tell him the baby was Lily's, and you were saving her from shame. We had promised each other to keep the secret. And I did. And so did Lily. And I watched her suffer. From the loss of the baby. From the loss of you. But, mostly, from the guilt.

"I know you left because you had to. You're strong, but not strong enough to keep your back straight under that shunning, that undeserved shunning, not to stay seeing all the hurt around you, *Da's* disappointment, *Maem's* heartache. Lily's remorse. But we missed you, Lily and me. We missed you."

"I came back," I said.

"But you left again."

"I couldn't stay. My beliefs had changed. I couldn't live again under the restrictions of the *Ordnung*."

She stared at me. It was a gentle stare. "You found another way."

"Yes. A better way."

"Jesus."

"Yes. Jesus."

"But I have Him, too." The pleading of her words carried to her eyes.

"I know." I understood she couldn't comprehend the increased intensity of faith that came with looking beyond the *Ordnung* and searching the scriptures. "Keep talking to Him. He'll always be there."

We sat quietly for a few minutes. The silence was good, comforting. Comforting for me—apparently not for Violet. When I raised my eyes to look at her, I saw her eyes lowered, focused on her hands pleating the folds of her skirt.

"Violet?"

She looked up. "You should go."

Her voice was wistful. Soft. I strained to hear it.

"They'll be coming soon. Willie and the midwife. You can't be here."

"I'm still shunned," I stated. "That's it, isn't it?" I didn't feel anger . . . hurt is what I felt. A sad, helpless hurt.

"Yes . . . and I shouldn't be talking to you."

"No, but you are."

"And Talitha knows it. At least she will when she realizes who you are. And she'll tell. She has to." Violet sighed. "Or baby or not, she'll be shunned."

"When will it end, the shunning?" I asked.

"For who? You? Me? Talitha?"

"All of us," I said. "When will it end for all of us?"

"For Talitha, she'll be okay. She didn't really talk with you, and the words she said, and because she told, and because she was in a state of pain and confusion, the bishop will understand and forgive. For you and me, the shunning will be lifted when we confess our sin in church, before our Amish brothers and sisters, though right now, you're not really one of them, and then our sin will be forgiven, and the *Bann* lifted. Then it'll be over."

"Our sin? We talked to each other. A sin? It doesn't make sense."

"You've been gone too long, Cora. It makes sense. To us."

"To you, Violet? It makes sense to you?"

"Yes."

"Then why do you talk with me?"

Violet lifted her hands, rubbed them over her face, and shook her head. "I don't want to, but for some reason, I just can't help myself."

I left before Willie and the midwife got there.

On my way back from the farm to the motel, I stopped at the cemetery to revisit the place where Lily lay . . . alone, outside the fence that kept her from lying with those whose sins had been forgiven.

I got out of my car and walked up the short hill, stood by the fence and looked over it at the gravestones. Those of the chosen ones. Deemed by a congregation of blackbirds to be worthy of consecrated soil. Lily, not there—Lily, shunned in death, buried outside the fence. My heart burned, struggled with the anger which the uncompromising, unbending brethren had planted within me, and at the same time, knowing the depth of their love and, though denied in my soul, their interpreted respect for God's justice, I understood their pain would have painted their decision with thick despair. Even so, I wanted to hate them, tear them apart, *hurt* them. But deep inside, where their strength and love were secure, I knew they hurt, too.

I sat for awhile, by the tree, outside the fence, staring at the space that was now Lily's home. Her body's home. For I knew, she was with God in Heaven.

I marveled at the beauty of that place, that place that held bodies within its rich, brown soil, both inside the fence and out of it. The same lush, green grass covered both sides of that enclosing white-painted, wooden structure. And the sky, a soft, moving blue, tiny clouds drifting beside and behind larger clouds—little lambs playing beside the mother sheep-cloud—roofed the whole of it. Peaceful. I wondered at the dying, Lily-of-the-valley bells spread over the grass, on Lily's grave. They stretched to a patch of those same flowers on a space near hers. Someone had placed them there. Perhaps, they were from a kindly soul that had loved Lily. But why was the plot of ground near her also adorned with flowers?

As I sat on the grass, there was a sad, yet soothing, peace that rested in my heart. Gentle, like watching a baby sleep, knowing the child would grow and know sorrow and hurt, but at the same time, knowing the child would have moments of such tremendous joy and completeness enhanced by the contrast of experienced pain. Then bowing my head, I prayed.

Father, I hurt. I sit on the ground that holds Lily's body, and I remember. I took her baby and gave it away. I never asked her; I never asked You. I simply took the child and gave her away. I thought I was protecting Lily, but I wasn't. I was robbing her. Of a child. Her child.

Maybe the placement of the seed within her body was an accidental happening, but the baby wasn't a mistake. And little Annabelle, now Talitha, should have been Lily's to raise. The Brethren would have forgiven her. Perhaps, probably, they would have shunned her for a period. But she would have confessed her wrongdoing, and she would have been forgiven. I robbed her of that. I took her baby and gave it away. The guilt is mine; it never was hers. I was never able to tell her I was sorry. I killed her, God. I took her baby and gave it away, left her with empty arms and an aching heart. I killed her with my thoughtless actions. I know You hold out forgiveness to me, but I'm too ashamed to take it.

Thank you, Father, for hearing my words, and, God, thank you, thank you for loving me. I pray in the name of Jesus, my Lord and Savior. Amen.

I stood, bent and lifted a lily bell from the grass, held it a moment, silky white in my hand, and then laid it, gently, back onto the grass.

I stepped carefully across the grass, past the fenced in cemetery and down the hill to my car. I didn't look back. My heart was too full to take in more.

I got into my car and drove back to Wander Lane. When I reached the motel, I went in, heeled off my shoes, pulled the pins out of my hair, and, fully clothed, crawled into bed, pulled the covers tight around my body. *Father forgive me.*

And I slept.

Chapter Eight

I woke, hungry, in the dark hours of night. I reached into the sack of snacks I kept on the bedside table. It was empty. I rose, shed my dreary, crumpled clothes, and replaced them with jeans and tee-shirt, grabbed my keys, went out to my car, and drove the streets seeking a place that sold food.

Harriet's Eatery was open. I smiled. Niece Bailey must have been bitten by the ambition bug. My ten-year, twenty-year, forever-year memories of her were far different. Lazy child. Lazy youth. Lazy adult. As a final feat before her fade into a mere shadow of knowing, Harriet must have used her last bit of reason to place the proverbial dynamite stick under Bailey's bottom.

And miracles of miracles, Bailey, awake and alert, greeted me as I walked into the restaurant.

The dining room was almost empty. There was a couple seated in one corner, two coffee cups sitting in front of them. Maybe empty. They weren't drinking from them. The woman, middle-aged and wrinkled, lifted a handkerchief and held it to her eyes. The man, gray-haired and black-suited, his back to me, sat rigid. She said something to him. I couldn't hear her words. He shrugged. A quick movement. I wanted to see his face. I imagined him impatient. Manly removed. Not understanding. The woman looked up at me, frowned, and I moved my eyes from her face.

"The sheriff's got a table over by the window. You wanna sit with him?"

"What?" I said, startled.

"You wanna sit with Sheriff Parker?" Bailey poked my arm with a menu.

I frowned, rubbed my arm. "Where?"

"With Sheriff Parker. Over there." She pointed to the only other table with a body sitting at it. "You blind or something?" Then she jerked her head at the couple. "Or maybe just nosy." I smiled and sighed. "I guess there are just some things Harriet forgot to teach you, Bailey—like manners."

"Almost closing time, no time for manners. Not even the ones you're not showing. You wanna sit with him or not?"

"Sure, why not?"

She lumped her way to his table, slapped the menu down hard, and grunted, "I'll be back in a minute. Less'un you know what you want right now."

"Grilled cheese and coffee."

She grunted again and walked away.

Lowell grinned. It was almost a smirk. "Got a friend there, huh?"

"She moves a little faster than she did ten years ago. But her pleasant genes still haven't kicked in."

He laughed. "Too old. They're dead by now. Sit."

I did.

"What are you doing up so late?" he asked.

I ignored his question, leaned forward and with a quick nod, bent my head in the direction of the couple in the corner. "You know who they are?"

"Yep. Schrock's wife's sister and her husband."

"I remember Schrock. He was Lily's age. Sometimes, he brought her home from Sunday Sings. Only mostly he had a liking for Ellie Miller. I think he married her. I know he did. I saw them when I was back here ten years ago."

"He did. Couple years after your first shunning . . . and leaving."

"And that can't be his wife's sister. Ellie is Amish, always has been, and she didn't have any sisters, Amish or otherwise."

"Ellie died, and he got a new wife. An Englisher."

I turned my head and looked full at her. She had her hands over her face and was shaking her head.

"Doesn't look too happy to me," I said.

"He probably didn't let her see her sister."

"Her husband? Why wouldn't he want her to visit her sister? Doesn't he like the Amish?"

"Not *that* husband. Schrock. He's the one. Keeps everybody away from Mattie . . . the new wife."

"Why?"

"Dun know; just ornery, I guess."

"What's she look like?"

"The new wife? Dun know. Never saw her."

"How'd Ellie die?" I asked, half listening to Lowell, while I watched Mattie's sister dab her eyes and push her chair away from the table. Her husband didn't help her, waited 'til she was up, then turned and walked to the door. He was a handsome man. Mattie's sister followed him.

"Childbirth."

"What!"

"Childbirth," he repeated. "Ellie died birthing her child. First one she would have had. A little boy. He died too. Least ways, that's what Herffort tells me."

"Can't be. When I left ten years ago, Ellie was a healthy, young teenager going to Sunday night singings and riding home with adolescent, hopeful, Amish boys in their courting buggies. She was too young to die."

"Apparently not."

"And you've never seen the new wife?" *That can't be so. He sees everyone.*

"Not much. Keeps to herself."

"I should go visit her."

"She won't let you in. She turned Amish. So, she can't talk to you."

"She doesn't know who I am, and if I dress nearly Amish, she probably wouldn't have a clue who she's talking to, and why she shouldn't."

"You think you can get past old Schrock?" Lowell grinned. "Not a chance."

"I'm gonna try."

"Schrock sold his farm and moved."

"Where?"

"Way back in the hills."

"I'll find him."

Lowell laughed. "I just bet you will."

Bailey brought my sandwich. No remarks. No smiles. Same old, scroogy face. Put the plate down. Put the coffee cup down. Hard. Liquid splashed. She looked at it, shrugged and left.

"Is everybody in this town a grouch?" I asked.

Lowell, sober-faced, pushed the sugar bowl across the table. I shook my head, and he pulled it back. "Serious time, Cora."

I waited, watched his fingers drum on the table. Then stop. He'd changed the tone of our conversation, and I wasn't sure I wanted him to delve into my mind or offer me words of wisdom. His wisdom. I didn't say anything. If he wanted to talk, he'd have to start it. And he did.

"Have you given any thought, Cora?"

"To what." And I knew my words rang belligerent.

"Don't play games, Cora."

"I'm not. She didn't commit suicide. Nobody knew Lily better than I did. She wouldn't do that. She just wouldn't."

"But she did."

"I don't want to talk about this."

"I don't want you stirring up trouble."

"She has a right to be buried with every other Amish person. She was good. *She didn't commit suicide.*"

"If I have to stop you, I will."

"I hurt. I hurt. Can't you hear me? *I hurt.*"

"You can't change what is." His voice was hard, cold. "You keep pushing this, you'll bring it all back and hurt others. Hurt 'em bad. Let it go. It was a long time ago."

"I can't. It was wrong what they did. They buried her in the wrong place."

He leaned across the table, spoke into my face slowly, each word staccato. "If the things you do cause others to hurt, and your behavior comes from the hurt you and others previously lived, and if they've overcome that pain, your questions and snooping spread your original maintained and nourished hurt, so that it not only controls you, but touches and hurts them." He drew in a deep breath. "Is that what you want to do?"

"Don't you understand? It was me that killed Lily. It was *me.* But for me, she wouldn't have died. She wouldn't have fallen into the creek. She would have been home taking care of little Annabelle. But I took her baby away, stole her . . . *gave her away."* I put my hands over my lips, wished I could hide those words, make them lying, never-happened words. But they were real. And true. And I didn't want Lowell to know that deep down, way down deep, I was afraid. Maybe I had driven Lily to hate herself, her life, so much, she ended it.

"I could say I understand," Lowell said, and I heard empathy in his voice. "I could tell you, it's possible what you say. And I'd like to be able to say that. But you're wrong, Cora. And until you accept what is and realize you're not at fault, and if you did make a mistake, accept that. Let it go. You can't change it, but you can dredge up the anguish and misery of resting sorrow. Why would you do that? Would it make you feel better? I don't think so, Cora. Let it go. Let it go."

"How do I stop it?"

"Forgive yourself, Cora. Just forgive yourself."

He got up to leave. He patted my shoulder as he went by me.

Bailey came and took my plate. "You done?"

I nodded and left.

I got in my car and drove to the motel, parked, opened the car door, slid my foot onto the ground, held it there a moment, and then drew it back in. I leaned forward and covered my face with my hands. I didn't want to go into a room that didn't know me. So, I started the car, and I drove—into the hills, into Amish land.

I don't know how long I drove, but, eventually, I found

myself near the cemetery. I stopped and walked up the hill toward Lily's grave. The air was cool, moved gently across my skin. When I reached the fence, I slipped my shoes off. The grass was soft, damp under my feet. Spring soil. Fresh beneath my soles. I passed the fence, trance-walked across its spongy surface, and sat by Lily's grave. I folded my hands together and spoke to her.

"Isn't it . . . I don't know, strange, sad . . . something happens, or a word is said, or a document written, and it's there forever. *Forgive.* One day passes into another and what is done or said or written sits there, and we're helpless to do anything to make it different. Except . . . maybe . . . I've been thinking, trying to rise above old thinking. Maybe we can change what is solid and done, at least in our hearts and head. We can forgive. We can let go. We can forget. No matter how hard, we can do that. It's a wonderous gift. Forgiveness. It takes us through those things that can break us. And if God did not forgive, I would be forever condemned. But, oh Lily, if He can forgive, if He can forgive *me,* how can I not do the same and forgive myself?"

I sat awhile, until I felt the damp of earth seeping through my jeans. I smiled and drove back to the motel and slept.

Chapter Nine

I had told Lowell I would do it, and I did. The next morning, I lifted the Amishy clothes I'd worn the day before and had dropped on the floor, smoothed my hand over them, figured they were adequately unwrinkled, and put them on. Then, I twirled my hair into a bun and wrapped a white kerchief over it. Hoped it would fool Schrock's wife into thinking it was a badly stitched *kapp* . . . or maybe with luck, she had poor eyesight. Anyway, if she had truly taken Amish vows into her heart, she would be too polite to utter a negative comment. I was looking forward to meeting this woman. She carried none of my sad memories. A refreshing thought. And just as I promised Lowell, I went looking for Mystery Wife.

The day was gorgeous. The thickly, packed together, larger trees and scraggly, smaller trees scattered outside the wood's boundaries were dressed with fresh, green, dewy leaves. Released from winter's heavy snow cover, the soil, richly darkened by spring rains, was patched with clusters of sun-spattered spring flowers, and the sky, a radiant blue, was filled with mounds of pure white clouds. Gorgeous!

It wasn't hard to find Schrock's buildings. I had a general

sense of their location and assumed when I found the messiest and neediest buildings, they would be his.

I was right. There was no mailbox, but the whole of the farm—house, barn, outbuildings, pasture, broken fences, rusty machinery, unkempt fields cried out, *put my name on the envelope, SCHROCK, and deliver it here.* No need for further identification.

As my car jerked down Schrock's rut-furrowed driveway, I glanced, when I dared, at the landscape around me. Apparently, Mystery Wife had been up early. Sheets, towels, black pants, shirts, and dresses hung from lines strung across the yard. They hinted at least one reasonably orderly soul lived there. A dusting of buttercups and daisies dappled the yard, while fresh plantings of summer flowers, impatiens and geraniums, just starting to bloom, lined the farmhouse's foundation. Encouraging.

I drove as close to the house as I could. Because the trampled grass path from driveway to porch steps appeared muddied and slippery, I considered my choices for reaching the building without falling. I could think of none. If I wanted to knock one's door, I'd have to risk the possibility of sliding and plummeting into a dawn-wet, sloppy mass of soil and grass. So be it. Clothes could be washed; and bodies, showered. Determined, I hefted myself out of the car and plunked my feet onto the path. It wasn't as bad as I thought it would be. Sturdy, soled shoes are not pretty, but I'd been sensible enough to wear them. And I hoped when I was done with this visit, the sun would have dried the mud . . . and sheets. Or miracle of miracles, Schrock would take time from needed work and lay some planks over the walkway. Probably not.

I made it to the front door and knocked. I waited. No one came to the door.

I knocked again.

Still no one came to the door. But I saw a curtain move.

I waited. No one came. I left.

The path had not dried, and the driveway was still potholed. I drove back to the motel.

I was tired. I shed my fake-Amish clothes, crawled back into scruffy sheets, buried my head into scroungy pillow lumps and tried to sleep. I couldn't. I guess I wasn't tired enough to overcome a lumpy mattress and mangy pillow. Since it appeared I wasn't going to make a quick, welcoming entrance into the arms of the Amish community, I decided it was time to find better housing. I got up, showered, and dressed in regular clothing. It felt good.

Daniel's framed photograph rested on my bedside table. Running my fingers over his face, tender remembrances slid through my mind engendering lovely, wispy feelings. "Time to move on again, Daniel. Any suggestions?" I whispered. His dear, smiling image—paper and permanent—stared back at me. "Guess not. Guess I'm on my own."

I packed. Didn't have much. Guess I thought I wouldn't be needing my Englisher clothes very long. Looks like I was wrong. The thirty-year-old shunning was still in effect. Strong as ever. Maybe, when every Amish body, with eyes that had ever touched me or ears had heard of me . . . was dead, I could live, unashamed, in their presence.

I returned my key to the office. Old Grumpy was there with her negative words of wisdom. I listened quietly, slid the required dollars across the counter, wished her well, and left.

Wander Lane hadn't changed much in the last ten years. A few more shops. Mostly Amish and small. A candle, cookie and candy shoppe. A tiny donut and cider café—two tables, four chairs. A second quilt shop. An outdoor display of baked goods, glass-jarred vegetables, and handmade brooms. Main Street was fairly empty of shoppers. That would change when summer arrived. I liked it that way. Quiet. The sense and smell of authentic Amish sinking into my skin. Real. Slow. Without the push of product, the hidden hand waiting to appear, to slide open for silver and dollar passing from Englisher purse to Amish open palm.

I stopped at the only Wander Lane realty. Exuberant and many-worded Gloria Snyder regretted although she had many and sundry homes listed for sale, she had almost nil rentals. However, Olivia's old house had been empty for some time and perhaps, with a little wheeling and dealing, Dianna might be willing to rent it out. Gloria was sure Dianna would be happy to do such a favor for her good friend, Cora. And it was fully furnished.

I shuddered at the sudden appearance of that house in my mind and shook my head, hoping to erase the clear vision of the chair upon which I'd laid and left baby, Annabelle, and the bed upon which Olivia had died.

"I don't think so," I said. "Nothing else?"

"Would you consider buying?"

"No."

"Not staying long?"

I said nothing.

"Hmm." She pursed her lips and stared at me. "Well, I guess

you'll just have to stay at the motel at the edge of town. I guess that's where you have been staying. A bit dingy, but I hear it's clean enough. I can't think of anywhere else to go. Maybe you should reconsider buying as an investment—a useful investment."

She wrinkled her nose, and I smiled inside. She was well aware a second motel was at the opposite side of town. A chain motel. Built for summer vacationers seeking the "authentic" sights of Amish life, but wanting electric lights, wi-fi, and hot showers. Pricier, and not needing her help to fill its rooms, and therefore no commissions. I shook my head and left.

Heeding the grumble of my stomach and the imagined drool of shoofly pie juice sliding down my chin, I made my way down Main Street to Wagler's Authentic Amish Bakery. Still there. Front window still shelved with pies . . . cherry, apple, peach, plum, and best of all, shoofly. My mouth watered.

I went in. Same Wagler girl behind the counter. Older, but still youngish pretty. She was busy with some paperwork and when she looked up, she was smiling. A welcoming smile. And when she looked at me, she recognized me. The smile disappeared.

"I remember you," she said, and so swiftly her hand drew up to cover her lips, as if to push the words back into her mouth.

"I still like shoofly pie," I said softly.

She didn't say anything. She knew the rules.

"Just a slice," I said.

With rapid movement, she turned, took a pie from the shelf behind her, put it on the counter, cut a slice, put it on a napkin. Held it out to me.

I sucked in my lips, held them tight together, kept them from allowing words to pass through. I knew this was hard for her. Awkward. I wished she had not remembered me. And I wished

I had remembered I was shunned and had stayed away from this place. She had been kind to me once, ten years ago, before she'd known my bishop had determined and declared my sinful state.

I took the pie, laid money on the counter, and left.

Outside the shop, I threw the pie in a trash container. I wasn't hungry anymore.

I got in my car and drove. Over the Amish hills. Bright-colored under a serene sky clouded with wispy bits of flimsy white. Lush, green fields. Rich, brown soil. Pastures welcoming frisky milk cows, released from stanchions, greedily attacking fresh, sweet pastures, their hides gleaming clean, washed by sun rays. Rabbits, out of their holes and running. Amish wee ones, rolling in the grass, running, giggling, lifting dirt and pebbles, spreading their fingers, watching nature drift and shape the ground to look a little different.

I drove and drove. Not thinking. Feeling. Feeling earth. Feeling security. Belonging. Amish peace. Innocence.

And then the tears came. I wanted it so badly. What they had used to be mine. And at the same time, it wasn't at all what I wanted. I had stepped out of the prison of rules and rules and rules. No deviation. No creativity. No thinking. Just rules. But love in abundance was there for me, if I narrowed myself to fit. If I was sorry. If I confessed. If I stopped thinking outside the rules. But I couldn't do that. I knew I couldn't do that. Yet, I knew I couldn't let go. Not until I got Lily placed into ground that held the birthright of her community. Sacred ground. Deserved ground. I'd stay and vindicate her. Whatever it took.

I still needed a place to live. Something more personal than a motel. It was pointless to keep driving around looking for rent signs. There had to be someone in Wander Lane who knew the ins and outs of every soul in the village. Ten years ago, that would have been Harriet. Not anymore. And as the thought of her went through my mind, I reproached myself for not yet seeking her out, knowing it was selfish not to. I was afraid to. She wouldn't be the same. Old age had robbed her, ripped out a part of her life and left her in an arid land of lost memory. I didn't want that to be my memory of her.

But there were some. Some who knew every ounce of the weighty substance of Wander Lane. Tilly. And good, old Sheriff Parker. He knew it all too, but he would be too judgmental and factual. Tilly would be just right. She would know all rental possibilities, and she would know the juicy incidentals of each of those potential properties and its owner. And she would relish the telling of them.

Tilly wasn't at her desk. I considered approaching Lowell's office, but decided I wasn't in the mood for his critiques, thereby saving brain cells that would have been wasted by listening to his unwanted and unappreciated words. However, as my hand reached for the doorknob that led out, my ears heard the rumble of heavy feet attacking the floorboards. Lowell. He must have heard the buzzer on the door. I turned and saw it was, indeed, he. Not acknowledging I was there, he slammed a pack of papers on Tilly's desk and then glared in my direction.

I lifted my eyebrows and shrugged.

"You here to see Tilly or me? And if it's me, make it short."

"And if it's long?"

"Okay." He shook his head. "Maybe if we talk, we can get this straightened out, and you can head back north."

He turned and stomped back to his office.

I smiled. There was a certain satisfaction that came from annoying him. I hurried and followed.

"You'd miss me," I said, as I stood inside his office door surveying the messy room, and then shaking my head, I pushed papers off a chair to make space for me to sit.

He glowered, plunked down on his desk chair, slapped his hands on the desktop, and said nothing.

"Actually, I'm here to ask Tilly to help me find a rental."

"Long term?"

"Maybe."

"What are you really here for, Cora?"

"I told you. I'm looking for a place to rent."

"Besides that. Why are you really here in Wander Lane? Besides thinking you can find proof Lily didn't commit suicide. Which you can't." He bent over his desk. "And you know it. There's nobody else agreeing with you, and the only person who could give you any help is Jacob Lapp, and he's long gone. Stay if you want. But make it a vacation." He leaned back in his chair. "A short one."

"Maybe you're right," I said quietly, "but I don't think so."

"Look, you want something you're not going to get. So, let it go."

I heard a faint gentleness in his voice. I didn't want sympathy. I wanted help. And I wanted a place to live.

"It wasn't your fault, you know," he continued. "Lily was the one who got pregnant. And she just wasn't strong enough to deal with it. But you were. You did what you had to do. Sometimes we're right, sometimes we're wrong. Who knows? But it's done and over with. Let it go."

"And sometimes we can fix what we did."

"Cora, I'm sure you've done a lot worse in your life. So what else is on your mind?"

"No, that's it. Mostly. She's still in sullied soil, Lowell." And as I spoke, a flash of Talitha's child blazed in my head. *And you're right, Lowell Parker, sometimes we're wrong. Way wrong. There was more than just Lily buried outside the fence. More for me to be guilty about. There was a wee child born from an incestuous coupling. What do I do with that, Lowell Parker? What do I do with the secret I know? Oh, God, I should never have taken that child, Lily's baby, away from her. Lily's baby, Talitha. She, a new mother of her own child . . . one child, both son and nephew. Oh God, what do I do now?* I swallowed and tried to push Talitha's child out of my head. "All I want from you today is a bit of your brain. Do you know of any places for rent?"

"No. And you go do what you have to do, Cora," Lowell said, ending my thoughts of Talitha and her baby, leading me back to the guilt and search he already knew was mine. He picked up a pencil and motioned toward the door. "Just don't cause trouble."

I got up and followed the direction of his pencil, but when I got to the door I stopped, turned, looked at him, tightened my face and scowled.

"It would be easy if I turned back to the Amish, repented and accepted that life. Again. Fully. Without reservation. Or thought. Just followed the rules. The Amish don't bend. Nor do they break. No reason to. It's all spelled out, in the *Ordnung*. And in all their actions and thinking, all of them are monitored by the bishop to make sure no one forgets what's in that oral book of rules." I sucked in my cheeks, drew in a deep breath. "But I

61

bend. And I don't break. Not because of some frivolous rule, but because I have a mind that thinks, contemplates, deliberates, and I keep going. Searching. Stretching beyond the obvious, and, sometimes, beyond the *Ordnung,* sometimes beyond acceptable behavior. It's God I look to, not a book of Amish rules. He won't lead me wrong. So listen to my words, Lowell Parker. Listen hard. I know I can't be Amish, and I can't let go; I won't let go. Not yet. Trouble or not, I won't let go, until there's nothing left to find." Defiant, I lifted my chin and glared at him. "That's who I am. And because I'm Cora Pooler, strong and determined, I'll stand fast in what I know is right, and like I said, I won't let go. Not until I'm done."

He nodded, said nothing for a moment, and then he smiled. "Looks like we got a fight going on here, Cora Pooler." His smile widened. "And you won't win."

Chapter Ten

Tilly still wasn't at her desk when I marched by it. It didn't matter. I'd find my own place to live, and if it had to be in a motel at whichever end of town, so be it.

Jittery, angry, I jammed myself into my car and headed out of Wander Lane. I was hungry, but food could wait. Getting away from people, Amish and English, and their efforts and declarations, their attempts to make their values and opinions mine, was the compelling force that fueled the desperate need to get them behind me. And driving through the strength and harmony of solid earth and sky, soothed my soul to amity.

I drove far beyond Wander Lane, passed little towns, farms, great expanses of changing countryside . . . forest, field, pasture . . . and, over all the beauty chained to earth's floor was a massive, moving sky, streaked with shades of blues and whites. And I lost the sense of separate and meshed with all that was living outside the bars of my incarcerated body. It was good.

Eventually, my body made its needs known, and I stopped at a diner. I left it refreshed and full, turned my car around and headed back to Wander Lane. As I drove slowly over the winding country roads, familiar from years of riding over them as an Amish girl, in a black buggy, visiting neighbors, going to suppers, quiltings, weddings, Sunday services and sings, I relaxed and remembered good times, love, companionship. I'd been a happy child. It was all good. Until Lily got pregnant, and I gave away her baby. And even then, it was good. I found a satisfying life among the Englishers. And I found Daniel. Love. Wonderful. But he died. And now I'm alone—searching. I'd tried once before to return to Amish life, be a solid part of it. It didn't work. It wasn't me. I needed to accept. Let go of a lingering, wispy desire to lose myself in that rigid, creative-killing, but loving and secure, life. Time to draw into my wealth of strength, do what needed to be done, and leave. I relaxed, let myself drink in God's presence, accept His care and wisdom, and enjoy the natural beauty of His creation.

I came upon a dirt road that twisted off the county highway I was on. I didn't remember it. Unencumbered, body and mind mellowed, I decided to explore. On either side of that narrow, bumpy road were plowed rows of soil ready for planting. Probably corn. I rolled my window down to catch the rich scent of turned earth. It made me feel Amish.

I saw simple houses, rockers on porches, blue front doors, curtains hung the same in all house windows. Big barns. Doors open, airing the stench and clutter of long, unventilated winter months. And near the outbuildings were large, manure piles ready to be shoveled onto wagons and spread over fields, feeding the land with nutriments. Close to the barns, tall fence wired silos were almost empty of corn. Farm implements and equipment ready for use were strewn over thawing ground. As I drove down the road, it pleasured me to see straw-hatted Amish men, bodies bent back, shirts rolled up to their elbows, walking behind their great, stately workhorses. Men holding tight to the reins and to the handles of sharp-bladed plows as they, together with their horses, turned spring-softened soil into rows for the seeds that would grow and produce product to eat, to sell, to feed their animals. And it pleasured me to see Amish women washing winter grime from their windows, hanging laundry on lines strung outside for the sun to dry their clothing, soft and sweet-scented, and other dark-dressed, Amish women planting gardens for food and flowers for beauty. A peaceful life, uncomplicated, constant . . . decreed. Nostalgically, remembered. Realistically, unwanted.

The road took me to a great stretch of woodlands. Trees on either side. Thick. Pines mixed within maples and oaks and elms. Limbs free from the dread of winter cold and howling winds, stretched upward to the sun. Those same limbs, dressed with an abundant hoard of lush, green leaves, shadowed the ground provided hiding spots, resting spots for small forest animals. I was tempted to stop and roam through the trees. Touch the bark's rough textures; slide my fingers over the silky smoothness of new foliage; draw in the sweet, musky, mingled scent of many different trees and shrubs and woodland plants; sink my feet into the damp sponge of the forest floor. But I didn't. I needed to find my way back to Wander Lane and make arrangements for my night's dwelling.

The forest stretched for many miles, but eventually thinned and the rolling hills, bare of trees, lay green, ready for field or pasture. I wasn't exactly sure where I was, but I felt I was close to the outskirts of my Amish community. And I was. As I passed an Amish buggy, I recognized the wheels unique to my Wander Lane Amish. A feeling of home washed through me. Would it always be so?

I saw a path veering off the road. It was buggy-wide, almost hidden by clumps of grass and a sea of early dandelions, but even though a little leery, considering I'd seen few other cars or buggies on this road, I decided to explore it. I had legs that could walk long distances over rough terrain, if they had to, and a can of pepper spray in my purse, if that was needed. A refreshing rush of excitement swept through me, and I opened all my windows to absorb and enjoy the sounds and smells of country. Happy, I turned the car onto the path, and gunned it.

It wasn't so bad. A bit bumpy, but under all the foliage, there were hints of tracks my tires could follow. Though I drove slowly, there was enough breeze to lift my hair, and my body was pleasantly warmed by sun rays streaming through the windshield. I relaxed and enjoyed the scenery.

After driving about a mile, the path wove beneath and through an enchanting wooded expanse, with old and stately oak trees on either side of the roadway. Their lush, green-leafed limbs stretched upward and over the road, meeting those across from them, entwining and forming a majestic arch above my car. It shadowed the air, and I basked in the magic of driving through a sun-streaked veil.

As I came out from under the sweeping curvature, the path ended. Before me was a massive meadow of unfettered grass, thick and rich in color. And in the middle of the field was a building. Small. Weathered brown. There was a porch. A place for rockers. And maybe a few potted plants. Geraniums. And, surely, a basket of yarn.

But it was falling apart. The house. Old. Discarded. Maybe not. There was a path of trampled grass leading from the back of the house to the place where the meadow ended and a scraggly, wooded area began. I thought to leave the car and explore, but the field was too open, too far from the country road, and I didn't know what or whom I might find in the cabin. And I dared not drive the car onto the grass. It might be covering softened spring soil. Ground that would sink a car.

I needed to get back to the dirt-packed country road I'd left. The hours were passing, and I hadn't yet found lodging for the night. Looking at the expanse of field before me and the horde of oaks on either side of me, I wasn't sure what to do. There was no safe place to turn the car. I feared the spring-dampened field would be far too spongy to hold the vehicle's weight. I could try. But if I got stuck, the legs of which I'd felt such confidence, with practical thinking, would take forever to get to a place of people, particularly when I wasn't sure how close people were. I really had only one choice. I took it and began the backward trek of the car making its way down the rutty, bumpy path.

It took a long time. And it took away every bit of my patience and the pleasure of beauty turned obstructive. My neck cricked, my legs cramped, my back strained muscles. My temper rose and flourished.

But I made it. *Thank you, God. And please forgive my temper. It was justified, but I probably should have curbed my anger a bit better.* I was back on the welcomed, hard-packed-dirt country road.

I aimed the car to go the same direction it'd been going, before I erred and turned on that miserable path. It seemed I must be fairly close to Wander Lane. And I was. The road made a sharp turn. I rounded it, and there, a short distance before me was Schrock's farm. It looked to be a walking distance from the rough path I'd explored. I pulled over to the side of the road. Pondered. Visualized the meadow, grass trampled behind the ramshackle building that led into a thicketed area. I was too far to see if the grass beyond the brush was trampled. Something or someone had made a path to that old building, and I wondered if it could be the grouch, Schrock himself, who had walked that path. It was hard to tell from such a distance.

I watched for awhile. Then I saw Schrock, swinging a milk pail in each hand, coming out of the barn and trudging across dirt and lawn to his house. My eyes strained to see. Schrock kicked the back door, hard, immediately, it opened part way. Then I saw an arm stretch out and take one pail from him, retreat, return and take the other. A glimpse of those quick actions revealed a portion of black skirt skimming the house floor. Schrock turned and stomped back to the barn.

I determined it was not a good time to attempt a meeting. I sighed and drove the short distance to the county road, and, still following the boundaries of the Schrock farm, turned onto it and headed for Wander Lane.

Chapter Eleven

I stopped at a fast food chain outside the village and filled my stomach with a hamburger and fries. Greasy, but tasty. A treat to temper the rumble in my head. It seemed uncertainties had invaded my mind, each one bumping against another, vying for preferential resolution. Lily. Lowell. A baby born that shouldn't be. A place to sleep.

The last was the easiest. I registered at the better motel. Newer. Flashier. Probably cleaner. Costlier. The clerk was pleasant. She checked my credit card, examined my license, and handed me a key card—all the while smiling. I took the bulk of my luggage to the assigned room, threw it on the bed, checked the towels, and left the room. I elevatored to the lobby, returned the wave from the still smiling clerk, went through the motel front door, and walked into fresh, clean, darkening air.

I stopped a moment, drew in the sweet scent of new grass, felt the soft, slide of evening slip over my body. I relaxed.

My feet took me across the portico onto the stretch of cement that led to a sidewalk. I paused, dropped my head and closed my eyes, absorbed the peace of dropping night. Pacified, mind cleared of thought, body attuned to the feel of earth and air, I continued along the sidewalk, crossed the street and onto the walkway that followed the park side of Main Street.

The air had cooled. Pleasantly. Across the evening-shaded street, I saw Hattie Shackleton come out from her quilt shop and step into the black buggy waiting at the curb. I wondered if she remembered me, and if this time, if I were to address her, would she still turn away? Did the rules of shunning still pour visibly over me? Probably. Definitely. Ten years would not have faded an aged, given ban.

I walked on. The deepening dark had smudged the outlines of objects around me. Streetlights glowed mellow, waiting to shine full when the sun had ended its drop and was swallowed far into the ground.

My eyes fell on a huddled, dark shape on the bench directly across from Harriet's Eatery. Though the falling night shrouded its form, I knew it to be a person. As I drew closer, I recognized Harriet. My Harriet. A tremor of joy slid through me.

I slipped silently, gently, onto the bench, sat quietly waiting to decipher her response to my presence. There was none. She seemed locked in a world that only she knew. I put my hand on her knee, leaned back against the bench and, eyes looking straight ahead into the evolving night, spoke "It's me, Harriet. Cora. Cora Pooler." She said nothing.

"Think, Harriet. Look deep into your heart. It's me. Cora Pooler. Do you remember?" I paused. When still she said nothing, I continued. "Do you remember the Amish girl who ran down the hill, with her little sisters, bringing you tomatoes and cucumbers and green beans.

"Fresh from *Maem's* garden. And onions. Sometimes, onions. Big, white, juicy ones. Remember? You skinned their outer layer and squeezed them, made their juices run. Tears. You said the onions cried, were sad, didn't want to be eaten. Violet and Lily laughed at your words. They loved you, not because you gave them candy. Hard as rocks. Enough pieces for each to have plenty with extras to take back to their brothers. They loved you because you loved them, and they knew it.

"And do you remember when that Amish girl, woman, gave away a baby? Do you remember her shunning, her banishment? Do you remember her coming back years later to find that baby? She went to you. And you consoled her and finally told her where the baby was. And even more, you made a way for her mother to talk to her shunned daughter. A secret place. Never told. And do you remember holding, comforting that Amish woman when she came to you, broken-hearted and shunned, not able to go to her sister's funeral?

"That Amish girl, woman, loved you . . . loves you. Do you know that? I need you, Harriet. Just to listen. To hear, if you can. Because I'm hurting, floundering, scared. And you are comfort to me."

I waited. Silence, only silence. But even so, it felt good, sitting with her. After a bit, I felt her hand light on my cheek. It stayed there awhile, then slipped slowly to her lap, slid, and rested over mine on her knee. I nodded. Sometimes, we don't have words, we don't have understanding, yet sometimes, we can feel the soul of another. Empathy. It soothes the one in need. I would come back another time. Talk again. Speak the sorrows, the questions, the fear in my heart. Another time. I creeped my hand from under hers and moved my arm across her shoulders, held her. Tonight had been enough for her, and for me. There would be another time.

It was fully night when Bailey dimmed the eatery's lights and crossed the road to claim Harriet. Her face showed clear under the now bright streetlamp. I couldn't read its surface.

She didn't look at me, glided her arm to rest firm against Harriet's back, and with a solid, strong grasp took the hand that had covered mine and raised the old woman to her feet. She led her away.

I watched them walk into the darkness. When I could see them no longer, I turned and walked back to the motel.

Morning came. I rose and looked around the room. Sterile. Clean, but sterile. No personality. If I were going to stay in Wander Lane for any length of time, I needed to leave this room, this motel, and find a place that mirrored me.

I went to Tilly.

She was at her desk, head thrust forward, eyes concentrating on the screen before her.

"Tilly?"

She lifted her head, rubbed her eyes with the heels of her palms. Smiled. "Cora."

"Good morning," I said.

"You're lucky. He's not available. Got a meeting going on with the deputies in the back room. And I've seen him in way better moods than he's in this morning. Like I say, you're lucky."

"I didn't come to see him."

Tilly raised her eyebrows.

"I came to see you."

"Okay?" She tilted her head and leaned forward.

"I need a place to live."

"You're staying in Wander Lane?"

I nodded. "For awhile. I'm not sure how long. But I think it could be a fairly long while."

"I see." Tilly bit her lower lip and frowned. "You want a place to rent?"

"Uh-huh."

"The problem is, Cora, there aren't many rentals. At least not close. There will be in the summer. But not now. The locals kind of only like to rent rooms in the summer and even then, full apartments are scarce." She scrunched her face. "But I can think of a possible solution. Maybe."

She paused. I waited, watched her finger tap her teeth as she seemed to consider the situation.

"How much are you willing to pay?" she finally asked.

My answer was immediate. "Whatever it takes."

"Daniel left you well off?"

I smiled. "Very."

"Then it turns out your luck might just have changed."

"You know someone?" I questioned.

"Lots of someones."

"And who might they be?" Quickly scanning possibilities in my mind, I came up with nothing feasible.

She didn't answer at once. As I watched her run her tongue over her lip, I sensed a reluctance. Then she expelled an audible breath and rushed an answer. "The Amish."

My stare focused hard on her. "What?"

"The Amish," she repeated. "Lots of them rent out rooms to vacationers wanting to taste the simple life."

"In the summer," I stated.

"Yes," she agreed, "but you know as well as I do, the Amish

like to make money."

"I'm shunned."

"I repeat, the Amish like to make money."

"*I'm shunned,*" I repeated.

"They don't have to talk to you. Put a plate on the table, clean sheets on the bed, hand you some towels, take your money, and you're both happy."

"It's a way to get in," I said softly.

"That's what you want, isn't it?" She cocked her head and gave a quick nod. "Right in the middle of it all. A way to get answers."

I smiled. Tilly was a clever lady. Apparently with big ears. Good ears. Listening ears. And a head that could put two and two together. It wouldn't be easy. I'd have to get permission from Bishop Herrfort. My smile widened. He was a good man, but he liked money too.

"Yes," I said. "It's worth a try."

Chapter Twelve

I didn't go directly to Bishop Herrfort's house. I needed to be prepared with words that would reach through his Amish rigidity—humble and polite words that would touch and resonate in a place where oral-branded words commanded his every thought, word, and deed. It had been long since I'd thought as an Amisher, and I struggled to squelch the reluctance and fears that bade me not go back there again, lest I lose the strength that kept me from sinking back into the simplicity that kills the mind's ability to stretch. But I needed to remember the words, the directives of the *Ordnung,* words seared on the mind, not written on paper. Herrfort would know every one of them . . . and he would use them. Twenty years ago, he had told me I didn't speak like an Amish woman, nor did I behave like an Amish woman. I tried, then, to put together the rhythm and words of an obedient disciple, to adhere to the rules of The Way, and to live with invisible, unyielding bars bound strong around my body and soul. I couldn't do it. I failed. As I drove over the twisting roads and low, rolling hills to the dirt pathway that led to Bishop Herrfort's home, I prayed God would lead me to be respectful and honest.

I drove slowly. As I grew closer to Herrfort's farm, I tried to empty my head of old thoughts, my heart of old hurts. I was afraid. Herrfort was a wise man, a discerning man. I wanted to say true words, but I did not want him to know the secrets and fears of my heart. If he perceived the scope of my search, my reason for returning, he would turn his back and remain that way, until I was gone from Wander Lane. Without his blessing, there would be no way I could find housing in his community, and so I drove slowly, postponing. Even so, my car, eventually, came to his house and stopped there. I got out.

There was no one in the yard. The barn door was shut; the farm implements lined and clean. Behind the barn, I saw cows grazing in the pasture, and with them the large muscled horses used for hauling and plowing, and the sleek, retired racehorse that drew his buggy. Though the yard grass was cut, flats of seedlings lined the house borders, and more of them lay scattered down rows of the newly turned soil by the barn, a waiting garden ready to be planted. I saw no one doing the work.

I looked at my watch. A little too early for Amish dinner. I smiled. But Martha Herrfort would be working at it.

As I went up the porch steps and across the wood floor, I smelled beef boiling and yeast rising. I closed my eyes, pressed my lips together, parted them to release a deep sigh, and knocked on the door.

A woman, skin loose and seeming to slide down her body, a late-winter snowman melting beneath a springtime, hot, noonday sun, opened the door—Martha Herrfort. The bishop's wife. She led me into the house. I don't believe she recognized me. She had hesitated, appeared puzzled, leaned forward and squinting, slightly shook her head, said nothing. Then she raised her hand, quirked her finger, and with that gesture, bid me follow her. I did. She took me into the kitchen.

Bishop Herrfort sat at the kitchen table, a bible open before him. Without seeing the words on the pages of the book, I knew they were not English words. It would be a German Bible he was reading. I smiled. It would be good to hold that book in my hands again, the old, first-learned language still remembered in my heart.

He had aged. Ten years had worn hard on him. When he lifted his eyes to look at me, they were the milky white of eyes that had seen long and were tired. But I could tell they knew me.

Their lids did not close for a challenging length of time.

His nod was slight. "Cora Pooler."

There were tears in my eyes. I didn't know where they came from. The loss of years in the comfort of knowing this man that would have given me the ease of a straight-formed, unchallenging life? The stretch of time without family, not knowing their touch, their acceptance, their unquestioning love? The soothing balm of all questions answered before they were asked? Was it regret, or the sorrow of knowing my words would hurt this godly man?

"Bishop Herrfort," I said softly. "It's good to see you."

"It's been a long time you've been gone." He sat back in his chair. "But you're back." He stared at me. His look was intense, but I could see no animosity. "Will you stay this time?"

"I don't know."

"Why are you here?" His voice was gentle.

"I need a place to live."

"We would welcome you back."

"As an *Englisher*?"

"You know the rules."

I heard a stirring spoon hit the side of a pan, as unobtrusive Martha went about the business of making dinner—a tomato sauce, for the beef. It smelled of home. Amish.

"I know Jesus." Though he had not actually asked a question, I answered him with words that indicated a resistance, but should not hurt. I stood by the table and waited for his reply. He had not asked me to sit.

"You know the rules," he repeated.

I hesitated, and then whispered, "I do."

"Are you ready to confess and obey?"

"The rules? No. To live as Jesus' child? Yes."

He brought a hand to his face and rubbed his cheek. "Then why are you here?"

"I want to buy the use of an Amish bed for several weeks."

"A room. For yourself."

They, too, were not questions, but I answered them. "Yes."

"Ten years pass, after twenty years gone, and you come back. I told you then that you didn't speak like an Amish woman, or live like one. Car. Clothes. Coarse words. Challenging words. English. And you heard me. I gave you time, and you lived again, here, as Amish. Proved you were Amish. Confessed. Repented. You lived The Way, for a while. You tried. I know you tried. Yet our ways didn't suit you, Cora Pooler. You rebelled and left. Shunned again." He pressed his fingers against his eyes, then dropped his arms onto the table and leaned into their strength. And slowly shaking his head, he spoke, his words falling upon the table. "And you don't speak like an Amish woman now. A shunned woman. You speak like a shunned woman."

My chin trembled, as I focused my eyes on his bowed head.

I wanted to say Amish words of comfort and agreement. I could not.

"We want you back, Cora Pooler. You belong here." Still not looking at me, his words were said with gentle firmness.

"Will you let me come and live among you? As an Englisher who loves the Amish?" I asked softly, wanting to put my hand on his shoulder, but I dared not.

He didn't move. I knew he was thinking. Reciting the words of the *Ordnung* in his head, measuring them. Perhaps, he was hoping to fit me into them, but I knew he could not. They were his Scripture. He obeyed them. Then he raised his head and looked at me.

"You're Amish. Still Amish. Shunned. No one here could speak to you, listen to your words, touch you with love. For them your entity, body and soul, would be as invisible. I would ask you not to speak to them. I could not stop you. You are already shunned." He smiled, a mournful smile. "I know of no double-shunning. But I would ask you to obey that rule. It would be a kindness to them."

I couldn't nod agreement, and neither could I speak to affirm his words.

"Does this mean you will allow me to live among you?" I asked.

"Perhaps if you live among us, you will remember the peace, honesty and unity of our community. Security. Kindness. Love. Perhaps you will remember who you are."

I bit my lip and lowered my head. I saw my hands clasped tight against my clothing. I'd heard the words he'd said. Words tangled within my head unable to join together to form acceptable phrases to speak in return. There will always be a struggle within my soul. But the scale tips. One way calls louder than the other. Not love. The love is equal on both sides of the scale. But the understanding of the desires of its Source, the total obedience to its Source, is shaded different. It tips. It tips the scale to the call of the English. How could I say this to Bishop Herrfort.

I raised my head, stared at him, willed him to turn and look at me. He did not. "Do you mean then that you give permission for me to seek housing within the brethren?"

"*Ya.*"

Still he did not look at me. I waited.

Martha came up behind me. She reached around me and laid a plate before him . . . a knife, a spoon, a fork. She moved to the other end of the table and placed a setting there. Her setting. None for me. As she turned to go back to the stove and passed me, I felt a brief, gentle pat on my shoulder. It was enough. It was time for me to go.

I gazed down at the bishop. He sat so still. I knew sadness and regret, the failure to bring me back into the fold, were full in his heart, but he did not acknowledge me further.

"*Denke,*" I said softly, leaning forward so he could hear.

Martha led me to the front door. As a loving, Amish woman would do, she opened it for it me. Again, there was a passing touch on my arm, tender. And again, I felt the pain of shunning.

I wasn't sure how to find a family that would house me. Although it was too early in the year to find painted wooden signs stuck in the yards advertising Amish rooms for rent, Amish suppers to share, Amish baked goods to buy, I drove their Amish roads hoping for a rogue sign placed prematurely. I could find none. Discouraged and hungry, I headed back to the village, perhaps Tilly would know the names of those who might give me board.

Chapter Thirteen

Tilly wasn't at her desk. But Alice Morgan was—snooty Alice Morgan. I knew her from long ago. She was the lady who bought tomatoes and corn from *maem's* front-lawn vegetable stand, who pinched every tomato and stripped the husk from every ear of corn, eventually buying the plumpest and the fullest. And here she was, white-haired and scrawny, sitting at Tilly's desk. "Alice Morgan," I stated.

She looked up from the files she was reading, probably marked *confidential,* read on the sly, and frowned. "Cora Pooler?"

I smiled. She didn't.

"Where's Tilly?" I asked.

"Gone for the day." She offered no explanation. "And the sheriff ain't seeing nobody." Haughty.

I lifted my eyebrows, shrugged and turned toward his office, waited a moment, looked at Alice, smiled, and took a step in that direction.

"I told you, you can't go there." Her words rang harsh.

"And I heard you," I said softly. "I'll tell him you tried to stop me."

"Humph."

His office door was closed. I peered through its frosted window. Hard to see clear, but he was there, head fuzzy but recognizable. Now if I could only defuzz some of the notions in his head, we might have a compatible conversation. It was worth a try. I opened the door, went in, moved papers, and sat.

He didn't look up from his reading, mumbled, "Maybe I should get you a bed."

"That would be thoughtful," I said. "It would save me some money . . . and shoe leather."

"You're here. What do you want?" His eyes continued to rove over the file on his desk.

"It isn't you I really wanted to see."

He looked up, tilted his head, squinted. "Then why are you here?"

"'Cause Tilly isn't, and Alice told me I couldn't come back here, and I don't like to be told by her what I can or cannot do."

He sighed and shook his head. "Go home, Cora Pooler. Just go home."

"I can't. I don't have a home."

He slammed his pencil down. "Then get one."

"I'm trying to. That's why I'm here. To see Tilly. She knows the Amish families that rent out rooms in the summer, and I don't." I paused. He was staring at me like I was crazy, a nuisance, a fly in his ointment. I bent forward and stared into his face. "Do you?"

"If I give you a list as long as the pathway to the sun, will you take it and read it and not bother me again, until you have seen and talked with everyone on it, rented a place, satisfied your soul that you're on a useless quest, thank me, and then go back to your factory in the north, and never set eyes on me again?"

"Yes," I lied.

He pulled open a drawer, reached in, pulled out a large, yellow paperback, and tossed it across his desk onto my lap. "Now go."

It was a telephone book.

"This isn't funny, Lowell Parker."

"Neither is the work piled on my desk. You're not the only problem in my life, Cora Pooler, but you're getting to be the peskiest one. Now, get out." He hesitated. "Please."

I did.

Defeated and hungry, I took my depressed body to Harriet's Eatery, took a seat near the back of the room and, without glancing at the waitress, ordered a large piece of chocolate cake, with mega scoops of vanilla ice-cream.

"All our slices are large and is it two scoops of vanilla or one? I have to know."

I looked up. It was Bailey. I should have known. Who else could I have been . . . lucky? . . . enough to get for a waitress.

"Two," I said, "and if they're actually less than large scoops, three."

"A little piggy today, aren't we?"

"Yes, and rightly so." Looking straight at her, I scowled and spoke sharp words. "Is that a problem?"

She didn't comment or ask why I was grumpy, simply took the menu from the table and left.

When my food came, I saw it was brought to me by a young waitress, not Bailey. I glared at her. She turned her eyes from my face and set the food on the table. Then even before she took her first step away from my table, my fork with a big chunk of chocolate cake topped with a glob of soft, white, vanilla ice cream was rising to my lips.

The first bite—ambrosia, food for the gods.

The second bite, good.

The third bite, a little less.

The fourth bite, grainy.

My mouth would not accept the fifth bite.

I felt a little guilty. Perhaps I had hurt Bailey's feelings. Probably had hurt Bailey's feelings, and probably the feelings of the young, stranger-to-me-waitress who'd brought me the goodies. Sensitivity didn't seem to run strong from me on that day. It seemed that the crust of my too full brain, usually filtering mean observations and tempering cruel, careless comments slipping through and traveling down the coils that dropped to the tunnels that led to my mouth, had cracked and allowed venomous, thoughtless words to leak from my lips. Ashamed, I dropped my head and covered my face with my hands. *God, forgive me*. I sat still and silent as I waited for Him to empty my head of distress and fill it with His calm, His peace.

Minutes passed and eyes still closed, I heard the chair across from me scrape against the floor, and I sensed someone sit.

"Are you all right?" The words fell soft into my ears.

I opened my eyes. It was Bailey sitting in that chair. Watching me. Seeming concerned. Unusual demeanor. Not familiar. Not expected.

"Just a little tired," I said. I waited. She said nothing, and I whispered, "I'm sorry."

"Eat your cake. And your ice cream. It's melting." She got up and left.

I couldn't eat more. I tried. It looked so good. And I wanted it. To savor and enjoy it. But my hand, mouth, and stomach rebelled and did not let me. So, I reached in my purse for my wallet, looked for my cost ticket, and when I saw Bailey had not left it, put a tip, generous, on the table, and went to the counter to receive the bill and pay what I owed.

Bailey was at the cash register.

I opened my wallet.

She reached and touched my hand. "You don't need to pay."

I looked at her.

"You didn't eat it all," she said. "The cake didn't pleasure you. You don't need to pay for what you didn't consume."

"Of course, I do. I ordered it."

"It didn't satisfy."

"It was good. I just couldn't finish it."

"Harriet would have given it to you. Whether you ate it or not, she would not have charged you for it."

My face scrunched in disbelief. "You're not Harriet." I knew I'd seen a radical change in this woman, but this was too much. She made me uncomfortable. I would have felt better if she'd be herself . . . mean, old, miserable Bailey. Predictable. That I could deal with. Not this.

"I want to be more like her."

"You do?"

"I love her."

I didn't know what to say.

"She's dying. And I want her to know I'll carry on . . . same as her."

I still didn't know what to say. What I thought was, *good luck, you've got a lot of shoe to fill.*

And glad I'd left a generous tip, I half-smiled, nodded, and left.

The clouds were heavy in the sky, their bottoms darkened by the moisture they held. It seemed appropriate, a match for the thick weight in my mind. I'd driven for hours through the Amish countryside. Looking. Seeking. Remembering. Wanting. *God, give me an answer. Do I belong here?*

I stopped at the bottom of the hill that led to the cemetery, leaned my head against the steering wheel and closed my eyes. *Please, God.*

The rain started, pelt hard against the windshield. I sat as I was, my mind empty of thought, and absorbed the crash of thunderous drops of water, meshing, and forming a brigade of an attacking force that threatened to smash through my windshield and sweep me away.

It seemed it rained long. Then it stopped. I looked through the water-streaked windshield and saw a washed, green world wavering sharp through the wet glass. Glittering. Green. Beautiful. I got out of my car and ignoring the sinking pull of my shoes into rain-softened soil, slushed through the grass and up the hill to Lily's grave.

I wasn't alone. There was a black-clad body sitting on the saturated ground near Lily's grave. A woman. Large. Her back to me. But I knew her. Vaguely. I'd seen her before . . . picking Lily-of-the-valley petals in the woods.

Her shoulders were hunched; her head bent. I didn't want to frighten her. I touched her on the shoulder, gently, and spoke, "Hello," just loud enough for her to hear.

Her body jerked, and I sensed a shudder run through her—an anxious movement. And as her head lowered closer to her chest, she clutched her body tight.

Confused, I pushed my fingers against my lips and waited. She didn't move. I didn't know what to do.

Finally, I moved closer to her, leaned my head near to her ear. "Can I help you?" She slumped a bit, as her arms loosened their grasp about her body. I saw the rigidity in her back ease. She did not turn to look at me, so I moved and crouched in front of her.

"I'm Cora Pooler. I used to live here among the Amish, and I knew all my people. But since I left and was gone for many years, there are some new brethren, and I don't know them all. I don't know you," I paused, "but I'd like to."

The woman lifted her face. "I'm . . . Schrock."

I bit my lip, tried not to show shock. "Isaiah's wife?"

"Yes."

Her response was sharp, distinct, and English. I wondered if it was intentional rebellion or an unassimilated language adjustment. *Ya* was neither a difficult word to retain nor to pronounce.

"I think I've seen you. In the woods. Picking flowers? Lily-of-the-valley." I rambled. "They are beautiful. Among my favorites."

"They're useful."

Useful? She didn't seem to be a woman of many words. But useful? Maybe to perk up her house? But anyway, she needed to get up from the damp grass.

"Can I help you up?" I reached to take her hands.

"No." Abrupt.

I backed away and tried not to watch her struggle as she hefted herself from the ground. It was hard not to help, and I didn't want to embarrass her, but my eyes ignored thoughtful discretion and kept rolling her way.

She made it. Awkward, but successful. Then pressing her hands against the small of her back, she looked down at the matted grass she'd risen from. I stared at her and tried, but couldn't determine the source of hinted need that lay upon her face. A distorting mask of unreadable emotion scrawled over the whole of it. Pain? Sorrow? Fear? I couldn't tell.

"Let me drive you home," I said.

"I can walk."

"I'd be happy to. It's cooling down pretty fast and looks like it might rain some more."

"It's not far."

"It is far, and if I'm going to be living among your people, it'll give me a chance to know you a little better." I'd got her attention and she gave a quick, inquisitive look.

"I'm not much for talking," she said.

"A few words can start a friendship."

"Schrock don't like me talking to strangers."

"I'm not really a stranger. I used to live here, and I know the Amish ways."

"Don't matter. He don't like me talking to nobody."

"Why not?"

She turned and walked away from me.

I wanted to follow, but I didn't. Instead, I stood by Lily's grave and watched her walk away, watched her slip on the grass, catch herself, pause, lift her shoulders, bend forward, and resume her march. She didn't slip again. When she reached the road, I bowed my head and prayed silent words for her safety . . . however it was needed in her life . . . and I prayed God would let me know her better, to clarify the whispering need I felt to help.

Shoes soaked and body, cold and wet, I got in my car to drive back to the motel to change and deliberate, justify, solidify the purposes of my being in Wander Lane, the possibility of reaching my goals, and most of all, the selfishness of my quest. How much of my wanting and searching answers would hurt others? *And oh, God, what do I do with the knowledge I have of Talitha's birth and the unintentional, incestuous birth of her and Willie's baby?*

Chapter Fourteen

It was nearing evening as I drove from Amish country and drew close to Wander Lane. The clouds had emptied their store of moisture and floated free, before a sun that was disappearing above them as the earth turned and drew the village farther from the sun's rays. Despite the discomfort of sodden clothing, I stopped at the top of the last hill leading into Wander Lane and watched the sun's wonderous departure. The spreading swirls of the reds and pinks and oranges of the vanishing sun filled the sky, tinged the edges of waning clouds, flashed a moment of brilliant power, and, with a lingering beauty, brought dusk. It seemed to last a long, wonderful moment and then the magic of a darkening earth was done. Night had come, and a mass of graying cumulus clouds covered the sky's stars. Within that darkness, the only penetrating light was the soft glow emanating from the far-off streetlamps in the village.

I waited and watched, not wanting to think, just feel, and when the procrastinating was done, mind and heart empty, I drove to the motel, parked, entered, went to my room, shed my drenched clothing, put on soft, warm apparel, and left to find an uncrowded place where I could eat and mull over the direction and worth of my quest and decide the next viable course of action.

As I stepped into the night, shivers ran the length of my body. The air had turned cooler. I thought to go back to my room and add a sweater or light coat but decided not to. If I walked briskly, it wouldn't take long to walk to Harriet's Eatery, and I'd be warm there. Easier, lazier, faster. And I was really hungry.

I was right. It didn't take long. And the immediate restaurant warmth was a balm to my body. My eyes, however, were not as pleased by what they saw, as was my warming body by what it felt. Sheriff Lowell Parker was among the lingering, late diners.

I frowned.

He saw me, shook his head, lifted a finger, crooked it, wiggled it, and, with it, bade me 'come over.'

I considered. His face did not match the welcoming finger, and I really wanted quiet time all by myself, all *for* myself, with no human distractions, especially his. But my Amish mother had taught me well. Polite. Always. Not that I always listened to her long ago, respectful lessons, but tired and hungry, not wanting confrontation, I succumbed. I went to his table and sat.

He chewed and swallowed. Took another forkful. Chewed.

I waited.

Finally, food swallowed, and his mouth empty, he spoke. "I talked with Herrfort."

"Bishop Herrfort."

"We can argue what we call him, or I can tell you what he said."

"What did Herrfort say?"

He took another bite, chewed.

I waited.

He swallowed. "He said you could go live with Aaron and Violet, and Violet could talk to you. But only necessary words. That's all."

"And what are necessary words?"

He shrugged. "I dunno . . . where's the towel? How many plates should I put on the table?

You figure it out."

"Okay, I will." I stared into his eyes. "Where's Jacob Lapp? Who was at the creek with Lily when she fell in?"

"Or jumped," Lowell interjected.

"Or was pushed," I said, my words fierce and deliberate.

He lifted an eyebrow and shook his head.

"Well, it could have happened that way," I argued.

"Right," Lowell said, "and somebody's gonna come up to you one day and say, 'Oh, it's me that murdered Lily Pooler. Sorry.'"

"Why am I sitting here," I said. Not a question. A statement. A disgusted statement. I rose to go.

Lowell grabbed my arm. "Sit."

I looked at his hand pinching my skin. I was tired. Residue Amish courtesy, patience, and meekness ignored, I thought I would like to stretch my head down to that hand and bite it. Hard.

"Look," Lowell said, taking his hand from my arm, "sit. I'm sorry I upset you. Sit and we'll talk civilly. No sarcasm. No accusations. No nasty remarks."

"I never make nasty remarks," I said, sitting.

He looked at me and grinned. "Okay. What I wanted to tell you is that Herrfort understands realistically you can't live in the Amish community without someone being able to say something, anything to you. So, he bent, and you should be grateful. Herrfort never bends."

"He must be getting old!"

"Be nice."

I leaned back and relaxed. This was a major concession from Bishop Herrfort, and I was grateful for it.

"How come he picked Violet?" I asked. "She's the least likely of the whole community to monitor her tongue with me. She's my sister. I practically raised her. Modestly, I say I could probably talk her into anything."

"She's done a lot of growing up in the last ten years . . . got married . . . to your old boyfriend. The stubborn, *Ordnung*-strict, never-ignore-a-rule one—Aaron," he said, grinning, scrutinizing my face for probable reaction, hopefully finding none. "She watches over your parents, oversees her brother. Well, thinks she oversees Willie. He doesn't listen to her. She thinks he does, but he doesn't. Amish men are pretty independent. They know who's boss." He chuckled under his breath. "And deep down, so does she."

"It's the Amish way," I said. "The men might be the heads of households, and the women respect that, but they still have a strong influence on their family. Men know they need us."

"You counting yourself an Amish woman now?"

I set my face stern and didn't answer.

"You eating?" Lowell asked. "Bailey's over there watching us, waiting for a spot to break in."

When I nodded, he motioned her over.

"You done?" I asked him, hoping he'd leave.

"I'll just sit here and drink my coffee." He grinned. "Keep your mind from doing too much misthinking."

"Did the bishop say when I could move in?" I questioned, ignoring his dismissal of the pact we'd made to erase antagonizing remarks from our conversation. And, at the same time, judging his in-your-face satisfaction, wished we'd added irritating facial expressions to the list.

"Nope. Left that up to you, I guess."

I sighed. "Do you ever try to make things easy for a person?"

"Nope. Don't try to make 'em harder neither."

I shook my head. "I can't figure out if you've got a complex, thinking mind, or it's just a simple, useless, insensitive mass of wasted coils."

He laughed. "Maybe both. And if you look up, you'll see that Bailey is right by you, listening to your unkind words." He lifted his head, tilted it and winked at the space beside me.

"Right, Bailey?"

"Never listen to my customers' talk, so I guess I didn't hear no unkind words."

"Smart lady," Lowell acknowledged.

"Miz Pooler?" she questioned—pencil poised over pad.

"Just Cora, Bailey," I said looking up at her. "Grilled cheese and tomato soup, please."

She nodded, and ignoring Sheriff Parker, left.

"More coffee," Lowell called after her.

She didn't respond.

I lifted an eyebrow. "Maybe you should have said 'please.'"

"She'll bring it."

"Sometimes, I really don't like you."

He laughed.

"Maybe you should take your cup and move to another table."

He laughed harder.

"Let's be serious, Lowell."

The laughter stopped, his face emptied of expression, and he looked at me for a moment before he spoke. And then his words dropped firm. "Sometimes laughter, whether funny or not, covers unwanted or painful or unfigured-out thoughts."

"And you're having those thoughts?"

He smiled. "Try doing my job for a week." He paused. "A day."

"And I add to those troubles?"

He didn't answer. I saw his hands, fingers laced, tighten around his cup.

"Do you ever pray, Lowell? Go to Jesus?"

"No."

"Never?"

"I tried. Didn't work."

"That happens," I said softly.

"To you?"

"Uh-huh. Sometimes I feel like I live in the in-between land . . . that place that sits between what was and what will be, and it feels like I can't get out. And I pray, but sometimes, I can't connect. And I wait, struggle, until I let it become a healing time, a learning time, until I can step out of that place, out of holding onto a want and a dream for what can't and shouldn't be, and until I'm ready to walk into a new world of promise and hope . . . the path God means me to walk, with steady tread. That's where I am now. In that in-between land. And when I'm truly ready, I know God will lead me out and onward, and it will be right."

"Sounds like a lot of work to me."

"It is." I looked at his face, into his eyes. He lowered his head, stared at the table.

"You know, Lowell, to reach the core of truth, the center of who we are and why we are and whose we are, we have to travel through the layers of self, confront the damaged soul, and discern what is real, right, and good." I paused. "No, Lowell, it isn't easy. It's hard, and it hurts. But when you're able to work yourself out of the in-between place, it's worth it. And you do have help whether you know it or not, whether you feel it or not, whether you acknowledge it or not. God is always there. He's patient and loving, and He'll wait for you to know and learn."

"You sound confident."

"Sometimes, I waver," I said, thinking right now, yesterday, maybe tomorrow, "but He always forgives." *But I don't. I can't forgive me.*

"And here comes Bailey," he said, pointing, "with grilled cheese and soup."

I smiled. "And relief for you. Lecture time over."

"Yep." He scraped back his chair, rose, saluted Bailey, and left. Apparently, forgot he'd wanted more coffee.

Chapter Fifteen

Before the sun rose the next morning, I had packed, checked out and was sitting in my car waiting for the earth to bask beneath light revealing rays and to give Violet time to scramble eggs, flip pancakes, pour coffee, send Aaron off to the barn, mix flour and lard, set it to rise, and clean the kitchen. Then while, hopefully, she sat at the kitchen table prioritizing the day's tasks, I would knock on her door and be welcomed.

And that's what I did. And hoped I would be.

Violet was quick to answer the knock. But there was no polite, welcoming Amish smile or hospitable words bidding me to come in. She said nothing. No 'Hello, Cora.' Apparently, per the dictate of Bishop Herrfort, those were not necessary words. But his rule was not inflicted upon me, so I said them to her, "Hello, Violet." There was no visible reaction. She motioned me to follow her, and we went up the stairs to the second floor. She opened the door at the top of the stairs and pointed me into a bedroom. I went in, looked around. It contained a bed, dresser, straight chair, and hooks for clothing. A calendar, an accepted Amish adornment, picturing a mass of fall-foliaged trees hung on one wall. There was no closet. No mirror. The room was clean. Adequate. I turned to thank her. But she was gone. And I wondered if an unseen struggle had raged within her. Surely, she hadn't forgotten strong, sisterly ties. Warm memories. Shared memories. Deep love.

I put my things away. The things I'd packed that should pass muster with the Amish. Gloomy clothes . . . black, navy, dark green and burgundy. Simple shoes. No headwear. No jewelry. But mounds of fancy, flimsy, lacy underwear. What Amish eyes couldn't see, couldn't offend.

Violet didn't call or fetch me to come down for the midday meal, but when I heard a door slam, and the clomp of Aaron's, probably muddy, work boots cross Violet's polished, hardwood floor, I knew it was time for food to be ready and on the table. I was hungry and bored. I'd forgotten to bring books. And since I paid board, I figured dinner would be ready for me, too.

And it was.

But not as I, as a former Amish woman, should have anticipated, but didn't, and so, I was taken aback. Chagrinned, I set my face to not reveal my hurt. The big table held plates for two. A little table, apart from the big one, held a single plate—thus was the tone of my presence declared.

On the big table, large bowls of boiled potatoes, green beans, corn, and yeast rolls were heaped with food, as was the platter of fried chicken. My table also had heaped bowls, small bowls filled with more than I could eat. Sorrowfully, a sad smile whispered within me. She would feed me well, my Violet, with unspoken pride, and without acknowledgement of me, her sister, by blood and community, about to sit in the same room, to eat the same food she had prepared for herself and Aaron. Yes, she would feed me. Speak to me? No.

I sat and waited for Aaron to finish washing his hands. When he was done and seated, not once looking at me, I dropped my head for the Amish silent praying moments, before eating moments, and I thanked God for giving me time in this Amish home, and I prayed He would nudge Violet to speak words to me. Many words. Silly words. True and enlightening words. Any words. And then at the clunk of Aaron's fork against his plate, I lifted my head and brought Violet's delicious cooking to my mouth.

Through the whole meal and after, neither Aaron nor Violet gave any inclination that there was, and had been, another person, close to them, eating near them, putting her dishes by the sink, wiping her little table, existing with them in the kitchen. They mumbled a few words to each other, too quiet for me to discern. But I tried unobtrusively. When Aaron was done, Violet walked him to the door, touched his arm tenderly, watched him walk to the barn, and, even then not acknowledging my presence, began her cleaning of the kitchen.

I'd had enough of this.

"I'm going to be here for a goodly time," I said.

Hands in dish water, Violet paused in her task. She didn't look at me but stared out the window, above the sink for a moment, and then resumed scrubbing a plate.

"It seems a word or two, now and then, might not bring the wrath of God upon us," I said to her back.

Violet brought her hands out of water, shook suds from them, rubbed them against her apron, and turned to me.

"I don't know how to handle this," she said, and I saw a sadness in her eyes. "It was the bishop's idea to bring you here. I didn't want it. It would be too hard." She bit her lip. "But he's the bishop. And Aaron said we must obey him." A soft sigh escaped her lips, and she lifted them in a half-smile. "And Aaron reminded me that he is my husband, and I must also obey him."

Another sigh. "So, I am . . . and I love you . . . and I don't know how to handle this."

"What if I talk to you, and you just listen?"

"I don't know. I just did talk to you, said forbidden words. I don't know if I could just listen. I want to talk to you . . . and I can't. It's wrong. And already I have to confess the few words I have spoken to you."

"Violet, who says you can't talk to me? The bishop? Aaron? Maybe, God? Maybe only God? He's got a lot more authority than the bishop or Aaron. So do you think God, a loving God, might want you not to talk with me? Not to show your love, with words? How could that be?"

"You're shunned." Flat, simple, condemning words.

"Why am I shunned, Violet? What did I do that was so wrong? All that I did . . . taking the baby, claiming her as my own, so Lily would not be shunned? Worshipping in another place, wearing clothes of beautiful colors, loving Daniel, loving you and *Da* and *Maem* and Lily and our brothers . . . believing Jesus comes first, even superseding the *Ordnung*? All of that? Why is it all so sinful that I should be put under the *Bann,* that I should be punished forever?" I dropped my face into my lifted, tented fingers, sighed, and then dropped them. "That any of it is sinful at all? Except maybe taking the baby away from Lily. Not giving her a chance to know her child." I could feel the anguish in my words. I could hear it. I wondered if Violet did, too. But though I hoped, I didn't think she did.

"If you confessed, I could talk to you."

"The Amish are a good people, Violet. I know they believe what is written in the Bible, and they can be such beautifully forgiving people. But the beliefs, so often, *too often,* are tucked behind the words of the *Ordnung,* and Jesus is hidden by rules that are sometimes just plain silly and debilitating. And they forget that He is to be worshipped and obeyed, only He." I put my hand on hers. "I can't give my life to a world that places, preaches, a rule book to be more precious, more immediate, more revealing than my Savior, Jesus Christ's Word."

"This is my life, Cora, I'm Amish. I can't change," Violet said. She dipped a scuffed pan into the water and vigorously scrubbed at the sticking food pieces.

I stood and watched her awhile. She was done with me, for awhile. I left the house. I needed to be away. We would work at it again. We were sisters. One Amish. One, partly so. But still sisters.

The afternoon stretched before me. My mind drifted to thoughts of Daniel. He had found me; a simple, frightened Amish woman forcibly ostracized from her known and protected world, lost in a maze of clamoring progress and braying, raucous, piercing, attacking blare. He had rescued me, loved me, taught me, pulled all the new pieces, into a sea of awareness and joy. And I swam in that exciting world, peaceful and productive, until he died. And, a second time, I returned to my first home—the Amish.

They would take me into their community again, erase the years I'd lived as an Englisher, cleanse me with the waters of their ways, if I would confess my sins before them and accept their rules. Promise to obey. No questions. No deviation. They would forgive, and I would be Amish again. Protected. Loved. Empty-minded. Safe. *God, why did You take him? My Daniel. Why did You take him?*

It does no good to ruminate on what could be, should be. It is what it is. Facts don't lie. But neither are they stagnant. I could lay them all before me. Shuffle them. Pile them one way. Shape them another. *You gave me choice, God. And a brain for thinking, deliberating, solving. And emotions, feelings that can make a soul soar, if chosen. And You gave me the wisdom to look to You for reason, purpose and guidance. I'm not alone. I have You. Always.*

I drove through the country of my old life, youthful years remembered. The hills. Fields. Rolling terrain. My home. Growing up a black clad, barefoot, sheltered, mirrored in the likeness of community girl children, stagnating in a lake of rules but happy and secure, until a rule was broken and I was banished.

My heart was filled with smiles and tears. Memories.

What do I do, God? Resolve the mysteries . . . Lily's death? Lily's child, Talitha, grown and married, the mother of her own child, that child born of an incestuous coupling? Or is it best to keep silent, let the lies cover truth? Is there peace in that? Honest peace? Lasting peace? Does not knowing . . . or seeking . . . relieve pain, dissolve pain? But I know, and I hurt from the knowing. And I know You will not take that pain from me if I quit, if I turn from seeking truth. And the answers are here, Lord. Help me find them.

Deep in thought, I continued to rove the Amish roads. Clouds were gathering in the sky, their underbellies a light gray, readying to release their burden onto earth. Those bellies, not full and dark, would drop a gentle rain, sweet upon the ground.

They did, and it was. A tender kiss against the grass, a brush of wet over a line of newly dried diapers hanging from the roped line on Mary Graber's front yard. Passing her house, I saw her leap from her porch and run toward the diapers, straw basket banging against her hip. Without thinking, I pulled my car to the side of the road and ran to help her. We pulled the diapers off the line, hers shoved into her basket, mine stuffed into my arms. She laughed when she took them from me, squeezed my hand, and said, *dank*. I laughed with her, and then hearing a baby's squall plunge loud and persistent from the house, squeezed her hand back, and pointed to the sound. She nodded and with another fervent *dank* ran toward it.

I went back to my car, stood by it, and lifted my face to the drizzling residue of the near empty clouds. Their sprinkles drifted soft and comforting against my cheeks. They were cleansing drops that washed and dissolved the spread of dust over God's creation and man's fabrication. The world glistened with beauty, and I felt calmed and complete.

I drove farther into the hills, looking and feeling a part of the whole, a part of the essence, a part of the mystery and magic of connection, a merging of body and universe.

It can't last. That feeling. It's too large to keep. Focus reels its way in and the world shrinks to what the eyes can see, what the mind can know. Even so, it leaves a vestige of harmony, a buoyancy, a rightness.

I passed a familiar grove of stately oaks presaging the emergence of a dense mass of multi-heighted pines. Anxious to physically experience their wonder, I opened my window to draw in the heady, dusky scent, of the freshly bathed woodland. It was a moment of falling into another world. A world where nature reigned. A world where people were not counted as primary. I stayed awhile, and then when fullness was reached, and I couldn't hold more, I drove on.

I came to a pond, a pocket of water so small it was more like a large puddle. Shoes off and skirts held high, two laughing, shrieking, little girls danced and splashed within its boundaries. Not able to resist, I scooted from my car, toed off my shoes, lifted my skirt and jumped in with them.

They were startled. The wee ones dropped their skirts, widened their eyes, and covered their mouths with raised fingers. I laughed. Then one, brave girl tilted her head, dropped her hand, twisted her lips, and frowned; the other, just stared.

I shrugged, lifted my eyebrows, and utilizing and enjoying the use of my old and still familiar first language, Pennsylvania Dutch, spoke, "It looked like fun, so I hopped in with you."

The taller, valiant little girl nodded.

"I'm fifty-eight," I said, smiling as that child's lips formed a circle, obviously knowing that number was large. "How old are you?"

She lifted five fingers. The second child, eyes still on me, raised three fingers, then quickly hid her hand behind her back, only to bring it forth and lowering her eyes, slid her thumb into her mouth. Immediately, the five-year-old grabbed the thumb and pulled it out of the little one's mouth.

"Shame," she said in a loud, firm whisper.

I smiled. "Does your *maem* know you're here?"

The older child shook her head. "Where does she think you are?"

"Aunt Elsie's."

"Okay. One last splash and then you'd better hurry, put your shoes on, and run as fast as you can to Aunt Elsie's house. You don't want your *maem* or auntie worrying about you. And it's always best to obey."

I watched them, still in the puddle, lift their legs and jump one last time as hard as they could, splashing mud-heavy water onto their hanging skirts. And I hoped Aunt Elsie loved these children dearly . . . and had an understanding sense of humor.

They put their shoes on and ran, the older half-dragging the younger. I wished I'd asked them their names.

Back in the car, present life merged with the past, whole, I wandered the roads, not thinking, just being.

When the sun hinted its impending fade, I turned the car to ride the road to the village. Amish men, and their families, having labored hard and knowing the next day would be the same, bedded early. Suppers would already have been eaten, kitchens cleaned, and preparations for sleep completed. Doors would not be locked. I could return to Violet's home at any hour. And there would be no questions.

I went down the darkening hill to find dinner at Harriet's Eatery.

I was not surprised to see Lowell Parker sitting at his usual back corner table, but I was surprised to see his backside facing the dining room. Usually, he sat face forward, his eyes inconspicuously searching, tracking every movement of personnel and patron.

I stepped behind him and poked his shoulder.

Before my finger left his shirt, he was up, chair pushed back against me, and as I swiftly jumped away, he twisted and turned to confront me.

"For God's sake, what'd you do that for?" he spoke, his voice spewing anger and disgust.

"I only poked you," I rebuked, "with my finger and don't swear at me."

"It could've been a gun. How would I know? Couldn't see you." His voice was cold. "And I'll swear if I want to."

"My finger doesn't have bullets in it," I mumbled.

"If you're going to eat, just sit down," he said, scraping his chair against the floor, centering it, dropping his bottom hard onto it. "And where'd you get that godawful, rusty red sack you're wearing?"

"It's a burgundy dress!"

He shook his head and scowled. "It's ugly. And if you're trying to look Amish, it doesn't work."

"I'm not trying to look Amish. I'm just trying to fit in."

"By looking ridiculous?"

"I think I'll go," I said, anger growing. Justifiably.

"Just sit. If you're hungry, just sit and eat."

"With you? That certainly would be pleasant."

"Don't be sarcastic."

So, I did sit. He looked miserable, and since everyone deserved a miserable day now and then, I'd tolerate his attitude . . . though I did feel a bit of resentment that he'd tarnished my overall walking-into-the-restaurant-contented disposition.

"You look tired," I said, hoping to dispel animosity.

His squinting eyes looked directly into my waiting ones. He rubbed his, looked down. I kept mine on him.

"Sometimes," he said, "it's better to not see. Sometimes, I'm so tired and discouraged, I don't want to see. Or know. Or listen. Or decide."

"You're talking to the table, not to me."

He lifted his eyes, grinned. "The table's got a lot more sympathy than you do."

"You're tough, you don't need sympathy."

He laughed.

"What's got you so worn down today?" I asked, curious and, though I hoped not apparent to him, sympathetic.

"Herrfort."

"Herrfort? Bishop Herrfort? *My* Bishop Herrfort?"

"He's dying."

I reached across the table and put my hand over his folded ones. "He's old. It happens. You grow old and you die. But he's lived a good life, and you know, when it's time, and you've done the work God gave you, it's not a bad thing. Death. It's not a bad thing."

Lowell looked at me, shook his head, lifted one side of his mouth in an apparently reluctant half-smile. "You're a tough one, Cora Pooler."

"No. An experienced one," I replied.

"He's my last tie to Honor."

"Your wife."

"My wife."

"Is she still alive, Lowell?" I knew Honor was Herrfort's baby sister, and I knew she'd married Lowell and then, after tasting a bit of the English life, had left him. Lowell had not gone with her.

"No, she died. Many years ago."

"You still love her?"

His laugh was almost a chuckle. "No. Maybe. A little. Love who she was while she still had a little of the Amish left in her."

He shook his head. "A long time ago."

"Grilled cheese and tomato soup?"

I looked up. Pen and pad in hand, Bailey was standing by Lowell, looking at me. I shook my head. "No. Just a drink. Diet cola."

She nodded and left.

"Didn't mean to take your appetite away," Lowell said, sliding his chair away from the table, making ready to leave.

"Don't go," I said.

"I think enough words have hit the air tonight." He rose, saluted, and left.

When Bailey brought my drink, I asked her if she'd like to sit and rest a bit. She smiled and said she had work to do in the kitchen. It was almost closing time. I smiled and nodded. She patted my shoulder. "But you stay as long as you'd like."

I told her I wouldn't be long, just needed a little thinking and recovery time.

She nodded. "Like I say, I've got a lot to do and it takes lots of time, so you just sit there and take as much time as you need."

And I did.

Chapter Sixteen

The months moved spring into summer. They turned the dewy birth of lush, green vegetation and the rich, brown of damp, supple soil into plowed, seeded, sprouting fields, cattle-trampled pastures, and forests trimmed of fallen limbs to be harvested for winter woodstoves. Summer for the Amish is a time of hard work and preparation for the harsher months of winter. It is a time women tend their large gardens, a time they pluck and pick and can and store, and I was of great help during that time to Violet and to neighboring households. My reward was an occasional nod or smile or, less often, the brush of a hand on my arm. Each small tribute was a treasure to me.

During that time, I found a welcome in a most unusual place of comfort. Where there should have been the most evident site of discipline, there was an air of unbidden forgiveness. I never asked for it. Forgiveness. Not from him, not from Bishop Herrfort. In my eyes, in my heart, I felt I had done no intentional wrong. I had made decisions, painful decisions, that led to unhappiness and destruction, but never had I set out to hurt anyone. The only forgiveness I sought was from God. I didn't think I would find it in an unyielding, rule-laden Amish man. Yet in that home, where discipline was of highest priority, I found unconditional and practiced love. I found it there in Bishop Herrfort's home. I sat by his bed, read the words to him, as best I could, from his German Bible. It soothed him, and it gave his wife a time of respite. There was love in that house, a piercing sense of what true Amish was meant to be.

In this Amish community, it was the custom of the brethren congregants to determine the successor, and in this case, it would also be they who would designate and thereby title the chosen one as preacher or deacon, and that man would fill the loss created by the permanent incapacitation of the bishop. It would be done at a regular Sunday service. Therefore, before Bishop Herrfort died, a service was scheduled to select his successor. As a shunned Amish woman, one of the favors still granted me was permission to attend Sunday church services, a privilege I accepted, sometimes with trepidation, and so I was at the service when a new spiritual leader was chosen.

The Amish singing of hymns is beautiful. Their strong and devout voices need no instruments. I sat, a former Amish woman, dressed in true, Amish, dark apparel sewn by an Amish friend of Bailey, relishing the return, for a moment, to being a part of a people whose life was simple and needed no new thought or adornment to be complete. I relaxed, as best I could, on the hard, backless bench in the certainty of near acceptance, even knowing it would not take long for me to be discontent and wanting more. But for those early service moments, I closed my eyes and simply listened and enjoyed, until the singing was done and the Deacon's words began.

The sermons seemed long that day. Music finished, the first sermon wasn't too bad, less than one hour. Then we prayed, and then a bit of Scripture was read—all words in German. Then we heard another sermon, the second preacher's spiel, a bit longer than the first, but again not terribly long, even though it seemed so. Undisciplined thoughts rambled through my head, and thus my ears were only half-opened to moments of Biblical truth and Amish rules. And my bottom was getting numb. Truly anxious for the choosing of the next leader of the brethren, the man who would replace Bishop Herrfort, to start, and ignoring the disapproving glances and pokes from Violet, I squirmed against the hard wood, under my restless bottom.

And finally, it was time. As the preachers and the deacon went behind a boarded-off section of the barn, the Amish males, oldest first, then, queuing in age-order, formed their line. When the deacon stretched his neck and showed his face around the boarded divider, each Amish man, in turn, whispered in the deacon's ear the name of a married Amish man whom he felt should be ordained as Herrfort's replacement. When the men's preferences had been recorded, the women took their turn, again in age order. As a shunned Amish woman, I could not participate nor make my predilection known. I would have chosen Aaron. He was honest, intelligent, and fair. Although, thinking about it, he was not very nice to me. Totally ignored me. Not too Amish in that behavior. Especially since, at one time, he regularly drove me home from the Sunday evening sings, a precursor to marriage. However, I was shunned, and he stood staunch in his faith. Always had. Always would. Though I sometimes wondered if he ever remembered our tentative, almost romantic relationship. Probably not. The *Ordnung* would surely wave a squelching flame over that reminiscing.

Beside me, Violet pinched my thigh hard. She apparently

could tell my mind was wandering, and, in her mind, church was not a place for idle thoughts.

When all were seated again, and after a fair amount of time passed, the two preachers and deacon stepped out from their boarded enclosure. They held, among them, four songbooks. The deacon called four men to approach the front. They were the men who had received the most votes. Each man took a book, opened it, and if he found a leaf in it, he became the deacon, replacing the spot formerly held by Bishop Herrfort.

The names rang clear. Joseph Schlabach. Eli Miller. John Hilty. Isaiah Schrock.

Isaiah Schrock! I drew in my breath. Who would vote for him? And wouldn't it be funny if he picked the book, with the dried leaf in it? Deacon Schrock! I twisted my neck trying to find Mattie among the women. Violet gave me a really sharp jab. I jerked away from her and smashed into Ida Truber, who gave me an "unchurchy" dirty look. Not a good way for me to find favor in the Amish world.

He wasn't chosen. A gush of air whooshed from my mouth. It was Eli Miller who found the leaf. And the whole Amish congregation should have joined me, with their own great sigh of relief. But they didn't. Later, cleaning the kitchen alongside Violet, when I voiced that thought, she told me, or rather told the kitchen sink, as her words were spoken to it and not to me, the community thought of him as a hard worker and a good man. She spoke her words loud and clear. Must be they were necessary words.

Bishop Herrfort grew weaker. Stews, casseroles, yeasty rolls, pies, cakes, and cookies found their way to his house. Food to sustain him and food to serve his loving brethren—the unceasing trek of Amish brothers and sisters arriving to pay homage to his service and his love. I went with Violet to his house. We took cookies battered heavy with home-churned butter, lots of sugar and plumped raisins. Martha came to the door, greeted Violet, and without speaking to me, but sneaking a wink, took my arm and led us to see him. There were several women in the room. Violet crossed the floor to stand with them, but Martha kept her hand on me and walked me to her husband's bed. There she bent and whispered my name into his ear. He reached and slid his fingers over my hand. He didn't speak to me, just looked, met my eyes, and then smiled. Weakly. Beautifully. He knew. He knew *me*. *My heart*. As I stepped away from him, I glanced at the group of women standing near. Not one spoke to me or, except with pressed lips and averted eyes, acknowledged my presence. I didn't need them. His touch, his eyes, had been enough.

When Bishop Herrfort died, and the three day and night line of mourners paid their respects, Violet, ignoring sharp looks and "tskings," took me with her to his house to pass by his casket. It was brave of her. Even believing there could be no contact between the dead and the living, it was a special time of reverence and remembrance for the grievers. But apparently, my presence tainted their mourning. I never felt more shunned than that evening when I walked through the room and viewed the body. Amish breeding overcome, backs turned, and eyes dropped or stared cold, so discreetly, an Englisher would not have perceived it. The Amish in me felt their shunning deep in the marrow of my bones.

Violet didn't invite me to ride with her and Aaron in their

buggy as they took their part in the procession that carried Bishop Herrfort's body to his place of burial.

When that day came, I stood on the porch and watched the long row of buggies traverse the highest hill to the place where an open grave waited. A site within the fence. Though I loved the bishop and knew he should rest in an honored spot, a wave of rage and bitterness swept through my body. My Lily should be inside that fence, too.

The days that followed were somber days. Bishop Herrfort was not easily forgotten. The grief of the brethren was stoic. He was not remembered with words shared by one Amisher to another, but I knew their hearts were full.

Herrfort had been a special and faithful mentor and friend to Talitha. After his death, on the days she brought Baby Clare to Violet's house, her sadness was evident, in long silences and little laughter. It was as if her body, her heart, her face had forgotten the way to move lightly, to glow, to smile.

As Willie's oldest, non-shunned sister, Violet took it upon herself to console his wife, Talitha. And there were times when, thinking it would be good for the new mother to step away from daily, routine duties, she would harness Aaron's sleek, black, and restless, retired, racing horse, affix that horse to their buggy, and trundle Talitha, sans baby, into the vehicle. Off they would go. To quilting gatherings. Food preserving get-togethers. Sewing, embroidering, knitting sittings. Church and wedding preparatory bakings. And not to be admitted or confessed by the good Amish ladies, gossip fests. And, many times, Baby Clare was left with me.

She was an easy baby to care for. Rarely cried. Never squirmed during a diaper change. Didn't splash while bathed in the sink. And because of Talitha's physical inabilities, she was a bottle baby, and she, always, as she lay cradled in her mother's, or sometimes, Violet's or my arms, quietly, docilely suckled her nourishment. She was like a child's doll. Moved instead of moving. Stationary where put.

There came a day Violet took Talitha to Maudie Hooley's house to help with Sunday church baking, and I was left with Baby Clare. When it was her time to nap, I held her on my lap, stroked her arm, and slowly rocked the little girl, until she slept. As I looked down on the baby, my soul was filled with guilt. Only Harriet and I knew the secret of her conception. Only we knew her father was her uncle. Tainted blood flowed through this child. Unblessed blood. Unhealthy. And only we knew, Harriet and I. I didn't have the courage to tell. And Harriet didn't have the ability to tell. Our secret. My sin. *Forgive me, God.*

As I rocked, my mind filled with scenarios and words that would tell Talitha and Violet the heritage, the parenthood of this child. Sensible words, true words. Scenes depicting understanding. Acceptance. Absolution. Vindication.

And within my fantasy musings, I heard pardoning words coming from Willie and Talitha . . . *Oh, Cora, how silly. Of course, everything is fine. Look at her. She's a beautiful baby—a perfect child. There's never been one so flawless, so easy.* And supportive words from Aaron and Violet . . . *Oh, Cora. how silly. You never meant for this to happen. Your motives were decent and loving. You did what you thought was best for Lily. And it was. Can't you see how beautiful this child is?*

I burst out laughing. *Oh, Cora, how silly. Of course, their reaction would be different from that.* I lifted my arms and held the sleeping baby against my chest, and I cried. For a moment. Then I drew in a deep breath. I wasn't a crier. I was a doer. Enough of self-pity and misplaced guilt. I'd talked with God, asked for forgiveness. He'd given it, and I knew His grace was a cloak covering my soul, with warmth and love. Forgiveness. Direction. And I knew He waited for me to nestle in that place, absorb His wisdom, gather strength from it and with the guidance of the Holy Spirit, *do.* And with His help that's exactly what I determined I would do. Accept forgiveness, listen to His whisper, heed His dictates, and execute. If I could.

I knew I should speak to Violet and Talitha, give them words that spoke truth. I thought of the things I should tell them: *Ten years ago, I thought, knew, I saw Lily's child, Anabelle, now Talitha, living in Sugar Creek. She was grown, riding in an Amish buggy. Holding a child. She looked happy. And my heart filled with joy. She was all right. I couldn't tell you then. She had been gone a long time and was but an occasional fleeting thought in your minds. And Talitha, you were happy and thought the mother who raised you had birthed you. Your father and those around you thought the same. But she didn't. The woman you thought was your mother, birth mother, wasn't. It was Lily gave birth to you, in a house, abandoned. Violet and I with her, Lily gave birth to you. And I took you and gave you away. But it all worked out; it was fine. Until your husband died and Willie's wife died, and he saw you in Sugar Creek—a widow to love. And he does love you. But what he didn't know, nor did you, your real mother was Lily. And Willie was her brother. Lily birthed you, and I took you, and I gave you away . . . so Lily wouldn't be condemned. Shunned. She was too young. It was too much for her. And then, much later you met, loved, and married Willie. Your uncle, Talitha. Willie, your uncle. Much older than you. But you didn't know. Nor did he. And God, I am so sorry. But I didn't know either. That you would meet. Marry. Give birth.*

I should have spoken those words to Violet and Talitha a long time ago. They needed to know. It would be hard to tell them. But not impossible. I'd lamented the situation for days and weeks and months but done nothing that produced positive results. That was not me. I wasn't a weak-keep-it-a-secret-do-nothing person. I was a doer, a solver. It was time to grind my mind and body against the honing perfection of a whetstone molding me into a courageous and fearless English/Amish woman, steadfast and unwavering, in my quest to find answers.

All the shunning thrown at me was ridiculous. I'd made some headway. Even with the hampering death of Bishop Herrfort, there was a slow, but growing response to my presence—smiles, nods, non-blank faces, slipped words, an occasional touch. Enough to generate a bit of hope, but not enough to satisfy. At that pace, it would take forever to harvest the secrets and suppositions hidden in the tightly wound coils of Amish brains. I had to take action.

Fortunately, during my tenure with Violet and Aaron, I'd not kept myself isolated. I'd roamed the area not only with my car, but also with my feet. And though the diligent, hardworking, Amish men and women, and often their children, no matter if sun scorched, water drenched, or wind tossed went about their work, appearing to mind their own business and giving no indicators of what happenings their roving eyes saw and soaking brains stored, under white *kapps* and straw hats. Among them, surely there would be a maverick or two who would, discreetly, perhaps with a hint of naughty glee, share the secrets they'd gleaned. Like all God's people, the Amish, too, had the gift of rationalization, and those who stretched the constraints of honor could find a way to justify within their hearts and souls the release of the revelations they dropped, sometimes unaware, into my ears.

I would have set my sights on them. The sponges and the leakers. And I still would do that as secondary and less reliable sources. But it was the wisest and most reliable from whom I hoped to garner information. It would be difficult, for they held tight to the *Ordnung* and shunning was to be obeyed without concession. Unless—I bit my lip, tilted my head, and considered. The first vision that came into my head was the image of Bishop Herrfort. Obviously, not a possibility, but there must be others like him. Reasonable. Able to see the rare occasion it was prudent and just to slip outside the realm of the *Ordnung*. Rare. Vital. Defensible. While I hoped Violet would relent and be one who would help me, I wasn't sure who the others might be. I'd been away too long. Yet, there were still many among the brethren who would have been alive when Lily died. I should know them, remember them. But I was uncertain. Times change and sometimes people change.

I needed help.

I smiled. I knew exactly where to get it.

Chapter Seventeen

"Oh my, I hope it's me you're here to see." Tilly's eyebrows raised as she looked up from her desk.

"Nope," I answered, shaking my head. Then ignoring the look of dismay on Tilly's face, I tightened my face, bent my head forward, and spit out my words. "It's *him* I'm looking for."

"Lowell Parker," she stated, and I heard a sigh behind her words. "You're looking for Lowell Parker. My boss"

"Yep, Lowell Parker." I said the name once, and then again, distinctly. *"Sheriff* Lowell Parker."

"Not a good day, Cora. Not a good day." It was her turn to shake her head.

I waited. Impatience fueling the underlining fear of confrontation caused my temper to rise in rebuttal. "I need to see him *now."*

"He just had a major run-in with one of the deputies." She grimaced. "And the mayor. He's not in a good mood."

"He's never in a good mood," I said.

"And he didn't get much sleep last night. Big fight in Riley's bar."

"I'll take my chances."

"I'm not going to buzz you in."

"You don't have to. I've got legs. They'll take me where I want to go, permission or not."

"Don't do it."

"I'll tell him you weren't at your desk."

She shook her head. She wasn't smiling.

"I really will," I said softly. I met her eyes for a moment. When she didn't respond, I turned from her desk and walked down the hall to Lowell's office. I wasn't nearly as confident as I'd led her to believe. But it wasn't courage I needed now; it was guts. I needed help, and I knew what I was going to ask for. And I knew there would be resistance. But I had to do this now, or I'd lose my courage. I was stepping way beyond my abilities and his sensibilities, and I would never have the courage, or the absurdity, to ask again.

I hoped he was neither tired nor cranky.

But he was. I knocked once on his door. There was no response. I hadn't expected one. I let my body shudder once, drew in one gigantic breath, let it out, and steeled myself, with strength and resolve. I opened the door. He was there, sitting at his desk, glaring at me.

"Go away, Cora Pooler."

I shook my head. "No," barely more than a whisper.

"I mean it."

"No." Solid.

He pressed his lips together. I knew there were vile words throbbing in his mouth, wanting to escape, and I knew he wanted to release them. But he didn't. I took that as a shield and as a fleeting feeling of acceptance, and, maybe, admiration. From him to me.

"I need your help," I said.

"You came the wrong day. I don't have any help left. Not for anybody."

He took his eyes from me and stared down at the strewn papers on his desk, rifled his fingers through them. Picked one up, balled it in his fist, threw it across the room.

I waited. Trembled. Pulled myself together. I needed him. He could help me. This was no time to be a wimp. This wasn't for me. It was for Lily. She deserved exoneration. It was me that made a decision that altered and, ultimately, shortened her life, and it was me that should return her to be honorably remembered in her community's Amish history. It was worth fighting for. It was worth making myself seem foolish.

"You're not going to go, are you?" he said. He looked weary.

"No," I answered, "not until you hear me out. And really listen. And really open your stubborn head to what I say."

"No matter how stupid it is?"

"No matter how stupid it *seems.*"

He breathed a sigh of resignation. And I knew he would listen. Maybe not like and maybe not accept. But he would listen. It was a beginning.

"I've done a lot thinking," I started. "I thought if I could get into the Amish community . . . their land, their homes, their loving and sympathetic hearts . . . I could find a way to get some information, even just hints of what happened the day Lily drowned." I cleared my throat. It was filling with tears. "But it hasn't worked. Their stolid, shunning ways have glued their tongues within their mouths, and their hearts within their unwavering, *Ordnung* obedience. I can't puncture it deep enough to slip inside and touch their souls with my need—my justified need. Lily's need. They will not talk to me. They barely look at me. *I can't get through*. But I've thought of a way." I paused, looked at him. His face was set. "And I need your help."

He sat back in his chair, gave the physical appearance of listening, but I couldn't decipher what was going on behind his masked face. He seemed to be waiting for further clarity of my plea. I was waiting for a response that would indicate the tone my words should take. There was none, so I continued.

"I know the answers I search are there, within the brethren's knowledge. But I can't get the answers, unless they'll talk to me." I pressed my hands together, looked down at the floor, looked back up into his face. "And I think I know how to make that happen."

He grunted.

"But I need your help."

He lifted his hands, palms out, and shrugged.

I didn't know how to go on. But I was determined.

"Just a little bit of positive response here would help," I said, and surprising myself, an anger was surging from within me. It helped. Spunk begat courage. "I understand you've had a bad day. We all have bad days. Suck it up. *I need your help*."

His lips twitched, almost a smile. Then disappeared into a scowl.

"Spit it out, Cora. How can I help you?"

"They have to talk to me."

He shrugged. "I can't make them talk, Cora."

"Yes, you can."

"And how would I do that?" He dropped his shoulders and grinned.

"Deputize me."

Chapter Eighteen

The swift, solid thump of his hands landing hard on the desk and the first howl of laughter shooting from Parker's mouth sent my stumbling feet fast to the door, through it, down the hall, past Tilly, out the front door, and onto the sidewalk, where still the slap on wood battered against my ears.

Oh, Cora, how foolish you are.

Somehow, I made it to my car, a sanctuary on wheels. I sank, a dead weight, into its nonjudgmental seat and covered my face with my hands. Rocked. I had hoped he would listen. I had feared he would not. I should have heeded that fear. Of course, it was a foolish plan, but I needed a way to make Violet and Aaron and all the others talk to me. Tell me what they knew. And I could think of no other way to break through that shunning armor, that impenetrable barrier that allowed no words to break its seal. *I needed them to talk with me.*

Wearied, my body slumped, and I bent my head against the steering wheel.

Oh, Cora, how foolish you are.

I didn't want to lift my head. I wanted to close my eyes and stay there forever, safe, basking in an eternal vast space of nothing.

It doesn't happen. Reality creeps in. Legs cramp. A fly lands on the skin. A twitch comes unbidden. A thought travels through the brain. An emotion births.

Oh, Cora, how foolish you were.

Remorsefully, I smiled. *Okay, God. I learned a truth today. Relearned a truth. Right now. Right here in this car. An old truth. It isn't always that we have to learn new truths. Sometimes, we need to read or think or say the old truths as reminders of what we already know in our minds and hearts. And I know these old truths, and I'm saying these old truths now. You didn't create me to doubt what is right. You didn't create me to give up. You didn't create me to fail. Old truths. And You promised to hear me, to stand by me with strength and direction. I need that from You now. I ask for it. And I know You will give it. I floundered. But my plan isn't foolish. It's a way to get in. And I'm not giving up!*

Still a little shaky beneath my renewed resolve, I stopped at the cemetery before going back to Violet's home. For me, the ground wherein Lily's body lay, her grave outside the fence, was a place of unrest and a reinforcer of my commitment. And I would find the truth for Lily.

The day was hot. The clouds, unmoving, basked in the borders God had allotted them for the whole of that day. With a gift from His store of unparalleled beauty, He'd scattered their sculps throughout the sky like the spread of age-faded, multi-shaded, white hair on the heads of old ladies sitting in church, an expansive mural, a magnificent banquet for eyes and heart.

I walked up the hill to Lily's grave.

I sat by the spot where she lay.

I emptied my mind of all things but the image of her.

I cried tears of love.

Head down praying without words, I stayed there a long time when I heard, close to me, the soft rustle of fabric. I lifted my face to the sound. It was Mattie. She looked down on me, gnawed at her lip, and scowled. Not unpleasantly. Concerned, I thought. Kind.

"You okay?" she asked.

I nodded.

"You don't look it."

"It's a sad place." When she said nothing, I motioned with my head for her to sit with me.

"I can get down there on the grass pretty good," she said. "And it's kinda hard for me to get back up. But I can do it."

"I'll help you."

She frowned. "I'm kinda big."

"I'm kinda strong," I said, smiling up at her. "We can do it. I'm a good tugger. You grab my hands. I pull hard. We work together. We get you up. That's what friends do. Help each other."

"Friends?" A half-laugh, half-grunt spit through her half-closed lips. "Got none of those. Old Schrock sees to that."

"He could be wrong," I said. "Sit."

"Don't look."

"You got something I've never seen?" I looked down at my lap, then up to her. Grinned.

"Something I don't have?"

A chuckle whooshed out her mouth. "Don't reckon I have."

I looked back down, folded my hands, and waited. Heard the drop of her body onto the ground. Smiled.

"You can look now."

"Hmm." I turned my face to her. Tilted my head. Looked up and down her body. "You look like a regular person. Hmm. Am I missing something?"

She laughed.

I plucked a blade of grass, held it to my lips, and blew.

"You know," I said, "I never could make a grass whistle. Neither could my sisters. But my brothers could. Maybe it's a boy thing."

"Never tried," she said.

"Try now."

"No, I don't think so. It's not the kind of thing Schrock would like me to do."

I screwed up my face. *Why not?* I thought about it. Strange. It would be interesting to decipher their relationship. "Do you ever call him Isaiah?"

"To his face? No. Actually, I don't call him anything. We don't talk much."

"Bet he could make the grass whistle."

"Yeah, he probably could." She pulled a patch of grass out of the ground, looked at it, then threw it away. "He can do most anything he wants to."

I didn't respond to her remark, and we sat silent for awhile. It was a comfortable silence.

For me. For her too. At least it seemed that way.

"I saw your sister," I said. "Awhile ago."

She squirmed a little.

"At Harriet's Eatery. With her husband. I think it was her husband."

"How'd you know it was my sister?"

"The sheriff told me."

"I didn't see her," she said. "I knew she was here, but I didn't see her."

"The sheriff told me that, too."

"Schrock shooed them away."

Minutes passed. I waited.

"He thinks she's uppity. My sister." Her recitation remained monotonal.

"She didn't appear that way to me."

"But she is. Kind of." She shifted on the ground, pulled her skirt to cover her shoes.

"You're not uppity," I said.

"She's the favored one." Mattie smiled slightly. "She loves me, but she's got no guts. Pretty and smart. Never had to ask for anything. Didn't learn how to be strong." She looked down at the ground. "Didn't have to."

"Did you?"

"Yep. Early on. Pretty earns a lot in some places. But I didn't have no pretty in me, and when you don't have it, you gotta work for it. For what you get." Looking across the grass, she paused, and I wondered what pictures and feelings were tumbling in her head. "And that's the way it was in our house." She looked at me and smiled. "But it was okay. I was loved . . . just not the favored one."

"How'd you meet Schrock?"

"My father hired him to fix a roof." She yanked another clump of grass out of the ground, dumped it in her lap, pulled a blade from it, shredded it, tossed it, then another and another. Continued speaking. "He's a good worker . . . and he knows how to talk man talk. The kind other men understand. Blunt.

Right to the point. And he's good at picking the right words to use with different kinds of people. Fools 'em good." She shook her head. "Fooled me."

"Did he fool your parents?"

"I don't like to talk about this." She looked at me. "What's done is done. Talking don't change nothing." She picked at her skirt, squirmed. "I should go. Been here long enough."

"I've seen you here before. Here outside the fence." I wanted to keep her there, learn more about her. "You're the one who left flowers by Lily's grave, aren't you?"

"Not for her." She turned her body, set her knee on the ground, pushed her hand against the grass. Struggled to get up.

I stood to help her. She ignored me. Instead, with great effort, she hefted herself up, brushed her skirt, and made ready to go.

I sensed she would leave without a saying a word of departure, and not indicating a want to seal the start of an unsettled friendship. I didn't want that to happen. There was so much more I wanted to know . . . who she was inside her body, her mind, and why she wandered the woods and the ground outside the cemetery fence.

"I hope I see you again," I said.

"Not likely."

I watched her lumber along the fence, her hand trailing over the top rail. Then she stopped, turned, furrowed her forehead. "Maybe."

She stood there a moment. I saw pain in her face. Then she gave a slow nod and returned to the trek that led back to her home and to Schrock.

I sank back onto the ground, lowered my head, and covered

my face with my hands, pressed hard. Really hard. And thought, perhaps if I pressed hard enough, concentrated strong enough, I could force every challenging obstacle into one solid ball . . . Mattie, Violet, Lily, Talitha, *Lowell Parker* . . . and could come up with a magical solution that would solve every problem swimming in my head.

I shook my head and laughed. *Silly girl.* I'd conquered worse. Made it in the English world. Held it together when Daniel died. Prospered his company and left it in good, competent, and trained hands. *We'll do it, God. We'll do it.*

Before I left the cemetery, I went inside the fence and searched out Herrfort's grave. I'd not yet had the courage to do that. I'd walked by the fence and thought of him there in the ground, and it had saddened me, pushed me from entering and seeing, accepting. He'd been the one Amisher to whom I could say full sentences and have those words receive recognition, respect, and reply. There was no one left in black garb and willing heart to listen to me full. Thoughts of my mother flooded my mind. I had seen her twice since the confrontation with my father. Both times had been in the cemetery. Each time I saw her, I had been driving, thinking, and as I drew near to the cemetery hill, I'd spotted her tethered horse and buggy positioned at the bottom of it. I'd stopped, parked, waited for the tears to stop, and then walked to where she stood, her head down, hands clasped, standing by Lily's grave site. Both times, she either heard or felt my presence, for she turned and looked at me, and I saw increased sorrow spread across her face. And each time, I drew in my breath, and watched her eyes fill and drop fresh tears over cheeks streaked by those already fallen. She said nothing to me. She simply stared, smiled so slightly, and then she stepped toward me, came to me, and she leaned her aged body into mine, drew me close. I cupped her with my arms, and we held each other. Not long. But enough. It was good.

I slid my hand over Bishop Herrfort's marker, reflected on his gentle kindness, so like my mother's, and let the warmth of my remembrances slide through me. I felt my lips turn up in a wistful smile, sadly soothing. One last loving pat on Bishop Herrfort's granite, and I left.

Chapter Nineteen

It was neither a foolish nor frivolous plan I'd birthed in my brain. It would work. With careful planning and courage, and a hard and stubborn head, it would work. But I needed Lowell Parker, mulish Lowell Parker, to assist me. If he issued me khaki pants and shirt and pinned a badge on my pocket, it would give me power, authority, and I could do the rest. He could close his eyes, pretend I didn't exist, and rest easy. He would meet the pretend-I-didn't-exist part with ease. The rest might be a bit more difficult. I'd soon find out.

As soon as the day started its slip into evening, I drove into Wander Lane, hid my car behind the old, big, brick, telephone company building, sat in it and waited for full night to come.

When I felt it had become too dusky to be seen, I slid out of my car, slinked onto main street, slithered across it, and slumped onto the bench that faced Harriet's Eatery. It was kind of fun. A deputy rehearsal. No way could Lowell spot me. I sat and waited. He would come. No imagination when it came to dinner. Same place. Pretty much same time. Same food. But I knew, if he saw me, he'd find a different place, different food. I knew he'd not be in the mood to see me. But I was going to see him. And convince him, whatever it took.

It wasn't long before the lamplight showed his shadowed form moving towards the eatery. His lagging gait didn't reflect his usual solid, determined, marching step. It had been obvious earlier he was overburdened by work responsibilities, and it was obvious, as I watched him walk, they'd taken their weary toll. My unusual request had probably added to his fatigue, and a slip of guilt, tempered by unwanted sympathy, quivered through me.

I would stay strong. And get what I needed.

Through the restaurant's front, glass window, I watched Bailey lead Lowell to the predictable back corner table, and while he dropped himself into a chair, slouched, and ran his hand hard across his forehead, she set a menu down before him. Looking up, he waved it away and mouthed words I couldn't hear, though I guessed he'd ordered, probably, coffee and the steak dinner. As he always did. Bailey nodded and left.

I decided to wait on the bench until Bailey brought his food to him, and he had eaten a few man-size chunks of steak and gulped a few mouthfuls of strong, hot coffee. It might help make him just a little more receptive.

Waiting and watching, each time he chewed and swallowed, food or drink, I took a matching deep breathe, and when I'd sufficiently rehearsed my speech and gathered a warehouse of courage, I walked across the street and into the eatery.

With warning footsteps planted just hard enough that he could hear them, I went to his table.

He didn't look up.

"It's me," I said.

He grunted.

"It's me," I repeated, "Cora."

"I know. I could smell you."

"*Chantilly,*" I said smiling.

"Honor wore it. Sprinkled it all over her body and hair," he mumbled.

He still didn't look at me. I shuddered. This was not a good time to be having the name of his ex-wife mentioned.

"Try *Evening in Paris,*" he said. "My mother wore it. Better memories."

I smiled. Not with joy. Relief. He was talking. Not much. But there were words coming out of his mouth. A beginning. Though a smidgeon of trepidation still tickled my brain.

"Go home, Cora Pooler."

Trepidation grew.

"Seems like you say that a lot to me," I said.

He looked up from his plate. I saw nothing pleasant on his face.

"Go home."

"No," I said softly. "No, I'm not going home."

"If I say I'm sorry I laughed at you, will you go?"

"No."

He looked at me, his wrinkles deep, his eyes bleary. "Doesn't matter." He exhaled a long and deep breath. I watched his chest draw in and then collapse as the air puffed through his lips. "I'm not gonna do it."

"You have to."

"No, I don't. You don't know the first thing about deputing."

"Deputing? Is that a word?"

"It means I'd have to teach you." He shook his head. "And it takes a long time."

"All I'd learn is that I can ask anybody any question I want to,

135

and they have to answer me. And I already know how to do that."

"I don't have a uniform that would fit you."

"I don't mind baggy pants."

"No, Cora, I'm not going to deputize you."

"If I go away right now, not one more word out of me, and leave you alone in total peace, can I come into your office tomorrow and get a uniform and badge, then get out of your office, and leave you alone for evermore?"

"If I thought the evermore would be evermore, I just might consider it."

"I'll take that as a 'yes' and I'll be in your office bright and early tomorrow morning."

Before he could say anything, I turned, scurried, was at the door and out. But I did hear the slam of flatware against table. Steak and coffee had not helped.

I did go to his office the next morning. Early. Chaotic time. Me there, a pest. Me there, an aggravation to get rid of. How? Give me what I want. Shut me up. Get me out of your hair.

I envisioned him, patience gone, shoving khakis into my arms, pinning a badge firmly on a shirt pocket.

Didn't happen. Saw him briefly. Ranting, backside to me, down the hall, deputies on either side of him, scurrying to keep up with him. The pound of their feet sounded like horses racing.

"You'd better go," Tilly said.

"I brought him coffee," I said, holding up the Styrofoam cup.

"Won't work. Some of your boys got him out of bed last night. Dead-drunk kids. Alive enough, though, to fight and demolish. And right now, Maudie Henderson has called for help.

It's her husband again. Crazy woman. Won't leave him. And she insists she *has* to speak to the sheriff. Nobody else will do."

"My boys?" I questioned, ignoring Maudie Henderson's recurring nightmare.

"Your Amish boys. *Rumspringa* happy they were."

I sighed. Amish boys celebrating unlimited freedom before baptism. An ongoing problem. The breathern's voices would stay silent, but there'd be a lot of unseen tsking and headshaking going on.

"I'll come back later," I said, capitulating.

"Don't, Cora."

I looked at her. Her gaze was unyielding. "Why?" I whispered.

"It's not going to happen. Go home."

"Where's that?" I lifted my chin. "The place where nobody speaks to me? Or looks at me? Or wants me there?"

"Isn't that what you chose?"

Hugging my body with one arm, I raised my right hand to cover my cheek, closed my eyes and lowered my head, rubbed my fingers against the side my forehead, down the length of my face, then up again to cup and support my head. Then I opened my eyes and saw, with my uncovered left eye, an ant crossing the floor. I dropped my hand and watched it. It scuttled across the floor to the trim at the bottom of the wall and went under it. Safe.

"Yes, I chose. But I didn't get a home," I said, answering Tilly. "A home is a safe place. A place where you can be you." I pressed my lips together. "I wish I could be that there, in Violet's house. But I can't."

Tilly leaned forward. I could see compassion on her face. "Maybe it's time for you to leave here. Maybe it's time for you to go back to Daniel's world. That's where you found happiness, and that's where you grew to be who you are now."

"I can't. Not yet. I have to fix what I broke."

"It's done." Her look was intense. "God has forgiven you. Take it. Let your heart leave with Him whatever it is you think you did wrong."

"I want to. But I can't. My mind won't let me. It demands I make things right."

"Cora, you're in control of your mind. Push the responsibility of Lily's actions out of your head. It's over. You did the best you could with the circumstances you had. It wasn't only you who made decisions. So did Lily. So did Violet. So did the whole community. Not just you!"

I didn't know what to say to her. She was right about Lily and Violet and the community but she wasn't right about me. I *did* have to resolve the mistakes of the past. Did that make me stubborn? Maybe. But is stubborn always wrong?

"I've seen *maem* at the cemetery," I sputtered, "actually, outside the cemetery. 'Cause that's where Lily is. Outside the fence. Still a sinner, to them, the judging blackbirds. How do you think that makes my mother feel? And yes, I said 'mother.' That's what she is. Mother to an English child. Me. That's what I am, an English child. Isn't it obvious, Tilly? I can never go back to the brethren, be an accepted saved-by-Jesus person. I can't be Amish, not after being English." I grabbed at my skirt, bunched it in my hand, thrust it out at her. "Look at this. An ugly, dark Amish green. Same as the blouse. Fake. Doesn't fool anybody. Certainly not the Amish bunch that lives by Wander Lane. Well, I'm *not* Amish. I don't *look* Amish. I don't *think* Amish."

Tilly lifted her arm, palm out, as if to stop me.

"No," I said, "don't try to shut me up. I'm tired of trying to fit in, to being not-good-enough, shunned like I'm going to end up in Hell. What's the point of trying? I can't be like them, and I don't want to be like them. And they're never going to tell me what they know and what I need to know." Teeth clenched, I lifted my arms, fisted my hands and shook them. And suddenly, it was gone. The anger. The strength. The fight. Nothing left but weariness. Depletion. Defeat. My body slumped, felt like it was a melting mass, not able to hold itself upright.

Tilly came around the desk. She put an arm, delicately firm, around my shoulders.

"Let's go for coffee," she whispered.

I shook my head. "No. You have to work." Her arm soothed. I leaned my head against hers. Calm, then quiet crept into my ears. She didn't move. I relaxed against her. And then, after minutes had passed, I shifted my body, and we stepped away from each other.

"I'll leave a note for the sheriff and say, I'm taking a break, and we'll go get coffee and something deliciously sweet." Her words glided gently across the air. Concerned.

I smiled. "I'm really okay now. I just want to go sit in the park alone for awhile."

"You sure?"

I nodded.

"Okay." She patted my back. "But if you need me, I'll be here."

I nodded again.

She went back to her desk.

I left.

The air had cooled; the breeze increased. Perhaps, a forerunner to rain. It would be welcome. Scatter the dust of drying ground. Shine the green on fading grass. Sparkle hot sun-drained minds and bodies to think and move.

I went to the park, sat on the bench across from Harriet's Eatery, relaxed . . . limp bodied, no thoughts. It was restful.

Nearing noon, I watched Harriet's restaurant become a congregating place for hungry villagers, tourists, the occasional Amisher . . . and Lowell Parker. I hoped he wouldn't look my way. But just in case, I sat straighter, stiffened my face, crossed my arms tight over my chest, slung one leg over the other and nonchalantly swayed it back and forth. However, it was wasted effort. He didn't look. Unwillingly, I felt a trifle disappointed.

The rain began a slow drip. Drops unclaimed by wind rustling on the maple limbs shading my bench found their way to my head. Just a small, refreshing mist of moisture veiling my hair. Rather pleasant.

While I sat, I kept my eyes focused on the eatery's glass front, and I saw Lowell walk through the building's door. Briskly nodding smileless acknowledgment to customer greetings, he strode to his corner table and sat, as usual, facing the room. As he pushed his menu to the other side of the table, I envisioned his eyes roving the dining room. I sighed. All business. Always ready to fight the battle for justice. Always right. I smiled. But I was the fly he could not track, swat and kill.

I decided he needed company at his table.

I thought he didn't see me when I walked in. I was drenched. Just as I'd left my bench, the drips had united to form a solid mass of pouring rain, and I'd hidden myself within a group of giggling, female adolescents, fingers spread over their heads, crowding into the restaurant, apparently attempting to protect their hair from the ravage of downpour.

I was wrong. He did see me. As the girls huddled by the door, I broke free and moving to the front counter, I perused the room and saw him looking at me. I couldn't tell what he was thinking. I felt a hand on my arm.

"He wants you to sit with him."

It was Bailey.

"You sure?" I asked. Not possible. He was totally angry with me. No way would he want me near him. But I knew going in, I was going to sit with him. My choice. I certainly didn't expect him to suggest . . . demand . . . we share his table. Nor did I believe he had. Bailey's ears obviously needed cleaning.

"I'm sure." Bailey's hand stayed on my arm, but she wasn't looking at me. "You girls sit and order, or get out," and then turning to me, "Grilled cheese and tomato soup?"

I shook my head. "No. Just hot chocolate. Are you really sure Lowell wants me to sit with him?"

She gave me a shove. "Yes. I'm busy. Just go."

So, I did. Firm-stepped right up to his table, and scowling, stood there.

"Sit," he said.

"Why?"

Eyes opened wide, he threw up his arms, shook his head, and slammed his hands down on the table. "And you wanted me to deputize you?"

"Your point being?" I asked, still standing.

"You're stubborn and won't take direction."

"Just because I don't want to sit with you?" I questioned, not willing to reveal by word or expression I'd come into the eatery with the express purpose of joining him at his table.

He sighed. "Just sit, Cora."

"Okay, I will. For a minute." I sat. "And if you were a gentleman, you would have pulled my chair out for me and made sure I was suitably comfortable."

He laughed, took up a napkin, and swiped my wet hair with it. Surprisingly, the laughter was good to hear. It wasn't poking-fun laughter. It was amused laughter, low and lulling. But I could have done without the napkin action.

"Okay," I said, anger tempered, curiosity born, "why am I sitting with you?"

"First, I'm apologizing." He raised his eyebrows and focused his eyes on mine. "I don't do that often. Apologize." He lowered his eyebrows, still looked straight at me. "But I shouldn't have laughed at you. Not like I did. It wasn't right. And I'm sorry."

"It was cruel," I said.

He nodded.

"It hurt."

"I know."

"And you've changed your mind? You're going to deputize me?"

"No."

I tensed. Pressed my lips together. He stared at me, unrelenting. I released a long, weak breath of air. Relaxed.

We sat quiet for awhile. We let the 'incident' fade.

He cleared his throat. "Secondly," and he looked intently at me, "I thought I'd have a talk with Eli Miller. But I wanted to tell you first." A part of his face wrinkled, and an eye crumpled shut, as he lifted one side of his lips in a half-formed smile.

Uncomfortable, I thought. He feels guilty. And he should. Yet it made him look old, vulnerable.

"He's pretty much the main preacher now Herrfort's dead." Confident. Remorse replaced.

"I know," I interjected. "He's a good man."

"He's the guy I'll be dealing with. About Amish stuff." He scratched his head, rubbed his cheek. "We get along pretty well. He's a fair guy." He stopped and stared at me.

"And?" I questioned.

"I thought I might have a little talk with him," he repeated, paused.

I waited. He'd put his old face on again. Stern. Noncommittal. Secure.

"About you," he said.

I bit my lip. Said nothing.

"I'm going to ask him to do me a favor, but I don't like to waste favors, and I won't ask for this one unless you agree to follow through with what I ask from him." He paused. "Will you?"

My face scrunched from a little twinge of apprehension and a large measure of curiosity. "How would I know? You haven't told me what you're going to ask him?"

"No Faith, Cora," he remarked. "I know what I'm doing. I don't want you trying to tell me how to do my job, and I don't want you meddling. So, I don't want you there."

"Just tell me what it is."

"No."

"I think we need to get something straight here." I clenched my teeth and glared at him. "Not too long ago, I thought we were truly headed toward friendship. I know you can be a raspy sort of man. Sometimes the words you spit out haven't gone through even a smidgeon of filtration. And sometimes your words are so sharp they cut through raw truth, so fierce they inflict pain. Don't you know, even ugly can be softened with a little sweep of healing salve." I leaned over the table, softened my voice. "Empathy. Kindness. Awareness. I know you have them. I've seen you use them. And really, Lowell, they're far more effective than words turned into pounding fists."

I straightened, folded my hands on the table, and hoped for a response.

He leaned back in his chair, rubbed his chin. Finally, the words came.

"Cold, hard action. Piercing eyes. Steadfastness. Alertness. Knowing. Courage. Audacity. Power. That's what gets the job done."

"It's not what makes friends."

"What's your recipe?"

"I told you," I said, "and I can add to that. Respect. Honesty. Caring."

"If you think, I'm not all those things, you don't know me very well." He shoved his chair away from the table and got up. "You may think I don't know how to be a friend, but maybe, right now, I'm the best one you've got."

His words struck sharp and shrunk me.

"Like it or not, I'm gonna talk to Miller, and he can do whatever he wants with what I say." He'd bent over the table, his weight pressed hard against his fists on its surface. He glared at me a long moment. "And then I'm done."

And he left.

Chapter Twenty

Bailey set a cup of hot chocolate in front of me. I put my hands around it. Warmth comforts, even when you're not cold.

"Men are like that," she said, pulling out the chair next to me and sitting. She folded her hands on the table, nodded. "Just walk away when they don't know what to say. Look mad, but it don't mean they are."

"He knew what to say, and he was plenty mad." I lifted my spoon and shoved whipped cream down into the cocoa, swirled circles in the liquid.

"He's tired. Got big bags under his eyes."

"Well, I'm tired, too. And I don't go yelling at him."

Bailey grinned. "You sure?"

I pulled my spoon out of the cocoa and ran my finger over the whipped cream and chocolate that had spilled over the cup's rim, then licked my finger.

"Too bad Lowell can't be as sweet as your chocolate," I said.

"We were talking about you."

"I don't rant and rave like he does."

Bailey cocked her head. "Maybe not as much, but I've seen a bit of temper flare from your lips."

"Maybe," I conceded.

"Everybody does it," she said, wrinkling her face. "Yell, I mean. So, I guess we gotta learn to let people gripe a little so's they can get it out of their systems and start doing what they need to do. Cleaned-out heads think better."

I tilted my head, gazed at her, squinted. "I think I'm seeing a bit of Harriet in you." I squeezed her hand. "Not a bad thing."

"She's in the back room."

"Harriet?"

"Yep. She comes sometimes. I can tell when she's got a hankering to get a taste of this place." Bailey grinned. "Feed her head. Nourish old fading memories."

"Can I see her?"

She tightened her lips and drew them down; the cords in her neck stretched taut. It was a sudden reaction, quick to go, and I realized she didn't want me to see Harriet.

"Just for a minute?" I asked, puzzled.

"She's not doing so good," Bailey said. "Not looking too good, neither." She paused.

"She might not know you."

"That's okay."

My eyes on Bailey's face, I waited. I saw her concern, knew it came from love, from learning and growing and recognizing the truths Harriet's living had taught her.

"If you be careful," she said, her face without yielding, her words firm. "Don't you be getting her excited."

"I promise I won't."

"I'll let you go in there alone with her if'en you promise you won't get her upset." She rubbed her hands. "And I'll be right outside the door. You need me, you call me. Right soon."

"I will." And I wondered why she was so worried. When I'd sat with Harriet on the bench, not long ago, she'd been fine. Quiet, but I think she knew me, understood the words I spoke. Regardless, I'd soon know the cause of Bailey's reluctance.

The room was a dusky dark, the only light slipping through a single, small window, and that spotted with clumps of clinging dust. I reached for a light switch, and then thought better. Perhaps there was a reason for the darkness. Perhaps brighter light was painful for Harriet's eyes. I would wait for my eyes to adjust, and, slowly, they did. And as the room grew clearer, it took me back to the day, more than ten years before, when my disobeying *Maem* stood in this same small, dusty dark room and held me, her shunned daughter. I closed my eyes and sank in the memory of her arms around me, smelled her sensible, sweet, soapy, scent, and felt the caress of her breath against my skin.

A scraping sound, soft and steady, broke into my reverie. I covered my face with my hands. I was afraid. All those years ago, that time in this dingy, shadowed room, the mixed hurt and joy was back. I'd borne it, lived with it, and diminished it. Harriet. My *maem*. The pain, the weight of that shunning. Yet, memories leave a residue of what was before. And now with the creak of a rocker, I opened my eyes to face them again.

While conscious of the dreary, box-ridden background, dust and dirt on walls and on the floor, cobwebs and droppings, it was Harriet that drew my eyes. She had shrunk. In so short a time since I'd seen her, she had shrunk. Almost to nothing. She slumped small in her chair, and I wondered that her feet could touch the floor, had the strength to move the rocker.

"Harriet," I whispered, and when she didn't respond, "Harriet," a little louder.

Her head moved a little.

"It's me. Cora, Cora Pooler. Can you hear me?" I heard my words tremble.

She grimaced, twisted in her chair, just a little, and her shirt rose, just enough for me to see the scarf wrapped around her waist and tied behind the rungs of her rocker. I bit my lip. I'd wanted to talk with her, remember with her, tell her all that was happening, listen for her wisdom, a touch of revelation. I wanted to share, her and me . . . hearts, minds, souls. It wouldn't happen. Not with words.

The door behind me opened.

"I think you probably need to leave now."

I turned and looked at Bailey. Nodded. "She's gone."

"Almost." I heard large sadness in that small word.

Before I left her, I knelt before the rocker, put my head for a brief moment on Harriet's lap, and then looked up at her. Her lips had turned upward. I wanted to believe it was a smile of recognition. Perhaps it was.

I rose and stepped outside the room. Bailey closed the door and anger, within me, rose.

"Why do you put her in that ugly, dirty room!"

Bailey shrugged. "It's where she wants to be."

"How can you know that?"

"I just do."

She turned to go, and I grabbed her arm. "And how can you use such a filthy room for storage?"

"I don't!" She pulled her arm from me. "There's another room, for your information, clean and tidy, for your information, that is used for whatever it needs to be used for. Harriet likes the room she's in. She doesn't come often, but like I told you before, she likes the room the way it is and when I try to clean or change it, she howls and cries, puts up a real fit. A real, *big* fit. So, I leave it. I can tell when she wants to be in it, and she's an old lady without much time left, and I'll do whatever she wants. So you think on that, Cora Pooler, and you tell me a better way to make her as happy as she's able to be 'til they put her in the ground."

She was right, and I was ashamed. But it seemed unfair and foreign to whom she'd been.

Life? Not tidy. Not easy.

Later in the car, driving on Amish roads, needing to be near a place that brought a measure of comfort, a knowing of kinship, a wanting of rightness, I drove to the cemetery, and I walked up the hill, my feet stepping on the tracks planted by funeral buggies climbing the pathway that would take Amish mourners to the burial sites of those who were theirs . . . sanctified brothers and sisters, privy to a space inside the fence. My spot of fragile connection lay outside that barrier, and I didn't have the knowledge or the power to climb that fence and claim a space for Lily. Not yet.

Eyes averted, I passed the cemetery and marched through the grass until I stood by Lily's monument, and there I touched my fingers to my lips and then to the monument. After a moment of visualizing Lily, wispy young, and beautiful in my mind, I reached and rubbed the engraved letters on her gravestone . . . **Lily Pooler**. I wondered if I died right at that moment, would they bury me here, or would they send me back to the English?

I dropped my body and sat close to the marker, leaned against it, let my thoughts drift. Without control, they slid over grass and trees and sky. Soft colors. Sweet scents. Soothing. From a distance, a bird sang. And I felt my body loosen, slip lighter, slide into a peaceful emptiness. It was good. But it didn't stay.

Harriet. I thought of Harriet. Was this how she felt as she sat in her rocker in the storeroom that had been, was now, her place of refuge? Did she remember, sort through the past and command the good and pleasuring reminiscences to come forth and entertain? Did she drift to the corner of her mind that held old recipes, the smell and feel of rich garden soil, the touch of a heaven-waiting husband's love? Did she think of dear friends, dimmed and softened, but true? Simple peace, rightness, did she feel that? I hoped so.

It seemed I sat there a long time. It was good. Healing. And then a stirring of air, a rustle, crept through my ears, interrupting the flow of tranquility. I straighten, pushed my back firm against Lily's monument and looked up.

It was Maddy. She was crying.

I didn't think she was aware of me scrunched against the marker, or if she was, she paid no mind to me. Her heaving body was hunched against the tree that overlooked Lily's grave, and her hands pressed so tight against her face, they pushed it downward, and through her fingers came gulping sobs. I wasn't sure what to do. I think I might have been able to slip away without her noticing. But I wasn't sure whether or not she'd already seen me. It seemed if she had, she'd not be crying where I could see her. She'd been so reticent in the past, I thought it unlikely she'd reveal strong feelings before me. But I wasn't sure, and it could be her emotional exposure was deliberate, her want for me to know and to help surpassing her need to keep her inner self unknown.

I took a chance. I rose and slithered near her, touched her shoulder. She shook her head, and I dropped my hand. "Maybe I can help you," I said softly.

She took her hands away from her face and looked straight at me. Her eyes were dull. Tears still lingered on her lashes. The whole of her face was a mottled red, but it was a cheek that grabbed and held my attention. A dark burgundy streak ran the length of it. It could not be seen as anything other than a good, hard slap.

"Who hit you?" I tried to keep my voice gentle.

She swallowed and then, as she opened her mouth to take in air, a gurgling gasp, like a baby ending his sobs, rumbled from her throat and spilled through her lips.

I took a step closer to her. I wanted to hug her, but she seemed to sense my intent and raised her arm to stop me. Not wanting to pressure her, I moved back a little. Eyes glaring, focused on my face, hers expressed a wariness. She lifted a hand to her mouth and chewed on her thumbnail.

"I want to help you."

"Are you Amish?" she asked, dropping her hand, rubbing it over her skirt. Then, squinting, she leaned her body forward and pressed her lips together.

I shook my head, no.

"Are you trying to be Amish?"

I shook my head again, and then, rethought. "I don't think so."

"I don't like the Amish very much."

"You married one," I said, trying to keep my voice steady, calm. Not accusatory.

She grunted. "We all make mistakes." She paused. "And sometimes they're not choice. Sometimes they're pushed hard right into you."

Not sure how to reply, I said nothing and waited for her to say more. When she didn't, I offered her a ride home. She refused.

"I can walk. It's not that far." She had not yet looked away from my face. "You go. I'm staying put."

"Look," I said, "it is far, and I can't leave you here all alone. Not when you're looking so miserable. I don't know what happened, and I don't have to know. But I do know you're in trouble right now and probably need help. Maybe just a shoulder to cry on. Maybe just an ear open to listening. Maybe more. I don't know." I paused. "Maybe just a place to go where it's safe."

"He won't hit me again. Not if supper's on the table when he comes in from the barn." She lifted one side of her mouth and a small grunt passed through her lips. "Like nothing happened." She lifted her shoulders. "And maybe nothing much really did."

"That purple mark on your cheek isn't nothing."

"Maybe I walked into a limb. Some of 'em hang pretty low, you know."

"But you didn't," I said. "He hit you."

"Yeah, he did." She shrugged. "But I probably earned it."

"Do you really believe that?"

"Yeah. I know the rules, and when you break 'em, you pay the price."

She set her face firm, almost challenging, and I knew it was best to be silent, to squelch the words that ached to be spoken. But we don't always do the prudent thing, so I threw wood on the fire.

"That's ridiculous. No broken rule warrants an attack on the face."

She laughed. "Lady, a slap is *not* an attack. You wanna see attack, you better take a look at me after I break a *big* rule."

"An Amish rule?"

"The Amish don't make rules that cause you to be hit."

"What rule then?"

"The Schrock rule. Rules. There's a whole, long list of 'em. The personal *Ordnung* concocted by Isaiah Schrock for the exalting of his exemplary presence."

I hadn't liked what I'd seen of the man, but I remembered Violet telling me the community thought of him as a good man, a hard-working man. It was hard to match the man Maddy was speaking of with the man the community claimed to know.

As if reading my thoughts, Maddy grunted and continued her rant. "But the half-blind blackbirds think because his fields are always plowed first of everybody's, and his cows give the most milk, and he's quick to reach in his pocket to give a few pennies, he's the epitome of good Amish behavior. But they really do know. They must. They just close their eyes to it. And I don't think they look at me as real Amish. 'Though I got baptized. But I don't think I fit their mold. They don't know quite what to do with me . . . so they do nothing. And they probably figure I deserve what I get." She sighed, shook her head. "And maybe, I do."

"Of course, you don't"

"I don't love him." She grinned. "And sometimes, I deliberately provoke him with little things. Burn the edges of the steak. Switch the pillows on our bed." She laughed. "It really riles him to get the wrong pillow. Doesn't like soft." She smirked.

"Sinks his head right down to the mattress. Yanks that pillow right off the bed and throws it at me." She nodded as if well satisfied. "Little things. Only sometimes I hit the wrong time, when the wrong mood's simmering in him." She smiled dolefully. "I pay the price." She lifted her hand to her face, smoothed it over the red spot, sobered. "Not always worth it. But sometimes . . . sometimes, it is."

"What'd you do this time?" I asked, a little wary. I'd never heard her speak so many words. I didn't want to stop the flow, but I wanted to know why he'd slapped her.

"Asked him why he'd come in late for dinner."

"And?"

She shrugged. "That's it."

Shocked, I stood silent.

"I think he stores up all the rotten words he'd like to throw at his Amish *brothers*, but to stay favored by them, he waits and hoards, and when he's got too full and can't hold anymore, he hurls them at me. Sometimes words, sometimes more. And then he feels better. And justified."

"Why don't you leave?"

"Go where? He feeds me. I got a house to live in. A bed. Clothes. They're ugly, but they cover my body." She gritted her teeth. Her eyebrows came together. "But I *hate* him."

"I can see why," I said softly.

"No, you don't." A mask fell over her face. Ugly. Mean. Hateful. "You don't understand at all. Nobody does." With that, she turned and stomped away from me.

I reached out my arm, called to her. "Maddy. Wait." I moved to follow her.

She stopped, turned. Fast. "Don't you be following me. I

don't want you. Keep away from me."

Dumbfounded, I stopped. She was right. I didn't understand.

Chapter Twenty-One

Before I left the cemetery, I stood over the spot of grass next to Lily's which Maddy's conduct had marked out as her own. I stooped and ran my fingers though the blades, attempting to raise the grass, straighten it, from the trampling crush of Maddy's feet. As I lifted and smoothed, I pondered her words. Not only those bitter, but also those questioning. Was I Amish? Was it a forever stigma? Inbred? Irremovable? And did I get to choose? I would hope so. At least, in my own head. Yet, if I chose not to be Amish, would that penetrate the minds, hearts, and souls of the brethren or would there be a forever shunning?

My body was weary from the day's happenings. Even my mind was begging to droop. No more thoughts. No more confusion. No more anything. Just blissful emptiness. And what better place to find invisibility and nothingness than in an Amish home peopled with persons neither allowed to acknowledge nor speak with me. Though it seemed to me impossible for that to happen. Irrational. I smiled. I was a full-formed person with lips that spit out words. Poor Violet, she tried so hard never to speak to me. Mostly succeeded. But not always. She must be spending a lot of time on her knees.

I left the cemetery and drove back to her and Aaron's house.

Violet was in the kitchen throwing, kneading, and pounding a mass of bread dough on the table. Flour flew everywhere.

"Looks like a little, non-Amish temper has invaded you," I said. Her display of unsanctioned attitude and behavior sparked a bit of wickedness within me. Already, I felt a mite better.

She didn't reply. Kept attacking the poor, defenseless batter.

"I sense a measure of anger in your manner. Want to tell me why?" Grinning, I slid onto the chair across from her. She pressed her lips together, and I knew she wanted, ached, to speak to me. Probably not very nice words. I relaxed. This was good. Pushed Matty right out of my head. And this was an opportunity. Really angry people, Amish sister Violet being one of them, don't always think before they speak and are easily goaded. And maybe, I could draw on all the tactics I'd used when we were young and squeeze all kinds of information from little sister Violet.

"Violet," I sing-songed. "You don't look happy."

Like the ladies I encountered at church, Violet knew how to make unladylike, unchurchlike, nasty, little faces. And I became a recipient of the worst I'd ever seen.

I laughed. Swiftly, ignoring *Ordnung* rules, she picked up a kitchen towel and with face set stern and glaring, whipped it against the table. Which was only a little less Amish forbidden than whipping it against me.

"Naughty, naughty, Violet. Don't forget, naughty faces, naughty actions and naughty thoughts have to be confessed. Before the whoooole congregation. So that everybody knows your transgression. Ooooh, Violet, Carrie Yoder is gonna looooove to hear that confession."

And with clenched fist, Sister Violet, adamant Amish woman notwithstanding, punched the poor bread dough with all her might.

"Okay, you're mad," I said, "and since I haven't been here all day, it can't be me that festered all that anger. Right?" I waited and when she didn't respond, I questioned, "What's going on?"

Facing downward, Violet swished the towel over her flour flecked hands, frowned and said, "It is you."

"You're talking to the table," I said. "Talk to me."

"You know what," she said, lifting her head, and bracing her body with her palms flat and arms taut, she leaned across the table, and hissed, "I can talk to you. You know why? Because your good *friend,* the *sheriff,* talked to Preacher Kurtz, and he talked to me, and now I have to talk to you. Which means Aaron will be mad and won't talk to me."

I was confused. "I don't understand."

"Well, you should. And believe me, the words I'm speaking now are *necessary* words. Totally necessary. Would be sanctified by Bishop Herrfort. If he were still living. But I don't need him. Your *friend* made it possible for me to speak not only necessary words, but unnecessary words also. I want you gone. I can't tell you to go. I can't make you go. But I want you gone. You've messed up everything." She was rambling. It made no sense to me. "But I'm Amish. Deep in my heart I am Amish. So I can't say those words, not the words that *tell* you to go. No matter how much I want to say them loud and clear, I can't. They have to stay there, too, deep in my heart, those unloving, forbidden words, and I can't disobey. I can't say them. I want to, but I have to leave them in there, in my heart, silent, and make them dissolve."

"Maybe you can't say them, but I heard them," I said softly, the hurt too big to let my voice be strong. "You want me gone." I swallowed. "I thought you liked me here."

"Sometimes I do. Did. But not mostly." I heard sadness in her words. "I keep remembering Aaron loved you. And I know it was a long time ago. But you're pretty, Cora. English pretty. Bright lips and shiny hair. Amish can't compete with that. And you laugh. Even when things aren't funny. You always did that . . ."

"Not always," I murmured even as she spoke.

". . . even when Lily and I were little. You brightened lives. You don't do that so much anymore, but you still have that positive presence. I can't match it."

"You don't have to," I said.

"I'm practical and plain." I heard an urgency in her voice. "Would you pluck a dandelion, if a tulip was growing beside it?"

"Dandelions last longer," I said.

"He looks at you sometimes. And I worry."

"You don't have to."

"Maybe not. But maybe so." She bit her lip. "And Baby Clare likes you better than she likes me."

I threw up my hands. "You're being totally ridiculous. And besides, all this foolish stuff you've got swirling out your mouth has nothing to do with the sheriff or the preacher. Just tell me, how did they make you able to talk to me?"

"I don't know. Probably the sheriff made a deal with Preacher Kurtz. Maybe he promised not to punish the *rumspringer* boys. Maybe he'll turn his back on some things he thinks are his business and let the preacher handle Amish wrongdoings. I don't know. I only know, if you ask a question about Jacob and Lily . . . ,"

She paused. Her lower lip quivered, "I have to answer it." She fastened her eyes on my face, and I saw an anger bordering on hate in them. "You got what you wanted, Cora. You came here to rile things up, and we have to let you do it."

"I came here for truth. It's that simple. I love you, Violet. I didn't come here to hurt you. I came here to help Lily."

"Lily's dead. It doesn't matter where she's buried, she's dead. It's done. And you can't change the past." She shook her head. Sighed. Reached and touched me. "I love you, too." Defeated words, neither of us winners, but I welcomed them.

"It'll be okay, Violet. I know it's been hard for you. And there's not a bit truth in the Aaron thing. I know he can be a hard man, rigid, *stubborn,* and you can't always be sure what he's thinking, but he's also a good man, true to his faith both in mind and heart. You've nothing to worry about."

I know," she whispered. Then she smiled. "And you know, Cora, I'm glad I can talk to you again. It'll be a big relief . . . and maybe we should clean the flour off ourselves before it hardens to paste."

But, unlike the Violet I knew, she didn't ask my forgiveness. In my mind, I knew the anger was still there. Fed by insecurity and fear, it would fester, grow, and be hard to contain.

I needed to know more. There were two possible persons who could clarify Violet's sketchy explanation. Preacher Kurtz and Lowell Parker. Preacher Kurtz was a good, kind, easily manipulated man, popular with the Amish populace, but a mite underbearing. And a tad less bright than most. Lowell Parker, on the other hand, was a probably good, sometimes kind, obviously overbearing, and admittedly smart man. Both tended to be truthful. But I had to choose one, and reluctantly, though wisely, I chose Mr. Self-Perfect Parker to explain what he had done. So I took in several deep breaths, let them out slow, went to my car, got in, put my flour-free hands on the steering wheel, breathed deep again, turned the engine key, put my foot on the accelerator, and drove.

I went to his office.

"He's not here," Tilly said.

"When will he be?"

She lifted her eyebrows, shrugged. "God only knows."

"Before closing?"

"When's that?" Tilly tilted her head, scrunched her face. "Far as I know, the man sleeps here."

"Tilly, I'm serious."

"I know you are. And I wish I could tell you, but I can't. I leave at five o'clock. Theoretically. And it's already past that, so I would guess he'll be in either soon, or later, or not at all. But one thing I am sure of," and she nodded, "when his stomach gets so empty that he can't function, he'll be at Harriet's. But I can't tell you what time that will be. If he hasn't eaten all day, which is possible, then he could be there now, but if he grabbed food on-the-run, he might not be there until near Bailey's closing time . . . and she's been known to stay open way past closing time. Just for him." She looked at me and made a moue. "Who knows?"

"I think I'll give it a try." I gave a quick nod and slapped her desk. "Right now."

"Don't," Tilly said, "his day has been hard enough. Give the poor man a rest."

"Maybe I should," I replied, "but I can't. I know it's selfish and I know he's tired. And I'll try to stay calm. But I need to know what he did or said that allows Violet to speak to me now. I truly don't understand it. And I promise, Tilly, I'll hold my temper and control my tongue."

She smiled ruefully. "I'm not sure you can."

"You'll see." I turned to go, got to the door, heard her call out to me.

"Cora?"

She was standing by her desk. Her face foretold serious words were about drop from her mouth.

"What?" I said.

"You don't give him enough credit. You think he doesn't do enough for you, doesn't listen. But he does. He just doesn't always think like you do. But he's smart, Cora. And he knows how to do his job. You need to listen to him. You might not see it, but he goes the extra mile to make things right. For everybody. Even you. Hear what he says, Cora. Consider what he does. He cares. And he doesn't have to tell you his every thought and movement, and he doesn't have to ask for your permission to do his job." She stopped, stood quiet. I knew she wanted to say more, but her final words were brief, spoken quietly, firmly. "Before you go looking for him, ponder the words I've given you . . . if you've got a lick of good sense in you now."

I didn't. I'd promised Tilly I'd control my anger, but it was a surface promise, and I knew from Tilly's last words, she intuited I wouldn't keep it. She was right. As I drove to Harriet's, the anger promise faded. I went into Harriet's ready to vent.

He wasn't there. Determined, I marched to the back corner, sat at his table, and faced the front door. I would wait for as long as it took.

"It might be long before he comes." Bailey slipped into the chair beside me. "His clock runs different from most." She smiled. "It doesn't ring consistent."

I studied her. She was far removed from the emerging woman of ten years ago, time had matured her, moved her from the sullen, resentful, aging, lazy girl to this sometimes wisdomed, compassionate, productive woman.

"Sometimes you remind me of Harriet," I said.

She lowered her eyes, and when she raised them, looked at me, I saw them swollen with tears. Memory tears? Regretful tears?

"I'll never be her," she whispered.

I said nothing. We sat, silent, for awhile.

Head cocked, face intent upon mine, Bailey was the first to speak.

"How long will you stay here?"

"In Wander Lane?"

"No. Here." She poked the table.

"'Til he comes."

"Eventually, and I mean tonight, I'll close up." Sliding forth on her chair, she made ready to rise. "Why don't you go home? Take a pill and go to sleep. Come back tomorrow." She pushed her palms against the table and lifted herself. "You're all wired up now. Not the best time to confront a busied, tired man."

"How long before you close up?"

"Another hour."

"And if he comes just before that hour ends, what will you do?"

"I'll feed him and let him stay as long as he needs, then he'll tip me well, walk out the door, and I'll close up."

"I'll wait."

She sighed. "I'll bring you some ice cream."

"And cake?"

"And cake. If you promise you'll tone down your words, if and when he comes in."

"I've already promised that."

"Then it's double important that you keep it." A stern mask slid over her face. "I'm not joking. I know you're older and wiser than me, but I'm smarter on this one. If he comes in, you hold your temper . . . or you're out the door. For a long time."

She'd taken a few steps when she turned and looked at me.

"You know, I remember when you were young. Happy before the Lily thing. The baby thing. The shunning. You gotta get that back." She tilted her head, furrowed her forehead. "And what you gotta see is that world isn't against you. Not even your shunners. They're really not so bad. You hurt them. Broke their rules. And they got a right to their rules. If you'd gentle down a bit, they'd probably treat you a little kinder. It's their world you're trying to live in now. So you gotta figure how you can get what you want within their rules. . . ."

"I do try," I interrupted, "but some of those rules are ridiculous."

"It's their world and you gotta admit they want you back in it . . . Amish. But there's something you gotta understand, Cora. Not about the Amish. But important." She bit her lip. Waited a moment. Bent her head toward me. "You wanna know what?"

I pressed my lips together. I didn't like how this conversation was going.

"Well?" She lifted her eyebrows.

Reluctantly, I nodded.

"You gotta open your eyes and *see* Lowell Parker. More than just the sheriff. The man. I know he doesn't always think like you, but did you ever consider that sometimes he might just be thinking better than you do? That man's got a heart, and he's trying to help you. Let him. And be grateful. It's getting pretty bad when I see things better than you do. You're supposed to be the smart one, but you're pretty dumb about him. He knows what he's doing, and he's one smart cookie. You better straighten up." She twisted her lips and shook her head. "Maybe a little cake and ice cream will clean out your head, make you a little sweeter."

She turned and walked away.

I felt shame. A bit. Not enough.

I finished the ice cream and cake. Truly tasty. Stomach pleased, energy fueled, I felt better. Multi-caloried food could wilt a seething sulk. A little. Enough. It's easier to be civil when anger's been tempered with sugar.

Lowell came in shortly after I'd finished the sweets.

His voice was mumbled as he dropped into his chair. "What do you want?"

"What did you do to make Violet talk to me?"

"It worked, so what do you care?" He rubbed his eyes and cupped his face, blew a big sigh through his fingers, and then dropped his hands and looked at me. "You can talk to her as much as you want now. Within reason. But you gotta ask the right questions."

"How do I know what the right questions are?"

"For God's sake, Cora, what are you doing here in Wander Lane anyway?"

"Vindicating Lily . . . and don't swear!"

"So if you know what you want to know, you figure out the questions . . . and I didn't swear. I was calling on Janus and Pluto for help."

"You should have tried Tellus and Proserpina. . . . I imagine even among those phantom deities, female goddesses do the dirty work." His lips turned up in a weary grin.

"And I need to know exactly who I can talk to and exactly what restrictions there are."

"You can talk to Violet and Aaron. Just like I told you. You should listen better, Cora Pooler. Seems obvious to me what questions you should ask. Use your head, Cora. Think."

"So I can ask anything?"

"Sure, but you'll only get answers to the right askings. And don't be demanding any answers yet. The preacher won't be letting the congregate know that you and Violet and Aaron have restricted speaking privileges, until the Sunday meeting." He rubbed his eyes and squinted. "Except Violet. I already told her. And she probably told Aaron. Amish women aren't good at keeping secrets from their husbands."

"Ha," I scoffed. "Whoever gave you that little piece of information was way off base, and why'd you pick just her to tell?"

"She's your sister. It's been hard for her. I thought I'd make it easier for her a little sooner."

"Easier? Ha!"

There came a quiet time in which I pursed my lips and

seethed, and he waited, his lips sealed. Fortunately, for my temper, Bailey came to the table and put a plate piled with steak, fried potatoes, and green beans in front of him.

"How'd you ever get all that food on one regular sized plate?" I asked her. "Absolutely astonishing."

"Wasn't easy." Bailey lifted her eyebrows. "And wait 'til you see the basket of rolls I'm gonna bring out." She shook her head. "Doubt if he'll offer you one. He'll eat 'em all himself."

She paused. "You want some more ice cream?"

"No. I don't think so," I said. "I think watching him stuff all that food in his mouth is enough to kill my appetite."

"I agree," Bailey said, "and he does it nearly every night."

Lowell shrugged and kept eating.

"Okay," I said after Bailey left. "I do know the questions I need answered. And I know whom to ask." Perturbed, I looked at him, not sure he was listening. "Can you put your fork down for a minute and open your ears."

"I can hear you," he said, opening his mouth, and I marveled that food didn't fall out of it.

"How did you do it? How did you make Kurtz agree?" I asked.

"He's easy."

"How?"

"He's a good guy. Simple, but cooperative. And he likes me to stay away. Thinks he can handle Amish law related problems with Amish discipline and prayer. When I agreed I'd let him handle much of it, he agreed Violet and Aaron could answer Lily-related questions from you. The timing was good. For me. The *rumspringa* boys have been having a particularly good time lately . . . and I'm glad to get 'em off my hands.

He was done talking. I was too.

I sat and watched him eat. And he ate it all. Steak, potatoes, green beans and rolls. When he was done, he wiped his face, pushed back his chair, rose and told me it was time to go.

"I see that," I said. "The food's all gone."

Then he pulled out his wallet, threw money on the table, and as he walked to the front counter, shouted, "Hey Bailey, I'll take some cake with me."

"He eats like an Amish man," I muttered to Bailey, as we reached the counter. She rolled her eyes, nodded. I didn't stay to see him get the cake, but I'm sure the piece was huge. I'd got the answers I'd wanted, and I'd had enough of Sheriff Lowell Parker for that night. Without a doubt, I knew he felt the same.

I went to my car, drove back to Violet's to sleep. The next day I would find a new place to live.

Chapter Twenty-Two

While I'd waited for and pulled information from Sheriff Lowell Parker, the earth had turned from the sun and had continued its slow rotation beneath a blackened sky relieved from full darkness, by a scattered shower of shining stars.

The drive to Violet's house was long enough to soothe the edges of anger and guide my thoughts to rational. The news was good. I could ask my questions, and Violet and Aaron would comply with the preacher's directive. But many times, good has a nether side, an underside of lurking gloom. And my Amish community was careful with words. They could parse them to shape what seemed to answer an unwanted query, but, in fact, did not. I would have to be careful. Question succinctly. Listen well.

My head too tired to linger on possible negatives, I shifted to frothy, inconsequential thoughts. It didn't matter whether or not I dressed drab any longer. It hadn't helped before, and it certainly wouldn't make a difference, after Lowell's mandate. And I wouldn't wait for Sunday's proclamation. Freedom was given me, in my mind, at Harriet's Eatery. I could pull the pins from my hair and let it flow. I could wear shoes that didn't need laces or weigh a ton, I could wear yellow and pink and soft, pale green. Soft and silky and velvety fabrics would cover my body. Skirts that almost showed my knees. Necklines that drooped. Pants. Jeans. No aprons. And I could spray my body all over with sweet aroma. I was free to look English. Bliss.

Violet's house was dark. I had thought it would be so. It wasn't prudent to leave oil lamps burning with no one awake to monitor them. Fortunately, there was enough light from the stars to guide me. I opened the car's trunk and pulled two full suitcases from it. English clothes. Packed tight and abundant. As I struggled to haul them to the house, their weight felt good. It would feel even better when I repacked them and their weight was calculated by Amish-style clothes, no longer needed or wanted.

Violet had left a lamp and matches on a table by the door. Amish thoughtfulness. If I chose to leave this community, I would miss their attentive concern, their kindness. Kindness afforded even to me. Me, the shunned one headed for Hell. And I knew they didn't want that for me. Hell. Eternal damnation. And I knew they prayed for me. It would help when they could talk to me. If they spoke full truth.

It took two trips for me to haul the suitcases up the stairs. One hand for a suitcase, the other for a lamp. But weariness couldn't conquer me. I relished lugging those valises step by step up the stairs, emptying their cargo of beauty, refilling them with mundane, and then dragging them back down the stairs, through the great room, over the porch, down the steps and driveway, and into the obediently waiting, appreciated open trunk. Actually, if I could have done it quietly, not waking anyone, I would have shoved them clattering down the stairs and kicked them all the way to the car. But, again, there was enough Amish residue in me to accommodate the sleeping patterns of my Amish hosts. Even so, it was good.

By the time morning came, everything was lovingly folded and neatly put away into dresser drawers. And on the doilied, glossy dresser top were combs, perfumes and cosmetics.

I'd slept long. And well.

When I went downstairs, Violet didn't mention the scrape marks on her polished, hardwood floor. Amish breeding. And I knew I was already forgiven for it. And I knew an apology for harsh words spoken on the prior day would be uttered. Sincerely. Eventually.

She'd set a place for me at the little table placed apart from the family table. Grateful, though not surprised, I smelled biscuits warming in the oven, saw ham slices on the counter, and a bowl of eggs beaten and ready for the frying pan. Violet was at the sink, hand washing what appeared to be her undergarments.

"Good morning," I said.

She nodded, and back to me, she poured the eggs into the frying pan. She didn't mention a request for forgiveness for the words she'd said when we'd last spoken, but I was confident she would.

"I saw the sheriff last evening," I said. "He affirmed you were allowed to talk to me now."

"Am I hearing a question about Jacob Lapp?" She didn't look at me as she stirred the eggs.

"Not yet, but I'm leading up to it, and I thought 'good morning' was a good place to start."

She put the eggs on a plate, added the ham, and opened the oven door. She said nothing.

"Okay, let's try this," I said, looking over her shoulder, through the window over the sink, at the sun heating the glass, shining through an unstreaked pane. Morning chores. Kitchen spotless. "Do you remember the day Lily died?"

"What's that got to do with Jacob Lapp?" She took the biscuits from the oven, closed the oven door.

"Was she with him that day?"

"Maybe." She dished the ham and biscuits onto the plate with the eggs.

"Was she?"

"Probably." She set the plate of food in front of me. "Milk or orange juice?"

"Was it a workday?"

She looked at me, face set tight.

"The day she died . . . drowned? Was it a workday?" I repeated.

"It was. Only it was late . . . late in the day." Her words trembled. "Jesse Miller found her, driving home from raking hay. He saw her clothes on the bank."

"Her clothes were off? Why?"

"I don't know. There was a water jar beside them." She pressed her lips together. "She must have been taking water to the men in the field. It was hot. She must have stopped for a quick dip in the creek."

"Was there still water in the jar?"

"I don't know. I just know what Brother Miller said."

"But Jacob wasn't there? Is that what they say?"

"Nobody was with her." I saw the heave of her chest, and

I felt the weight of her words telling of that time of what must have been unbearable sorrow. *"Nobody was with her.* I know what you think. You think Jacob Lapp was there, maybe knew about the baby, maybe she told him, and maybe he pushed her. But he wouldn't do that. He was a good Amish boy, and he would have done the right thing." She leaned toward me, her face close. "He would have married her."

"Why? The baby was gone. Remember?" My voice rose. "I took the baby and gave it away."

"I'll do your dishes when you're done," she said and walked away.

"I'll leave, if you tell me where else I can live in this community."

Aaron neither looked at me or spoke to me, just kept pounding the broken rack on his hay wagon.

"I know you don't want me here."

He glanced at me, looked away and, with a final blow to the rotten wood, smashed the board to smithereens.

"You can't ignore me," I said. "Well, you can, but if you do, I'll just stay until you don't."

He walked around me, picked up a slat from a pile by the barn, walked back to the wagon and measured it against the length of the board laying on the ground. "If I ask you a question about Jacob, you have to answer it."

Still he said nothing. Totally ignored me.

"If Jacob came to you on the day Lily drowned and asked where she was, did you tell him? You have to answer, Aaron. The sheriff told Violet she had to answer Jacob questions and if she's your wife, it's the same as if he told you."

He scrunched his face and shrugged, and then he picked up the slat and shoved it into the empty slot on the wagon bed.

I didn't really think Jacob would have gone to Aaron with such a question, but I thought Aaron might react, even negatively, and say one word, one single word, that *might* lead to others. I waited. Nothing. He just kept messing around with that miserable rack. "You're not going talk to me at all, are you?" Temper was beginning to rise.

He looked at me, lifted an eyebrow and grinned. A self-satisfied, antagonizing grin.

"Okay," I picked up a stick and held it out to him, "if you won't talk to me, then draw me a map to a place where I can sleep tonight."

"I'll answer your question." He smiled. No, not a smile, a smirk. "No. I didn't see Jacob that day."

I bit my lip. "Okay, what about a place to stay?"

"For Jacob? He's got one in Sugar Creek."

"No, for me!"

He laughed and turned back to his slat, vigorously shaking it to fit into the flatbed's groove.

I'd get nowhere with him. I started toward my car. Then I stopped. Turned. Went back.

"You know, Aaron, you're as stubborn now as the day you wouldn't speak to me, in the vineyard. You remember that day?" He stopped his work and stood, his back to me, didn't move. A drop of sweat slid down his neck. "I brought you cookies. I was shunned then, too. Ten years ago. You wouldn't talk to me, but finally you did. Sometimes we have to break rules. Man-made rules. None of them are written in stone. They're not rocks in our hearts. I know it's hard for you, but, please, help me. Talk to me. You knew Lily. You were like a brother to her . . . and to Violet. Two little girls down the road. Remember? You gave them rides in your buggy. And pennies. You gave them pennies for candy. You made daisy chains with them. And now you're married to one of them. Do you think Violet never wonders about Lily? How she died? Why she died. Do you think she never looks in *Maem's* eyes and cries at the grief she sees there? Help me find answers. Tell me what you know."

He didn't turn, but I heard his voice.

"See Schrock. He'll take you in."

Chapter Twenty-Three

I drove to the far end of the community where the hills were beginning their roll. Gentle slopes, and where the climb was in its infancy, they invited the ambitious farmer to cultivate, seed, and harvest on their rising surfaces. Continuing their upward journey, they harmoniously mounded in an increasingly challenging topography. As they rose and peaked, one of them, somewhat wider than the rest, stood as if separated, appearing not to be a part of them, though, in fact, it was simply a slightly higher mound of the same grouping, and it seemed mysteriously flattened at its peak and shaped into a vast expanse of richly, greened soil, suitable and correctly positioned, for an Amish cemetery. Upon discovering that space, the Amish had smoothed the soil, built a fence, and constructed a pathway up that hill. And so, having completed the required rudiments for the establishment of an Amish cemetery, it was there they buried their dead. Peaks reached, on the farther side of the cemetery, the hills, in near unity, began their flow downward and settled on the edge of the many-miled flatlands.

It was at the edge of those hills, as they began their rising on the side that was near Wander Lane, Schrock had relocated stock, farm equipment, buggy, and house furnishings, and had reconstructed a falling, abandoned barn and had repaired staggering outbuildings. There were two separate structures that appeared to have been used to house human creatures. Those buildings, except for minor repairs making the larger one habitable, remained as he found them.

Schrock's first wife, Edith, had died shortly after they'd moved to their home at the edge of the hills. She'd died giving birth to their first child. Neither did that infant live beyond birthing. Both were buried in the cemetery on the hill, and Schrock continued living alone in their house, until he took a trip and brought back Maddie to live with him.

This all had been told me by Sheriff Lowell Parker as we sat, one evening, at his back-corner table at Harriet's Eatery. He had told me, too, that Maddie came to Wander Lane as an Englisher. But not for long. First wife replaced; Schrock redid Maddie . . . clothes, religion, demeanor, responsibilities. And she was accepted, in a sense, by the brethren. The other wives greeted her, brief nods and smiles, attempted verbal exchanges, but she could not seem to melt into their harmonized flock, was just a little, unchangeably different. And so, she stood, tolerated, outside the circle. And, per Sheriff Parker, was satisfied with her allotted position.

I remembered all this as I drove to their farm. He'd told it all at one of the better times of our tenuous, reciprocal civility.

As I reached Schrock's house, I recognized the road I'd been driving to Schrock's farm was the same county road I'd driven several months before. I realized if I didn't stop at Schrock's and continued down this road, followed the bend and continued along the border of Schrock's farm, farther down the road I would find the place where I'd branched off and driven down a narrow, dirt path. I remembered it had taken me through a beautiful, almost romantic, archway of great, oak limbs meeting from either side of the road and forming that splendid structure. Where that road ended was a large, uncut, grass field with a small, shed-like building sitting alone in the center of it. And I remembered as I backed my car off that path, and, with great relief, got back on the county road, it wasn't far from there to Schrock's farm. And I remembered there was a trampled grass path that led from the building to Schrock's house.

Strange what we remember. It sometimes comes back to haunt us. Sometimes with good reason.

Though I saw no one in the yard when I reached Schrock's farm, there was a horse, harnessed and tethered to a rail, next to the barn. A buggy, Schrock's, I assumed, waited close by. It was near enough to noon to suppose he had returned for dinner, probably from visiting somewhere, though crop harvesting time called for men to be out in the field working, dinner or not. Dinners can be carried . . . in a bag or a pail. I shrugged. It didn't seem consistent with his nature to leave his farm work, or shorten his visiting to go back to the house for a meal, but from what I'd seen, he was a complex man. And a determined man. A chameleon? Lowell's workhard, good-man impression certainly didn't match Maddy's slap on the face. But it really wasn't my business, and, right then, I needed a place to live. Though, I had to admit, it was hard to understand why Lowell had suggested, almost commanded, I search for lodging at Schrock's.

Looking at the condition of the house, I wondered that

he would recommend it to me . . . to anyone. And maybe he wouldn't. Maybe just me. He was anxious to get rid of me. Maybe, he couldn't think of any other place . . . or maybe it was just a ghoulish sense of humor. Although, I don't recall a sense of funny in him when we were dating. He was nice to me then.

At the same time I stepped out of my car, Maddie stepped out of her house. The first thing I saw was her flower-filled apron. Pink and white yarrow, blue bachelor button, and Queen Anne's lace . . . sturdy ditch flowers . . . bulged lumps in the encasing, white fabric. As a clump of pink yarrow spilled from her grasp, Maddie paused, looked down at it, shook her head, and clutching her apron with one arm, as best she could, grabbed the latch behind her and pulled the door shut.

And then looking straight ahead, she stopped when she saw me.

"You going somewhere?" I called, realizing the buggy wasn't for Schrock at all. It was for Maddie. "I can come back later."

She shook her head. "No. Stay."

I watched her stumble over the stoned dirt driveway to the buggy and dump the flowers behind the front seat. She motioned me to move my car out of the driveway. I did, and then I saw her motion me to the buggy.

"You can help me heft this buggy onto Millie's harness." She looked at me and frowned.

"You know how to do that?"

"You forget," I said, moving to the horse. "I was raised Amish. Bringing a horse and buggy together is second nature to me."

I untethered the horse and backed her up to the buggy. Together we attached animal to vehicle and were ready to ride. I climbed into the buggy. She followed and took up the reins.

"Where we going?" I asked, once seated and moving, "and where's Schrock? It's dinner time for him."

"Packed him a big lunch. Enough to feed Millie. He won't be back 'til supper."

"What if he comes before you get back?"

"Never does." She lifted the reins and slapped them against the horse's back. "A little faster, Millie. We ain't got all day."

"Millie? Isn't that a little close to Maddie?"

"Yep. Schrock named her. Says he can't tell one from the other. Me or her."

I bit the side of my mouth. "Doesn't it bother you?"

"Better'n a whack on the face."

"True," I said softly. "But not good. Ridicule can hurt worse than a slap." I don't think she heard me. The clop of horse and the rustle of buggy could easily overpower my weak words.

I lifted my voice and asked a second time, "Where are we going?"

"Same place I always see you."

The flowers, I thought. "The cemetery."

She nodded. "You're right."

"You're going to put flowers under the tree."

"Yep. Under the tree and spread all over the grass."

"Even on Lily's grave?"

"There, too. If that's what you want."

"There, too?" I waited, repeated, "Too?" She didn't respond. "Maddie? Why do you go to the cemetery?"

She slapped the reins hard against the horse. "We're almost there."

"You walked before. It's a long way to your house. Why'd you take the buggy today?"

"I always take the buggy. At least when Schrock's gonna be gone all day . . . or most of the day. When I'm sure. Otherwise, when he takes the buggy, I hitch a ride. Not too often. And I make 'em let me get off way before the cemetery. So's they don't know where I'm going. And I only ride with nontalkers." She snorted. "Which most of the Amish are . . . at least to me."

"I've never seen your buggy when I've been at the cemetery."

"I hide it. The other side of the hill. Lots of trees and bushes there. You'll see."

"What if Schrock finds out?"

She looked at me. Lips pressed together, eyes squinted. "Then I get punished."

I sensed I should say no more.

We did as she said. Drove the horse and buggy into the trees and behind some bushes. She didn't unhitch the horse but did allow her enough leeway to drop her head and munch grass. Down from the buggy, Maddie reached behind the seat and carefully lifted the flowers and held them against her. I lifted my arms to help her, but she turned away from me. I knew not to try again. Side by side, we lumbered our way up the rest of the hill. When there, beside the tree shading Lily's grave, Maddy, slowly, carefully, put the flowers down, spread them out.

I waited.

Then, she picked the stems up, one by one, sucked in her lower lip and, holding them close to her breast, stood quietly, looking down at the grass, then the sky, turning her head slowly, all the while, looking, absorbing, as if God's work, His creation, was gently soaking into her whole being. Then she closed her eyes, and I thought she might be praying.

When she opened her eyes, she turned and looked at me.

"If you want to help me, you can. But you have to know this is a special place. When bodies rot under the ground, their spirits, their souls can't rot. They're there forever. I like to think they can smell the flowers, feel their nectar drip into the ground and slip into the leavings of the bodies. If you can't do that, it's okay, but you can't poke fun of what I do. You have to honor what I said, or you can't help me."

I held out my arms, and she walked to me, leaned over them and dropped some flowers into my waiting circle.

I didn't know what to say. Never before had I heard her speak so many words at one time. I'd seen the hurt. She'd spoken her hurt, the physical hurt . . . the hand slapping pain against skin. But this was more. Deeper. *Hers.* And she was sharing it with me. Yet, I was confused. Whose were the souls she was speaking of? Lily? But she was only one, and Maddie had said "*souls.*" I didn't know how to respond.

"Shall I put all these," I said, needing to say something, "on Lily's grave?"

She nodded, and then shrugged. "Unless you want to give some to Bishop Herrfort. I know he was special to you." A soft, throated grunt passed through her lips. "Sometimes, Schrock speaks to me." Her lip rose, just slightly. "Sometimes, he tells me things and doesn't realize he's doing it. Like Herrfort had a special thing for you." Her smile widened. "He has no idea what my brain grabs and holds."

"Why do you stay, Maddie?"

"Where would I go?"

I tilted my head, drew my eyebrows together, examined her

182

face. "Home. Go back home, to your parents—your sister. She looked like a fine woman. Nice."

"She is. But I don't want her to know what life has been, is, for me. She has a tender heart. She would hurt for me. More than she already does from what she hasn't been able to see." She paused, looked down at the flowers in her arms, stroked the stems. "Schrock is good at hiding truth."

She paused and I saw a wistful veil slide across her face. She started to speak again and stopped. I supposed she'd rethought the advisability of spontaneous revelation and was done. She was not.

"He's also good at molding a situation and making money from it."

"He made money from marrying you?"

Her head jerked, and her eyes roved the space around us.

"I'm almost done here." Her words spit hard against my ears. "Why don't you just go put those flowers on Herrfort's grave, and then we can go back."

As I climbed the fence, slid over the rail, and dropped, I stumbled a little. Quickly regaining my balance, I looked back to see if Maddie had noticed. She was staring at me, face expressionless. I hurried to finish my task.

When I was done, I turned to motion I was finished with Herrfort's grave, but she was gone.

I hurried to the buggy. She was there, already seated, reins in hand, waiting for me. We didn't speak further on the ride to her house.

As we turned onto Schrock's driveway, Maddie drew in a

sharp breath and pulled the horse up short.

Schrock was sitting, whittling, on a stool by the barn.

"You'd best get in your car and go," Maddie said. Her eyes were focused on him.

"I want to talk to him."

"Just go."

"Maddie, I'm not afraid of him."

She turned her eyes from him and looked at me. "Maybe you should be."

"He won't hurt me."

"No, he won't. Not now. And he'll say he's happy to see you. But he's not. He don't like uninvited company. And if you stay, he'll hurt me more."

"Why?"

"Just go."

I slid from the buggy, looked at Schrock. He was watching me. He nodded, lifted his eyebrows, smiled. Confident. Cocky. He kept his eyes on me but made no move to come near us.

I feared for Maddie.

"Please let me stay," I said, looking up at her. "I can tell him I asked you to take me for a buggy ride."

"You don't know him. Now that you're here, he wants you to stay, and I can't make you go. He plays games, Cora Pooler. And he always wins." She didn't look at me, kept her eyes on him. "Stay away from here, Cora. Just go. And don't come back."

Chapter Twenty-Four

It was past noon. I was hungry. The sun was bright overhead. The car was hot from sitting. Schrock's leer lodged in my head. And I was edgy.

I pulled to the side of the road. Turned the engine off. Covered my face with my hands. Held it there a long time. 'Till the shudders faded to trembling, and then they too disappeared. I straightened, set my lips in a firm line, and drove. Angry. Uncertainty, fear turned to anger. Schrock. He wouldn't best me. I wouldn't let him. I'd find a way.

I didn't know where to go. I wanted to go to Aaron and scream at him, *why did you send me there?* And I wanted to go to Violet and say, *please, please talk to me, can't we find a way to behave as sisters, loving sisters?* And I wanted to take my car, trunk filled with the wrong clothes, grab, dump them in a ditch, and go to Violet's bedroom, grab back the clothes and all I'd brought with me from the English world , stuff them in my trunk, and drive to a place far from the Amish. Get myself to my safe place, a known place. Daniel's place, mine now. Me, Cora Pooler, appreciated, wanted and understood there. I sighed. But I'd find no answers there. Neither to vindicate Lily nor to wave a magic wand and make Baby Clare whole. Yet here, in the Amish community, if my mind and heart acceded, she was accepted and cherished as she was. I sighed. But not yet. I couldn't go yet. I had to be here, in Wander Lane. I had to finish the promises I'd made to myself. And also, resolve thickening as a shield around me, I *knew*, without a doubt, I had to best Isaiah Schrock. And I knew I could. Anger can strengthen. And this anger did. Although I didn't rule out nasty verbal confrontation, I hoped for Maddie and Violet's sakes, not to feed or acknowledge Aaron or Schrock's arrogance, with words or a demeanor too gentle. And I neither needed Violet . . . nor Lowell Parker . . . as protector or comforter. With God's help, I could take care of myself. I sighed. *Where do I go from here, Jesus? Where do I go from here?*

And anger can make a hungry stomach lay dormant—for awhile. But it does awaken and wants to be fed. Procrastination fades determination. I needed to eat and to plan. Right away. I could do that . . . think and appease my stomach all at one time.

I drove to Harriet's Eatery. It was lunch late, so I shouldn't encounter anyone. I could ponder and partake without pestering persons present. Paradise.

Of course, it was not to be. In the whole of the dining room was just one table occupied. And of course, it was the back corner table. And there he was. Sheriff Lowell Parker. I made a moue. Bailey must have placed a permanent, invisible sign, **Reserved for Sheriff Lowell Parker**, sitting forever, on that table. And all patrons seemed to intuitively understand. I'd never seen anyone, other than Lowell, in *his* seat.

It was too late to turn away. He had seen me.

"Lowell Parker," I said moving across the room and sitting, "how is it our stomachs so often seem to desire sustenance at the same time?"

"I guess they need retraining."

"That could be." I looked at his plate. One huge lettuce-tomato-bacon-cheese burger, and one massive pile of fries, on one plate. One half-eaten, probably only one bite taken, hamburger in his hand, and a great, big chunk of apple pie waiting on a second plate.

"How can you eat so much?" I asked scrunching my face. "I'll bet you'll come back tonight and get a great, big, gigantic, steak dinner."

"Yep. I work. Eat when I can. As much as I can. How come you're here so late?"

"I was at Schrock's."

He frowned and put his hamburger down. Leaned back and crossed his arms. "Why?"

"Violet kicked me out. Aaron told me to go to Schrock's."

Lowell looked at me, shook his head, and sighed. I visualized wagon wheels turning, no, spinning, fast, in his mind.

"What's wrong?" I questioned.

"You tell me." He leaned across the table. "Obviously, Aaron knows Isaiah has an extra house on his property . . ."

"Shabby," I interrupted.

He shrugged. "Shabby, but fixable. A day of Amish men working on it . . . good to go. And Aaron knows Isaiah to be a good enough man, albeit a bit rowdy. But a hard worker . . . Aaron's words, not mine. So why didn't you stay?"

I stared at his half-eaten burger. I wasn't sure how to answer him. I was scared *of* Schrock, and I was scared *for* Maddie.

I wanted to say that to him, but I wasn't sure how he felt, and I didn't want to start something, say something, that would end up hurting Maddie. Yet I wanted to know what feelings or knowings were whirling around in Lowell's head.

He twisted his lips, bit one side of them. I would have bet money that, at one time, he'd been a smoker. Then he pressed his lips together, rubbed a finger in the crease alongside his mouth and chin. I could tell he was thinking.

"You hungry?" he asked.

"I can wait."

He plucked a napkin from the dispenser, smoothed it in front of me on the table, grabbed a handful of his fries, dropped them on the napkin, and shoved them over to me.

I raised my eyebrows.

"Eat," he said.

"I don't think so," I said wrinkling my nose. "I'm not into finger germs."

He scowled, held up his hands. "They're clean."

"Could be." I waited for him to say more about the Schrocks. When he didn't, I figured he didn't want to talk about them. But I did.

"Do you know why Maddie goes to the cemetery?"

He didn't answer.

"Do you?" I pressed.

He rubbed his fingers over the bottom of his chin. Hard. Opened his mouth. Hesitated. Grunted. Muttered, "No. Just suppositions."

"Tell me."

"Just maybes. No facts. And if there were, I still probably wouldn't tell you."

"Do you know Schrock hits her?"

"Yes."

"But you don't do anything about it?"

"What I do is my business, Cora . . . and I'm good at my job."

"And you won't tell me why she goes to the cemetery?"

"If she wants you to know, she'll tell you."

"But you won't?"

"I think you've asked enough questions, Cora. Probably be a good idea if you just order your lunch, eat it, and go back to Violet's and make nice with her, so you've got a place to sleep tonight. She'll take you back. And I'll talk to Aaron tomorrow."

I ignored his unwanted advice. I didn't want to go back to Violet's. Pride. And I could always sleep in a motel. And besides, I wanted to talk about Maddie, not me, and where I was going to sleep.

"I think everybody knows Isaiah smacks Maddie," I said. "Probably he does it a lot. How can they not know, especially the women; they don't miss much. They don't wear makeup, and the bruise on her face is going to turn into many, stand-out, spreading colors, and she can't hide her face forever." I narrowed my eyes and stared, intently, at him. "So why don't you do something about it?"

"I probably could. But if I did, I might not be able to go back into the community, with the same freedom I've got now. I walk a fine line, Cora. The Amish like to do their own condemning and punishing. They don't like interfering. Sometimes, I have to. But I'm careful, Cora. I use authority when there's no other way, and when it's big—but not always. And sometimes, I bargain. Sometimes, I give. Sometimes, I get."

I grabbed a french fry, stuck it in my mouth.

"Yuch. These are cold."

He pushed his chair away from the table and stood.

"I got work to do, Cora. Tell you what. Change of plans. You come to my office around 6:00. We'll go to Violet's and talk. Aaron'll be done with chores by then, and I want him there too. This is getting ridiculous. If you can't get answers by fall, you have to let it go and get on with your life. Here or back north. It's up to you."

"You can tell me what to do, Lowell Parker. But you can't make me do it."

"Don't count on that."

He was gone before I could say more.

I was there, promptly at 6:00 p.m. Tilly, looking a bit haggard.

"Aren't you done here at 5:00 p.m.?"

"I've got a demanding boss with high expectations. He's had me out running all afternoon, and, unfortunately, there's paperwork needs to be done today."

She sighed. "Good thing I've got a husband who knows how to make peanut butter-jelly sandwiches."

"Do I go right back to his office or do I wait till you buzz?"

"Go on back. My finger's too tired to buzz."

I smiled and patted her desk. "Sneak out. I won't tell him you did."

"Some people got ears behind their heads. He's got ears that hear through walls. I can stick it out. I'm almost done." She sighed and shook her head. "And there's a part of me, a very little part, that thinks he's a great guy . . . only not so much today."

She stood and picked up a pile of files. "Here, take these to him. Maybe he'll feel a little sympathy and tell me to go home when he sees how much work I got done."

She handed me the files. Stacked paper heavy. I groaned and called on muscles for help. They cooperated.

"It's 6:00 p.m., and I'm here," I said entering Lowell's office. I dropped the files on his desk, grinned. "Looks like I brought you some reading."

He grunted. "Sit."

"You don't look ready to go anyplace. Thought we were going to Violet's. You were going to solve all my problems, magician that you are."

He leaned back in his chair. "Change of plans."

I raised my eyebrows. "Again?"

He ignored my sarcasm.

"Listen, I don't have time to mess around. I've had Tilly running all afternoon rounding up preachers and men to meet at Aaron's tomorrow after chores and supper. Might as well do this with one swoop of directives. You be there. You can sleep wherever you want tonight, but you be there tomorrow—6:00 p.m. sharp."

"What are you going to do?"

"I told you, I'm busy. You want to sit around and talk now, or do you want to go so I can get work done, so I can have time to take on your tangled problems?"

"And I'm grateful," I said sincerely, and left.

Chapter Twenty-Five

There were already buggies parked in Violet's yard when I got there. I didn't see the sheriff's car. Probably intentional. His presence would be far more authoritative, if he didn't socialize before he talked. And it wasn't friendly I was hoping for. It was information.

Though I really had no idea what loner Lowell was going to say.

I hesitated, before I got out of the car. *God, help me hold my temper. I know these are people who love you . . . in the Amish way they've been taught. Please give me patience, and if I have an opening to speak, rope my words tight, so no antagonizing or untrue ones can escape. And please, do the same with these Amish men waiting in Violet's house to hear what Lowell and I have to say . . . and, also, please monitor Sheriff Parker and plant some tactful words in his head. . . ."*

I heard the sheriff's car before I saw it. I lifted my head from prayer and looked out my rearview mirror. He was speeding up the driveway, spun dirt nearly rising to his windows, and I thought he really should give himself a ticket. This meeting wasn't a big enough emergency, except to me, that it called for unreasonable, show-off speed.

When he stopped, got of his car, and looked around, he saw me and motioned me to get out and follow him. I did and had to half-run to keep up with the speed of his steps. Thoughtless. But then, it was Lowell Parker. What else should I expect?

"Slow down," I said. "The Amish are a patient people. They aren't going to run away or yell at you just because you're a little late."

He ignored me.

My chest pounding, his not moving, we reached the front door. He grabbed my arm before I could knock.

"Now listen. I'm gonna talk first. Then you talk. And don't you be accusing anybody of anything, and if I motion you to shut up, then you shut up."

"I know how to handle myself. And them. Remember, I've got Amish blood in me. I know how they think, and I know how they feel."

He grunted, dropped my arm, and glared at me.

"You've been away a long time, and Cora, you don't think Amish anymore. There's no meek dripping off *you,* no indication of female Amish submission in your bearings. So watch yourself. Soften yourself. Show a little humble."

"Do you really think I'm a tough, heartless, *hard* woman?"

"Do you want to stand here and argue, or do want to go in there and let me help you?"

I knocked on the door. Aaron opened it. Yet even before the door was fully opened, I knew the room was full of Amish men. Grain, fermented corn, digested hay, dung . . . male Amish barn-smell, and it clung, everlasting, to their skin and clothes. Accustomed to the odor, Amish women were not repulsed by it. For them, it reeked of love and livelihood. For me, it reeked of family and home. I didn't know what Lowell thought about it. Stepping farther into the room, I saw church benches had been brought into the great room and the men, preachers at the fore, sat patiently waiting for the meeting to begin. Violet was nowhere in sight, but she had left plates of cookies and donuts on the dining table. The confections would be eaten, after the meeting was done. A chair had been placed for me apart from the men.

Lowell greeted the flock and then got down to business.

"You know me. You know I leave you to yourselves unless something big comes up that goes against the laws of the country or unless severe misbehavior in the village calls for me to intervene. But for the most part you take care of your problems, and you do a good job at it.

"We've come up with a situation here that looks like it needs a little help from me. Seems a while back, an Amish girl, Lily Pooler, drowned in Wander Creek. And I let you handle it. You took it in your hands and determined Lily was the cause of her own death, and so, acted accordingly. At that time, I found no reason to not accept your decision. Now, much later, questions have arisen that force a look back to that time."

He paused, briefly, gave the men enough time to comprehend, but not to mull.

"My workload is big, and this search could be long and intense. I've sought out and commandeered a person, familiar with the situation and with Amish ways, to help me. Cora Pooler. I realize she is shunned, and that she is the sister of the victim, Lily Pooler, but because of her Amish background, she has learned integrity, honesty, and discernment, and therefore, I am giving her, paid, legal authority to work on this case, to ask questions . . . and get answers. Lily died a long time ago, so the search for the truth in this case will be intensive. Cora will not have the authority to arrest or accuse. She is merely searching the circumstances of Lily Pooler's death. And as sheriff, I'm ordering citizens to cooperate with her. When she has completed her investigation, I will take it over.

"I've spoken with Deacon Lapp, Preacher Jesse Miller, and Preacher Eli Miller. They understand and accept that, in this situation, communication with the shunned Cora Pooler is accepted, as needed and as restricted to words used only for investigative purposes.

"I've worked closely with your community. You are a people I respect and admire, and because of your principled way of life, I'm confident you will assist in this investigation, and we will bring the matter of Lily Pooler's death to resolution.

"Thank you for appreciating the need for this search for truth. I understand it will, sometimes, be difficult for you, but I know you are a strong and honest people, and you'll do what is right.

"I'm asking you now to hear Cora Pooler. She can clarify the reasons for this investigation. And after she is done, you can ask questions. To me. Ask whatever you want to know, and I'll answer."

He sat down, and I stood, faced the men, composed my face to look gravely serious, and roved my eyes over them. They stopped. Briefly. Schrock was in the back row. Leering. Silently, I warned myself not to glance at that section again and began speaking.

"Some of you are old enough to remember when I was a

part, an Amish part, of your lives. I'm a Pooler. Of good, sound Amish background. But I was foolish. I gave away a baby. I took her from her mother, and allowed you to think I'd given birth to the baby. Lies are wrong, silent lies, lies that misdirect, and for that, I was shunned.

"Lily Pooler, my sister, was the child's mother. Because of my actions, she suffered. I'm sure all of you who are fathers can understand a mother's anguish upon losing a child. Lily suffered that anguish. I couldn't see or communicate with her that time between the loss of her child and Lily's death. I didn't see the emotional torment from losing her baby. Nor knowing where the baby was, how the baby was faring. Five years of not knowing. I was neither allowed to return to Wander Lane to be at Lily's funeral, nor was I allowed to grieve with my family.

"Shunning hurts not only the person banned, but also those affected by the shunning."

I heard Lowell clear his throat and knew it was a signal for me to move on.

"I came back ten years ago, and for a while, after confession and rejoining the church, I wore the Amish *kapp* and was a part of the Amish community. During that time, I could not bring myself to visit Lily's grave.

"And again, though I respected the Amish Way, I chose to leave, and was, again, shunned. Now I am back. Ten years later. Still shunned.

"And I visited Lily's grave." I paused. My lips were near trembling, but I would not let them see me weak. I lifted my chin, and, perused the assemblage. Spoke. "You know what I saw." From the corner of my eye, I saw Lowell shift in his chair. "You had determined Lily died in a state of sin. You labeled her an Amish woman who had committed suicide. And you buried her outside the fence." I paused again. "I needed to know why, why you thought as you did, so I came into your community and lived in an Amish home and tried to discover the circumstance of Lily's death. I understood, as a shunned woman, this would be difficult, and it was. But I did glean some information that led me to think she had not taken her own life, that a thorough investigation had not been done, and that all possibilities were not considered.

"I understand it must have been a difficult decision for you. And I truly believe you did what you felt was right. Yet, it is a huge and terrible thing to declare someone a sinner at the time of their death and to determine that person is unfit to rest in hallowed ground, unless you are *sure* and have done everything you can to determine the circumstances of Lily's death.

"I cannot reveal conversations I've had that have led me to know there is more to learn. I will respect the anonymity of information I received from anyone to whom I speak. The only person I will confide in is Sheriff Parker, and he will be the one to decide what to do with my findings.

"In closing, I ask you to recall my earlier words . . . *lies are wrong, silent or spoken, and for that I was shunned.* It was a correct decision. Lies *are* wrong." I set my lips and glared.

"No matter who tells them."

I heard the scrape of Lowell's chair.

"Thank you for cooperating with this investigation, and thank you for honoring my paid and legal position as an investigator. I promise I will not forget or disrespect the character or rules of your Order. Thank you for listening to me."

I went back to my chair.

Lowell stood and faced the group. "I'm here for questions, and Violet made cookies and coffee for you. They're looking good." He turned and looked at Aaron. "My guess, Violet made 'em." He ran his tongue under his lower lip and completed one brisk nod. "So, go on up to the table and Cora will fix you up with the goodies." He motioned toward me and turning, looked at me. No smile. No expression. But I smiled just enough that he'd know it wasn't real.

Several of the men went up to Lowell with questions. No one came to the table for cookies. After a few minutes, I lifted my chin and went outside.

I considered not waiting for Lowell to come out, but decided to be a good, passive, Amishy woman—for the moment. There was a rocker on the porch, as good a place to fume as any. I thought it would be long before men started coming out the door and getting their buggies. I was right.

Last to come out was Lowell, or rather last to *stomp* out was Lowell. He closed the door behind him.

"Well," he said, "you know, Cora, I've told you, I choose when I use my sheriff power, and I did this for you, so you best be thanking me, 'cause I'm not gonna be thanking you for this night. I've lost a whole lot of bargaining points, from this little episode."

I raised my eyebrows. "I did what you told them I'd do. Explained why the further investigation."

"And a whole lot more."

"I thought a little explanation, a little background, would help. I don't think I was overly critical. Besides, you said you'd tell me to 'shut-up,' if I went beyond your boundaries. And there weren't any 'shut-ups' that I could hear."

"I gave you hints."

I shrugged. "Not clear enough, I guess."

He started down the porch steps and turned. "Looks like I've got a bit of orientation to do before I set you loose on them."

I smiled. "Do you want to go to Harriet's for coffee?"

"*No*. And be in my office bright and early tomorrow morning."

Chapter Twenty-Six

"You're in early," I said to Tilly, as I put a rose on her desk. "From *Maem's* bush. I drove there early and plucked it before anyone was up."

"She's always grown the best." Tilly lifted the flower to her nose, sniffed, smiled, put it down. "The sheriff's waiting for you."

I pressed my lips together and sighed.

"I can't tell you what kind of a mood he's in. He looks tired, but he wasn't scowling when he plopped all these papers on my desk. So, good luck."

"Could be I'll need it. Packed in a great, huge parcel." I lifted my hand, wiggled my fingers at her and started down the hall.

His door was open. I went in.

"Sit."

I moved papers and sat.

He wasted no time.

"I've pretty much given you free rein to ask whatever you need to ask to get the facts you want. The only boundary I've given is that you keep your questions pertinent to Lily's death." He drew in breath. I watched his cheeks puff and deflate, and his lips purse as he let the air out slowly. He folded his hands and leaned across his desk. I sensed a forthcoming lecture. "I know you're not going to do that. Boundaries seem to be unable to curb your tongue. If I could, I'd pile all the words you *should* say and stuff them in your mouth . . . ."

"And burn all the words I *shouldn't* say," I said, though I knew this probably wasn't a good time to interrupt.

He frowned and continued. "You can't be accusing or criticizing, indirectly or not. The Amish aren't stupid. They know what your words mean."

I pulled in my anger.

He glared. "You've grown a cement cast of revenge around yourself. Lose it!"

I sucked in my cheeks. Said nothing.

"You know, Cora, they're the ones with power now. You want what they can give. And they're not real anxious to help you. You can't yank words out of their heads. They have to give them to you. And you have to remember, too, they're not wanting to talk to you. They will, because their preachers said they have to, and they know they have to obey the law and they have to obey them." He leaned farther over the desktop. His brow was furrowed, and I saw no give in his face. *"You're still shunned, Cora Pooler, and they won't forget that."*

"How'd it go?" Tilly's voice broke through my chastened defiance.

"You look kinda dragged out. Come on," she said, taking my arm. "We'll go sit in the people-with-problem chairs, and get you revived."

Unresisting, I let her lead me to the waiting area. We sat. She waited. I think for me to let loose with a not-too-kind word rendition of Lowell's reprimand and recitation. I wasn't ready to offer up my inmost and confused feelings to anyone. To avoid facing, acknowledging, what I felt, I picked a puzzle piece off the table in front of us and held it up with thumb and finger, and examined it.

"The edges are frayed," I said. "Looks like someone tried to shove it where it doesn't fit. You need to buy some new puzzles, Tilly. Make them easy ones. No one wants to sit in these chairs long enough to figure out the right spot, for a miserable, little piece of pictured cardboard."

Tilly smiled sympathetically. "The budget doesn't stretch much for entertainment. Besides, most people sitting here have big stuff . . . troubles . . . on their minds. They don't concentrate much on enjoying the surroundings." She paused, took the puzzle piece from my hand, laid it on the table, turned her eyes on me. "Looks like you might have a few troubles."

"I'm not sure." My face scrunched. My eyes stared at the table. "I think I'm near to crossing the line from selfishness and unfairness and step into sensibility and concern." I felt an ease from the pressures I'd tried to store, to hold from sharing. I raised my fingers, placed them against my lips and patted that softness. Thought. Looked down at my lap. Spoke. "It's hard being shunned."

Tilly put a hand over mine.

"It's not fair, you know," I said softly. "I'm not an evil person. I'm not headed for hell. Those black-clad isolationists don't have a monopoly on heaven. Their Jesus is mine, too, and I say this humbly, with reverence and reluctance . . . I think I know a fuller

Jesus than they. Sometimes, it seems their *Ordnung* speaks louder than God's biblical words, words given through His Spirit, for us to know Him.

"And yet, though they are so judgmental and critically blind to a lifestyle different from theirs, there is so much love within the brethren. Safety. And I would say truthfulness, but often, lies are spoken with unsaid words. And if an unspoken truth stays intentionally hidden or twisted to sway another's thinking, is it not then a lie?"

Tilly squeezed my hand.

"You know what is right," she said. "You can take words and parse them and know what it true."

"I don't think I can always do that."

Tilly said nothing.

"I do know I have to be careful not to do the same as they might. Twist truth. Manipulate it. I so much want answers that prove what I want to be is what really is."

"What will you do if it turns out that Lily did commit suicide?"

I looked at her. Her face was fixed with intense concern.

"I don't know."

Chapter Twenty-Seven

I needed clothes. Except for a the few items I'd purchased at Wander Lane's *Claire's Boutique,* I had nothing other than the dull, fake-Amish, baggy clothes I'd been wearing while living in Violet's house. And if I had to choose naked or those togs, I'd wend my way through life bare as a defeathered chicken ready for roasting.

I had a choice. I could buy more clothes, or I could collect those already my own, folded and stored, in Violet's guest bedroom's bureau.

I left the motel, got in my car and headed for Amish country. It was an easy choice. Practical. Not only could I gather my clothes, now that I was an official law employee, I could talk to Violet. About Lily and her death. And it also seemed possible, likely, I could maneuver the conversation to all manner of topics. Self-satisfied, I pushed my foot a little harder against the gas pedal.

I'd wiled away the morning reading favorite Bible passages that lead me from maudlin, self-deprecation to reinforcement of the realistic and productive wisdom, of knowing self and purpose. I did love the people of my young years. Although I didn't agree with the whole of their doctrine or the unquestioning set of their minds, they were, for the most part, good people, and they did deserve respect.

While I drove, I juggled words in my brain to put them in an order that would come through to Violet as serious, lawful, and loving. And I realized, as I opened the car's window and smelled the clean, sweet scent of fresh-cut, tall grass and visualized it drying on the ground to a practical, serviceable, golden winter fodder, it would retain its own lingering scent . . . even from the ground, into the barn, and into the season of cold. And I thought, shades of change, linger, and we, too, can rot on the ground, or live as fodder in the world. I would know the words to speak, when the need for them came.

I knocked on Violet's front door and waited. Minutes passed. The door stayed closed. At the same time as I thought I should leave and try another day, though I really wanted those clothes, Violet opened the door. I smiled.

"I thought you might not be home, but . . . ," I stopped. Violet's eyes were dull; her hands were twisting a dish towel, tighter and tighter. "Are you all right?" Foolish words. Of course, she wasn't.

"I thought you might be Schrock," she murmured, looking beyond me.

I turned and looked toward the barn. I saw nothing amiss.

"Schrock's doing the milking," she said.

I glanced at my watch. It was late to be tending cows. They should've been let out from their stanchions and into the pasture long before. And why would Schrock be doing the chores?

"Is Aaron ill?" I looked at her cheeks. Pasty. Pale. Loose. "Are *you* all right?"

"I'm all right. You can't help."

"Where's Aaron?"

"You should go. I can't talk to you."

"You can," I said softly. "I'm here on business."

"I can't talk business now."

"Violet, we can turn any talk into a semblance of business conversation." I thought, hoped, I might be able to convince her that we could stretch the business requirement and just be sisters.

"You shouldn't be here," she said. "I don't think Schrock likes you."

"Why don't we go in, sit on the couch, rest a little. No words. Just quiet . . . until it seems talking, gentle talking, would help, would be the right thing to do?" I slid my arm around her waist, pushed the door shut with my foot, wished for a lock to keep Schrock out, and cautiously moved her to the couch.

When settled, I asked again," Where's Aaron?"

"Sleeping."

"In your bedroom?"

She nodded.

"Is he sick?"

She shook her head.

"Then what?"

She rested her head against the back of the couch, looked up at the ceiling. Her chest didn't move. It was as if she wasn't breathing. "He smelled of whiskey."

I drew in my breath. "How'd he get home?"

"Schrock."

"Was he gone all night?" I asked, bewildered.

"No." She paused. "Just most of it."

"I've never seen this happen before."

"It's not regular. Just sometimes." She dropped her head into her hands and rubbed her forehead. "I had the baby here all of yesterday. Baby Clare. Aaron doesn't like me to watch her, so, he got mad and left. Guess he went to Schrock's. Don't know what he does there. Maybe just drinks. I do know Schrock always brings him home. Does his chores for him. Can't figure him out. Schrock. Talks mean sometimes, but always does Aaron's work, when Aaron can't. Guess he's got two minds and hearts. Schrock, I mean. But they don't always seem to work together."

"Do you like him? Schrock?"

"I don't know." She shrugged. "Sometimes, I do. Sometimes, I don't."

"Want me to go talk to him?"

"*Schrock?*" Her head jerked away from her hands. "*No.*"

"Why not? He could probably explain things."

"He doesn't like you, Cora. Not at all." She shuddered. "And I don't think he likes me much either." She tilted her head, furrowed her forehead. "Another thing, he doesn't like his wife to come here, unless he's with her. Don't know why."

"Do you talk about this with the other women?"

"Gossip, you mean? No."

"Do you want me to come back and live here again? I came to get my clothes and take them back with me to the motel. But I can stay."

"Cora," Violet whispered, and I could hear sadness behind her voice, "Aaron doesn't want you back."

"Why?" I asked, thinking I probably reminded him of youth . . . and me. Us. Pure arrogance. On my part. He probably didn't think of me at all. Except to wonder why I ever thought English life was better than his.

"He thinks you influence me against the Amish Way," she sighed. "He's wrong, I'm Amish through and through." She smiled ruefully and looked at me. "Except for the times I miss you so much, I slip around the shunning, and talk to you. Like now."

"Okay," I said, sliding closer to her, placing my hand on hers folded on her lap. "It is now, and we are talking now, and we *need* to. God would bless the seeking of Truth. And that's what we're doing, Violet, seeking truth. And if we can figure out what is true, we can erase wrongdoing and replace it with peace. So, right now, I'm going to go out there to the barn and get a little truth from Schrock. And after that, I'll go looking for it from your Amish cohorts."

Violet withdrew her hands from under mine, rubbed them against her eyebrows and up across her forehead, pressed them hard, dropped them, peered at me. "Don't you know the trouble you'll cause?"

"I won't cause it. It's already there. Old Schrock does his part in creating it. All of them do. Secrets. Shunning. Hiding from what's real. There must be so much pain harboring in so many hearts here within the brethren. How can they look at me and not know I hurt from the doing of what they're shunning me for? It all goes back to the taking of Lily's baby and giving her away. And Lily's death. And if they truly believe she committed suicide, how can they not feel guilt for not understanding and helping her. Maybe they all should be buried outside the fence. Right next to her so their souls can mix and mourn together."

"Stop it, Cora."

"And you, Violet. How can you not look at Talitha and Baby Clare *and not see Lily?" Oh, my God! What have I done?"*

Mouth opened, Violet turned her eyes to stare into mine. "What are you saying, Cora?"

Her voice pierced my ears . . . quietly stern and unyielding. I closed my eyes. "What are you saying!"

"Have you not noticed it?" I tried to keep my voice steady.

"Noticed what, Cora?"

She was unrelenting. I shuddered. "I don't know if I can say it."

"I don't think you have a choice." Her words spit out and hit me hard.

"I told you, ten years ago I told you. I saw Talitha, was sure I saw Talitha, the face was Lily's, in Sugar Creek, riding in a buggy. Annabelle. It was Annabelle. Renamed Talitha. Lily's baby. The one, the wee child, I gave away. Annabelle. Talitha. Grown."

"You told me. What does that have to do with Baby Clare?"

"Willie went there, didn't he—to Sugar Creek, after his *fraw* died. Didn't he?"

"He did."

"And he brought back a new wife. A young wife."

"He did."

"And she looked like Lily."

"She did. Does. As many Amish girls do. Blonde. Blue eyes. Pretty." I heard a touch of anger steel her words.

"How many named Talitha? Child raised up from the dead by God?"

"None that I know." Still firm.

"She, Baby Clare, born of Talitha, fathered by Willie, the grandchild of Lily."

"No! How can you know that? Lily's baby could have grown up anywhere. Who knows? Maybe even, an Englisher."

"No. I knew where she was."

"How?"

"I told you, I saw her. In Sugar Creek. And more than that, Harriet knew, and she told me."

"Get your clothes and get out. I don't want you in my house."

"Violet?"

"Just go."

I went up the stairs to the bedroom she'd given me to use. I walked, with deliberate speed, across the room, yanked the bureau drawers open and grabbed as much as I could hold. And then, not spending one minute more than needed, tramped back down the stairs to Violet.

She stood by the opened door, her hand on the doorknob, waiting for me to go through.

She would not look at me. I stretched my hand to stroke her arm. She didn't resist. Neither did she acknowledge by word or movement.

"Please, Violet."

She said nothing. As I stepped out of the house and onto the porch, I wondered if the door would slam shut behind me. It didn't. I turned and looked. It was already closed. Amishly, quiet, closed by long-trained, acquiescent, Amish hands.

"You leaving already? Mighty short visit."

So anxious to get to my car, shove my clothes into the trunk next to those suitcased, phony, Amish clothes already stuffed in there, I hadn't looked toward the barn, hadn't remembered he was in there. But he wasn't *in* it any longer. Big as life, he stood outside the barn, one foot propped on a hay bale, mouth lifted in a leer, and then mouth closed, lips pushed out and pursed ready to send out a stream of tobacco juice; he did it. A thick, brown spurt of liquid arched high, flew far, landed on the ground before me, but not near enough to me to bring him joy. Schrock. Failed. Good.

"You still lookin' for a place to live?" He dropped his leg off the bale, looked to the house, seemed satisfied, and walked toward me. "I still got that building next to my house. Little cleaning and it'd be fine for you. Less'n you're too English fancy." He smirked. "And you could keep your eye on Maddie. Make sure I don't *abuse* her." He was getting closer. "That's what you think, ain't it? That I abuse her? Smack her around."

He was very close. I could see the spittle on his chin. I could *smell* him. "I don't, you know. Just keep her in line. She doesn't know the Amish way clear enough yet. But she'll learn. I'm just helpin' her." He was at the car.

Inside my skin, I could feel my whole body shudder, but I wouldn't let it loose for him to see. I bit my lip hard and concentrated on that pain. Stood solid. Kept my face expressionless and my eyes glaring straight into his.

He smiled. "I'll give you a good price."

I said nothing.

"Think on it." He grinned an ugly, lecherous grin. Then walked away.

I was in my car and backing down the driveway, before he reached the barn.

Chapter Twenty-Eight

It struck me as strange, but the place I wanted to go was to Sheriff Lowell Parker's office. And I did. I went there.

I heard Tilly's greeting. At least, I think I did. But I didn't stop. And neither did I pause at his door, nor did I knock on it. I simply walked in. I remember him rising, coming toward me, and then he was holding me. I remember comfort. Relief.

He didn't say anything, simply led me to a chair, shoved papers and files onto the floor, lowered me down to its seat, walked back to his desk, and sat.

I looked at him. Elbows on his desk, forearms lifted, hands clasped, chin resting on them. So calm. Waiting for me to speak. I closed my eyes and fell into his stillness. I could sense his patience and, not having a store of such previous comportment from him, I wondered at it. But I was grateful for it.

"You've been sleuthing?" He lowered his hands and leaned back in his chair.

"Not exactly."

He waited.

"I went to Violet's." I smiled. "To sleuth."

He nodded. "And?"

"I went to Violet's," I repeated, "to get my regular English clothes, and I did hope to delve a little into Lily's last days with Violet . . . her moods, her words, her behaviors. But I didn't get a chance to. My tongue slipped and released words I wasn't ready or intending to say, and they jarred Violet into an awareness of their meaning."

His eyebrows went up; his forehead creased. "Explain."

"She figured out I was hinting, no, saying, Baby Clare was the offspring of a coupling of our brother, Willie and our sister, Lily's granddaughter, Talitha. Incest."

"Hmm." He shook his head. "Bad move, Cora. That one needed preparation."

"I know," I said, peering at my lap . . . for a moment, looking up, intense. "She kicked me out."

"So that's why the pale face and shaking," he stated.

"Partly. The beginning of a fear . . . total and permanent rejection. Violet turning away from me. I'm not sure she can grip or acknowledge the news I dropped on her—not intentionally. Incest. Unthinkable. Unacceptable. Lowell, she's my sister." I ran my fingers through my hair, pushed it back behind my ear. "My blood. I need her." I sighed and shook my head. "Too much. This morning. Too much for me to handle."

"What else?"

"Schrock was there . . ."

"In Violet's house? What . . ."

I lifted my arm, palm out, to shush him. "He was there when I left the house. Outside the barn. Looking at me. Ogling." I stopped, didn't want to think more. Not yet. I was safe in Lowell's office. I wanted to stay there, quiet, until the shameful weakness inside my head and body left, and I was in control of myself again.

"Did he hurt you?"

"No."

"Were you afraid he would?"

"Not then. There. Maybe, a little. No, a lot. But even through that fear, I knew I could yell, and Violet would hear, and she'd wake Aaron, and later tell the Preacher. He knew that, too. Might lose some of that good reputation he'd fooled others into thinking of him, fooling those always-looking-for-good-and-seeing-the-good-brethren into believing. But later, if he can, if he has the chance, he will try to hurt me. More than just with words."

"You need protection?"

"No, I won't let him hurt me." I pressed my lips together, wimp time over; strength returned. "I might not be physically stronger than Schrock, but I'm smarter, and I'm not going to let him be the victor. This has been a lesson for me, and I'm a good learner."

I rose and leaned over Lowell's desk.

"You helped me," I said softly. I felt moisture gather in my eyes. "And I know if I need you again, you'll help me again." I paused. He looked at me, straight-faced, but I knew his heart was listening. "And I thank you."

"You need protection," he affirmed.

I left.

A big chunk of the day remained to be filled. I could go back to Violet's and retrieve more clothes. If she opened the door to me. Amish blood bid all welcome . . . except those, me, shunned or bearing news of a child, a relative, a niece, born from an illicit pairing. And I'd met the shaming criteria of both. I needed no more judgement.

Or I could give Violet time to absorb and accept that which is, at first, wholly unacceptable.

Or I could go rescue Maddie. Gallop my four-wheeled steed to her castle, leave it full throttled, straining to surge forward again, as I loosened my hands from the steering bridle and leaped from the saddle. Then I'd rush to her, grab her, hoist her into the back of my carriage, and trot away on fast rolling tires to a place too well hidden to ever be found. And I'd hold her hostage, until she told me what I needed to know about Schrock. And I'd then return her to her palace . . . if she desired to return to bondage.

Or I could hit Schrock over his head, with a tire iron.

Or I could mull over the list of people in my head who might have secreted in their heads a clue, a word, a sighting of Lily's last days. It could be profitable to rummage through their stocks of memory . . . a thought of their musings, a release of their *knowings*. I should pick one who knew her well to start my search for truth.

I chose Hattie Shackleton.

I went to her shop, **Hattie's Quilt Shoppe**. But the sign didn't read **Hattie's Quilt Shoppe**. Instead was printed, in large and swanky font, so unlike plain Hattie's, **Joyce's Amish Quilt Shop**. And then it hit me, and I remembered. While I was struggling to melt into English life, Hattie had married my brother, Willie. Thirty years ago, during my first return to Wander Lane, Violet had told me of their marriage and the birth of their Baby Alice. In fact, I had seen the wee, sweet child. And recently, in my current tenure in Wander Lane, in a weak moment of ignored shunning, Violet related that soon after the birth of Willie and Hattie's fourth baby, they'd heard of the prosperous market for authentic Amish quilts in a northern Amish population and had moved there—Lancaster, Pennsylvania. Land of Amish entrepreneurs. Unfortunately, they were forced to return when our oldest brother, George, married and moved, leaving a need for the next son to work the Pooler farm. That would be Willie. So, he came back. They raised their children and saw them settled with homes and families of their own. Then Hattie died. And Willy, missing a wife to perform Amish wifely chores, went roaming. He found Widow Talitha, young Widow Talitha, in Sugar creek. Needs meshed, and they married. Together, they started a new family . . . Willy, Talitha, stepdaughter Katy, and now, new Baby Clare.

As I walked away from the shop, I tried to remember any Joyces living within the brethren. I could not. It troubled me. I didn't want to see a strange face in Hattie's shoppe. I stopped. Turned. Briefly brushed against a vacationing English looky-loo, ignored her aggravated expression, that probably wouldn't have been given if I'd been in Amish attire, apologized, and walked back to the quilt shop.

I stood outside the shop for several minutes looking at the bright colored "authentic" quilts in the storefront window. Apparently new patterns had found their way to the needles and threads that expert and loving Wander Lane Amish hands had sewn, stitch by stitch, familiar and cherished designs, quilts on their beds and quilts flung over chairs—beautiful, useful coverlets comfortably warming cold, Amish bodies.

Moving quietly, expectantly, I turned the knob and pushed the door. And a treat to my ears, sleigh bells jingled a melodious, welcoming greeting. I smiled. That was new. I think Hattie would have liked it.

A middle-aged lady, Amish clad, but to my discerning Amish eyes, an Englisher, stood behind the front counter. There is an Amish demeanor, enhanced within the presence of the English. Amish ladies . . . reticent, demure, a bashful bearing. A hiding of self. There was none of that evident in the woman at the counter.

"Look around, ask if you need help. My name is Joyce."

I ran my hand over the top of a quilt lying on a shelf close to the door. It was non-uniformly lumpy. I lifted a corner of the blanket of joined squares, bent, brought it closer to my eyes. Scrutinized it.

"Beautiful, isn't it." Joyce spoke. A definite opinion. Not a question.

"Did you make it?"

"Not that one. But many of them."

"Are you Amish?" I asked.

She laughed. "Can't you tell?" She smoothed her dark skirt, tapped her starched cap.

"I can. You're not."

"Why would you say that?"

"I've been Amish. And you're not. Not even close."

"Then why would I wear these clothes?" I heard a voice perturbed.

"The Amish are more than the clothes they wear." I looked directly at her, raised my eyebrows. "You can sew a dress, put it on, wear it. But you can't sew a heart or a soul to be what they aren't."

"Well, *you* certainly don't talk or act like an Amish woman. They would *never* be so rude."

"You're right, and I'm sorry. I could have said nicer words . . . but they're true."

She pressed her lips together, said nothing.

"Why do you pretend?" I asked sincerely. I really wanted to know.

She shrugged. "It sells quilts."

"They're not authentic, are they?"

"Yes." She made a moue. "They are."

I smiled, again, a wistful smile, sad. "My words aren't nice. Yours lie."

"Why do you say that?"

I held up the quilt. "The quilt tells me. Strange pattern. Sewing machine stitches. Amish quality is learned early and stays long."

Joyce bit her lip. "Will you tell?" I heard the fear in her voice.

"No. I'm sure the Amish already know . . . and laugh. And, perhaps the English are satisfied thinking they've bought authentic. I'll leave it to your conscience."

"A woman needs to make a living."

"God be with you." And I left. Once outside on the sidewalk, I stopped, thought. I'd been harsh, not thoughtful, not helpful. I went back into the shop. Joyce's face did not radiate happiness.

"You know, I can help you." I raised a corner of the quilt I'd left on the counter. "See, here? The stitches are machine made. The Amish have a particular, symmetry in their stitchery, unique enough that it stands out from those made by a machine." I smiled. "Perhaps, it's from the love sewn in them." I looked at her, listening, her eyes directed toward quilt. "Look here, at this square, and this one, and this one." I moved my finger from one square to another. "They are beautiful. Colorful. But they don't tell a story."

"A story?"

"Uh-huh, a story, a meaningful premise, a lingering thought." I smoothed my hand over the quilt. "Yours are colorful and they are lovely, but they don't make tears fall or take you to a memory of meaning. I'm sure they bring momentary joy, surface joy. Amish quilts bring joy that seeps into your heart. Shared joy." I patted the afghan. "A piece of the Amish heart goes into each of the quilts she and her sisters make."

"You don't understand," Joyce said. "These are cheap for me to buy, and they sell fast. I have a family to feed."

"I do understand. And I truly am trying to help you. My guess is that it's mostly vacationers that buy your quilts. Am I right?"

She nodded.

"I grew up, Amish, near Wander Lane. I've seen the buyers then, and I've seen the buyers now. Many of them, most of them, have full purses. They want, and can afford, quality . . . authentic quality. It's more likely they will return as second quilt buyers, if they are happy and satisfied as first quilt buyers."

"Where do I get these quilts to sell?"

"I'll give you names, and you can get more from other townspeople. Ask around. Let it be known what you're looking for."

"Even if I could find the quilts, there's no way I could afford to stock an inventory."

"Does the word contingency ring a bell? Amish ladies like to make money, too, and you'd be offering a fresh market for them," I said, as I tapped her arm, gave a quick, sharp nod, and winked.

"I'll think about it," she muttered.

"Good enough," I said, "for now . . . God go with you." I looked intently at her. "He will, you know. He wants you to succeed. He wants the best for you . . . and from you."

Chapter Twenty-Nine

In my determined quest to find the last influential happenings and their impact on Lily's thinking and the actions before her death, I still hadn't made my first official contact with a shunning Amisher. I ached to talk with Violet, but that wasn't yet a viable connection. She needed time to recover from the upsetting, the horrendous news, I'd inadvertently, without preparation, laid upon her.

I didn't know why Hattie's death had left my memory. Maybe a subconscious wish. If she hadn't died, there'd be no uncle/niece marriage filling a space in my head that would have much preferred a simple, solvable complication. But, with the remembrance of Willie's first wife, it was back, large in my head, the knowing because she died, Willie married Talitha and they conceived a child. A beautiful child. A miracle as all babies are, and worthy of a life without shame.

And so, two problems loomed large within me. Both too big to stay locked inside the caverns of my mind and heart. Lily's death and Baby Clare's birth. I had accepted the responsibility to shine a revealing and healing light on both. It had all started with my taking a baby that was not mine and giving her away. *God,*

221

forgive me and guide me down the path that would make things right.

There was a person who'd been a part of the Amish community for a long time, who would have known Lily . . . at least, who she was. Maybe more. He was around her age. Maybe a little older. Not much. Stayed mostly in the background. I couldn't recall him attending Sunday sings, with the young people, but he could have. He had a father who kept a tight rein on him. At least, tried to. Yet neither Lilly nor Violet mentioned him in their boy-talk giggle sessions. I did recall Aaron expressing a concern for the young man's lack of appropriate behavior. I didn't remember elaboration of the implied deviant conduct. It was Schrock. Kind of in the background then, certainly not later.

I didn't look forward to confronting Schrock, but sometimes, it's best to tackle the worst, to overpower trepidation and dig in . . . swim fast out of the deepest wave and the rest are easier to conquer.

I considered stopping at the cemetery and consulting Lily, but I was wise enough to know that wouldn't help; it would neither take apprehension away, nor increase the strength of my wavering determination, and, realistically, a dead person gives only the assurance that already dwells within self. Again, I admonished myself, it's wisest to hit a problem head on.

Nevertheless, I didn't press harder on the accelerator.

Schrock's farm lay on Amish land that was farthest from the village of Wander Lane. It gave me time to contemplate various approaches that could lead him to divulge old thoughts of Lily, old memories of his contacts with her. If any. And I was sure, whether Lily had been aware or not, there been many. Lily was pretty. Schrock was bold. My gut told me his brain forgot nothing, but also, I intuited he carefully sifted the contents of that brain to shape and reveal as was beneficial to himself.

As I drew close to Schrock's homestead, I pulled to the side of the road and looked to the sky for God's presence and peace, His mighty strength. *Lift your eyes and look to the heavens:* (Isaiah 40:26). I did that, and like wind ripples waves across the expanse of a lake, it looked as if God had spread His hands under the water, turned the lake upside down and filled the sky with rippling waves of clouds. I sat there a long time and drank in His magnificent magnitude.

And then I drove on . . . ready to confront Schrock.

Even a slow pedaled car makes it to its destination.

I drove onto Schrock's driveway. Parked near the barn. Got out. Looked around. Other than a few ground-pecking chickens, I saw no activity. Temptation to leave loomed heavy.

You're not a coward, Cora Pooler. Look at this opportunity as a challenge. Hunt him down. You can outwit him. I smiled. *Yes, I can.*

As I walked closer to the barn, I heard a steady pounding coming from within. I paused, imagined a hammer in Schrock's hand. *He's not going to kill you. Move.* I shrugged, and feeling like a prowling character, in a dime store-novel—the victim, no, the female gumshoe. Back bent, head thrust forward, I grinned and walked, almost on tip-toe, into the barn.

Back to me, Schrock was nailing a wood piece over an opening in a horse stall. He dealt a pretty good swing. Glad I wasn't a board. I saw a second hammer leaning against the wall. I nodded and picked it up. An equalizer. I was beginning to enjoy this encounter. Just a bit.

I tapped the side of the wall.

He turned. Quick. Hammer at the ready. Then smirked.

"You here for a duel?"

"No," I said, laying the hammer down on a broken stool. Close to me. "Just here as an employee of the village legal system."

"The little lady, with the questions about her sister's death." He looked at me, smirked.

"That's me."

"Shunned little lady, with the sheriff's okay for me to talk to you."

"That's still me." I lifted my hands, palms flat and upward, tilted my head, lifted my eyebrows, and shrugged.

"Don't recall needing his permission before. Don't need it now. Always been, if'n I want to say something, I say it."

I squinted. "Seems to me, you don't listen real well. Seems to me, the bishop made it clear, I'm off limits for your words. Except for now when you've been told to answer my questions, . . ." I clenched my teeth, . . . "about Lily."

"I do what I wanna do."

"Are you really Amish?"

"You know I am. And you know I was here when you stole that baby and got rid of it."

"Did you know Lily?"

"Pretty girl." He put his hammer down, crossed his arms.

"Did you know her?"

"Yep."

"Let me ask it another way." I ran my tongue over my lips. "Did she know you?"

"Yep." He grinned. "Everybody knew me. Still do."

"I didn't."

"Sure, you did." His grin widened. "Maybe not. You're a lot older than me. Guess I could even call you, right now, the far-edge of middle-age." He laughed. "Yep, I could."

"Yep, you could," I mimicked, "but you know, with age comes wisdom. And this wisdom, within me, says I'm a lot wiser than you. So, let's get down to facts and you tell me about the last times you saw Lily."

"That was a long time ago."

"It was," I said, "but I'm sure you remember all the pretty girls, what they did, and when they did it."

"You're right. I had a good eye then and a good memory now." He sneered, and I wanted to swat the smirk off his face. "And she was one mighty fine looker. Feisty one, too."

"We're talking about Lily. She was pretty. She was bright. She was not *feisty.*"

"You want to hear truth, or don't you?" He leered, obviously trying to intimidate me, and I wished I could put a mask over his face or, at least, tape over his mouth.

"Just tell me what you know."

"She was running with one of the Jake's. Can't remember which one. Lapp or Mueller. I just know she was lookin' to marry." He shook his head. "You Amish girls turn breeding age, and all you think about is to hook a good, or any, Amish man, and you're set up for life."

"Did this Amish boy like her?"

"All the Amish boys liked her."

"She was well into marrying age when she died, but she wasn't married," I said. "If all the boys liked her, why do you think that was?"

"Don't know."

"Where'd you go that you saw her?"

"Sometimes the Sunday sings. When we were younger. Not too often there though. I didn't go to them too much. Kind of boring. But you know, kids can slip away now and then. They get good at it." He chuckled. "The Amish work pretty hard. They sleep hard, too. It's easy to walk right by their bedroom and out the house without causing even a snort from *Da*."

"And Lily did that?"

"Yep."

"Often?"

He cocked his head, grinned his aggravating grin. "Enough."

My body tightened. It held firm the growing anger even though wanting to repudiate all the words he was saying. "What about later? After I was shunned. Did you see her much in those years?"

"Some."

"Did she seem happy?" I asked.

"Mostly." He frowned. "Not always, though. Like I said, she was feisty, a lively one, sometimes almost hysterical . . . laughing, loud, talking a mile a minute. But there were other times she dried right up, wouldn't talk, moped, pulled herself into a tight ball. Couldn't get near her." He paused, seemed to be thinking. "Kind of like she was off in some other world. Try to talk to her? No response. Sometimes, I felt like giving her a good, hard poke, just to wake her up."

"Did you see her in the days just before she died?" I questioned, not remembering a frantic Lily. Not ever. Exuberant, yes. Frenzied, no. "Think hard."

"I don't think so." He frowned. "I remember thinking, before she got herself drowned, I hadn't seen her for awhile, and I thought maybe she was sick or something."

"Do you think it was an accident?"

"Dunno. Maybe. Prob'ly. Don't think she would've jumped in and stuck her head in the water all by herself." He looked at me, shook his head, and hmphed. Then his face turned hard.

"Why don't you just let this go. It's done, and you might find out things you don't wanna know."

"Like what?"

He picked up his hammer. "Got work to do. Time for you to go."

"What," I repeated. "What wouldn't I want to know?"

He laughed and walked back to the stall.

I watched him put a nail against the wood and lift the hammer to strike it into place. I hoped he'd miss and hit his thumb. Smash it hard.

He didn't. Disappointed with his meager information and healthy thumb, I turned to go, and then, thought, no, he knew more. I wanted to know what his vague insinuation meant. Angry, I picked up the hammer I'd dropped on the stool and tapped the wall. It drew his attention once; it would do it again. And it did. He turned and scowled at me.

"What now?" he asked, as his eyes dropped to my hammer. "Another duel?" He grinned. "You won't win."

"You must know more," I said. "You're all over the community. You see all kinds of things, and you've given me almost nothing I didn't already know."

"Lady, I've given more than you realize." He turned away from me, raised his hammer to slam another nail and shouted over his shoulder, "Think on it."

Puzzled, I left the barn, got in my car, sat in my car, and pondered his words. I could think of nothing to say I'd not already said. Frustrated, I left his farm and drove to the cemetery.

"Lily, I'm trying." I reached, touched her monument, slid my hand over the engravings. "Lily, I know I've just started, but already I feel inadequate. I don't know the questions to ask, the detail-getting. I don't know them. And I don't think I know how to dig the right information I do get from my paltry answered questions. I probably started with the wrong person. Schrock likes to provoke. If he really did hint he knew pertinent and exclusive facts, and it seemed that might be so, I don't know what they are. But, as you know, Lily, I've got a brain, and I can use it. I can examine, sift, sort, evaluate, and conclude. And I'm going to do just that. I won't fail you, Lily. *I won't.* Before I leave Wander Lane, you're going to be inside the fence."

Chapter Thirty

As I drove, thoughts, questions, fears swirled in my head . . . scrambled, connected, broke apart, clashed together, separated again . . . a frenzy of words, not much sense.

I stopped at the side of the road, covered my face with my hands, sat quietly and settled my mind. I felt the sun's rays slip through the windshield and warm my hands. I lowered them and felt soft sun heat, caress and comfort my face.

I don't know how long I sat there, but I rejoiced in the calm that came.

I was ready to continue my quest for truth.

It was soothing to roam the rolling hills, spotted with fields of growing corn stalks, not quite ready to tassel, and cows moving through pastures, inherently knowing the time they should be at their barns for milking, and gardens, continuously grazed for ripened vegetables, already stripped of peas, and exhibiting semi-dirt filled holes where carrots had been pulled from the ground, and often eaten right there by little mouths before they made it to the kitchens of those young ones' *maems*. I came upon crop land, stopped, and rolled my window down to inhale the rich, scent of limed soil nourishing a huge field of tomato plants. I remembered regularly skimming the field for table and canning tomatoes, but the majority of the crop waited for the full, fall harvesting of fruit grown for marketing, tomatoes picked when the vines, spread wide over plowed rows and heavy with product, yielded their ripened crop for consumption. I couldn't resist. I got out of my car and plucked a tomato, pushed its stem off, buried my nose into the space it left, and drew in the heady, dank, musty scent expelled from the separation of fruit and its attachment to the vine. And for a moment, I was Amish. Young and gathering tomatoes for *Maem's* rich, red, meat sauce.

Contented, I got back in my car and drove, roamed, enjoyed.

A while later, I saw Preacher Kurtz coming down the road toward me. Reins in hand, he was standing at the front of a horse-drawn, hay-filled wagon. I'd just passed his house and surmised he was going home for evening chores and supper. Wanting to thank him for speaking with Lowell and agreeing to let me talk with the brethren, I stopped the car, got out, and flagged him down.

He pulled the reins taut, stopped the horses, and nodded in my direction. Expressionless, he waited.

"I want to thank you. What you did, what you're allowing means a great deal to me."

He nodded, again, and I knew he understood what I meant. And then, surprising me, he asked me to have supper at his house. His words were few. A simple invitation. A time. After chores. I wasn't exactly sure how that would register on a clock, but I agreed anyway. It would be easy to watch his home from a distance, and when the cows were released from stanchions to pasture, and Silas Kurtz walked the distance from barn to house, I would give him time to greet his wife, Annie, and to wash the day's grime from his face and hands. And then I would go to his door and knock.

I knocked, and Annie answered. I smiled. She did, too. Then she touched my arm briefly, turned, and walked to the kitchen area. I followed.

Silas was already seated.

Annie turned to me. "I believe you're here to speak with us about Lily." She smiled. "We both knew her . . . and you," she said, laying her hand briefly on mine, "and would be proud to tell you what we know." She motioned toward the table and I saw there were place settings for three. "Please sit and eat with us. We've not yet said the blessing."

I nodded, whispered my *dank,* and sat.

Three heads bowed and 'said' silent words to God.

Annie rose, took a dish from the oven and brought it to the table. I watched and absorbed the scent of rich, Amish cooking, as she placed cheese slices over the baked layers of cabbage, potatoes, carrots, onions and ground beef. Radish salad and dilly rolls were already on the table.

When it came my turn, I took a roll and a generous helping of both casserole and salad, and as the food touched my tongue, I remembered and savored the tang of the lemon and garlic that dressed the salad. Violet had fed me well, but these were the tastes and smells of *Maem's* kitchen . . . home.

"Save room in your stomach for a *snitz* half-moon pie," Annie said softly.

"Ahh, dried apples wrapped in pastry." My taste buds watered. "Annie, I love you."

She smiled. We ate. Silently. Until all were sated. Then Silas led me to the living area, and Annie began the kitchen clean-up.

It was time. We would talk of Lily.

"What do you remember of Lily?" I asked Silas.

He didn't answer.

"You were like a big brother to her. Do you remember the magic stone? She thought if she tossed the stone in the creek and whispered a wish, it would come true. My wisp of fairy, Lily, sweet and innocent. Endearing." I bit my lip, closed my eyes. She danced behind my lids.

"We will wait for Annie," Silas said, his words so sharp. "She will sit with us when we speak of Lily. She knew her better than I. She was more Lily's age. I was more yours."

"I'll help her," I said, starting to rise from the wonderfully comfortable, soft-cushioned chair . . . that might put me to sleep after eating so much. And so well. But he gestured me to stay where I was.

"We can wait. She's efficient and won't take long."

I swallowed. His strident words sent me back to the years living with *Da*. A child. An Amish child. And a well-disciplined Amish child argues not with an Amish man. I sent my mind to gather pleasured pictures. We had played together, Silas and I, schooled together, went to Sunday sings and a buggy ride, or two, together. Smiling memories. But we were grown now, and certain rules, matured relationships, had changed, stiffened. We would wait for Annie to be done in the kitchen. We would wait silently. A preacher is not given to frivolous words. And I knew he, Silas, when we talked, would rein in his words to adhere to Lily. He was a preacher, a man of rules. But I hoped the gentle in the boy I remembered was still there.

Annie was done. She came and sat in a chair similar to mine. Only Silas, Preacher Silas, sat in a straight-backed, hard chair.

Now it was time.

"You came about Lily," Silas stated.

"I did." I nodded.

"What would you like me to tell you?"

"First, I want to thank you. . . ."

"You already did," he interrupted. "Sheriff Parker requested we speak with you. About Lily. I agreed to do that." His gaze on me was steady, not disagreeable, but composed. "What would you like to know?"

"Will Annie be able to speak, too?" I questioned.

"Yes, I agreed. I told you that. She may speak freely. She knew Lily better than I did. There was a twelve-year difference between us. That's a vast space when you're young. Not so much now."

"I'm going to take you back," I said, "to all those years long ago. When we were young. And friends. You, Annie, with Lily. You, Silas, with me." I looked at Silas. "You and I weren't as close as Annie and Lily, but we were friends. And so you were both privy to the personality and behavior of Lily from the time she was little, until the time of her death." They nodded.

I turned my face to Annie. "How do you remember the young child, Lily, before the time she would have become pregnant?"

"She was kind and fun and . . ." She paused. "Elusive. Like a sunray that drops and shines on you for a moment and then,

233

leaving its warmth on you, springs away. She laughed a lot."

"And you, Silas?" I asked.

"Like Annie, I remembered she laughed a lot." He turned to his wife. "I don't remember anything special about her. She was just a kid. Far as I could tell, a regular kid. A girly kid."

"Did she stay that way?"

"I guess. Didn't really notice her that much. I was busy with my own life: *Rumspringa;* the farm; Sunday sing; buggy rides. Look, I was at an age where it was all fun or work." He smiled. "Mostly fun. Then it was settle-down time, baptism, and the farm." He glanced at Annie. "And courting."

I looked at Silas. "You married Annie," I said. He sat stolid. "Before or after Lily died?"

His face didn't change. I looked at Annie. Hers showed hurt.

"After," Annie said. "After Lily died. It was small. Just family. I didn't want big."

"Because of Lily?"

"Yes."

"Do you think she killed herself?"

Annie jerked. I knew she hadn't expected the question to come so soon. But I wanted her answer before she could think what it should be.

"I don't know."

Her words bit, and I thought it might be harder to dig answers from her than I thought.

"The bishop said it was so. Said she jumped in the water with purpose." Silas jumped in, his voice stern, authoritative. He glared at me. "Why do you doubt him?"

"I don't doubt he did what he thought was best, but I don't believe Lily would have committed suicide," I stared back him, "and I'm going to prove it."

"What if you're wrong?"

I didn't answer.

"I don't have anything to add to this," he said rising abruptly, voice strident. "I'm going out to check out things in the barn, maybe walk the fence awhile, see what needs mending." He looked at Annie. "I admonish you to remember you are only to speak of things pertinent to Lily's death." He nodded toward me. "I know you, Cora Pooler. You've always been honest and respectful. I trust that hasn't changed." He stood before me a moment. "But Annie will tell me if you have."

He strode purposefully out of the room.

"This is hard for him," Annie defended.

I heard a sad appeal in her words. But I couldn't yield. "This is hard for all of us," I said.

"You. My family. Me. *Me.*" I felt tears gather in my eyes. Remorse? Uncertainty? Anger?

My hand went up. Fisted. Came down hard against the chair's arm. "Lily's outside the fence. How can you not *hate* that?"

Annie covered her face with her hands, shook her head, dropped her hands, looked at me. I saw sorrow in her eyes, and I heard a sigh that seemed to travel from a deep place, slip from her lips.

"Cora?"

A plea? Surrender? I wasn't sure. I sat silent, waited for her decision.

"She'd changed. Before the baby." Head down, Annie spoke to the floor. "She was afraid. She wouldn't tell me why." Annie raised her face, her eyes stared into mine. "I thought it was the Jakes. They wanted her to choose. I thought she didn't know which one she wanted. She laughed when I told her what I thought. It confused me. Sometimes, she'd be talking to me and she'd start shaking, sometimes, even crying. But she wouldn't tell me why." Annie leaned her body toward me. Her voice strained. "It was worse after you left, when you said the baby was yours, and you wouldn't tell the bishop who the father was, and he put you under the bann, and she, me, nobody could talk to you anymore. And you left. And she got worse and worse, sadder and sadder."

"Why didn't somebody help her?"

"I don't think they knew how bad she was. She was a good hider. She could look happy when she wasn't happy. *But I knew her.*" Annie bit her lip. Her hands clenched. I saw, heard, her struggle to say the words. Then very softly, more slipped through her lips. "She let me hold her when no one was looking . . . and Cora, it lasted so long. So many years."

"Five," I said, guilt rising. "Five," I repeated whispering, "and I thought I was helping her, doing the right thing. The baby was hers. I should have helped her, not robbed her."

We sat, saying nothing, for what seemed a long time.

"Annie," I said, breaking the silence, "do you think she killed herself?"

"Yes."

Chapter Thirty-One

I drove to the cemetery, walked up the hill, and sat by Lily's grave. When it was near dark, I walked back down the hill, got in my car, and drove to Harriet's. I parked in front of the eatery and sat. Empty.

Lowell found me, got in my car, sat. Body tilted forward, hands clasped, arms resting on his thighs, eyes on the floormat, he shook his head. "Not a good day?"

"Not a good day," I agreed, looking out the windshield, absorbing the deepening darkness shrouding the buildings, the trees, people . . . hiding the village dirt. I wondered if I could open my window, grab it, and swallow the night and hide the dirt in my heart. Magic. Illusion. Useless.

"Annie believes Lily killed herself." I said, not looking at Lowell. I rubbed my eyes with the heels of my palms, slid them hard down my cheeks, folded my hands together, rested my chin against them.

"The preacher's wife," Lowell stated.

"Uh-huh."

"And Silas?" He sat back against the seat, stretched his legs, looked through the windshield.

"He didn't say. He left. He hid." A short, grunting laugh escaped my lips. "The preacher hid."

"You giving up?"

My head jerked. I glared at him.

"*No.*"

He grinned, "That's better. Thought I'd lost you there for a minute . . . 'though I'm not so sure that wouldn't be a good thing."

I shrugged my shoulders and grimaced, not amused by his attempt at humor.

"You hungry?" he asked.

"No, I had a huge supper at Annie's. Besides, I want to think on what Annie told me."

"Well, I'm starved. You can sit here and think, but I'm going into Harriet's and eat." He opened the car door and swung his legs out. I watched him walk as far as the eatery's door, and then, his hand against the door, ready to push, Lowell turned. He looked at me, frowned, came back to the car, and tapped on the window.

I opened it. Reluctantly.

"Two heads think better than one," Lowell said, bending, talking through the window. He grinned. "And full or not, ice cream melts and can slide around all that good Amish cooking sitting heavy in your innards. Besides, doing as opposed to moping, spurs your mind to think smart."

"You know, you're probably right. Ice cream can solve anything." I shook my head. "I just wonder what flavor is right for this problem."

I went in with him, ate ice cream, and I talked. He listened.

I'm not sure the ice cream gave me any concrete advice. But

it tasted good—Butter Pecan. With a thick coating of chocolate syrup. My favorite. From Lowell, I got a small bit of advice, *Lighten up and keep plugging along. Eventually perseverance pays off.* Not very helpful. Neither concrete nor new. But sometimes, it's nice to know someone is aware of your dilemma. And cares. Maybe. Probably. Certainly.

I decided to spend the next weeks honing my investigative proficiency. I practiced my skills on those who had few, clear memories of Lily, but were aware of the circumstances of her death. It had been long since Lily had died, and old happenings grow dim. Yet, all were firm in their belief the church had made the right decision when it resolved Lily should be buried outside the cemetery fence. Their vague memories painted Lily as a troubled and depressed young woman. When asked for facts determining their presumptions, they were ambiguous. The women tended to lay their opinions upon their husbands' words; the men, upon the bishop's.

I had hoped for, but not anticipated, firm clues as to the state or circumstances of Lily's death and burial. I didn't receive much helpful information, but my questioning had increased my acuity and ability to ask questions that would produce meaningful answers. I was ready to interrogate those I felt would offer pertinent facts and opinions, and so, it was time to speak with those likely to hold relative thoughts and facts within their banks of memory. I went to the motel to sleep a night of building and storing a vat of energy.

I slept well. Dreams not remembered indicate they've been good. Mine had cleansed and freshened my spirits. Ah, joy.

Drapes closed, early sun pushed through their thin fabric, to softly shadow and reshape, smudge the edges, of objects in the room. I rose and stumbled to the bathroom. Then showered, and towel-wrapped, I went into the bedroom. Moving within the meager light slipping around the half-closed bathroom door, I pulled clothes from drawers and the miniscule motel closet, and dressed. Then morning hungry, I went down to the motel dining area.

Several late summer tourists were eating breakfast there. I poured a cup of coffee, added sugar, grabbed a Danish, and by shifting my chair to various positions, as if I were a hard-to-please and annoyed traveler, I sat close enough to hear the comments of several tete-à-têting vacationers. With my ears attuned to their conversations, I was privy to some interesting observations. Marvelous quilts. Drool worthy desserts. Adorable children. And it seemed most thought the Amish were shy, simple, honest, faith-believing-and-living, hard-working, productive members of their community.

Hmm, I thought, I knew some like that. And I knew some not like that. I rose, frowned, and enjoying my playacting, impatient, tourist role, wended my way through the close spaced tables, snatched a banana from the food counter, screwed up my face and sniffed its peels, put it back, and then shuffled a cranky, old lady pace to the outside door. As I pushed the door open, I dropped my disguise and laughed.

There is a magical day when summer fades and the annual foliage retreat begins. It's a day that hints the promise of fall cloaking the earth, with a rich, colorful complexion. I passed through the door and walked into that day of beginning change. Rusty-orange leaves, some fully colored, some less, some with orange and yellow tinged edges, hung sprinkled through the still dominant green leaves, but they, too, in a staggering dance, would eventually flash color and die. As their stems grew brittle, and the drying leaves lost connection with the trees' limbs, they would linger a brief moment, and then drop, scatter, fall through the trees' residual, thick, green fullness, peppering them with vibrant color. Before long, they would be gone, piled by children, jumped on, rolled in, raked, the first fallen to be followed by the dropping of the remaining leaves, frost kissed, flamed, dried and drifting, one by one, to the ground. And branches would be empty, naked, killing frost the victor.

I shuddered at the thought of fall's demise and the weather that would follow. Cold was slithering through the calendar pages. Too fast. I hoped to be done with my search, before snowfall. I slid the vision of winter out of my head, drew in a deep breath, and relaxed, for this day was glorious. The sun hit the hint of fall with a shimmering glow and a soothing, embracing heat. It was good, invigorating, and, maybe, I could keep those feelings all day.

My first stop would be at Mary Graber's, now Mary Rissler's home. When I was fully Amish, she had been a close friend. After she married, as she had no brothers, her husband, Paul, came to live with her and her parents. When her father was no longer physically able to maintain the farm, Paul, with her father's consent and advice, had taken over that responsibility, and a *dawdi haus* had been built for Mary's parents.

When I'd last seen Mary, ten years before, she had given birth to eleven children. Two had died in infancy, the rest had thrived on rich, Guernsey milk, butchered cows, pigs, and chickens, and farm-grown fresh and canned fruits and vegetables . . . and Amish baking. Her youngest child, Lisa, had been nine years old then. She was the lowest rung in a ladder of many children. The years had passed and now all were adults, unless more had been born during my last length of absence. It was possible, but I hadn't seen signs of it in current days. Yet there had been the diapers hanging in the yard. Those I'd helped a younger version of Mary pluck from the clothesline before the rain soaked them, and she did look so much like Mary, I'd assumed the diapers covered the bottom, or bottoms, of Mary's grandchildren. Mary did seem to follow the pattern of a many child Amish family.

I was anxious to see Mary. It would be good to catch-up. I went to her door and knocked.

Amish reserve abandoned, she screeched and hugged me when she opened the door. Our bodies entangled, our cheeks touching, we laughed.

"I know you've been here a goodly time." Still holding me, she pushed me away, enough that our faces were close but discernible. "I wanted to see you, to talk to you. But I couldn't, shunned as you were . . . are. But now I can, about Lily anyway. And it seems to me, all things, all topics could somehow be related to her. *Yeah?*"

"*Yeah,*" I returned and smiled.

"Come in," she said, letting me loose and dropping her hand to hold mine. "We'll talk."

"It's legitimate, this visit," I said, standing firm. I didn't want to cause Mary trouble or put her in a position of having to defend herself. "I really did come to talk about Lily. She pours into so many memories, so many times we were together . . . and with Annie, too." I paused, bit my lip, held Mary's hand tight. She kept her eyes on me, said nothing. "I need you to be honest with me. Even though it might hurt."

"Me or you?" Mary asked. She stood by the door. One hand in mine, the other on the doorknob. "Or both of us?"

"I know you're friends with Annie, but I have to know your thoughts and knowings. I don't know what you'll tell me, but it has to be truth."

"I know what Annie thinks. We've talked of it. A little." She sighed. "But Cora, we're Amish, both of us. We don't lie . . . and we respect the words of one another."

"That's not always true, Mary. You want it to be, but it's not. Not always."

"Come in, Cora. We'll talk." She said again. She opened the door and led me in. "The men are gone and Lisa, my youngest, has taken her baby to the woods," she smiled, "to look for birds and flowers. But mostly, I think grass will be pulled and little legs will run and fall, get up, run and fall again. She's a handful, that little one."

Mary led me into the kitchen. "Do you mind if I peel the potatoes while we talk?"

"Of course not." I sat, watched her take a bowl of potatoes and a pan off the counter and put them on the table.

"Paul loves potatoes. Mashed. Roasted. Fried." She smiled. "Even sliced raw."

"Do you have another knife?" I asked. "I can help."

"That would be *gut*."

We sat for awhile, peeling, not talking.

"I know Annie thinks Lily took her own life," Mary said softly, breaking our silence . . . a calming, peaceful silence. "I don't know what happened. I have thoughts, but I don't know."

"Do you think she could have killed herself?" I asked.

"I don't know. She was very . . . volitant . . . those last days, the last days I saw her." Mary furrowed her brow. "Flighty. Always moving." She pressed her lips together. "No, I'm wrong. Not all days. Some days she was so quiet, so pale, you'd think an angel had dropped down and lifted her spirit from within her, gathered it against her angel breast and flew away with it."

I covered my face with my hands, blew into them, gently. "Mary," I asked, again, through my fingers, "do you think she killed herself?"

"You ask a question I can't answer. Some days I do. Some days I don't."

"It's a sin," I said. "A sin that can't be forgiven. Her last act on earth, a sin." I shook my head. "Not Lily," I moistened my lips. "Not Lily."

"You're right, Cora. She would not be forgiven. Not by this Amish brethren."

"But how could they be sure?"

"That her death was deliberate? Done by her own will?"

"Yes."

"I don't know. There were stories," Mary said, then grunted, "'though the Amish don't gossip." She shook her head. "But everyone has opinions, and sometimes, they get said."

"Were there some who didn't think she," I swallowed, this was getting ever more difficult to say, "killed herself?"

"Yes."

"And you were one of them?"

"I told you I wasn't sure. There were some, good sisters and brothers, who were adamant that she'd done it. And others, just as pious, who thought she didn't. I listened to all and was sorely confused." She looked intently at me. "I still am."

"What would make you think she did?"

Mary hesitated, pressed her lips together. She put her knife down and leaned over the table. "She was so different. One day so angry. The next day . . . withered. Walked the road. Where it went by the creek. So slow. She kept her arms tight around her body. Wouldn't talk. I tried. I even drove the buggy alongside her. But she wouldn't get in. And she wouldn't talk.

Nothing. Not one word."

"Was she crying?"

"No. No tears. Just a face with nothing written on it."

"The other days? You said she was angry."

"I had a couple wee ones then, and Mahlon, he was a little older. Lily'd scream at them. Screech. Once she grabbed Mahlon's arm so hard, I saw bruises when I took his shirt off that night. I'd make her leave when she got like that. The little ones shouldn't see such behavior." Mary paused, looked at me a long time, and when she spoke, her words wavered raw. "That day she gave Mahlon the bruise, I made her go. That day she was crying. Gulping tears. It frightened the children. I made her go."

I wanted to touch her. She looked so forlorn. But Mary wasn't done. I sensed words yearning to be let loose, and I knew she didn't want to say them. But she did. And by the time she was finished, my head was bowed and my hands, clenched tight in my lap, wanted to cover my listening ears.

"Before she left that day, the day she hurt Mahlon, she said your name, Cora. Bookended your name with foul words. Then she looked at me as if I were her worst enemy. Me. A friend it seemed she wanted to hurt. Her face carried hate. And I think pain. She glared at me, spit her words at me. 'If Cora had let me have my baby, I wouldn't need another.' And then she left.

Stalked out the door. Slammed it. I'd asked her to leave. And she did. I wanted to follow her. Grab her and hold her, take her back into my house. But I couldn't. My children were there." I felt Mary's eyes on me. "You wanted to know, Cora. I've told you truth that should have stayed within me, but you wanted it, and I showed you a hurting Lily, an *angry* Lily. But she wasn't always like that. Could Lily have killed herself? Yes, Cora, on that day, I think she could have."

Chapter Thirty-Two

I went to the cemetery. I needed that place of rotting death, a place to lament, to release my howling heart from pain, to spread my tears over Lily's grave. Had she killed herself? Could she kill herself? *No.* But did she? And if she did, my Amish heart should bid me accept the place of her internment. But I knew I couldn't do that.

I lowered my body to rest against Lily's marker. The stone was cold against my back; the grass, damp under my clothes. It seemed fitting. Uncomfortable. Less than it should be. Like Lily under the ground. I looked up to the sky. Dawn's soft, gray-bottomed clouds, their meager store exhausted, had faded, disappeared. Their replacements, streaks of wispy white, feather clouds, drifted over the blue. I closed my eyes and tried to pray. But I couldn't do that, either. God seemed a long way off. I wondered if I'd lost Him, if I were doing wrong, and He went away. And I wondered if He'd left Lily, too.

If we're wise, we allow ourselves those moments of doubt and despair. For a time. And then, depleted, if truly wise, we realize how foolish are our flimsy fantasies, and we fill our souls with renewed strength and determination. I wasn't done. Lily didn't kill herself. And I would prove it.

I don't know how long I'd been sitting there, my struggling thoughts consuming time, when I was startled by the rustle of a new and pleasantly scented presence. I looked up. It was Mattie, arms filled with late-blooming cabbage roses. With one swift charge, she plummeted her weighty body down onto the space next to Lily's grave. Her space. For whatever reason, Mattie's space.

"What are the roses for?" I asked.

"You know. Lots of times I bring flowers." Seated, legs spread, roses strewn in the half-circle her legs formed, she lifted a short-stemmed, thick petaled, pink rose and offered it to me. "Be careful, it's thorny."

I took the rose, lifted it to my nose, drew in the sweet scent. "It's lovely, Mattie. Thank you." I watched her separate and spread the flowers over the grass and wondered at their purpose. "Why do you bring flowers, Mattie?"

"Ain't no reason that I shouldn't."

"True," I said, "but what's the reason that you do?"

"Don't you like them?"

"Uh-huh, I do. But why do you bring them?" I asked again.

"Why do you come here and sit on that Lily grave of yours?" she retaliated.

"Because I love her, and I miss her." I moved my eyes away from her. "Do you love and miss someone?"

"I guess. My mother . . . my sister. Some. Not my father. At all."

"Do you miss someone in the ground under you?" I still kept

my eyes from her face. It was a bold question. I didn't want to bear more pressure on her than those words did, so I sat quiet and waited.

She didn't answer.

"You're a lady full of secrets," I said.

"Not so much. I told you about Schrock. He's a mean one. You saw that. And I told you where I came from, how he took me from my parents." She laughed a little. "Only what I didn't tell you was that he paid for me. Lots of money. More than a thousand." She turned her eyes from the ground and looked straight at me. "You worth that much?"

This was a Mattie I'd not seen before. Not sure how to respond, I said nothing.

"He needed someone to clean and cook. I could do that. Wouldn't be no worse than what I was already doing at home. Maybe, even more interesting. Different dirt, different food."

Her words flung from her mouth. Angry. Sharp. A dam bursting.

"Mattie, you don't have to tell me this."

"Sure, I do. You're the almost Amish saint that's looking for answers to everything, and so I'm giving you some." Her head flung back and short, staccato ha-has burst from her mouth. "And best of all, you know what he wanted? . . . A child, a wee baby to replace the one that killed his wife."

I reached to touch her arm, quiet her, but before my hand touched skin, she turned, glared at me, 'don't touch me,' and she drew her body away from me. Then she thrust her head forward, and her eyes glued onto mine. Intuitively, I drew away from her. Her face was too close, and, not recognized before, the putrid odor of rotting liquor spewed from her mouth to my nose.

"Mattie," I said sharply, then, thinking the unfairness she'd experienced, whispered, "I'm sorry."

She cried, put her hands over her face and cried and cried and cried.

I slid across the grass and held her.

I drove Mattie home. I saw no sign of Schrock near the barn or the house. Seeming to read my mind, Mattie, face forward, not looking at me, words sounding confident, as if she were fine, as if there had been no frenzied incident in the cemetery, spoke out, "You won't find him around here. He's over at Harvey Glick's place threshing. A whole bunch of blackbirds. Threshing grain. All day." She shook her head. "He'll come home hungry and dirty."

"Won't Lovina Glick feed him?"

She shrugged. "Maybe. Probably. Both dinner and supper. Even so, he'll expect food.

Most likely, a full meal. With fresh bread and pie."

"Would you like me to come in?"

"What for?" She opened the car door, got out, walked to her house, and went in.

I was tired, so very tired. If the morning were a sandwich, it would've been a five-decker. And thinking 'sandwich,' my stomach bade me feed it, so I headed the car in the direction of Wander Lane, specifically Harriet's Homemade Soups and Hearty Sandwiches. Lunch. Just the thinking of it, a consistent and tension relieving event, sparked my foot to push heavily on the gas pedal. It would be a late lunch. Which was good. Fewer consumers. Less prospect of unwanted banter.

There were no cars parked near the eatery, and the sidewalks were relatively empty of shoppers. As I eased my car into a space near the restaurant, a quick glance from my window into the eatery showed few people still eating their lunch. *Good timing, Cora.*

But it wasn't such good timing, for as I stepped in, I saw at the back of the dining room Lowell sitting in his corner. And worse, he looked up and saw me. I raised my hand in a weak wave, but there was no response. He kept his eyes on me for a moment, then lowered his head, lifted his fork, and shoved some food around on his plate.

Obviously, he didn't want to talk to me, which was fine. I didn't want to talk to him either. I considered leaving, then reconsidered. I was tired and hungry, and I wasn't about to let a moody sheriff dictate where I sat and to whom I spoke. I surveyed the dining room, pondering my choice for sitting.

"Best to leave him alone," Bailey said, sidling up to me.

"Didn't intend to do anything else." I lifted one eyebrow. "Even my nonjudgmental, gentle speaking, Amish mother would have recognized the man had, in her words, a bee in his bonnet."

"Not a bee," Bailey said softly, "a grief."

"What are you talking about?"

"Deputy Kenyon's son died this morning."

"Oh." I took a step towards the sheriff's table and felt Bailey's hand grasp my arm, in a tight hold.

"Let him be."

"How'd the boy die?" I asked, saddened. It always touches the heart when a young one dies. There's always the brief, *why?*

Until the believing soul remembers, *knows,* God foreknows when that day that will be, and on that day, the deceased will be met with just love. For the living, the grief lingers, but if a believer, it's tinged with joy.

"Cancer," Bailey answered. "Been sick a long time."

"I didn't know that."

"No, you wouldn't have. You've been too busy mourning the death of someone who's been gone a *long* time. A long time. Not entitled to tears any more. You, not to give them. Her, not to receive them. Don't matter where she's lying. God determined her place years ago." She let loose my arm, and walked away mumbling, "Inside the fence or not, don't make no matter."

"Bailey" I called after her.

She didn't turn, stopped her waitress, Lucie, and without looking at me, jerked her head toward me. Lucie nodded and moved in my direction.

"It's okay, Lucie, I won't bother him," I said, a bit perturbed.

"There's a good table right by the window," she said. "You can look out at the park. That be okay?"

"That would be fine, Lucie."

"It's okay, Lucie." I heard Lowell's voice boom. "She can sit here, if she wants to."

Lucie looked toward Bailey. Bailey shrugged and nodded, and Lucie led me to Lowell's table, took my order, 'Just diet cola,' and left.

"You look like of peaked. You shoulda ordered some food." His words were harsh.

"You look kind of not-too-great yourself," I said quietly. I wanted to pat his hand but wasn't quite sure it would be a welcomed gesture, and, also, not certain what I should say, I simply pushed out the only words I could think of. "Bailey said Kenyon's son died. I'm sorry. It's a hard thing to take in."

"Yep."

I waited for Lowell to say more. He didn't.

"She said he had cancer. A long time."

"He did."

"Does Kenyon have other children?"

"Three. All girls."

I sat quietly hoping he'd say more. Again, he didn't. Relieved to see Bailey make an appearance, I breathed a short sigh of thanksgiving. She'd come to take his plate away. It was full of food. He'd eaten almost nothing. Bailey made a moue, shook her head slightly and placed a piece of chocolate cake, frosted thick, in front of him.

"If you won't eat normal, nourishing vittles, then eat the cake. I was gonna put ice cream on it, but I figured it'd get you too sugared up. Gonna be hard enough to get through this without riling up your blood," she admonished, her voice gently stern. "Now you eat. Kenyon's gonna need ya."

Lowell looked at me, half-smiled and winked.

I smiled back. "Eat your cake," I whispered. "It'll make *her* feel better."

"Humph," Bailey said, "As if my ears can't hear you, and yes, it will make me . . . and *him* . . . feel better." And she stalked off.

"Seriously," I said, gazing at Lowell, "what can I do to help?"

"Me or Kenyon?"

"Either. Both."

"For Kenyon, pray. For me, tell me how your sleuthing went."

"I kind of think that's not too important right now."

"Shifts my mind to another track."

So, I told him the day's happenings. Filtered. Just who I saw, chatty words said, no substance. He'd had enough grief that day, he didn't need more.

Chapter Thirty-Three

Lowell and I sat at the table, me talking, him listening. I'm not sure his ears absorbed my words, but his eyes never left my face. I'd pause, now and then, hoping for a response, either by words or facial expression. Neither was forthcoming.

After a bit, Bailey came to our table. She bent and whispered into his ear. He nodded and rose. He handed some money out to her. She pushed it away. He dropped it on the table, laid his hand on my shoulder for a brief moment, and then he was gone.

"Don't matter what happens, life keeps comin' at ya," Bailey said, shaking her head. "But it don't seem right for a young'un to go." She slid Lowell's uneaten cake across the table. "Might as well get the sugar into you, since you're not eating healthy neither. Diet cola. Some diet that is. You and Lowell. Both of you. Eat like your bodies don't need nothin' decent today. Anyway, eat the cake. Looks like you could use it."

"I don't want the cake, Bailey."

"Eat it anyway. It's got energy in it."

"If I eat half, will you leave me alone?"

"Maybe."

I took a bite. It was good, but I didn't feel like telling her that. She was younger than me, shouldn't be bossing me. I didn't need a mother. I was perfectly competent to make my own decisions. Good or bad."

"Well?" She tilted her head with a know-it-all attitude.

"What?" Almost a pout.

"Don't I make the best cake ever?"

I grunted. She probably didn't even make it. She had good, young, Amish, baker girls working in her kitchen. Without a doubt the credit should go to them. But I succumbed.

"Yes, Bailey, it's good."

"Okay. Now then, you can't be living on just sugar. Tell me what you want that's good for your belly, and I'll get it here right fast."

"*I don't want anything.*"

"'Course you do. Don't be getting stubborn. Won't get you nowhere," Bailey said, and she raised an eyebrow and a pencil and a pad. "Okay, what'll it be?"

"Do you always win?" Bailey grinned.

"Yep."

"Tomato soup and grilled cheese." I spit the words out fast.

She was still grinning as she walked away. "Bailey," I called after her. She turned, frowned.

"How long was Sheriff Parker here?"

"What difference does it make to you?" Her brow furrowed. She looked puzzled.

"Who just called him?"

"Now that ain't really none of your business."

"Maybe not, but I want to know." I tried to cajole, but I don't think she was about to be sweet-talked. "And I won't tell anybody."

"Well, I ain't telling," she said. "I know your little games, and they don't work with me."

"At least tell me if it was important, if it was about me."

"Why would anybody be calling about you?"

"Was it? Was it the preacher? Preacher Miller?"

"He got a phone?"

"In the pasture. For emergencies."

"You been making trouble for the Amish?"

"No . . . but they might think so."

"Good thing Aunt Harriet don't know about your shenanigans. She'd be one mighty upset old lady." She walked away to get the food I wouldn't eat.

I put a tip on the table and walked out of Harriets Homemade Soups and Hearty Sandwiches. Petty? Probably. But I'd had a miserable morning and, childishly, needed someone to be sympathetic.

And I knew where to go.

Harriet's house was tucked in a pocket among pines and maples. There was a stream nearby. I remember when I was young and my brothers little, many hours I was entrusted with their care. Sometimes, I would take them in the pony cart, and taking turns with the reins, we plodded the trail to Harriet's cottage. It was before she had realized her dream of providing a place, a small stall, in the summer where she could sell her culinary treasures . . . cookies, cakes, pies, donuts, breads, canned jellies . . . before the fruition of that dream and then the explosion of customers growing it to Harriet's Homemade Soups and Hearty Sandwiches. Now a physically impaired old lady, she was bound to that home in the woods. A willing captive in a place of wonderful remembrances.

It was long since I'd been there, and I'd not seen Harriet, since those harrowing moments in her restaurant's storeroom. As I pulled in her hard-packed dirt and narrow driveway, I wondered if I should have called Harriet's home-helper, Bailey's young sister, Louise, to discern Harriet's well-being and her desire to receive visitors. Neither had I conferred with Bailey. The want to see Harriet had come to me as an immediate and pressing need. It was a pull I couldn't resist.

I sat in the car a moment, girding my soul with strength and discernment. When assured my intent was honorable and loving, I stepped from the car, walked with deliberate step off the driveway and onto the grass yard, walked through the thick and tall blades, up the porch steps and across the wood planked floor to the front door. Knocked.

Though I wished it were so, I knew it would not be Harriet answering my knock. And it wasn't. The questioning face surveying me was Louise's.

"I should have called," I said.

"You're Cora." She pressed her lips together, then yielding, "Cora Pooler."

"I should have called," I repeated.

"Yes." Louise hesitated. "But it's okay. She's awake. Just. Her nap was short, so she isn't exactly . . . coherent?"

"I just want to see her," I said softly.

"Why?"

I smiled. She seemed puzzled.

"She's a piece of my past that stays special," I said. "I don't need to talk. She doesn't need to talk. There's a connection that doesn't need words, but, even so, fills a body's spirit. We have that. I just need to see her."

"You won't get her upset?"

"I won't get her upset."

She led me to a room that was obviously an add on. It was large, sunny. The walls paneled with rich, mellow, light brown stained planks. Across one wall was a large section of sliding glass doors accessing passage to a railed patio. The patio was empty except for a large, rounded, metallic pan, appearing to be from an old barbequing structure. Filled with birdseed, it had been placed on the floorboards near the sliding glass doors. Inside the room where I was standing, a padded rocking chair, facing the glass, sat waiting for occupancy. Harriet's. It would be hers. I imagined her sitting there, watching the birds feed. I smiled, thinking of bluebirds, wrens, finches, and oh, the cardinals, the beast of small birds, attacking the others, driving them away, feasting alone.

I turned to view the rest of the room. There was a bed, single-size, its cover rumpled, pillow lightly indented . . . traces left from a resting body. And there, next to it, Harriet sat in a paisley, fabriced recliner, its bottom cushion barely sinking under her fading weight. Her eyes were closed; her hands, folded, resting on the Bible, lying on her lap.

I stood by the glass doors and watched her. Pale, the skin on her face sagged, and her scalp showed pink where her hair was not enough to cover it. My eyes followed the droop of her sunken body to the bones of remembered graceful hands, rising and falling with the rhythm of her words, now with fingers, twisted and swollen at the knuckles, and on the top of those hands, veins swelled purple. There was little left of physical beauty, yet she was lovely.

Sometimes our hearts see clearer than our eyes.

Her lids rose, closed, and opened again. She smiled.

"It's me, Harriet. Cora Pooler." I went to her, pulled a small chair from the nearby vanity, sat, and took her hands in mine. They were silky, soft and warm.

Bending close, I lay my forehead, gently, against her hair, and I whispered in her ear, "Do you know me?" There was a slight movement, and I moved away from her, less close, and looked at her face. She was still smiling. Yet, I wasn't sure she knew it was me. It didn't matter. It was good to simply be near her, to fill with the thoughts and feelings of her, of us, gathered together in my soul and my head.

"Do you remember," I said, as I smoothed my hand over hers, "the last times I saw you, in the park, in the storeroom, when we, I, spoke of old days? The twins. Violet and Lily. And you remembered how they ran down the hill, their pails filled with vegetables from *maem's* garden, to exchange for penny candy? And eggs. I brought you eggs. Fresh eggs. Nearly every day. And do you remember when I came back to Wander Lane, twenty years gone, and you sewed an Amish dress for me? And, do you recall how bravely you secreted *maem* in the storeroom where no one could see a disobeying mother holding her shunned daughter? You were always there for me. Even though I left Wander Lane a second time, thought I'd never come back, but did. You helped me then.

I paused, swallowed, sighed small, and spoke. "Yes, I did come back then, and I'm back again now. And I need your help.

"I need you to listen. I know there are pockets in your heart where love is stored. And love gives strength, even when it's silent, it reaches out. Sitting here beside you, I feel the accumulation of all the special moments we've had, that are, even when we're unaware, kept within our being, and even as memories and feelings grow old and fade, they leave a residue of the wonder of love and friendship and connection.

"It's enough to sit here, close beside you, and feel the oneness that is ours, feel the acceptance of the essence of me joined to you."

I lifted my hand and cupped the line of her face. She leaned her head into my hand, and it was comfort.

After a bit, I slid my hand from her face, across her shoulder and down her arm to rest again on her hands.

"There are things I want to know, to understand, to change. I'm bewildered now. I sit here so quiet with you, my body still, but inside I am roaring. Turmoil leaps and crashes against my soul. I came to Wander Lane and found Lily buried outside the hallowed place of her dead, Amish brethren. Punished for taking her life, deciding it was worth nothing and had to be killed. I couldn't accept that. I went looking for evidence that her death was an accident, but, Harriet, I'm not finding it. And a doubt is making a small, stealthy creep into my brain. Could she have done that?

"And Harriet, there's more. Who can anticipate the tentacles that stretch evil from a deed that is meant to bring solace and hope and a way to live without shame? I took the baby from Lily. I thought I did what was right. But it wasn't. And that one action stretched through the years and reaped a havoc that seemed not to be stoppable. Lily is dead. How she died, accident or intentional, I don't know. But I know she was haunted by the loss of her child. And I know her sense of obedience was strong. Could the guilt of her lifting her skirt, sinning, birthing a child out of wedlock, and the weakness of allowing another to bear the burden of her sin, plus the loss of the child that had lain in her body so long and so loved, could it have bred a sorrow so big it could not have been held any longer . . . and she ended it? Could my Lily do that? Could her grief overpower the beliefs, the pressure of right, the joy of life? I don't know, Harriet. I don't know.

"And added to that, there is a child, born of a relationship not sanctioned by God. Only I know that, and now I'm telling you. Because I don't know what to do. And you have never judged me, never given me false words, never turned me away. I believe you hear my words now, and I know you so well and so dearly, I think I can absorb the words you speak without sound. They come through the unexplained senses that travel from one heart to another. And so, I tell you, Lily's child, Talitha, has given birth. The child was born of her second husband, Willie. My brother. Her uncle. Not known to be so by Talitha. Also unknown to Willie. And I don't know what to do with that knowledge.

I moved my eyes from our hands, hers spread under mine, to her face. Her eyes were set on mine. I couldn't read them. I pressed my lips together and smiled wanly. My words were gone. I knew no more to say. It was then, a most opportune time, Louise came into the room. "You've been here awhile. It's time for her to rest."

I nodded. She'd spoken gently, but firmly.

"I'll leave you to say good-bye to her."

I nodded again. "Thank you."

I bowed my head and closed my eyes, listened to Louise walk away. When I could no longer hear her, I raised my head and looked long at Harriet. Finally, I looked away, lifted my hands from hers, and as I did, I saw a twitching, a slight tapping of one finger. I looked up at her face, again, and sensed a struggle, a yearning, emanating from her eyes. And I knew. I looked down at her finger slowly rising up and down upon her Bible.

"You're right, Harriet—God," I said. I smiled. A feeble tapping appendage, Harriet's finger showed me where to go for relief, comfort and direction. "He's always there. God. Thank you, Harriet. You help me still. You've sent me to the right place."

Chapter Thirty-Four

Three days later, Harriet died.

She'd left her Bible to me. Her hope. Her peace. Her legacy.

After her funeral, I took the Book and sat alone in my motel room leafing through the pages. A folded paper slipped from the Bible onto the floor. I lifted it, carefully unfolded it, and read it.

Dear God,

This will be the last time I'm able to write you. My mind grows fuzzy and my fingers stiff. I know I'm near the time I'll be leaving my home, the trees, the birds, the untamed animals, my family . . . those related by blood and those related by heart. There is so much I've watched through the glass doors. The soil I've trod and farmed. The animals you send to comfort, to remind there is life beyond me . . . four-footed, winged, tamed, wild . . . all living things made by You, loved by You. The clouds You ride in Your wind-driven chariot. And the family I've encircled in my arms and held as tight as I could. I'll be glad to be done with the pain and the weariness. But I hope there will be moments in heaven, or perhaps, hours, you will let me look down on them, check and make sure they're doin' good.

But Father, so many times, breathing and being, living the years You've given me, existing on this land where You placed me, struggling to live right on this hard-living earth, I've worried I'm not good enough to walk through the door that leads to Your kingdom, that leads to You. I've made so many mistakes, said so many unkind words, left so many things undone. And that's when I worry that You won't want me. I get scared. And that's when I go to Your words, here in the Bible, for assurance, for a reminder of Your love, and I read, hear with my heart, the words on the pages. Your words. Your Word. And it's true, I can't be good enough by myself. So, You gave me Jesus. And He loves me, And You love me, Father. Beyond measure. And it's okay. I'm okay. It's so simple. When I die, I'll be with you in Heaven. While I live, You're here with me on earth.

Thank you, Father.

I love You.

Harriet

I reread the note, the letter to God, and I wondered how many times, as she grew feebler and feebler, had she read and reread those fading words now on paper grown fragile at the creases and no longer white. I slid the note back into the Bible and sat quiet for a long time, not really thinking, but pondering, visualizing Harriet sitting in the rocker by the glass door, Bible on her lap, watching the birds feed and the trees beyond the yard sprout tiny, lime-green, spring buds . . . limbs, sun, and rain nourishing them to bright green, a lush home for summer birds, nests, egg laying, and bird birth. Summer leading into to fall. Weather changing and beginning its phase of drying the leaves, but as compensation, exalting them with color . . . red, copper, orange, yellow. And finally, stems brittled, the leaves separate from the tree and drop to the ground.

Cycle completed. Months to pass before new leaves burst forth. But during that time of waiting, the magic of white, sparkling flakes falling from above, settling on trees and ground, painting a splendid new picture beyond the glass doors. Not always placid. Sitting in furnace heat, afghaned in her rocker, watching the winter world outside, Harriet had, also, been also privy to vast living murals of hurling winds shooting piercing snow pellets against the glass doors, and other times, flakeless winds lifting the snow, spinning it in flimsy curtains of white, sometimes a fragile twisting mass, sometimes a delicate, swirling pattern, sometimes a solid bulk. But as she sat in warmth and watched, always beautiful.

I was happy Harriet had seen the splendor of fall. I wondered, hoped she'd be able to look down on the coming exquisiteness of winter. Then I smiled. Would she want to? Heaven promised to be more glorious than earth. And Harriet was wise. She would choose well.

I kept the Bible in my car. It was there I found myself each day. It was good to have Harriet's Bible by my side. And it was good to open its pages daily. Grounding wisdom.

Gentled by Harriet's death and admonished by the finality of it, I tempered the anger and pressuring gravity fed by my own negative retention of events occurred years before.

As the mourners stood before Harriet's coffin, sadness reigned. *Sadness*. No harsh words. No reprimands. No scowls or hateful faces. All petty, or great animosity, melted away or, at least, was set aside for a time. An interlude of common sensitivity. It left a pocket of peace within my heart. I hoped it would last.

And so, I made my way to Violet's house. To mend. To find words that would fuse our sisterhood. To explain. To touch. To repair.

I'd seen Violet at the funeral home. Standing with *maem* and *da,* with Aaron and Willie and Talitha. They stayed apart from me. Not maliciously. There was more a sense of demureness, dignity. When our eyes met, I saw no rejection. I thought, hoped, I saw love. Even so, as I drove, apprehension mingled with the want for full acceptance. I was scared. Home territory is security, fosters the release of the heart's reality. Violet reflected no animosity in the funeral home, but I couldn't be sure it wouldn't surface in her house.

I knocked at her door. She opened it.

We looked at one another. It seemed a long time.

Then she opened her arms, and I went into them. I didn't know if she'd forgiven my accusation of Baby Clare's conception, but we were sisters, and time can dull unwanted words, true or not, when they are enclosed within love. And in that moment, for that moment, I knew we were, in the deepest apprehension of the word, sisters.

Arms locked, we went into the living area. We sat, each in a rocker facing the other, chairs spaced in a manner that encouraged the easing and deliberating of thoughts, needs, opinions. On the floor next to Violet's choice of chair, a basket of yarn with a pair of thick, wooden needles stabbed into a pink yarn ball, sat waiting.

"You're knitting?" I said.

She smiled. "Mittens for Baby Clare. She'll need 'em come winter."

I swallowed. Took a deep breath. "Is she doing well . . . it's been long since I've seen her?"

It took awhile for Violet to answer.

"She's healthy." She straightened, hesitated, then blurted her words. "She's slow, Cora. Not doing like the other babies did. Willie's babies, grown now, working their own farms. And not like Talitha's little girl . . . that girl is sharp and doing regular stuff a little girl does . . . same as other little girls."

"You mean Katy?"

"Yes, Katy. She's a real help to her *maem*.

I waited. I wanted this visit to go well. I didn't want to anger her or cause her to withdraw. She lowered her head and clasped her hands in her lap, and I could see a tremble in them. I stayed silent. Violet was hurting. Before, when I'd left her house, I'd given her cause to deliberate an unwanted and shameful circumstance. I doubted she'd shared that burden with anyone, including Aaron.

"You know, Cora, this talking has to wind around Lily. I can't speak of other things. Aaron has been stern with me. He'll not tolerate me saying words not pertaining to her." She rubbed her fingers over her eyes. "He would have me shunned."

"I understand. And so far, we have done that. Baby Clare was born of Talitha, Lily's daughter. It wouldn't be so if I had not taken Lily's baby, if I had left her for Lily to raise." I shuddered. "Nor would the child be as she is, if I had told of her whereabouts."

Violet bit her lip and shook her head. "And oh, God, I wish you had done that."

"Have you told anyone?" I asked, hoping she had not. It would stir a cloud of anguish.

"I can't. I can barely think the words. How could I ever say them . . . and who would I say them to?"

"I don't know, but maybe we should think about it," I said softy.

"Telling?" She leaned forward. Looked intently at me.

"We can't let Talitha have more children. Not with Willie."

"Maybe, she won't. She's getting old."

I smiled. "No, Violet, she's not. She's got a lot of baby-making years ahead of her."

"What about Willie? He's getting old. Maybe he's too old." She gave a sharp nod. "That would be *gut*."

"Yes, that would be good, but since he doesn't produce the egg that grows the child, I don't think his age makes much difference."

"Probably not." Violet scowled and shook her head. "Who else knows?"

"No one." I hesitated. "Except Lowell Parker."

"The Sheriff."

"Uh-huh."

"Is he going to arrest them? Willie and Talitha?" She brought her hand up and slapped her head.

I laughed. "No, this one he'll leave to the Amish . . . actually to me.

"It's not funny, Cora."

"No, it's not," I agreed. "And we need to decide what we're going to do about it."

"Maybe, nothing. Maybe, she just won't have any more kids, and maybe, Baby Clare won't ever marry and have babies. That would take care of everything."

"That's a lot of maybes, Violet." She wrung her hands. "I know."

I bent my head, rubbed the furrows in my forehead.

"We have to do something," I said. "I'm just not sure what."

"No, we don't. We don't have to say anything."

"And if we don't, and she has more children?"

"They could be fine." She set her face firm and glared at me. "And if they're not, we love them and take care of them. Just as we would any Amish baby. Child. Adult . . . Baby Clare."

"We can't do that," I said.

"We can. I can. You can. And Sheriff Parker will keep quiet."

"And the Bible says?" I looked at her. There was no softness there. In that moment, there was no Violet softness.

"I know what it says. And I also know the shame and pain . . . one child shunned, the other lying outside the fence . . . do you think *maem* and *da* could live through this, too?"

"Yes," I answered, "their faith is strong."

"And what about me?" She stood, walked to the door, hit it with her fist, walked back. "What about me? You think Aaron wouldn't take that news and lay a big part of the blame on me? And no, I'm not responsible for any part of it. But he still would. He'd say I let you take the baby and give her away to who knew who, so I played a part in all this." She pointed her finger at me. "But *You*. *You* don't know Aaron anymore. He's got that *Ornung* seared strong in his head, every unwritten clause, every unwritten

270

sentence, every unwritten word in it. There's no deviation, no interpreting . . . except his." She clenched her teeth. Gasped. "And if we told, I'd hear it and hear it and hear it. The shame we brought upon this Amish community." Her shoulders slumped, and she closed her eyes. "We can't do it, Cora. We can't tell."

I rose, nodded. "You're right. *We* can't." I ran my hand down her arm. "It'll work out, Violet. I promise. It'll work out."

I left her house. *I'll work it out.*

Chapter Thirty-Five

I'll work it out. Those unspoken words hung in my head. Good words. Positive words. Determined. But how would I do it?

I drove the Amish roads, deep in thought, eyes straight ahead, seeing only the dirt bordered, blacktopped road, black, brown, and spotted horses, black buggies, and sometimes I saw, as I passed those slow trotting former racers, a flash of black garb and whip. I wondered if those horses missed the thrill of flat-out speed, heads stretched forward, haunches wet with sweat, hoofs pounding ground. But like people, animals grow old. Old humans are put in resting homes. Old horses are put out to slaughter or pasture . . . or Amish buggies.

Finally, I stopped at the bottom of the cemetery hill. My eyes followed the path up to the gravesites, to the fence that guarded the privileged dead, to the tree that shadowed Lily's lonely burial spot, and I thought how embittered I'd become.

I felt tears locked and wanting release behind my eyes. If I let them loose, I knew they would drown me. I had no answers to still their pushing fullness. The only thing I had to offer was guilt, and if I gave them that, their force would amplify, and I would be lost in their mighty drench.

Laying on the seat next to me, was Harriet's Bible. Now mine. Given to me to *use*. I ran my fingers over the textured cover. I knew the words on the pages inside. I'd read them many times, studied them, memorized some. It seemed long ago. I still prayed, told God my sorrow, asked for His help, but foolishly, thinking only of my own selfish need, I didn't quiet my words and listen. To Him.

I picked up the Bible, remembered reading verses that had always, before overwhelming guilt soaked my soul, brought sorrowfulness and happiness into reasonable perspective and solution. I searched and found their pages and read those words again.

Who has measured the waters in the hollow of his hand, or
with the breadth of his hand marked off the heavens?
Who has held the dust of the earth in a basket, or weighed
the mountains on the scales and the hills in a balance?
Who has understood the mind of the Lord, or instructed
Him as His counselor?
Whom did the Lord consult to enlighten Him, and who
taught Him the right way?
Who was it that taught Him knowledge or showed Him the
path of understanding?
Do you not know? Have you not heard?
Has it not been told you from the beginning?
He sits enthroned above the circle of the earth.
The Lord is the everlasting God,
The Creator of the ends of the earth.
(Isaiah 40:12-14, 21-22)

I looked through the windshield and up to the sky. Great, white, majestic clouds moved slowly over the incessant blue.

You're up there, God. Beyond my eyes, but not beyond my heart. And I need you. My wisdom is slight. Your wisdom and love are endless and perfect. I need you. I can't solve these dilemmas alone.

You know my needs, my inability to settle and make right the conundrums of loved ones. I've prayed for clarification and resolution so many times. "Help me find and sort and resolve the events of Lily's death. Help me know what to do with the knowledge I have of Baby Clare's parentage." These pleas I've prayed to You, over and over, but I've not heard Your voice reply. So attuned to my own thoughts of resolve, I haven't listen to Yours. Thank You for Your patience. Please forgive my reliance on self.

I wait for Your answers, Your guidance. Please open my mind, heart, and ears to know

All glory to You.

I pray in the name of Jesus Christ, my Lord and Savior.

Amen

I got out of my car, walked up the hill to the cemetery, sat by Lily's grave, and waited.

Prayers are not always answered as quickly as wanted or with the simple resolution desired. I sat on the grass by Lily's grave for a long time. Though my will concentrated, strained, to hear God's voice, through thought or feeling or ears, I didn't. And finally, I left.

There were still many hours left in the day, but the weight of my failures, my inadequacies, tired my body, my mind, the depths of reason, and I drove, weary, purposelessly, until my car, finally, took me back to Wander Lane and to my motel.

The day was still bright with sunlight, but the darkness in my soul bade me sleep. I walked, empty of thought and feeling, from the car, to the motel, through the lobby, into the elevator, out of the elevator, down the hall, into my room, and fell on my bed. Slept.

I didn't wake until morning.

A sleep that is birthed from the heaviness of burden, when wakened, should leave one groggy, attacked by a bright, glaring sun pouring through unstreaked glass into glazed, slant-shut eyes, and then tackled by furniture sitting in the path of an unsteady body.

That wasn't me.

I woke refreshed and happy.

And I knew what to do.

God had done His work.

I readied myself for the day, went down to the lobby, grabbed a banana from the free breakfast spread, and went to my car.

I drove to Jesse Miller's farm.

It was early morning when I arrived. It seemed, Jesse and his sons had already readied the cows for milking, for he was taking what must have been the first pail of milk from the barn to the house. He saw my car and came to it.

His greeting was brief. As this was the beginning of the harvest season, I knew he had much work to do and his time was, therefore, limited, but this was important, and he was a preacher. It was his job to settle matters of dispute and impropriety.

"I need to talk with you," I said.

He nodded. "Is it urgent?"

"Urgent is of individual relevance," I said, "and I can wait until it's convenient for you." It was difficult to be patient, but my problem was long in the making. His situation was immediate. Before winter settled in, there was much work to be done. He needed the hours of daylight to care for his cattle and crops.

"Then a time after dinner would be *gut?*" he asked.

"Afternoon would be fine." I said, and then thought of his fields needing to be tended.

"Perhaps, after supper would better. I know you have much work to do."

"This afternoon. After dinner. The sons will take care of work."

I nodded. "After dinner. That would be *gut.*"

The morning hours sat free waiting for me to fill them. I thought of going to Violet's, then thought not. The ease of body and mind upon waking was still with me. I didn't want to muddy it with argument or ill feelings. From the same reasoning, I thought it best to delay questioning any of those who might have information regarding Lily's demise.

I knew a place of pleasure.

I drove to the schoolhouse. Children. When one is filled with dismay or delight, it makes no difference which, the sight of children mends or enhances the mind's inner workings.

I parked where the views of the school's front door and playground were clear. Mid-morning, the children would spill out that door and for a time of bodily freedom, shed the cloak of classroom restriction, run, laugh, kick and toss balls, punch and roll, and share secrets . . . play.

As I waited for school to release its captives, I thought of how I might direct my appeal to Preacher Miller. He was the same age as Lily and probably was thinking our meeting would involve his contemplations regarding her death, but I didn't want her to be the subject or even an underlying shadow in our discourse. It was imperative we stay on topic—the resolution of Willie and Talitha's relationship. And I would need to be ever cognizant of his Amishness and his position, otherwise it was likely he would grow reticent, and I would fail to accomplish resolution for Willie and Talitha's untenable situation.

I watched the children come out of the small, white schoolhouse, the last a little lad, probably this fall was his first season of learning. And while the others came swiftly and easily down the building's stairs, he, little legs scrambling to keep up with the others, tumbled from the last step. Apparently hearing his cry, a little girl, not much bigger than he, perhaps a sister, turned, shook her head, helped him up, brushed him off, and ran away, off to a group of long-skirted girls, gathered and giggling, beneath a huge, old oak, the tree already changing its summer green to fall orange, yellow, and red.

The little boy stood by the stairs, observing the circled boys tossing a ball at the dodging boy in the center of the circle. He frowned, and I thought he might think it odd that the boys were trying to hit their friend with a ball. Violence against a fellow Amisher was not a desired behavior, and young though he might be, he would know that.

I smiled and got out of my car to view his reaction sharper. He watched a while, then, apparently satisfied, moved his foot around in the dirt at the bottom of the stairs, then bent, picked up a stick and dragged lines in that same dirt. Perhaps a budding artist. When he seemed to tire of that activity, he threw the stick as far as he could, and half-hopping, looked around the area. When his eyes turned on me, he stopped. Stared. Tilted his head. Put his thumb in his mouth, not to suck, but to hold between his teeth. After a bit, he walked toward me, stopped, glared, then came closer. He stopped and wrinkled his face.

"Are you a man?"

He was a brave boy. I was sure his mother would not have approved and had made it plain to him that he was not to speak to people he did not know.

"No. I'm not a man." I spoke in German, as had he. I realized he wouldn't know English yet. He was too little and would only be starting to learn English words as taught in school, but never used in the home. "I'm a woman."

"You're wearing pants."

I smiled and looked down at my jeans. "You're right. I should be wearing a skirt. Do you think I should go to my home and put on a dress?"

He nodded and ran away.

I did go back to the motel and change my clothes. The child was brighter than me. Of course, it was *unseemly* to go to the preacher dressed in *unseemly* clothing. *Unseemly* to him. And I wanted him to concentrate on my words, not my attire. Thus, I chose a simple skirt of dark color and a high-necked, long-sleeved, white blouse. Flat shoes. Washed off makeup. Pulled back hair. Suitable. I looked in the mirror. A gold neck chain flashed in the glass. I removed necklace, watch, and ring. Even more suitable.

I was ready to make my case to Preacher Miller.

Chapter Thirty-Six

As I drove onto his driveway, I saw Preacher Miller settled in a rocker, on his front porch. One leg crossed over his knee, he pushed the wooden floor with his other foot, affecting a slow, soothing sway, apparently lulling him enough to close his eyes and droop his chin against his chest. I left the car and walked up the porch steps, and as I drew nearer to him, wondered if I might hear snores. I didn't. Just a couple of low snorts. I smiled. Even as he slept, he kept the rocker moving.

I bent to bring him back to awareness, and then thought better of it. It didn't seem the best of ideas to embarrass him. Awkward moments are not always conducive for beginning a congenial investigative interrogation. I really did not want to humiliate the preacher. So, I went back to my car, opened the passenger door and slammed it shut.

It worked. Head jerked up and crossed leg hit the floor.

He rose and came to meet me. A simple '*greesa*,' a returned 'hello,' and he led me up the porch steps and to a second rocker.

He was the first to speak. Firm. Polite. Amish frugal.

"The sheriff instructed us to help you determine the events of Lily Pooler's last days, so how can I help?"

"That's not why I'm here."

"Then I can't help you."

"It's not me that needs help. It's Willie and Talitha Pooler that we need to talk about.

And Baby Clare."

"I'm afraid I can't discuss them with you." Looking at his hands folded on his lap, he spoke kindly, a shade apologetically. Then he raised his head and turned to me. "Are you forgetting the rules of shunning? It's only Lily of whom I may speak."

"Hear me out," I said, "because this *is* about Lily."

Face emptied of expression, he raised his eyebrows, spoke, "How is that so?"

"You were here, a young man, Lily's age, when I was shunned, shamed before the brethren for bearing a child, giving her away, and refusing to name the father." I spoke directly to his face, and though I could not read his thoughts, didn't know if he was judging or accepting, he didn't turn away. "No one knew, then, the child was, in fact, Lily's. Except me and Violet and the woman who helped us, Olivia. And my mother suspected." Silent, he kept his eyes on me.

"A home was found for her, the baby I'd called Annabelle. An Amish home. A way from here. Sugar Creek. She was given to a woman who had birthed a dead baby. No one knew. Except Olivia's Agency from which the baby'd been placed. The midwife. And the new mother. And later, me . . . and Harriet."

I paused and when the silence grew too long, Preacher Miller spoke.

"So how did you know where she went?"

"I saw her as a grown woman in Sugar Creek. In an Amish buggy. She was golden-haired and beautiful, the image of Lily."

"It could have been a young woman not Lily, but looked like her."

"No. It was verified. By Olivia." I looked across the yard to the barns. Jesse Miller's sons were hitching two majestic work horses to a wagon, and then, finished with that task, they jumped on the wagon and made ready to head out. One of them, the son with the slender body, younger, as he'd walked to the wagon had brushed his hand over the sun-glistened red-gold hair of one steed's massive flank as he passed it. I smiled. It was good to see an Amish animal appreciated.

"So, you know the whereabouts of Lily Pooler's child. What does that have to do with Willie Pooler's family?"

"Your sons appear to be helpful to you," I said, watching his muscular son lift the reins and drop them heavy on the horses. I knew I was delaying the passage of words that would spill from my mouth to his ears and reveal the unintended sin of Willie and Talitha.

"They are," Preacher Miller answered, his eyes on his sons.

"Are they going to be bringing in a second cutting of hay?"

"They're going to load hampers and take tomatoes down to Wander Lane."

"A good crop this year?"

"Plentiful."

I pressed my fingers against my lips. Closed my eyes and swallowed.

"Cora?"

"The adopting mother named the child, Talitha," I said quietly. "And that baby, Talitha, is Lily's daughter.

A soft swoosh of air expelled through his lips. His measured, steady rocking stopped. I waited for him to speak.

"Then Baby Clare is Willie's niece."

"Yes."

"I see." The rocking resumed. "A sin."

"Unintended." I sat rigid in my chair, not rocking.

"You read the Bible, Cora?"

"Yes."

"Numbers?"

"I've read that book."

"Then you know God required the Israelites to make offerings for both intentional and unintentional sin."

"For forgiveness."

"Yes."

I waited for him to say more, but he didn't. In my head, clear and vivid, was the image of Willie and Talitha, holding Baby Clare, standing before the brethren, confessing to a sin they didn't even yet know they'd committed.

"Can the confession be made just to you, Preacher Miller?" I asked, breaking the silence. "In private so there is no shame."

He looked at me. His eyes were gentle. "There is no shame, Cora. They didn't know. But there has been sin, and they must ask for forgiveness. And God will give it. And the brethren will respond with love, acceptance and understanding."

"And Baby Clare?"

"She is God's child. She will be loved and cared for. By all of us." His eyes were gentle; his words, spoke calm. "It will be all right."

"Done? Will it all be done with the confession?"

"No. I will speak with Willie and Talitha. Some things must change."

"In their physical relationship?"

"Yes."

I struggled to know, if I could ask more. I could tell he perceived my quandary.

"My job is to direct, explain and counsel." He bit his lip, nodded. Half-smiled. "Yours is to accept and love."

I drove to the cemetery, parked my car, and as I walked up the hill to Lily's grave, I smelled fall. Air cleaned by an early morning drizzle had gifted the area with a teasing breeze scented with the releasing crisp tang of drying, dying leaves and the sweetness of damp grass. I played a tantalizing game with my nasal senses. I took my shoes off and stepped from the dirt pathway onto the grass, paused to wiggle my toes in the green blades, and then walked the moistened ground to the top of the hill.

Once there, I stood a few moments looking over the fence. My eyes wandered over the monuments, plain, simple, alike. A modest beauty . . . for those free of sin. I turned from the fence and looked towards Lily's resting place. Outside the fence. Plain, simple, headstone identical to those inside the fence. I shook my head. Same ground, same monument. Different resting places.

My eyes slid to the space next to Lily's grave. Mattie's spot. A mass of golden rod lay over that grass. There was nothing on Lily's plot. No matter. Mums would be prettier, and though it was a bit too early for their blossoms to spread resplendent in color and fullness, I vowed, when that day came, I would fill my arms with pink, maroon, and white flowers and cover Lily's grave, with a plethora of color, and put none on Mattie's space. No, I would pluck one white flowered stem from the abundance of Lily's and lay it over whatever or whoever was buried in Mattie's spot. Dog, silver bracelet, diary? Whatever. I was convinced there was something there of value to Mattie.

I smiled a smile of repentance. Of course, I would share my flowers with Mattie. Though a bit of pettiness is sometimes a release of unrealistic thought and unjustified jealousy, and if acknowledging pettiness retained is useless and inhibiting, it clears the mind and makes room for joy to flow back in. Even so, I still wanted to know what secrets that bit of ground held. Perplexed, I spread my sweater over the grass by Lilly's stone and sat. Thought. Pondered Mattie's changed behavior. I could think of no reason for it to be from my words or deeds towards her, so, logically, the source of her attitude was Schrock.

I took a deep breath and emptied my mind of wondering thoughts. Serene, I closed my eyes and spoke a silent prayer of thanksgiving. God had been good to me that day. I smiled. My heart was pleasured that I *recognized* God had been good to me. I needed to share that goodness with Violet. I wasn't sure she would agree.

Chapter Thirty-Seven

As fall sets in, the lingering remnants of summer spewed forth a final blast of beauty, filling the ditches, with masses of pungent yellow, white and pale lilac yarrow, sturdy Black-eyed Susans and delicate Queen Anne's lace. My eyes feasted on the colors; my nose, on the wafting aroma; my heart, on the splendor of nature's generous bounty.

I knew late afternoon would not be a good time to visit Violet. She would welcome me with words but having been Amish and thus knowing the spreading time needed to prepare an adequate meal, though less so for supper than dinner, I would see in her eyes and her likely taut face, unintentionally expressed displeasure. I went anyway. Her need, my need, to be done with dawdling over Willie and Talitha's unacceptable relationship and to move in a direction that could resolve the problems within it were of far more importance than the preparation of an adequate meal for Aaron. Surely a left-over bowl of stew, a slice, or two, or more . . . if his hunger was at a horrendous level of want . . . of dinner's left-over bread, and an apple should be adequate. At least for one night in his life. But, again, Violet probably would not agree with me.

She didn't. When I told her I had something really important to talk about with her, she said, "later" and continued her bustle about the kitchen.

"It's about Willie and Talitha," I countered.

"Doesn't matter. Aaron's been working long in the fields today. He has to use every hour of daylight he can get. Days are getting shorter. Makes his day longer. Even does the barn chores after dark." She turned, looked at me, and scowled. "He comes first. Willie and Talitha, after."

I sighed. She meant it.

"You can eat with us." she said. "But no talking."

I lifted my eyebrows.

She shook her big, wooden spoon at me, "Not even about Lily," turned back to the stove and stirred. "No talking, just eating."

I smiled. Maybe, left-over stew. Looked that way from the smatterings of juicy red the swung spoon had made on table, stove . . . and my sleeve.

"Just as soon as he's done eating, he'll go right to bed . . . and sleep. Won't ask any question if I tell him we, you and me, are going to be talking about Lily and nothing else." She shook her head. "Probably won't even hear me. The man's dead tired."

He came in. He washed his hands. He sat. We sat. He bowed his head. We prayed. Silently. I heard his spoon hit his bowl. We lifted our heads. We ate. We finished. He went to bed.

Violet accepted my help, and we cleaned the kitchen quickly.

"You want to sit on the porch? The evening air's cooling. Pleasant," Violet said. "And Aaron, if he's too tired to find sleep come easy, won't be able to hear us."

I nodded, hoping her suggestion Aaron wouldn't hear us

indicated we might speak of topics excluding Lily . . . if Violet would accept Preacher Millers' resolution, and we could get beyond Willie, Talitha, and Baby Clare. And for this evening, this one time, even disregard Lily. Just talk about the rest of the family—*Maem* and *Da* and the brothers. Their current lives. Our memories. What was, before I changed the color of our lives.

We went out to the porch and settled in roomy rockers. Violet had brought quilts, in case the air grew too cool. I took mine and hugged it to me. Not for warmth, but for the comfort of loved, Amish moments remembered, as its scent and softness encompassed me. We rocked for awhile. Silent. The darkness wrapped a calm peacefulness over us. I prayed it would last. And it did. For a time. A short time.

"I don't like to fight," Violet said softly, breaking the silence.

"I love you, Violet," I answered, just as softly. "Do you remember Plumpy?"

Violet smiled. "That fat, furry, little dog Lily found and claimed."

"Found him in a ditch . . . she said."

"Stole him from the Hershbergers."

"She really loved that dog." Violet laughed. "He was ugliest dog I ever saw."

"*Maem* made her take him back."

"Not before *Maem* scolded her for calling him fat . . . *not nice to call a body, even a dog, fat. He's just a little large in the belly. Plump.*"

"I miss *Maem*," I said.

"Easy enough to see her. Just confess. That simple."

"Confess what?"

"That you were wrong to leave the brethren, and you want

to be Amish again. Accepted Amish."

"*Accepted* Amish?"

"You'll always be Amish, Cora. Right now, you're just a wayward Amisher, a practicing Englisher." Her rocker kept moving, and she didn't look at me. "Easy to change."

I bit my lip. Peace seemed to be leaving. I thought it time to move from my Amish status and tell of my meeting with the preacher. Get it over with. Hope she'd be satisfied, and we could go back to amiable reminiscing.

"I talked with Preacher Miller."

Her rocking stopped. She didn't look at me, fixed her eyes on something straight ahead, kept them there the entire time I spoke of my meeting with the preacher, his assessment of the situation, the conclusions he made, and the meting out of chastisement.

When I was done, she turned her head and glared at me.

"*He's going to put her in front of the congregant and make her tell everybody she had sex with her uncle.*"

"Maybe not so crudely. But, yes."

"Isn't there any other way?" Face pale, words hollow, her words fell as helpless.

"He makes the decisions."

She put her hands over her face and shook it side to side, as if she could shake those words, those thoughts, out of her head.

"The Amish have heard worse," I said.

"I don't think so!"

"Yes, Violet, they have. How many sins, deliberately done, have you heard confessed before the brethren? Hundreds. This one was not deliberate. Are not those done with knowledge worse than those done without one knowing wrong is being done. When you pray, Violet, do you not ask for forgiveness for intentional sins *and* for those you have done without knowing or meaning to—unintentional sin? And does not God forgive those sins? All those for which you have asked forgiveness? Of course, He does."

I placed my hand on Violet's arm. She dropped her hands from her face and looked at me. Tears were thick on her face, and her pale cheeks were mottled with blotchy patches of red.

"It will be so painful," she said. "For them . . . for *Maem* and *Da.*"

"It will be," I agreed, "but you're forgetting, the Amish are a loving and forgiving people. Sincerely so. Preacher Miller will explain the situation, and he will pray *with* the brethren. And Violet, they will understand. They will *help* Willie and Talitha through this. There will not be criticism. The Amish are strong and accepting. It's, probably, the thing I miss most about not being a part of this community anymore. The oneness. The knowing whatever the problem, you're not alone. Your difficulty and its rectification are shared by all. So, leave it all in the hands of Preacher Miller. He'll lead in what is right."

"I love you, Cora," Violet whispered.

"I know." I slid my hand down her arm and took her hand in mine.

"Remember Lily's stone?" Violet smiled wistfully. "She thought if you threw it in Wander Lake, all your wishes would come true."

"I remember." I squeezed her hand and smiled.

"She kept it. I found it, after she died. In her drawer, under clothes. I have it now in my drawer."

I felt tears slide down my cheeks. "I'm glad you have it."

"Cora?"

I turned my head to her.

"Do you think Lily can see us? Do you think she knows her child had a child, Cora?" She whispered her words through the air to me. A plea. "That she's a *mommi*? Do you think her spirit is locked in that box outside the fence? Punished. Unable to get out, rise, and walk through God's door into *Himmel*? Cora, can none of us, alive or inside that fence, help her?"

"I don't know if she can see us, but I believe she is with God. She was a good, Amish girl. When she was little, I remember sitting with her, kneeling with her, hearing her prayers. Sweet voice, so earnest. Yes, I believe she's with Jesus."

"Then why don't you let this cemetery stuff end?"

"Because she was a good, honest, loving Amish girl, and she deserves to be thusly remembered. Inside the fence. Untainted. Her remains honored the same as the others."

We sat silent for a long while watching the evening sky darken to night. A restful peace dropped over us. It stayed as we rocked, slowly, gently over Violet's Amish, porch floor. And I thought it would be hard to leave this place of my youth. But I knew I would. Eventually.

Chapter Thirty-Eight

Sun poured light and warmth across my face. I snuggled into heated blankets and resisted that great source of brightness piercing through Violet's sparkling spare bedroom window urging me to open my eyes and rise. But finally, reluctantly, I did. And fortunately, Violet had left two, large, white washbowls of water and a bar of handmade soap on top of the dresser. One basin for washing. One basin for rinsing. Thoughtful. Amish.

I dipped my hands in one bowl and splashed my face with water. Cold water. Shivering cold water. I washed my body as quickly as I could, then opened bureau drawers looking for the clothes I'd left at Violet's. There were none there. Instead I saw a pile of the clean, folded clothes Violet had stacked on the chair next to the dresser. Amish clothes. Happily, I noted, not black. Dark green. A little better. Not much. However, I knew I'd left clothes, not only from the previous day, but also from my prior stay with Violet. Again, I looked in the bureau drawers, all of them. Nothing there, nothing hanging on pegs, so, I put on the Amish clothes. A pleasant smidgeon of Amish-feel came with the drop of their cloth over my body, along with a satisfaction from my fingers knowing to place straight pins in the right order and location on the Amish dress.

Even so, I wasn't bursting with happiness. My own clothes, except for my shoes, were missing. Even my underwear. Not good. I felt manipulated. I went to the window, looked, and, as I'd feared, found my clothing. Jeans, sweater and shirt pinned and drying on lines strung over Violet's front yard. For all to see and disapprove. But not my underwear. Flimsy and lacy, that would be drying in the house, secluded from curious eyes, in some hidden place. Not a surprise. Even if plain white and simple, they would not be fluttering on a clothesline, in the front yard. That would be shameful, for Violet—anger inducing for Aaron.

I shuddered. I should have ignored Violet's plea to stay the night, braved the lonely, dark roads and driven to my motel home the night before. On second thought, a few clothes on the line, though a reason for more shunned Cora head-shaking fodder, wasn't worth a worry. But criticism focused on Violet for washing a shunned sister's wardrobe might bear a bit more concern, might not be to the preachers' liking.

Dressed, I went downstairs, found the kitchen to be clean and empty. I'd really slept late. Breakfast had come, gone, been cleaned up, and Violet had taken my clothes without waking me, washed them and hung them to dry, and now it seemed Aaron and Violet, even as I still had wisps of the previous night's dreams stirring in my head, were about somewhere performing the work and responsibilities of dutiful Amish folk. I shrugged, glad I wasn't under the rules of Amish productivity, and hungry, I peeked in the refrigerator.

"Ahh." It looked like Violet had also prepared Aaron's dinner dessert. Flat rock pudding. Chocolate chip cookies sandwiched with peanut butter, broken, and stirred into fluffy whipped pudding. Heaven.

I spooned a good portion into a bowl and took it to the table. There was a note laying on the table. Big lettered and bold. **ESSA.** Eat. So, I did. I ate. She didn't say what I could eat. Just eat. So, I ate what was in the refrigerator. Aaron's pudding. But I'd left enough for him. At least, what I thought was enough for him.

It was good.

I was nearly finished when Violet came through the door, her arms laden with carrots, onions, and a cabbage. She looked at me, looked at the pudding filled spoon rising to my lips, said nothing with words, walked past me, and dumped the vegetables in the sink.

"You said eat," I defended myself. "There's plenty left in the refrigerator."

"You're welcome to whatever food is there," Violet said, her back to me. She picked up a brush and scrubbed at the garden dirt clinging to the vegetables. Her arm was moving fast, and I could hear the brush scrape hard against the vegetables' skin.

"You're angry," I said. "This is Aaron's pudding, isn't it? I probably took too much."

"I can't talk to you. Unless it's about Lily."

"You're being ridiculous. We've talked word after word without mentioning Lily, or only hinting at it, as we rationalized *Ordnung* rules. Many times. Many words. Let's just forget the silly rules and *talk*."

She turned and looked at me. Her face was pale. "It's not silly, Cora. It's how I live. It's what I live. You should know that. You lived that way once yourself. It wasn't silly to you then."

"No, it wasn't," I whispered.

"But," Violet said, taking the vegetables out of the sink, putting them on the table, taking two knives from a drawer, handing one to me, pointing to the carrots. She picked up an onion. "Today, I'll talk. About anything you want. And on Sunday, I'll confess. Maybe, be punished. Shunned for awhile. Probably not long. And Aaron will be mad. But that's what I'll have to do. And after this, Cora, no more."

"But you'll still be able to talk with me about Lily?"

"Yes."

"Then, while you're breaking your silly rule, I want you to tell me all about the brothers. Where they are. Their families. Why they left. How *Maem* really is. She looks so old. And *Da*. He's so angry with me. And Aaron. Why has he grown so angry? And what do you know about Mattie and Schrock? No Lily talk. Not now. I just want to know what is going on in my old, loved, missed Amish community. The whole of it. All the brethren gossip. I hunger to know everything, and there's no one to tell me. Just you."

So, while we peeled, sliced, and diced vegetables for Aaron's sausage and noodle dinner and his onion pie supper, Violet fueled my heart and head with a plethora of facts, images and emotions, all I'd missed, all that was still happening. I buried her words, current knowledge and remembrances, deep in my soul to be taken, treasured, and brought forth when I left Wander Lane and needed to reconnect the whole of whom I had been with the whole of whom I'd become. It was good. I was nearly satisfied. My brothers were well, busy, happy, familied. *Maem* and *Da*, growing old, but coping well with joy and adversity, content.

But there were questions that hadn't been answered;

circumstances and people she'd ignored. Most words she'd spoken had been spoken pleasantly . . . or near pleasantly. Easily accepted, not challenged by me.

When her synopsis was finished, I hoped she was ready to answer the hard questions. I was ready to ask them.

"Why is Aaron so hard, so angry?"

"He's not," she answered. Onion tears reddened her eyes. She swiped her hand across them.

"Don't do that," I said. "It makes the sting worse. Go wet a cloth and press it against your eyes. And tell me what's happening with you and Aaron."

"My eyes are okay and, anyway, I've got enough onions sliced. And I'm not sure it's any of your business what goes on between me and Aaron."

"I'm your sister, and it is. Besides, you said you'd talk about anything."

"I'm not sure I made such a definitive statement."

"Well, you kind of did. *Any thing I want to talk about.* Your words. And I want to talk about Aaron."

"Why?"

I didn't answer,

"Okay." She sighed. "There's not much to tell. He never paid much mind to me 'til after you left the second time. Ten years ago. He'd always been friendly . . . and helpful . . . with little things. He didn't have much to do with women. But after you left, he started giving me lots of attention. I kind of thought it was because he'd seen you and you brought back romantic feelings. And he courted me. He was fun to be with. Laughed a lot. Not excessively, but a lot.

"And you have to remember, we were getting older. It was

good, really good. And we got married. No kids. We're too old. But it was good." She paused and looked at me. "Until you came back this time. I don't know what happened. Or what he thinks. But he changed. Not much laughing now. Especially when you're around. It bothers me. Sometimes, I think he wishes I were you. I don't know. He's not mean. But he's different now. A threatening storm waiting to let loose a full outburst. That's what he's like. Only the pounding rain never comes. A few drops sometimes, but never a deluge." She looked down at the table, spoke quietly. "I think he still has feelings for you."

"Violet, don't be worrying about me being a problem. He's far from even liking me anymore." I paused, hoping my words alleviated doubt, but I wanted more. Something explaining such a great personality change. "What about Schrock? Could he be the problem?"

"I don't know. They've become real friendly. Wasn't that way before you came."

"If I were Aaron, I wouldn't pick Schrock to be a fun friend." I frowned. "More a trouble making friend."

"Aaron likes him." She mirrored my frown. "Schrock drinks a lot. I think Aaron does, too. I *know* Aaron does, too." She shook her head. "He didn't use to. It's that Schrock. If I were allowed, I'd hate him." She scrunched her face. "Unfortunately, shunning doesn't appeal to me."

I smiled. "Me either."

"Do you remember Schrock? From when you were young? Well, younger. He's more my age than yours," Violet asked.

"A little. You're right, he was in your Sunday sings, not mine or Aaron's. But I do remember he was a rambunctious boy. Not really mean, but he was an instigator. Aaron was never like that.

I'm surprised they struck up such a close relationship now. Aaron was quieter. Nicer. He took the *Ordnung's* directives seriously. The truth is when we were kind of special friends, and *Maem* thought there was a wedding in the works, he quoted those *Ordnung* rules many times." I made a moue. "He knew them all."

"I wish men talked more," Violet said wistfully. "Aaron. I wish he talked more."

"Some talk too much," I said, thinking Schrock.

"Anyway," Violet said, "I've got to get this food ready for Aaron. He wants his food when he wants his food. We'll have to talk about Lily another time. Can't do it now." She looked at me and shook her head. "And that's all we can talk about anymore. Lily. Just Lily. I've got enough confessing to do. Don't want to add to it."

"We can talk while you work . . . and I'll help you fix the cooking."

"No," Violet said sadly. "You have to go. If you stay, you'll just wheedle words out of me. Words I shouldn't be saying."

"I won't."

"You will."

"You're probably right," I conceded and shrugged. "Are my clothes dry?"

"Probably not."

"Where are the clothes I left here from before?"

"In a box. Under the bed."

Frustrated, I threw up my hands in disgust, turned from her, went upstairs, pulled the box from under the bed, opened it, took from it, took off the Amish clothes, dressed in my own, closed the box, picked it up, went down the stairs and out the door. I'd wanted so much to stay her Amish sister. Not just that day. But always. It wouldn't happen. I couldn't unshun myself. It would be a sham.

I didn't look at her. I didn't say goodbye.

Chapter Thirty-Nine

I kept my eyes aimed downward and walked carefully down the porch steps. The box of clothes was heavy, and if I fell and broke an ankle, Violet would, Amish helpful, insist I stay with her. Shunned. Not too pleasant a prospect. When I got to the bottom of the stairs, I looked up and saw Aaron and Schrock unloading a wagon full of chopped tree chunks. Schrock was throwing them off the wagon bed onto the ground, and Aaron was stacking them next to the barn. A harbinger of winter. I hoped my soul would be satisfied, and I would be gone before bitter cold came.

I tried to get to my car before they saw me. I was in no mood for Aaron's disapproving glares or Schrock's taunts. But of course, as this seemed to be a day of misery, they did see me, and Aaron glared, and Schrock taunted.

"Well, what have we here? More help? Equalized English woman in pants out to help her Amish cohorts, well almost cohorts. Gonna help pile these old wood pieces before the snow flies?" He saluted me. "Mighty nice of you."

I wanted to ignore him, but feisty rose up in me, and I couldn't contain it. "Seems to me, the blizzards are going to hit your house, too. Seems to me, a good husband would be thinking of keeping his own home warm, instead of worrying about his friend's wife staying comfortable. Or maybe he's thinking of keeping his *loved one* warm with punches. Just make her skin puff out with swelling and pad her pain."

He threw his head back and laughed. "Hear that, Aaron? The woman thinks I've got a thing for your wife."

Aaron said nothing, kept stacking.

I went to my car, turned the key, pushed hard on the gas, and hoped to scare the horse to prancing and rattling the wagon enough to make Schrock fall off.

Didn't happen. Startled the horse, but not enough. Schrock stood firm and laughed even harder.

I drove to the cemetery, walked up the hill, and sank onto the ground covering Lily. I dropped my head into my hands, pressed the heels of my palms against my eyes.

I felt the sun warm on the back of my head.

I sat that way a long time.

If we stay very still, empty our minds, a calm enters. A melting of emotion. A drift to a meshing with eternity . . . all that was, is, and will be. We're everything, and we're nothing.

I sat that way a long time.

Then it stopped. The vast vat of peace. I felt a leaf drop against my hands. Aware, I lowered my hands, opened my eyes to the leaf, held it and smiled at the colors and texture of that one small, drying, dying, completing its cycle, leaf. I felt the grass tickle my ankles, and the breeze lift my hair. I raised my face and a whoosh of breath sprang from my mouth, as the sky showered my soul, with a mass of magnificent, shape-changing, pristine, white vaporous mounds, moving slowly, gracefully over the sky.

I sighed. The earth still moved, the seasons changed, animals roved, and people lived. Ugly peeked through beauty. Difficulties squashed desires. But truth, coupled with strength and fortitude, could conquer both. I hoped I had enough of each.

Before I left, I climbed over the fence and stood by Bishop Herrfort's gravestone. I ran my fingers over its chiseled words. Simple words. Name and dates. There should have been more. He was more than a name and two dates. Strange how you remember a person after they're dead. It wasn't his face and body that mattered, that were sharp and clear in my head. It was his stance, his thoughts, his words, that I remembered. They were good thoughts, provoking. His words . . . wise, kind, and useful. His demeanor . . . loving, compassionate, with an authoritative demeanor. *You spoke through him, God. He was blessed to know You so well.*

I stood there a long time. Finally, I patted his monument gently and climbed back over the fence, walked down the hill, and got into my car.

Although the day was unusually fall-warm and sunny, I knew, if I wanted to leave Wander Lane before snowfall, I'd have to increase the pace of interviews. So, I spent the afternoon attempting to ferret out useful information from Lily's old friends—Crystal Schwartz, Fannie Hershberger, Effie Glick and Emory Fisher. Careful not to go beyond Lily related questions, they answered all I asked, with terse words and short sentences. I sensed and understood their reluctance to speak fully with me. They knew the rules and would not risk reprimand, by stepping outside those boundaries. I listened carefully to them, and almost entirely, their recollections were the same as I'd already heard. Lily was unpredictable. Often exuberant. Often maudlin. Often reticent. Even so, it was pleasant to see their children, their homes, *them,* and I although I left with little new information, I was satisfied.

But I would keep seeking.

Chapter Forty

The afternoon's sleuthing and cemetery visits had emptied my stomach of flat rock pudding calories, and it was rumbling. My tired body and empty digestive system deserved a treat. Ice cream would taste best, but prudence was clamoring health. Grilled cheese and tomato soup? Nutritious and relatively tasty. But mundane. Having performed well that day, taking me to places that, though not accomplishing desired answers, furthered my search, my body deserved better, and because it had been so good to me, I would treat it royally and suitably nourish it with delicious morsels. Bourbon chicken, broccoli, with enough extra sauce to drown them both. A small salad, generously drizzled with raspberry vinaigrette and, if room left, a tiny, *relatively* tiny, dish of ice cream with a hearty dose of chocolate syrup? Perfect. And I knew all that good food was on Harriet's menu.

I drove a little faster than I should.

When I got to the restaurant, the sky still showed light, but the days were shortening, the evenings cooling, and the sense of a day of diversified emotions ending well eased my being to pleasant contentment, lasting even though walking through the eatery's door, I saw Lowell Parker sitting at his back corner table.

He looked up from his food, noticed me. Frowned. Shook his head.

I waited.

His eyes stayed on me. I wasn't sure what he was thinking, but I decided to find out.

I walked to his table. Sat down. And I smiled.

He shook his head again.

"You should be glad to see me," I said. "I'm in a good mood."

He lifted one eyebrow.

"Say, 'Hello, Cora. What a wonderful surprise.'" I lifted my eyebrows, both of them, and kind of smirky smiled.

"Hello, Cora." His face still showed nothing. "Not a surprise at all. It seems wherever I go, there you are . . . or there you come."

"Like a bad penny?"

"Yep."

"Ah, but today, I'm a shiny, gold penny."

"Copper," he said. No smile. No grin.

"Want to hear what I did today?

"Probably not."

"I ate Aaron's dinner desert, had a mild confrontation with Violet, was taunted by Schrock, visited Lily, and talked with four of her friends."

He said nothing.

"And now I'm really hungry. And it would be pleasant to order a meal, receive a meal, and eat a meal in the presence of a welcoming and verbalizing dinner companion."

He bit his lip.

"Are you trying not to smile?"

He shook his head, though one side of his mouth lifted up.

"Let it out, Sheriff Parker. I can see you want to," I sing-songed.

And he did.

Smugly satisfied, I was ready to feast, and when Bailey came, I ordered all the good things previously determined to be the desires of my patiently waiting, but drooling, stomach . . . chicken, broccoli, bourbon sauce, and yes, ice-cream . . . with streams of chocolate syrup flowing over it and whipped cream topping it.

Food came.

I ate.

Lowell watched.

Food demolished, I wiped my mouth, put my napkin down, leaned back, tilted my head, gave a quick nod in Lowell's direction, and when he said nothing, queried his thoughts with a "What now? You're turn. I ate. You talk."

"Your belly happy now?"

I laughed. "A bit overly happy," I said and patted my stomach.

He leaned back and folded his arms over his chest.

I looked at him and grinned. "All you need is a toothpick between your teeth, a plug of tobacco, or a pipe, and you'd be the picture of a smug, self-satisfied, old man."

"I am a bit pleased with myself. Jailed two men. Warned three others. Gave a bonus.

Small, but she deserved it. Got a letter off to the governor. Talked to a bunch of fifth-graders. Interviewed a couple men . . . and a woman . . . for a probable detective opening and managed to get out of the office at a decent hour. All in all, a pretty good day . . . for an *almost* old man."

"No Amish antics?"

"No Amish antics." He wrinkled his forehead and rubbed his chin. "You say you talked with Lily's old friends."

"I did."

"And they said?"

"They all pretty much said the same thing." I leaned forward and folded my hands on the table. "Her emotions erupted at either end of the spectrum. From ecstasy to despair. Frenzied movement to weepy withdrawal. Unpredictable."

"How long had that behavior been manifesting itself?"

My head jerked up at his tone. "I'm not sure. I think it was the time pretty close to her death."

"You're not sure."

It was a statement, and I heard disapproval in it. "Should I have asked? I thought it was clear. Maybe not clear enough?"

"It could have been helpful." His words were clipped. "What else did you learn?"

"Nothing really. We just talked about the old days when I was part of the community, and Lily and Violet were part of their group. And how they looked up to me. I was older and they thought I was smart and kind. It was nice. The remembering."

"Did they mention any new friends she might have made? Before her death. Any new names?"

"No. Just the regulars. Their Sunday singing friends."

"Nobody else?"

"No. Just Harvey Kurtz. And oh, yes, they mentioned Vernon Erb and Aaron. They took turns taking the girls who didn't have buggy rides back to their houses, so they didn't have walk in the dark. Just good, safe, fun memories."

"So, what's your takeaway?"

I tilted my head and lifted my eyebrows. "Takeaway?"

"What did you glean from your talks? Did those conversations affect your thinking?"

"I'm not sure." I looked at him. There was no give in his face. I could tell he wanted a profound answer from me, a light bulb moment bright enough to break through to awareness. I couldn't give him that. "But they did give me a few moments of relief, a feeling that there wasn't an answer, and I should let it go. And I did, for those moments. I let it go and everything was all right. Good." I sighed deeply. "But it's not all right. And I still don't know."

"Maybe it is time to let go. Maybe there isn't a definite answer. Maybe if you accepted what was, is, and really let go, permanently, you could keep that good feeling and live in what is real now."

I smiled, ruefully. "I can't."

"It's choice, Cora, choice."

"I can't," I repeated. "I can't."

Sleep came hard that night. The day had been filled with a myriad of happenings, and though my eyes squeezed shut, and my head strained to vacate thought, and my body craved rest, those events clamored relentlessly for attention. I finally resorted to counting sheep. It didn't work. I wondered who was the fool who originated and touted that procedure as viable.

I got up and ate cookies. That didn't work either. I downed a sleeping pill. Maybe, two.

However many, it worked.

Chapter Forty-One

I dreamed of Lily that night. She was skip-running in the dark, stopping sometimes and twirling. Round and round. Laughing. There was a boy, no, a man, grown, chasing her. He had risen from the ground, from heavy, thick clumps of grass, blades shining green in the moonlight. He was running, fast, faster, to catch her. He wasn't laughing. She came to a creek. Wander Lane Creek. But it wasn't the gentle, flowing creek I remembered. This was a rushing, roiling, raging creek, its water roaring its way down the creek bed, splashing the banks on either side, softening their soil to a spreading, spongy, slippery slide.

I could tell Lily couldn't see the creek. She was almost there. The man caught her. Right at the edge of it. He pulled her away from it. She tried to get loose, but his arms stayed around her. They rolled closer and closer to the bank. Lily was laughing. The man was not. They fell over the edge, down the slippery slope. I heard the slap of bodies hitting water, as they rammed the charging creek. I called out to them. To Lily. The moon slid behind the clouds, and the sky blackened the earth. I heard Lily's laughter rising from the creek. Fading. Then it stopped. I listened, turned my ear to the silence. Waited. Heard splashing. Saw the man come out of the water. Alone. His body was darker than the night. He ran. I called for him to stop. "Where is she? Where is Lily?" But he didn't stop. I tried to see where he was going. I needed him to tell me where Lily was. The clouds moved briefly, and the moon flashed an empty earth and then was gone again. So was he.

I woke.

Dream images flashed bright in my head. They quivered my body, and then dimmed slowly, leaving a weakness, a sadness within me. I shivered and buried it, willed myself to remember the positive feelings and learnings gleaned from the previous day's encounters with Lily's friends.

I rose and made ready for the day, and then went down to the lobby, hoping there still would be motel coffee, hot, and donuts, untouched, waiting for me.

The dining door was closed. I'd have to go elsewhere for sustenance.

I went to the lobby. Stopped.

Maem was there. Sitting, quiet, pale, beautiful, facing me.

"Maem!" She smiled.

I went to her, held her, and although small in stature and fragile in appearance, her arms went around me tight as a vise closing firm.

I laughed, and she let loose, looked at me and nodded.

"What are you doing here? Does *Da* know? Can this woman standing before me, in Amish dress and cap, truly be *you?*"

"Indeed, it is." She took my hand and pulled me toward the door. "Now come with me. Hot blueberry-lemon, buttermilk muffins are waiting." She tilted her head and winked. "Maybe a little warm now. Or cold. But still good."

She led me outdoors, and there, alongside cars, pickups and SUVs, stood a sleek, black, adopted, Amish racing horse and a much used, black Amish buggy.

"*Maem!*" She was a trifle too old and directionally challenged to be buggying herself in town.

"Climb on up."

'What's *Da* going to say?"

"Nothing. He's gone to Sugar Creek with Willie. They've got talking to do, with Willie's wife's pa. Guess you know what about." She looked at me and puckered her face. Now, you want those muffins or not? If'n you do, you'd better heft yourself, right quick, into that buggy. Little Katy knows where they are, and she's just drooling to get at 'em."

"Is she at your house?"

"Nope. You and me got talking to do, just like Willie and his wife's pa," she said, hefting herself up and into the buggy. "But Katy smelled 'em baking, and she'll be watching out the window for me to call her over to get one."

"It's about Talitha, isn't it? What you want to talk about."

"You heard me say you knew why Willie and *Da* went to Sugar Creek. Same thing we got to talk about."

"How'd you know?"

"Violet told me. Wanted to prepare me for the confession."

"Are you prepared?" I patted her knee. My hand felt her knee bony under her skirt. Then I reached and took the reins from her. Contesting my takeover, she tugged at them, yet her resistance was minimal. When I'd returned to Wander Lane ten years before, she would not have allowed me to usurp her control of the drive. So much change since then. The touch of aging. A soft drop of grief whispered through my thoughts. How could I leave Wander Lane when her years, months, days numbered few? I'd done it twice before, could I do it again? Guilt.

Always the adversary. A forceful foe. She didn't answer.

We'd reached the place on the hill where thirty years before, I'd stopped on my trek to abandon Lily's baby. Remembering that night, I turned the horse so we were facing Wander Lane and could see the town as I had seen it that night then, with its streetlamps shining in the dark, magical, now clear and common.

"I stopped here, so many years ago," I said, putting my hand, again, on *Maem's* knee. Little Annabelle, that's what I called her, a flower name to match ours, Lily, Violet, and me, Corabelle, and I held the baby against me and felt the weight of what I was doing. I thought, how can I do this? But I could, and I did. I gave her away. I gave Lily's baby away. That pain has stayed with me all these years. Was I right? I thought so then. I'm not sure now."

"You were right."

I heard her words."

"You were right," she repeated. "If you had stayed, there still would have been pain. And the child would know the stigma of no known father. And a shunned mother. If she confessed. If Lily spoke truth. But she didn't, Cora, she didn't. She kept silent, and let you take her burden." *Maem* sighed. "Sometimes, Cora, there is no good answer. And to do what you believe *is* the best thing to do, *is* the right thing. For that moment." She lifted her head, looked to the sky. "Sometimes, we can't hear Him. Sometimes, our hearts and heads are so full, we forget to ask Him. But He knows, and it's never too late to ask for forgiveness when *our* choices bring grief."

I lowered my head into my hands and let the tears flow.

Maem sat quietly beside me. After a time, she patted my knee. Against my pressing hands, my lips formed a smile. A pat does bring a joining of hearts, and we'd both used that gentle source of comfort. I lowered my hands and sat up.

"We need to rescue Katy," *Maem* said softly. "She's waited a long time for those muffins."

"You're right," I said, as I guided the horse to turn and lead us back in the direction of *Maem's dawdi haus*. "It's the *right* thing to do."

We laughed.

Katy was waiting on the big house's porch. When she saw us, with arms lifted and waving, she jumped down the steps and ran to welcome us. Or perhaps to encourage us to hurry and ply her with muffins.

Which *maem* did.

In the kitchen, crumb-catching napkin on her lap, Katy gulped the first muffin. Stuffed it in her mouth and barely chewed it before she swallowed, then she lifted her eyes to *Maem,* in a plea for another.

"This time eat it slow." *Maem* putting a second muffin in the child's hand. "And I'll give you another to take home . . . and one for your *maem.*"

"And Baby Clare?"

"And Baby Clare." *Maem* winked at me. We both knew who would eat Baby Clare's muffin.

"I might have to help her," Katy said softly, looking so sweet and innocent.

We laughed.

Katy left with a napkin stuffed with blueberry-lemon buttermilk biscuits. We watched her run across the yards and then settled ourselves in cushioned rockers on *Maem's* porch.

We rocked awhile. Not talking. Absorbing the lulling spread of rolling hills, harvested fields, large patches of untilled ground sprinkled with thick masses of rich-hued yellow weeds, ditch-flowers stretching high and full in their trenches, trees glorious with color. Fall.

"Maem?"

She turned her eyes to me.

"I wonder," I paused, kept my eyes on the vista before me, "why is it you're speaking so freely to me?"

"You're my daughter."

"Your shunned daughter."

"Preacher Miller gave us permission to speak with you."

"True." I glanced at her. She was looking at me. I turned my eyes away. "But only about Lily."

"Yeah."

"You're disobeying."

"Yeah. But only the preacher, not God."

"And *Da.*"

She said nothing.

"The Bible says to submit to your husband." I looked at her. Her eyes had left me.

"And I do. Mostly. Except when he's wrong. God has given me brains, feelings, and good sense. He would not have me follow a husband's sin."

"Da's sin?" I heard a whinny in the distance, a bird call close by, a rustle in the tree by the porch, and I heard the absence of her rocking.

313

"He's to love his children."

"He does."

"He loves himself more."

I sighed and looked up to the heavens, God's clouds, His chariot. "Which cloud, *Maem,* do you think is God's road today?"

She smiled. *"He makes the clouds His chariot and rides on the wings of the wind.* (Psalm 104:3) I think it's a road your *da* is not following."

"And Preacher Miller? Did he not restrict you to conversation only regarding Lily?"

"He's young, Cora. He'll learn. I hope." She started rocking again. "Have you noticed how full and beautiful the flowers are this fall?"

I said nothing.

"I pray, Cora. During the day, He, God is my dearest company. And I read my Bible, words written on paper, to be studied, cherished and obeyed. Sometimes, the words written in the Preachers' heads are pulled out and tossed at us as the final and *right* directives, rules, words of the *Ordnung,* stern, senseless, petty, and," she turned to me, "sometimes ridiculous." She smiled. "Sometimes, wise. You know, Cora, I'm near dying age, and I want to have my children not only close to my heart, but close to my visible love. So, I will speak my words to you. Just as I want you to hear them and know them. If at some point, I have to confess this as wrongdoing, I will do it. I'll just leave out the word 'wrongdoing,' because it's not."

"I do love you, *Maem.* So much." And I thought it time to delve into *maem's* knowledge and thoughts of Lily's death. Directly. Precisely. "What do you know of Lily's death?"

"Right to the point, Cora." She reached and patted my arm,

shook her head. "I know she drowned, and I know she's buried alone, near her brethren, but not with them." She rubbed her eyes. "I don't know how it happened. But I don't believe it was intentional. Not on her part."

I straightened my body, leaned toward her. "You think someone pushed her, held her under the water?"

"I think she could have slipped. They say it happened at night. Dark can be a thief."

"Who said it happened at night?"

"Bishop Herrfort."

"Why was she out at night?"

"Sunday Sings, Cora. She still went to the Sunday Sings. She still was not married. It was a way to mingle, to feel a man's attraction. She was a beautiful girl, your sister. Beautiful. And there were still men without women out there, seeking to find the right one."

"Even five years after I left."

"She was still young. When she died, she was only twenty-one years old."

"So, she could have been anywhere with anyone the night she died?"

"*Yeah,* we would not have known where or who she was with. The old ones, your *da* and me, are in bed when the courting's going on." She shrugged her shoulders. "We trust."

"Was she going regularly to the Sings?"

"She was. I liked her too." She touched my arm and nodded towards a squirrel, under the oak by the big house. "He's getting ready for winter." Pushing at the floor with her foot, she set her rocker to moving. "It was a release for her. She could let go of memory and enjoy."

"Was she not happy?"

"It's not likely one is happy all the time." She put her hand on the arm of my chair and stopped its rocking. "Look at me, Cora Pooler. My beloved daughter. Your laughter. Your company. Your wisdom. You were a second mother to my children. We raised them together. Not intentionally, but it was as if you were born to be helper-daughter and friend to me. Special. A treasure. And then you were gone. The hole you left was deep, and it was a time of struggle for me. Inside my soul was turmoil. I knew it was Lily who'd had the baby. You were healthy, fine the morning they, the sheriff, brought the baby back to the community. Lily was frail, dragged out. And I knew she needed me. And I needed you. For support. For wisdom. But you'd done what you thought was best for Lily. And the bishop shunned you. And you left. The days," she gulped air and swallowed, "were muddled after that. I had to keep Lily . . . upright. We were living days that weren't real."

She stopped her rocking and clutched her chest. A sob escaped. Then silence.

I got out of my chair and sat at her feet. She stroked my hair.

"After a time, she took to roaming. Sometimes late. Missed meals. Forsook chores. Had this far-off look when *Da* scolded her absence, her ignoring household duties. Yet, there were days when her eyes danced and her lips laughed."

"When were those days, *Maem?*"

"Mostly after the Sings."

I turned my body and raised my face to look at her. "Why do you think then?"

"Forgive me, God. I think perhaps she was hiding memory and sorrow in a man's arms."

316

I saw her tears, but I couldn't stop the question. "What man?"

"It was Schrock who brought her home from the Sings. Most times."

Chapter Forty-Two

Talk of Lily's death ended. There had been enough lingering words of sadness, instead we reminisced over our history of joyful times, of those occasions of family strength and unity that tempered the residual pain settled deep in our hearts. *Maem* and I voiced words that spoke remembered joy . . . Pooler unity and community strength, laughter and happiness. Picnics and auctions and weddings. Baking, canning and quilting. Dandelion bracelets, dodge ball and pony cart rides. Because there were no men for whom to prepare a hearty, time-consuming dinner, the reminiscing stretched over a *lunch* of left-over muffins and glasses of cold milk.

I called Katy in from her weeding to eat with us. She didn't hesitate, dropped the wild, plant-choking weed in her hand, brushed the dirt from her skirt, waved to her mother watching from the big house, and ran to join *Maem* and me. When the last muffin was consumed, she patted her stomach and declared it the best dinner she'd ever had.

Before she left, Katy came to me, stood so close by my kitchen chair, I could feel her breath on my cheek. *"Maem* said to tell you she's very thankful that you helped her birth Baby Clare, and she would very much like to tell you that herself, but you're shunned, and she's sorry that you're shunned, and she wishes you would be Amish again, though she's never really known you as an Amish person, only kind of. But she thinks you'd make a good Amish woman."

I smiled and thanked her, told her to tell her *maem* that I was grateful for her kind words.

"Oh, and she said to tell you Baby Clare looks a little bit like you."

I motioned Katy to bend her ear close to my mouth. "Tell your *maem,* I've looked hard at Baby Clare, and, to me, she looks like you, Katy. And that's a really, lucky thing for Baby Clare, because you, Katy, are a beautiful little girl."

"Beauty doesn't count." Her face was set firm. "Wise and obedient. That's what counts."

I laughed. "Spoken like a true Amisher."

I left shortly after lunch. It had been a light, lovely, lady lunch. *Maem* urged me to stay longer, but I could see she needed to nap. So many years since I'd first left Wander Lane had passed, and the wrinkles on *Maem's* face and the bend of her back reflected the stretch of them.

"And I need a nice, long walk to burn off your generous use of sugar and butter in the best Amish muffins ever baked on this earth."

She put her arms around me, and as she held me close for a long moment, I slipped back into the comfort of being her child.

Looking back, I wish I had stayed longer, sat beside her as she slept, for shortly after that day, she had a stroke and lost all memory.

I considered walking the short distance up the hill to Aaron's house . . . Violet's house . . . but decided not to. I didn't want to roil the peace in my head. So, at the end of my old home's dirt-packed, flower-bordered driveway, I stepped onto the road and began my walk down the hill to Wander Lane.

It was a glorious day. One of fall's rationed, miraculous days when the sun falls hot and glistens the world, with a magical glow; a day for mind meandering, not thinking, and a day for relinquishing the body to a clean lightness. Just pleasant.

I was near the place where I'd stopped with Baby Annabelle and as I looked down at Wander Lane, I heard the steady clomp of a horse behind me. I stepped to the edge of the road to make room for buggy, or wagon, to pass me.

It didn't.

It stopped.

It was a buggy.

It was Schrock.

"Get in. I'll take you down to the village."

I didn't say anything. Didn't look at him. Began walking.

"Mattie says you haven't been at the cemetery for awhile." He kept the horse walking at the same pace as mine.

I still said nothing.

"She misses you."

"Go away, Schrock."

"She's sick." I stopped.

He stopped.

"Did you beat her?" I hoped the hate showed in my face.

"I've never beat her."

I scowled. "I suppose she did walk into a limb that day. A tree limb shaped like a hand with five fingers."

He laughed. "Quite an imagination you've got there, Amish girl. Oh, that's right. Almost Amish girl. Wanna be Amish girl. Enough to pick the brains of those who really are."

I scrunched my eyebrows and looked hard at him.

"Why don't you just leave it alone, Cora? Just leave it alone and go back up north."

"Am I getting too close to the truth?"

He slapped the reins, hard, against the horse, turned, and drove back up the hill.

My head full of Schrock and Mattie, I walked the rest of the way to Wander Lane. There, sun-dried and thirsty, I went into Harriet's for a cold drink.

And of course, like a bad penny turned up, there, in his ever-saved corner, was Sheriff Lowell Parker.

And there, of course, my feet took me to his table.

"You look hot," he said, greeting me.

"As in sexy?" I queried, knowing he meant, not.

He laughed. "As in sun-stroked."

"I walked from *Maem's* and it's hot out." I paused, looked at his glass of ice water. He grinned and shoved it toward me. I drank. "I saw Schrock. Mattie's sick."

"I know. Schrock brought her into the doctor."

"He probably beat her."

"He doesn't beat her, Cora."

"You told me he slaps her."

"Slapping isn't beating."

I frowned. "Sounds like you approve of slapping."

"Not exactly approve." His eyes were hard on me. "But sometimes, it's necessary."

"I can't believe you just said that." I shoved his water glass back across the table.

He shook his head. "I think it's best we drop this conversation."

"Maybe all conversations."

He sighed, shook his head, again, pushed back his chair, rose, and left.

Chapter Forty-Three

I sat there. Alone. Facing the wall. Which was better than looking at or thinking about Parker or Schrock or previous-almost-husband-turned-cold-fish-Aaron. Not as good as being with *Maem* or Violet. Especially if I could think of a way to get rid of husband-of-Violet, Aaron. Aaron, whom in the olden days, had courted me . . . kind of. A few Sunday Sing buggy rides. A few special smiles. A few encounters at after church dinners. Although in those days, I occasionally did think Aaron was pursuing me as possible marriage material. Good thing Daniel, though a few years later and me firmly ensconced as a budding Englisher, came along and spared me from that miserable happening. A marriage with Aaron would have been a disaster of the highest magnitude. Almost. Schrock would have been worse.

"Do you want some lunch?"

I looked up. It was Bailey. I scooted around the table and sat in Lowell's chair.

"I can see better in his chair," I explained. "The people. Only I don't wear a gun, and I'm not checking them out to see if they're crooks."

Bailey raised her eyebrows. "I would hope not . . . something to eat?"

"I'm stuffed to the gills. Had muffins at *maem's*."

"You're *da* there?"

"Nope. Out visiting with Willie." I grinned. "If he'd been there, I don't think I'd have a muffin-filled belly. More than likely it'd be a starving belly. His lips locked tight, and his eyes glaring at me, there'd be no crumbs offered." I tilted my head, thought a moment. "Except maybe a plate would be offered at a separate table."

"No doubt about it. Something to eat?"

"No, just some ice-cold water."

"You're *maem's* okay?"

"She's okay. Bailey, you know you don't have to beat around the bush. You can just come right out and ask me." I patted my stomach. "It's just way too full, Bailey. Even the walk down the hill didn't absorb *Maem's* good baking and make my innards shrink. But yes, *Maem's* fine, and I can't tell you what's going to happen Sunday at church. But keep your ears open, there's going to be plenty to hear."

"I see." Bailey pressed her lips together. "But how am I gonna know what happens in Church?"

I laughed. "Oh, Bailey, you've got more sources than a fish's got scales."

"That could be."

Her face radiated smug.

"Anything else?" One eyebrow raised; she poised her pencil over her pad.

"No, Bailey. Just water."

She brought me lemonade . . . and Tilley . . .

"Funny looking water, Bailey," I said wrinkling my nose at Bailey, and then turning my head to nod at Tilley. "You not working this afternoon?"

"Busy day. Late lunch," she answered dropping into the chair across from me.

"Good."

"Just coffee, Bailey, and . . . ," she thought a moment, "and maybe, if you've got it, a slice of carrot cake."

"That's going to be your whole lunch?" I said. "Coffee and cake. All calories and no nutrients," and I heard Bailey mumble 'look who's talking.'"

"There're carrots in it," she defended. "And besides I had an egg salad sandwich. Brought it with me to work."

"And my muffins were loaded with blueberries and lemon zest," I said, frowning at Bailey. "Fruit. Nutrious."

"Neither one of you get a blue ribbon for healthy eating," Bailey said. She took a couple steps, turned and glared at me. "Drink your lemonade. A lot of squeezed lemon and just a tad of sugar. Drink it." And she stalked off.

Tilley looked at me, and we laughed.

"Lowell was just in," I said.

"I know. I saw him outside, and he told me."

She stared at me, rubbed the side of her face. I saw a slackness in her skin. Tilley was aging.

Nonchalantly, I pushed the skin at my jawline up toward my ear. The skin moved loose and full, under my fingers. I sighed. It hits us all. I was aging, too. I lamented the months sped by.

I'd accomplished so little.

"He wants me to talk to you," Tilley said.

"He wants you to talk with me? Why?"

"Not talk with you, Cora. He wants me to talk *to* you."

I bit my lip. "Why can't he say what he wants me to hear?"

"I'm not sure, Cora. Maybe he thinks I can say things a man can't. Maybe he thinks you don't listen to him. Maybe he's just plain tired of this whole thing and doesn't know how to make it be over."

"Do you?" I kept my chin firm. "Do you know how to make it be over?"

"No, Cora, I don't."

"What does he want you to say to me?"

"He wants you to leave Schrock alone."

"Why?"

"I don't know. He just told me to tell you to leave Schrock alone."

"You have to have thoughts, feelings. Opinions."

"I do." Tilley paused as Bailey put her cake on the table, and then she smiled as Bailey raised her eyebrows, looked at me and pointed at my still full glass of lemonade.

"I wanted water," I said petulantly, "but now I want diet cola. With lots of ice."

"You're the boss," Bailey shrugged and took my drink. She turned to Tilley and spoke with a kinder voice. "You need anything else?"

Tilley shook her head. "No."

I watched Bailey walk away, sorry I'd been so bitey, but I could be nice later. Right now, I wanted information. I leaned across the table and fixed my eyes on Tilley's face.

"Why do you think Lowell wants me to stay away from Schrock?"

"He likes Schrock. I think that's one reason. Schrock's mouthy, but Schrock has never done anything to hurt another person."

"He slapped Mattie."

"Maybe . . ."

"I saw it! I saw the mark on her face."

"Maybe she got it some other way."

"It was a slap! And she said Schrock did it. And Lowell said he knows Schrock sometimes hits her. And then, he said, *today*, sometimes it's all right to hit a woman."

"Lowell said that?"

"Lowell said that."

She looked down at the table. When she raised her face, I saw a weary sadness.

"I just don't believe that," she said. She raised her hands, put them to her cheeks, closed her eyes, and shook her head. "And if he did say that, he had a reason, a *good* reason. Cora, you know him. He's fair and just and *kind*." She paused. "To everyone."

"Maybe not if you're Mattie."

Tilly looked at me for a long moment, then she pushed her chair back and stood. "He told me to tell you to leave Schrock alone. I've done that. There's nothing more for me to say." She reached and touched my arm. Gently. And walked away.

Her cake was left, untouched, on the table.

Bailey brought my iced soft drink to me. She stared at Tilly's empty chair and uneaten cake, then at me.

I shrugged.

She put the drink down, slid the cake toward me, stopped when I raised my hand against it, took her hand away from the plate, bent her head toward me as if to speak, then straightened, turned and left.

I looked at the cake a long time. How could anything so pretty and delicious cause such a bitter lump to rise and stick in my throat?

I rose, laid money on the table and, hoping not to see Bailey, walked to the front door. I sensed her presence, but I did not see her. A gladness Harriet had not seen this day flashed through my mind.

The sun was still firm in its brightness. It would hold that light for awhile. It was too early to hide myself in a deep slumber. I needed a place to go, something to do. Someone to explain Lowell's defense of Schrock. Other than Tilly, I didn't know who that could be. And Tilly had indicated she didn't want to have that conversation. The realization that I hadn't made many local connections, and even should an Amish person be allowed to freely converse with me about topics other than Lily, there was no one who would share negative, or troubling thoughts regarding Lowell or Schrock.

I had no choice. Tilley was the only logical person to go to. Perhaps she'd tempered her emotions, and if I promised to only listen and not criticize, she might speak with me, help me understand Lowell's tolerance towards Schrock.

It was worth a try.

With a hearty smattering of anxiety mixed within my roiling stomach, I went to Lowell's building, paused beside the official vehicles parked alongside it, tsked at their muddied exteriors, then straightened my shoulders, and went through the door.

Tilly was at her desk. She looked up at me, frowned, and shifted her eyes back to the papers on her desk.

"Please, talk to me . . . ,"

328

"How will it help?" She picked up a pencil and began writing.

I walked to the chair by her desk. Like Lowell's, it was piled with papers. I removed them, stacked them on her desk. Sat.

"Please?" I said.

Face rigid, she glared at me.

I waited.

"Three things," she said. "One, Lowell doesn't hit women . . . or approve of it. Two, Lowell likes Schrock . . . with good reason. Three, Lowell thinks you don't listen. And Cora, often you don't."

"I listen."

"And too often his words bounce right off you, Cora. If Lowell were to spread a thick layer of glue on them and smash them onto your body, I think you'd find a way to pull them off. You don't listen to him, Cora. Not intently. Your mind stays on what *you* think should be done."

"That's not fair."

"Do you want to argue, or do you want to talk?"

"Now you sound just like Lowell."

Tilly said nothing.

"I want to talk," I whispered.

"And listen?"

"Yes," I agreed.

"Good." She sighed. "First, I want to preface my words by saying Lowell actually has a great respect for your thinking . . . and your actions. But you have to let go of predetermined results. You're not looking for truth. You're looking to make truth be what you want it to be."

"I don't think so," I interrupted.

"Of course, you don't think so. You're bound and determined

to prove Lily didn't kill herself."

"Is that wrong?"

"It's predetermining based on what you want. Don't you think that colors what you hear and how you interpret?"

I pressed my lips together, relaxed and swallowed. "I do want to know what happened to Lily. And I do want the truth."

"And you want the truth to be that she didn't kill herself."

"*Yes.*"

I hope you're right, but you might not be." I heard sympathy in Tilly's voice. "And if you're not, what will you do?"

"I don't know." I set my face and straightened in the chair. "But I do know Schrock is somehow involved in all this . . . and Lowell knows it." I bit my lower lip, slid my teeth deep into it, waited for a response. Didn't get it. "I want to talk to him. Now. I've got questions . . ."

"This isn't the time, Cora. He's not too happy with you right now. Best leave him alone. He'll settle down, and *that's* when you need to talk with him. If you really want his advice, and if you'll listen to it, give some time."

"Buzz me in. I'll be careful what I say."

"No, you won't. You're not in a listening mode, and I'm not going to buzz you in." She clenched her teeth, and sympathy gone, I could feel her anger pushing tight against her teeth wanting to be let loose. "It's best if you just go now."

"I don't want to," I said. I watched her quiver. "But I will."

And I did.

I went to my motel room, rooted a drugstore romance from my underwear drawer, took it along with a pillow to hug, entrenched myself in an almost comfortable motel chair and read, until my eyes grew weary enough to sleep.

Chapter Forty-Four

I didn't sleep well, and I woke grouchy. Couldn't figure out what to wear, and automatically following my established routine, I reached in the shower and adjusted the temperature, apparently moving the indicator to a higher heat than desired. I jumped when the water hit me, fell. Didn't get hurt but got mad. Fixed the water temperature, got back in, scrubbed hard. Still couldn't decide what to wear. Had to be something suitable for Lowell's eyes. 'Cause that's where I was going. To see him. Question him. And if my mood was still rotten and didn't please him . . . too bad. After all, he was the cause of my mood. Partially. Mostly.

I put on a midcalf, dark skirt. Black. Matched my mood. Slipped on a white blouse—long-sleeved, touch of lace at the collar. Boring . . . which I intended not to be. Cosmeticed carefully. Put on hooker shoes. And lastly, dabbed my most expensive perfume behind my ears, in the hollow of my throat, and on my wrists.

I wiggled a little in front of motel's slimming mirror and smiled. I looked like a good girl, except for my shoes, and I hoped I smelled like a harlot. Stuffed my purse and was ready.

331

When she saw me, shook her head, sighed, and covered her mouth with one hand. A useless endeavor. I'd seen the smile before she hid it.

I lifted my shoulders and leered. "Is he in?"

She nodded. "He doesn't want to see you. But." She grinned. "He looks like he had a good night's sleep. He can handle you. I'm going to just step into the ladies' room for a moment. You do what you have to do, and if he says anything to me, as in reprimand, I'll tell him I thought you'd left." She looked at me. "So why don't you leave, so I can step away from my desk for a few minutes."

"I'll do that." I nodded, said good-by, went out the door, waited a few moments, opened the door, went through it, passed by Tilly's empty desk, and walked into Lowell's office. Stood by the open door a minute, and then closed it, hard. Stomped across the floor to the chairs facing his desk. Apparently, the slamming door and floor-pounding shoes caught his attention. He turned an unresponsive face toward me, turned it away from me, and concentrated on the papers on his desk.

As seemed to be the necessity of those entering his office and wanting to sit, I cleared the papers from the seat of one chair and laid them atop the papers on a second chair. And sat.

He continued working.

"I'm sorry," I said softly, and I thought I probably was. A little.

He whooshed a sigh, put his pen down, folded his arms across his chest, and tilted back in his chair. Said nothing.

"I'll listen if you'll talk. I'll do what you say." I crossed my fingers. "And I won't smart mouth."

He raised his eyebrows.

"I need help."

"How?" he asked, leaning forward, arms on the desk, hands folded.

"I've talked with a lot of people, Lowell," I said, not quite answering his question. "Her friends, Amish friends who knew her pretty well." I crossed an arm over my waist, pressed my other elbow against it and raised my thumbnail to my teeth. Bit on it. And I waited for a response.

Lowell lifted his eyebrows and frowned. I figured he'd surmised I was either mulling over possible mollifying words or was just plain nervous.

"And?" he said.

"The consensus was that she either *did* end her own life or that she *might* have."

"And your conclusion from that?"

"I don't believe she killed herself." I said, looking at him intently, then less sure, "I don't want to believe that."

"And you want me to do what?"

"Help me."

"I've tried to help you."

"I know. But I need more." I bent forward. "And I will listen. And I will do as you recommend."

"Preacher Miller isn't happy with you." Lowell's tone was terse. "Which means he's not happy with me. I need to have a good relationship with him. I've always been able to work with the brethren. And I want it to stay that way."

I drew in a deep breath.

"You've gone way beyond the limits, Cora. You know the

Amish. You know the weight of disobedience is heavy. And the consequences, harsh. Miller knows his flock, and he knows his responsibilities. One of them is protecting. Another, monitoring. Another, punishing. He made a substantial concession when he let you in, a *shunned* Amisher, to talk with the brethren . . . ."

"I'm not Amish!"

"In his eyes, you are."

"I know. Shunned. Forever for them. Even though, I'm really not Amish anymore."

"True. Probably. But even so, to them you're shunned. Amish shunned. And that means you had no right to talk beyond the boundaries agreed upon . . . Lily's death. That's all. Nothing else. Lily's death. And you did agree to those conditions."

"I didn't go beyond those limits," I half-lied, convinced within my mind, I was justified.

"Of course, you did."

"They were willing."

"You connived."

"Most of the time they liked being connived. They were happy to talk with me. *Wanted* to talk with me."

"Listen to me." He slammed his fist onto the desktop. "They're not happy when then they have to stand before the whole congregation and confess they were bullied, by you, into breaking their vows."

I bit my lip and shuddered.

"If you want me to help you, then you listen to me."

"I told you I will."

He leaned on the desk and put his forefinger on his lips, scrunched his forehead. Looked at me. Thoughtfully?

"I told you I don't want you to see Schrock anymore. I mean

that. No talking. No going to his farm. Nothing. Stay away from him!"

"Why?"

He grabbed his hair with both hands and shook his head. Grunted.

"I think he had something to do with Lily's death."

"Go, Cora. Just go. And keep away from Schrock. He did not kill Lily."

"You can't know that. I have to talk with him." I pursed my lips and breathed deep. "Before Lily died, he drove her home from the Sunday sings. That's not done lightly. It's usually a signal the boy likes the girl. And it sometimes leads to more intimate things. And maybe, Lily wasn't ready for that."

"Just go, Cora," he said softly. "And if you're ever really ready to listen, come back in . . . and maybe, I'll even listen to you."

I walked to the park and sat on the bench across from Harriet's, now Bailey's, eatery. I thought of her, Harriet. She had been such a lovely, loving, woman. Wise. Kind. Giving. I wondered how a person got that way. Faith. For her, it was faith. When I held her Bible, the cover supple in my hands, loosened flakes of dried leather leaving patches of bare lining, thin and pliant god-trimmed pages smudged and winkled from fingers tracing their words, I thought of her . . . simple, steady love.

Daniel had those qualities. So absorbed with Lily's death, I'd forgotten that, put him aside. It had been long since he'd filled, or even touched, the tentacles of my mind. Instead, they'd stretched to places he'd never truly been a part of. He'd taken me, a young Amish girl, and taught me the English world. He hadn't questioned the world I'd come from, simply accepted who I was and led me to become more. His hold was firm, but not so demanding that he questioned my need to go back to my old life, my Amish life, and then when I left the Amish again, he welcomed me and loved me and took me as his wife. Patient love. Gentle love. Steady and deep love. Daniel.

I had been a gentle, loving person. As a young Amish woman. As an Englisher's wife. Now? Not so gentle. Not so loving.

I wanted to be that person again.

Thoughts of Harriet and Daniel segued to thoughts of Sheriff Lowell Parker. Guilt. That's what I thought. Felt. Guilt. I hadn't listened to him. And he was wiser than I in the ways and thoughts of the Amish. I'd been gone too long. Anglicized. Englishcized. I'd been a nicer, stronger-in-a-good way person in the English world than I was here in the Amish world. I'd brought most of the Englisher somewhat, somehow, good strength I'd acquired with me to Wander Lane, but I'd left most of the niceness behind in New York.

On this day, remembering, evaluating, I didn't like the Wander Lane Cora very much. *I had to bring the better me back.*

Even so, I still needed to talk with Schrock.

Or, I thought, as I saw Lowell go into Harriet's eatery, I needed to talk with someone who would tell me about Schrock. If that someone would still speak with me.

Chapter Forty-Five

"I'm really ready to listen."

Lowell had watched me walk across the floor to his table, heard me say those words, kept his eyes on me, but said nothing.

I couldn't read his face. An empty mask. I waited, not perturbed, but curious and cautious. Hopeful. When no change of facial expression came, when no words were mouthed, I sat. Slowly and carefully, quietly.

I folded my hands on the table and waited.

He still said nothing.

"I've been sitting in the park . . . thinking," I said. "About Harriet. And Daniel. They were important in my life. They taught me." I paused, waited for a response. When there was none, I continued, "It was their character, their conduct that taught me. Their consistency. And I did learn, and I did reflect those qualities. For a time. A long time." I drew in a breath. "Then I came here. And found Lily, my Lily, buried outside the fence. Unworthy. A piece of garbage. And all those noble qualities I'd learned . . . patience, ponder, compromise, reasonable acceptance . . . faded. Almost to nothing."

The cords in Lowell's neck drew taut. He was listening.

"I needed to know how Lily died. What put her in an unconsecrated grave. I *had* to know. I went to you for help. And you gave it. And I did use it. But not always rightly. I listened, but used only part of your wisdom, the part that jelled with my thinking. I foolishly stretched your wisdom to mesh with my rushed and selfish thoughts and actions.

"I'm sorry. I need your help. And I will listen."

Elbows on the table, hands raised, thumbs under his chin, fingers tented and pressed against his lips, Lowell looked at me. I could not read his stare.

I waited. I waited. I waited.

Finally, he dropped his hands from his face, laid them folded, like mine, on the table, bent forward, looked straight at me, and spoke.

"Schrock is a good man. Was a good boy. Mischievous, but good. Still is. You see one side. The side he chooses to show you. A rougher Schrock than most see. To most he's bright, friendly, and quick to help."

Lowell must have noticed my sharp intake of breath, for he stopped a moment, his face noncommittal, and then he resumed.

"I don't know why he treats you differently. I've asked him. He said he simply treats you as he needs to. He wouldn't say more. I didn't press."

Lowell paused again. I think to let his words settle.

"You think he might be involved with Lily's drowning. Either directly or indirectly," he stated.

I nodded and replied, "He's proven he can be violent, with women." I hesitated, not wanting to cease Lowell's commentary, but needing to explain my reluctance to agree with Lowell's assessment of Schrock. "I've seen the marks on Mattie's face."

"You need to know a little of the background between Schrock and Mattie." He squinted, his face intent. "But you understand, you don't discuss what I say with anyone? *Anyone.*"

I nodded, and he continued, "Schrock had a bad time for awhile. He married and the marriage wasn't good. I think he married for beauty, for she was beautiful, Edith, his wife. And vain for an Amish woman." He shook his head. "Pinched her cheeks hard to redden them, tugged strands of curly hair from her *kapp,* pulled her apron tight over her body. That kind of thing. Silly little things not worth confessing. And Schrock loved her. A lot."

His forehead creased as if struggling for the right words. "You understand, she loved him, too. In her own way. But as she got older, she seemed to need more than an Amish marriage could give." He paused, bit his lip, continued, "She left him. Went to explore the English world. Came back pregnant. Said it was Schrock's child. Impossible. She was gone too long. But Schrock bought it. At least, he said he did. And he claimed the child was his. A little boy. It was a hard winter the year she came back. The infant died. So did his wife. Pneumonia. Are you getting all this, Cora?"

I nodded.

"Good." He looked hard at me. "Schrock was devastated. You know his parents were gone, left the farm and just moved out? No one knew where or why. Not even Isaiah. Signed the farm over to him and were gone."

"No, I didn't know that."

"Anyway, the farm was Schrock's and when his wife died, he went wild, left the community, and gambled it away. Drinking and cards, those were his partners, and he lost it all . . . parents, wife, child, the farm." Lowell tilted his head and scratched behind his ear. "When he finally came back, Mattie was with him and his pockets were filled with a pile of money."

"He already had money . . . from somewhere," I interrupted. "Mattie told me he gave her parents money to buy her as a cleaner-cook for his house."

"Not true. She lied," Lowell snapped. "They paid him to take her. She was pregnant. From somebody. Not Schrock. And he'd had enough of carousing. He wanted to go back to the brethren. And Mattie was relatively attractive in those days. Even more, for him the unborn child was the greater enticement. A second chance for a family." He snorted. "Redemption."

"He beats her," I said, anger rising toward Schrock. "He took a woman he didn't love and purchased her and a packet of money, with his selfish soul."

"She came with conditions. And he's never beat her. Bound her with his arms. Slapped her. But never beat her."

"Slapping's enough to condemn him."

"What would you do if someone came at you with a knife . . . or a pan of boiling water?"

"She wouldn't do that. I don't believe she ever did."

"You're not listening."

"I am. I'm trying to understand." I leaned forward. "And why does she go to the cemetery?" I asked softly, easing my anger, changing the direction of his words, wanting to know everything, but not wanting to provoke Lowell. "There's a spot of grass there, outside the fence, where she puts flowers or sometimes, just sits."

"The baby died. Before it was birthed."

"The baby's there in the ground?" I shuddered.

"As far as I know, yes."

"Is that legal?"

"No one knew she was pregnant. Schrock told me. Made me promise not to tell anyone."

"You're telling me."

His hands were fists on the table. He lowered his eyes. I was sorry I'd confronted him with those words.

"You needed to know." His words were clipped sharp.

"But I still don't understand about Mattie. Granted, she's a little strange, but violent?

Enough for him to hit her?"

"Yes."

"Did he know that when he married her?"

"Yes."

"He wanted the money," I said, disgusted.

"Maybe. Probably. But I think even more, he wanted a family. And she could give him that. She's not a raving beauty, but I think he'd grown beyond that. He understood there were behavioral problems . . . but not the extent of them."

"Why didn't he divorce her? Better than beating her."

Lowell sighed. "He doesn't beat her, Cora. And the Amish don't divorce." He shook his head. "And you know that."

"You still think he's a good man?"

"I do."

"Okay, I promise I'll leave Schrock alone," I said reluctantly. "But I don't want to."

Lowell said nothing.

"I really will," I said softly, and thank you . . . you've helped me many times, and I really am grateful."

"You're welcome." He stared at me a long moment. "And I hope you mean it."

Chapter Forty-Six

I left the restaurant, got in my car and feeling an unwanted sense of depletion, quietly sat wondering where I should go, what I should do with the hours left in that day. I watched the diminished vacation populace trek in and out the Amish trade stores, some with packages some just curious, window-gazers . . . laughers, frowners, indifferent responders.

And I watched Lowell leave the eatery and head toward his workplace. My eyes followed his steps to the village office building, turn, walk along its wall, turn again, and disappear behind that structure. I pictured him nodding to Tilly, walking down the hall, opening his office door, stepping in, dropping to his desk chair, lifting papers from his desk, and tending to the needs they presented. And I wondered if he had emptied his head of all thoughts of me. Maybe a flash of puzzling curiosity flew through his mind, and then a deliberate erasure of all thoughts of me.

I pressed my hands against my face and shook my head. I needed to be away from him,

Wander Lane, the Amish. Just for awhile. A few hours.

So, I started the car and drove.

Eyes looking neither right nor left, I traveled roads that took me away from Wander Lane.

Several miles later, somewhat relaxed, still in Amish country, but not my Amish, I spotted a rough, wooden sign, Baked Goods, stuck in the tall, grassed, front yard, of an unkempt house. Though a bit apprehensive, I knew the baked goods would be authentic Amish and *good,* so I turned onto the stony, dirt drive and drove up to the house.

Two little girls sitting at the end of the path, a bowl of water and a pile of dirt beside them, were making mud pies. When I stopped and got out of the car, they held up their muddy hands, wiggled their fingers at me, and laughed.

"Ah, mud pies," I said. "Are they for sale?"

"They're not mud pies. They're cookies."

As if realizing they chanted the words in unison, they looked at each other and giggled.

"Are you twins?" I asked.

"No," they said, holding up three fingers, "we're three."

I laughed and asked, "Is your *maem* home?"

"She's making pies."

"Can I talk to her?"

"I'll get her," one little girl said, rising and wiping her hands on her already muddied apron. She ran up the porch steps, and the second little girl held out a mud cookie to me.

"I'm not too hungry right now. Maybe later."

She shrugged, dumped a little water on the dirt and continued her baking.

I watched her until their mother came out, introduced herself as Sadie, and bade me come into the house.

Her kitchen was immaculate. Smelled wonderful. Yeasty and

343

spicy. Bread in the oven, tomato sauce on the stove. I couldn't see any pies."

"The wee ones said you're making pies today."

"Everything is pies to them. But no, today it's bread for customers and tomato sauce for Elijah." She winked. "My husband. He likes his noodle and sauce. Too much." She laughed, open-mouthed. "His belly just keeps growing. But I like it." She lifted her brows and looked at me. "And what can I do for you? Sweet bread? Rolls? Plain white."

"I was kind of hoping for pie."

"Nope, not today." She shook her head. "But I got some left-over shoefly pie in the cooler and if you got a liking for that, set yourself down and I'll get you a piece."

"It's my favorite," I said.

"Then this is a good day for you. Now, set yourself down, right at the table." she pointed and left to fetch the pie. She brought back two forks and two plated slices of shoefly pie.

"What about Elijah?" I said as we settled ourselves at the table.

"Oh, don't be worrying about him. I always save enough of everything for my Elijah.

Now, eat your pie and tell me where you're from."

I smiled. "Both at the same time?"

"*Yeah.*"

"Okay." I took a bite, chewed and swallowed. "I've been staying at Wander Lane."

"Oooh, that's the place with the witch."

Startled, I sat straight in my chair. "Witch?"

"That lady that buried her baby outside the cemetery. The evil one. They say she practices *hexahrei.*"

Mattie, I thought. And here was an Amish woman who didn't mind gossiping. I'd hit treasure.

"That's a pretty harsh accusation," I said.

"Sure it is, but I've heard it's true." Sadie folded her arms on the table, leaned forward, and though no one else could hear us, spoke her words in a forceful, raspy whisper. "They say she's got a little house where she keeps the baby's clothes and cradle, even her toys and bottle. Out in a field hard to get to."

"Why would she do that?" I asked, and even as I said the words, I thought of the cabin I'd seen behind Mattie's house, and the tramped path connecting those houses.

"'cause she thinks the baby's spirit's there. Thinks she can connect to it 'cause she can't get to the baby's body that 'cause it's buried by the cemetery."

"Seems like a lot of becauses," I said. "You can't know that to be true."

"I know there was a dead baby, killed, and buried. And I know people who have seen her fits." Sadie shook her head. "She can be a wild one. Best, if you see her, to stay away."

"Best if we don't spread this kind of news."

Shrugging, she prattled on. Mostly local happenings.

When the pie was gone, I reached across the table and patted her arm. "The pie was delicious, and I thank you for it, but I have places to go and though I've enjoyed speaking with you, I need to leave."

She looked disappointed. She probably didn't get many ears that would listen too long to her endless chatter. Amish women have loving souls, but tight mouths. They would know how to leave gently . . . firmly.

The little girls, happy as wee birds testing their wings, were covered with mud. I laughed as I passed them. Gossip and mud. They were a happy family.

Driving the country roads leading to Wander Lane, I headed back to find the dirt pathway that led to the cabin behind Schrock's house.

I found it, and drove carefully, for though summer had packed the soil, it was still rough and rutty. Relieved, the solid footing assuring I would be able to drive onto the field at the end of the path without sinking, I relaxed and enjoyed the ride.

The foliage on each side of the road was beautifully colored with shades of fall—oranges, reds, yellows, golds, greens. Leaves fallen from the limbs gave slivers of space for the sun to shine through, with its glistening rays and to dapple the patchy, last, clinging leaves, in a splendor of color.

I gasped when I came to the archway of great maples dressed in colorful, fall finery on either side of road, their limbs meeting and entwining, over the center of the path. In awe, I drove through the arbor to the end of the road, to the expanse of virgin, lush, uncut, green grass spread before me. And in the center of that field was the small, wooden building I'd seen before, . . . with a narrow width of trampled grass disfiguring the pristine field. The trail to Schrock's house.

Mattie's footpath. Mattie, the presumed witch.

I got out of my car and tested the hardness of the ground, under the grass. It stayed firm beneath my stomping, and my legs felt no dampness from the tall grass. Dry and solid, the field would bear the weight of my car. I breathed a sigh of relief. The cottage was far enough from the roadway that it would be hard, without my car, to get away from it quickly, should someone discover me in the building. *And I was going to get in it.*

And I did. The drive across the field was perfect. The car plowed through the grass without a glitch. I hoped getting inside the cabin would be as easy.

It was. Neither latch nor lock slowed my entrance.

I was in, and mouth opened wide, breath drawn in deep, I surveyed the single room's content.

Dolls. Dolls everywhere. Baby dolls. All of them, baby dolls. Naked. Clothed. Plastic. Porcelain. Cloth. All of them, baby dolls. Bassinets. Cribs. Cradles. Highchairs. All full of baby dolls. Piles of them in corners and on shelves. Individual babies strewn haphazardly over the floor. And a single rocking chair, a child's book on its seat, sat in the middle of the room. And tucked among the babies sitting and laying on the shelves, were toy baby bottles, little cups and plates, plastic spoons, and plastic food.

The dolls were clean. The room was clean. Clean in an unordered room.

I heard the door close behind me. Then the plunk of something set on the floor.

I didn't turn. I knew who it was.

Chapter Forty-Seven

"They're my babies."

"I know," I whispered.

"The babies I'll never have."

"Is that why you go to the cemetery?"

"She was the only one that was almost real. But she never got there. Inside the fence. Not real, she wasn't. She was gone before she was a real, whole baby. But I loved her. They told me there was nothing to bury. But they were wrong. I showed her to them. But they wouldn't let me bury her in the cemetery. I did it anyway. Got her as close as I could. I put my hand on Mattie's arm, but she drew it away. She didn't look at me.

"I saw your car in the field. I don't let nobody in here. Just Isaiah. Once. He told me I needed to get rid of the babies. It wasn't healthy. He's wrong. He started picking 'em up, and I hit him. Hard. Over and over. He tried to get hold of my arms. But he couldn't, and I kept hitting him. Had a broom. He couldn't get it away from me. I just kept hitting. 'Till he slapped me. On my face. Grabbed the broom and slapped me. And I stopped hitting him. My fists couldn't reach him anymore. Neither could my heart."

"Does he hit you often?"

She turned and faced me. I watched her crumble. It was as if her body shriveled, a molten, shrinking mass. Then she straightened and smiled, a slight upturn of lips, almost a sad smirk.

"I wanted you to think so."

"Does he?" I repeated. "Does he hit you?"

"Only when I get too mad and can't stop. Don't want to stop. Not when he talks bad about my babies. Then I have to hurt him. Bad. However, I can."

"But he stops you."

"He slaps me." She grinned. "Only way to stop me." She laughed. "And then he's real sorry he hurt me." She stopped laughing. "He means it. He's really sorry." She paused, and then spoke . . . her words, soft. "You need to go."

I nodded and turned to the door. There was a broom leaning against the wall. And a pail of water, a stack of cloths on the floor next to the broom. I looked back at Mattie.

"I have to clean my babies."

I nodded again. "That's good, Mattie. That's good."

"I know they're not real," she whispered. "Not real to you."

I bit my lip and went through the door.

Schrock was standing by my car. I went to it and stood next to him.

"She okay?" he asked.

I nodded. He didn't move and we stood silent for awhile. Then he stepped away, so I could get in the car. But I didn't. I needed to know.

"Do you love her?"

"Yes."

"Why?" I raised my face to him. "Is it the money?"

"No." He shook his head, didn't question how I knew. "The money was a bonus, but I liked her. She was funny, smart before all this. Not pretty, not Amish, but she had an Amish heart and one thing about us Amish, the heart is more beautiful than the face. Her parents didn't see that. I did. And when like turned to love, I married her. And it was good, until the baby died.

Even before the baby was more than a shared knowing, it was gone. Mattie changed. And I'm hoping one day she'll change back. But you're asking, do I love her now? I answered yes, and it's so."

I didn't know what to say.

"She goes to the cemetery. To sit with the baby." He sighed. "You know what's in that grave?"

I shook my head, no.

"A baby doll."

Chapter Forty-Eight

I needed time to think. I drove to the spot on the hill where I'd stopped so many years ago, as I'd walked holding Anabelle, loving Anabelle, taking her away from Lily. Anabelle, the littlest Pooler, not ours to keep. Nor to love. Nor to *know*. How strange life is. I was wrong. She is ours now. A Pooler. Now blessed and living within the rules.

And this is where I'd seen Mattie gathering Lily-of-the-valley.

I left the car and wandered into and among the trees. Mostly pines, the woods would keep its green and shadowing limbs throughout the coming winter—not gloomy, but comforting. A place of soothing, seasonal sameness. The crunch of step on crumbling leaves, the slip of foot on hidden twigs, the scent of pine, the design of chipped bark on tree trunks, all absorbing myself into their silent singing. Fall woods. Matchless.

There was a pleasant, moist coolness in the air. As I walked far into the woods, it spread over my skin with a gentle softness that seeped into and throughout my body. Unexpectantly, I came upon a smooth-topped stump. I stopped and ran my hand over its hard, level surface, and then, as I wondered who'd fashioned such a fitting seat in such a needed spot, I sat upon it. A trifle damp but welcomed by tiring legs.

My thoughts went to Mattie and Schrock. I'd not, before now, seen them, *ever*, as a loving couple. But now, I'd seen Schrock as a loving husband. Totally unexpected. And obviously, real. At least it seemed that way. And according to Lowell, Schrock was practically a saint, and that should indicate a loving spouse. And I had to admit, reluctantly, Lowell usually was right in his thinking, but he wasn't perfect, and he could be wrong. Probably, I should think a little more regarding his feelings towards Schrock. Maybe. Hard to think the Amish man was Amish kind and honest beyond the few, short sentences he'd spoken to me. Yet, maybe there was a Schrock to whom I'd not been fair.

And Mattie. I'd just experienced one of her little, really little, fits at the cabin. And a few months ago, a big, really big, one at the cemetery. But she was Schrock's problem, and he seemed to know it. Hopefully time and patience, love and understanding would lead her and Schrock to an honest and peaceful merge. I sighed. I would be long gone before that would come about, if it could come about. I prayed that it would.

The damp was seeping through my skirt, and, unnoticed, so deep I was in thought, I hadn't heard the patter of raindrops on the trees or felt their trickle through my hair. I rose and walked quickly through and out the woods.

When I got to the edge of the trees, I saw an Amish boy, his arms filled with pine cones, stepping onto the road.

"*Shtobb,* stop" I called, lapsing into Amish dialect. "Are you going up the hill? I can give you a ride?"

He looked at me and shook his head, no. I heard a weak "*dank,*" and he continued up the hill.

"*Voaht,* wait," I cried out, continuing to speak Amish words, for I didn't know if he'd learned enough English in school to know what I was saying. "Would your *maem* allow you to ride in my car?"

He shrugged and kept walking.

"It will keep you and your pine cones dry."

He shrugged again and smiled. A little smile. Uncertain, I thought. Then he turned and came toward the car. When he reached it, he set his cones down by the side of the road.

"You can bring them," I said.

"They're dirty."

"Dirt can be cleaned. *Voaht*

I rummaged through the car, found a plastic bag, helped him put the pine cones into it, and laid it on the back seat. "They'll be fine there, and if a little dirt leaks out, I can wipe it up easily." I continued to speak Amish. I smiled. It was good. "Show me the way to your house."

"Just before the top of the hill, turn."

"The Oberholtzer farm?"

He nodded.

"That's a long walk from the woods. Can't you find pine cones closer than that?"

He nodded. "But these cones are best. The biggest. We paint 'em and *maem* sells 'em." He grinned. "The English buy 'em. There're pine cones all over the place for free. The woods are full of them. But the English won't go in there. Guess they'd rather pay for 'em." He grinned again. "Maybe they don't like to get their shoes dirty."

I laughed. He was a talkative one. Not usual for an Amish boy. Especially as I wasn't in Amish attire. But I figured since he'd seen me around his community, he felt safe.

"Well, you got yourself a batch of big ones. The English should like that. And your *maem*."

"I don't tell her where I go to get 'em."

"Why not?" I asked, surprised.

"The witch goes there."

"The witch?" I said, immediately thinking Mattie.

"*Yeah*. She goes there a lot. Sometimes sits and cries."

"You've seen her?"

"Once I saw her picking those Lily-of-the-valley flowers. Me and Henry. She got lots of 'em. Put 'em in her apron. We were kind of scared. Not too much. We're too big to get real scared. The little kids are though. Scared. She takes those lilies home and makes soup. Makes her husband eat it and get sick. It could kill him. They're poison you know."

"She wouldn't do that," I said. But, I did know she might. They could make Schrock mighty ill.

"Yeah, she would. My *maem* said so. Said she wants the evil one, she won't call her a witch, dead. But she is an evil one. That's what my *maem* says. And she don't lie."

"Well, anyway," I said as I pulled in his driveway. "It's probably best you don't spread that news around. I don't think your *maem* would like you to be gossiping, do you?"

"You gonna tell her?'

"No," I said shaking my head. "It's up to you to decide whether to tell her or not." And I hoped he wouldn't. It's kind of fun for young ones to have harmless secrets. Even though, this one might be true. And it's good not to squelch a young boy's talking. There's far too little speech flowing from the Amish male population as the men get older and their lips grow tighter and words can't get through them. Inclined to only say few and necessary words, it sometimes seems they've forgotten their voices need to be used more often than once or twice a day. Yet probably, that's not totally fair nor true . . . neither in the barn with friends nor in the bedroom with wives. At least they don't waste words. Probably, hopefully, most speak well thought out authority.

Poor Schrock. I wished him well. With Mattie. The witch.

After I let the boy off, I drove the Amish backroads, thinking, musing, Amish scenery drifting and coloring my thoughts. Winter was coming. The ground, the trees were readying themselves for the onslaught of that cold, bare season. Foretelling its approach were broken corn stalks, upright but staggering, drying, ready to bend and slump onto the soil. Unharvested pumpkins rotting in the fields, winter fertilizer. Bare trees, no leaves to break and slow the winds. Hay fields, dried stubble. Vegetable fields, plowed. Wood stacked. Yes, winter was coming. Cold winds, snow, sleet, early dark. I'd been in Amish land long enough.

Weary, a trace of nostalgia for what I would miss, a heaviness from all I'd experienced, a wandering sadness drifted through my thoughts . . . family lost, diminished, me essentially neither needed nor totally seen. A portrait on the wall. The surface clear and behind the canvas, shaded images. I bit my lip. But still, the face on the painting, the face that showed, could be loved, could be seared in memory, savored.

The dropping of the sun darkened the earth, softened and melded the shapes of nature and man. By the time I reached the village, the fullness of the sun's disappearance, aided by a bevy of star-hiding clouds was interrupted only by the soft glow of

Wander Lakes shops and streetlamps. Soothed by their gentle gleam, I drove slowly and made my way to Harriet's eatery.

I parked, looked through the restaurant's window and saw, as I'd hoped, Lowell at his corner table.

Bailey greeted me at the door.

"It's late, but you're welcome to stay." She sighed and shook her head slightly. "He just got here." She put her fingers against her lips, as if pondering further words, then said, "He's tired, Cora. Too many burdens in this town." She hesitated, leaned her body forward, spoke softly. "Try not to rile him." Her face tightened. "I mean it."

"Okay," I whispered. "I promise I won't upset him." As soon as the words left my mouth, I reconsidered. Honesty was important. I spoke louder. "I promise I'll *try* not to upset him."

"*Try hard.*"

I nodded.

"You eating?"

"Just diet cola."

"I'll bring it with his steak."

I smiled. Apparently, he wasn't too tired to chew on dead cow meat.

She left, and I went to his table.

He looked up and screwed his face. "Cora."

"I'll go if you want me to."

"Sit."

"I saw Mattie today. At her cabin. You know what's in there?"

"Dolls."

"You know then," I acknowledged.

"I know."

"Schrock?" I squinted. "He told you?"

356

"Yep, Schrock. Isaiah Schrock. He told me."

"He tells you everything?"

"Pretty much."

"Then you know all about why he married Mattie? And their problems?"

"I told you some of it before."

"I remember, but how come," I said, thinking back to Mattie's sister and her husband sitting sad at Harriet's, "how come he wouldn't let Mattie see her sister?"

"It wasn't him. It was Mattie. She wouldn't let them see her."

"Why?"

He shrugged. "Who knows? Mattie's a strange one."

"I saw her, fairly often, at the cemetery. I really thought we were getting to be friends." I drew up my shoulders, sighed deep. "Yet, there were times of sarcasm and anger. Apparently, too, moments of imaginative delusion." I visualized Mattie in my head. "I think there's a great deal of sadness within her soul."

"That could be." Lowell's eyes moved to see beyond me. "Bailey's coming with my food."

"Maybe it's time I talked with Schrock."

He said nothing, kept his eyes on Bailey, watched her put his steak and my drink on the table.

Obviously, he was trying to shut me up, but it wasn't going to happen. Eventually, he would say something. I folded my hands on the table and waited.

He cut a piece from his steak, shoved it in his mouth, chewed. I waited.

"Why?" he finally asked, as he sawed his meat into large pieces.

"I want to know why he's been so rotten to me."

"Doesn't sound like he was malicious up at the cabin."

"I caught him off guard. I guess he does have a bit of vulnerability secreted in his soul."

"Drink your cola."

"I'm going to do it. I'm going to see him. With or without your permission."

"Figured you would."

Chapter Forty-Nine

Depleted, I went back to my motel room and tried to sleep. Couldn't. Body and mind don't always work together, and this night, my raging mind conquered my sleep-wanting body. I finally got up, took a book, read, and realizing after reading five pages and remembering none of it, put it down, and succumbed to the multitude of thoughts battling in my head. Which to concentrate on. Which to resolve or let go. I curled into the cushions of the unusually comfortable motel chair, hugged my pillow, and contemplated my choices.

First, I could let go of Talitha and Willie. That was resolved. Sadly. But humans are able to acclimate. Pain lessens when solutions are seen by the recipient as right, are accepted, and adjusted to retain the essence of what is sought. For Talitha and Willie, love, and theirs was such they were able to accept their circumstances, live as loving friends and rejoice in their child. A struggle, but an acclamation of strength.

Violet. I couldn't leave Wander Lane, until I was confident our sister relationship . . . loving, respectful, joyous . . . was reciprocal.

Mattie. I think I finally understood her. There was a childlike sweetness about her. Most times. But like a child, she hadn't grasped responsible approaches to difficult or detested situations. Hopefully, Schrock's love would reach and soak into her heart and head, and there create understanding, acceptance, competence, and growth. Gone from Wander Lane, I would never know if she reached, or came close, to that pinnacle of adultness.

Schrock loomed large, an irritating enigma in my head. My mind couldn't comprehend a reason for the juxtaposition of his good Amish reputation and his miserable relationship with me. And I wouldn't be placated, until I understood his unjustified behavior toward me. I could think of no reason for it, other than misplaced malice, and unless I addressed it, I probably never would. Which was not acceptable. He knew more about Lily's death than he'd revealed. His little innuendos proved it. Confrontation, Lowell's commandment to stay away from Schrock, sanctified or not, was the solution. And I *would* confront Isaiah Schrock.

And Aaron. Whirling amid the myriad clashing visions inside my brain, was the avoiding, stern face of Aaron. Always rather prudent, we'd parted ten years before as friends. And, on most occasions then, he'd been a smiling, pleasant person. Yet even then, there were huge blocks of obstinacy. However, as long as he made Violet happy, he wasn't vital on my list of problems. I put him to rest in my head as a probable non-changeable.

Lowell. He was there. In my head. And I didn't know what I felt. I shook my head. Him, I'd ignore.

That left Lily. What should I do about Lily? I'd talked with so many that knew her, had seen or been with her the days before her death, and all who knew her well had spoken of her varying moods, the disparity of them, the intensity. But none had known her last moments. *None.* I felt my body constrict, the inside of my head strain to know what more to do, and how to do it. Fingers pressing hard into my pillow, I grasped it tight against my chest, as if it could hold me together, unjumble the mass of quandaries rolling and smashing inside my head.

When sleep finally demanded it be served, I crawled back into my bed, and tossing, turning, thinking, it found a way to overpower and give flitting, shallow hours of rest.

Chapter Fifty

I needed coffee. Thick, dark, caffeine-loaded coffee. My head pounded and my body, too heavy to move, begged to stay within blankets. I willed my eyes to stay open and dragged out of bed. Coffee was essential. I forced my feet to walk to the motel coffee maker, and my hands to fill it with water, dump packets, several, into it, plug it in, and I needed patience and prayer to wait for quick perking.

It did help. Patience or prayer. As did the shower, with its water as cold as I could stand. I toweled and dressed. Ready and reasonably alert, I set out to face Sister Violet.

The day was gorgeous. Bright sunned. Fall scented. Invigoratingly cool. It primed my person for possible confrontation.

As I drove up to Violet's home, I saw no sign of Aaron or harnessed horse and wagon, near the barn or in the yard. I hoped that meant he was off somewhere doing farming chores that demanded a full morning to complete. I wanted time alone with Violet. Aaron's judgment of my every spoken word, and

his scrutiny of my every facial twitch and my every reaction
to words said or mannerisms displayed was not conducive to
truthful, productive conversation.

I got out of my car, walked up to Violet's front door, and
knocked.

She opened it, looked at me, then tilted her head to the side,
smiled wanly, and said softly,

"Cora."

I nodded.

"I can't talk to you. Not even about Lily. Aaron forbids it."

"He's not the preacher."

"He's my husband." Her voice trembled. *"He's my husband,"*
she said again. Firmly.

"He supersedes the preacher: Preacher Kurtz. Preacher Miller.
Your spiritual leaders?"

Her shoulders slumped. "Cora, I have to live with Aaron.
He supersedes *you*."

I moved to step past her into the house.

She blocked me. "I can't talk to you."

I threw up my hands. "Why does Aaron hate me so?"

"I don't know. He doesn't really hate you. He just wants you
to leave Wander Lane."

"Where is he now?"

"He's with Schrock. They're tearing down the house next to
his . . . the house, he offered to you awhile ago."

"Why is he tearing it down?"

"It's an eyesore. . . ."

"Well said," I interrupted, "and probably offered to me
because it wasn't livable."

". . . so," she said, ignoring me, "they're taking the wood to build a new corn crib. Schrock wants to fix up his farm. Says he's tired of shabby. It's not the Amish way." She bit her lip. "But I think there's another reason. I think he wants to keep Aaron busy and away from you."

"Why?"

"I don't know. But sometimes they talk when I'm near, drop words when it appears they know I can hear. *Both* of them want you gone. I'm not sure why." She hunched her shoulders, ran her hand over her face. "Cora, I can't talk to you. Shouldn't talk to you."

"I can understand why Schrock wants me gone," I said disregarding her words. "Kind of. I think because of Mattie. Partly. But mostly I think he thinks I'm a nosy, pushy woman. And I don't think he likes strong women. Though just a little while back, at the cabin back of Schrock's farm, he said some gentle words to me about Mattie. Confiding words. Maybe he didn't realize he was talking to me."

Violet laughed. "You've got a lot of thinks rumbling around in your head." She grew serious. "And Cora, you have to go."

"I will, but first tell me, why is Aaron so strange with me?"

"I don't know. I've wondered about it. It seems like he changed right about the time you came back to Wander Lane. Never laughs anymore. Doesn't talk much. Only to Schrock. And when I think about it, it was at that same time Schrock started spending so much time with Aaron." She scrunched her face. "They'd always been friends, but it's like now, they're glued together." She frowned. "*Especially* since you came back." She shook her head. "Cora, you've got to go. I won't tell Aaron you've been here. Unless he asks. I can't lie to him."

"You could. I wouldn't tell."

"Oh, Cora." Violet shook her head. "You've got enough Amish left in you to know I can't do that. And also, I've done so much praying and confessing since you've been here, I think my knees are wearing out."

"How can I leave you, Violet? It'll break my heart. I wish I could pack you up and take you with me. You'd love the freedom."

"I don't think so. The Amish is too firm in me," she said with gentle voice. "Will it be soon you leave?"

I nodded. "It will be soon. I don't know what more I can do to prove Lily's death was not suicide. And I can't live partly Amish, partly English anymore. I have to go back."

Violet reached and touched my arm. I pulled her to me, held her. She whispered, "I'm sorry," drew away from me, backed into the house and closed the door. But not before I'd seen the tears on her face.

A desire to see *Maem* touched my heart. I glanced at my watch. The morning was passing quickly. It was already time for Amish wives to be at the stove, preparing midday dinner. Not wanting to be underfoot, I remembered *Da* staggered his workload, his trips into Wander Lane, and his neighborly farmer visits to coincide with that time. I wondered if he still did. If so, *Maem* would be alone, and we could talk. If she would. Shunned was still my fate, but painful restrictions sometimes yield to a mother's love.

I tapped on the door, heard *Maem's* welcoming *"nei komm"* resonate through the wood, and went in. *Maem* was at the stove, stirring. It smelled wonderful. And, when I spoke, she turned and smiled.

"Cora! Come sit."

"You sit and I'll cook," I said, moving to the stove. "Where's *Da?*"

"*Nay, nay.* It's only simple stew." She moved it from the burner and pointed towards the rockers. "We don't eat so heavy anymore. Our old stomachs have gone into retirement and need pampering, so's they won't rebel."

"Where's *Da?*" I asked again.

"Out walking. The doctor told him he needs to get out and move his bones."

"The doctor?"

"*Yeah,* down in the village." Bracing her back, she eased her body into her rocker. "He had a spell. She rested her hands on her lap and set her chair to gentle rocking. "We're getting old, Cora. And the doctor told him to take some pounds off and get to nudging his joints into getting some action going."

As I rocked beside her, I lamented the words I had to say. Biting my lip, I reached and took her hand in mine.

She seemed to sense a trouble was coming. She looked at me, and I saw dread in her eyes.

"Cora?" she said softly. "Are you going back to the English?"

"How did you know?"

"I know you, Cora."

"It's time, *Maem.*"

"Are you really ready to go." She squeezed my hand. "Did you find what you were looking for? A peaceful heart?"

"I think so. Almost. Almost enough."

Hands joined, we sat, rocked, in silence.

There came a creaking announcing the opening of the front

door. At the same time, I looked up, I heard a happy grunt from *Maem,* and then laughter.

Katy stood inside the door, holding Baby Clare. She came across the room and held the baby out to me.

"My *maem* said she wanted you to see Baby Clare."

"To hold her?"

"Yes. And *Maem* told me to tell you that you did the right thing. And she loves you."

"Can I go see her, Talitha, your *maem?*"

"No. She said maybe, the next visit. She does love you, but it's too hard now. But she wanted you to see how beautiful and loved the baby is, and that she will take good care of her.

And that Baby Clare is a blessing and she's happy to have her. She said to tell you, 'thank you.'

She *was* beautiful. And a blessing.

Katy took the baby from me and went to the door. Once there, she turned and looked at *maem.*

"I nearly forgot, *mommi, maem* said *dawdi* is eating dinner with us. You can come, too."

Maem looked at me and quickly turned her eyes back onto Katy. "Thank you, Katy. Cora and I will be eating here."

She left. *Maem* took my hand and squeezed it. "He's an old man and can't change his ways.

Maem's stew was simple and good. When we finished, I helped her clean the kitchen, hugged her, asked her to tell *Da* I loved him, and left.

As I walked by the big house, I saw Katy standing behind the backdoor screen. I waved at her. She smiled and waved back.

Chapter Fifty-One

With male, Amish appetite sated and energy renewed by, what I assumed, was a hearty, noontime, Mattie cooked dinner, it seemed logical Schrock and Aaron would be back at work, demolishing the dilapidated structure next to his lived-in house. Should be a good, and probably final time, for me to delve into their minds and extract Lily-memories.

When I reached Schrock's home, I saw him sorting through a pile of rubble and stacking those boards that seemed to be whole and sturdy. I didn't see Aaron.

"Where's your buddy?" I asked, approaching Schrock.

"Day's warm. Soils hard. Thought he'd get some late, fall plowing done."

I didn't expect him to stop working to talk with me. And he didn't. So I spoke to his back and his heaving, pulling arms.

"Why won't Aaron talk to me?" Might as well get straight to the topic. I had no idea how much time I had before he'd send me on my way. Not with kindly words.

"Guess you'd better ask him."

"Can't. I told you, he won't talk to me."

"You think he's gonna you tell something?" He smiled, didn't stop sorting and pulling and piling.

"I don't know." I watched for several minutes. I figured he would let me stand there for several hours without him responding, so I tried again. "What do you know, Isaiah . . . about Lily?"

He stopped, looked at me and grinned. "Everything." Went back to his work.

"You really do know, don't you?" I said, spitting out the words.

"Yep." He dropped a cracked piece of wood on the ground. Moved close to me. Face squinted, and lips drawn tight, he looked directly into my eyes. "Go home, Cora."

I pulled my eyes away from his and looked down at his hand. It was fisted. I swallowed, drew a shallow breath and let the air out slowly. "I have to know."

"You don't want to know." His words were sharp.

"I do. No matter what, I do."

"Okay." He dropped the board he was holding. "I'm tired of protecting you." He grabbed my arm. "Let's go."

He moved quickly, half-dragging me to my car.

"Get in," he ordered.

"Where are we going?"

"To find Aaron."

We said nothing on the way. When he wanted me to turn, he pointed, and I turned. Other than that, the only sound was the car running.

Then I saw him. Aaron. Back bent, flexed muscles visible beneath his shirt. Steadying the plow, he walked behind the heaving horses splitting the soil, burying weeds and corn stalks, row after row, beneath dark, earth-damp, broken loam.

We stopped at the field and got out, walked to the edge of it and watched Aaron, at the far side of the row, stop to adjust the plow. I looked up to the sky, a spread of open-faced, cornflower blueberry pie capped, with a cluster of peaking meringue. I drew in a deep breath, watched the clouds drift over the deep blue, and drank in the moist, heady aroma of fresh-turned earth. I bent and reached to fill my hand with the soil's richness, crumble it with my fingers, hold it in my palm, and bring its scent to my nose. The pungent inhalation of its odor drew me back to long ago years. Amish years. Home. Horses. Love. Security. Sameness.

I kneeled to spread the soil back where it belonged, but before my hand touched ground, Schrock yanked my arm and shook it. I looked up at him. His face showed impatience.

"Tell me why he's angry before he fixes the plow and culti-vates another row." I paused.

"Before he sees us."

"Stand up." He glared at me. "You want to ask questions? Well then, stand up straight and be ready for answers."

"From Aaron? Or from you?"

"From both of us. If that's what you really want."

"Truth?"

"Truth."

"It's what I want."

Schrock tilted his head, raised his eyebrows, and nodded.

We watched Aaron plow down the row, until he reached us, where he stopped, looked puzzled.

"Is something wrong?"

"You've wanted to spill your guts to her for a long time,"

Schrock said. "You want to talk to her now? Then talk.

"Just to her," Aaron stated. "Nobody else." He looked at me. *"You don't tell anybody what I say.* Agreed?"

I nodded.

"Nobody."

"Schrock?" I asked. "You want him to hear?"

"He already knows."

"Knows what, Aaron?" I said softly, a fear creeping through me.

"He didn't want me to tell you."

"Tell me what, Aaron?"

"Lily had *my* baby."

I gasped, looked hard at his face. "Annabelle, Talitha, was *your* child?"

"Is, Cora. *Is.*" His eyes on my face, his words fell brutally harsh. "And there's more."

"And you were with Lily when she died?" I whispered.

"There's more," he repeated.

I crossed my arms, held them tight against my chest.

"I saw Lily the night she died." His words spit out terse, abrupt.

I reached to grab his arm, but he pushed me away, walked to the plot of broken earth, righted the plow, lifted the reins, slapped the horse, and ripped into a new row.

I turned to Schrock. "You *knew.*" The world was turning black, whirling my head.

He nodded, put his hand on my elbow. "We need to go."

I yanked it away from him.

"Cora, we have to go." He grasped my arm and dragged me toward the car.

"I can't. I have to know more." I insisted, struggling, kicking against Schrock's imprisoning hold.

Face stoic, he pulled me to the car and pushed me into the passenger seat. Then he slammed the door, and I watched him stomp to the driver's side. He got in, sat and turned the key. A jolt hit my brain. He was Amish. He didn't know cars.

"You can't drive," I said.

"*Rumspringa* teaches an Amish boy a lot." He pushed hard on the gas, and we were fast out of there.

"Where are we going?" I asked.

"I know a place."

"I don't want to go to the place you know. I want to go back and make Aaron tell me more. I want to punch him. *Hard. Talitha. Talitha was his.*" I could feel tears gathering in my eyes. Not now, I thought. I needed to stay focused and work through this.

We drove down a twisting, narrow road, a mass of trees on either side. I tried to keep my mind empty. I couldn't, Aaron's words kept running through it They couldn't have been true. He lied. But Aaron didn't lie. He was the epitome of Amishness. Maybe, he was wrong thinking, or protecting. Of course. It was Schrock. Schrock who was Talitha's father, and Aaron was protecting him. And because Schrock knew Aaron would break and tell me, he stuck around Aaron and wouldn't let me get near him. It explained the nastiness Schrock threw at me. He had to keep me away from Aaron. That was better. Though devastated, it was easier to accept Schrock had impregnated Lily, than my older and former boyfriend had.

But still, I wanted answers. Schrock's confession . . . I wanted to know about Lily.

"*You* were the father," I blurted wanting it to be true.

"No, Cora, I wasn't. I'm not. Talitha is not my child."

We went a bit farther. Him, probably thinking of excuses, quiet. Me, satisfied I'd determined the proper culprit, fuming. Schrock. He was the father. It had to be Schrock.

We reached the end of the dirt path. He turned off the car and pointed.

"In there."

A thick woods. I shuddered. Alone with Schrock? No choice. I got out the car and followed him.

Chapter Fifty-Two

We moved into the woods and tramped a sodden-leafed, earth-damp path. A dank, musty odor slid through the air. I shivered and wrapped my arms around myself.

"Cold?" Schrock asked. "I saw a jacket back in the car."

I shook my head. "I'm fine."

After a bit, he stopped and pushed into the trees.

"Just follow close. I'll bend the branches for you." He spread his arms and stretched a space to get through. "Stay close, so the limbs won't hit your face."

It was only a short distance to a small, shadowed clearing. Leaning against a tree were a couple beat-up aluminum chairs, and near the edge of the clearing was a chunk of chopped off tree trunk. In front of it were signs of a recent campfire.

"This is your place," I observed. "Where you get away."

"Mattie has the cemetery. I have this." He pulled a chair from the tree, unfolded it, motioned me to sit. "It's safe. It'll hold you." He sat on the trunk.

"Why are we here?" I asked. I needed to know. All of it. Fear weakened. I wanted no part of it. I willed it away.

"To deliberate. Understand. It's where I come to think out

hard thoughts. Hard situations." He paused. "Settle them."

"Did you rape Lily?" I looked straight into his eyes. "Did you?"

"No."

"She was just a baby herself." I squirmed in the chair. It was not comfortable. "When she got pregnant. Just a baby . . . the first time. Sixteen. Innocent."

"Not a baby when she died. Twenty-one, she was. Same as me." Again, Schrock paused.

"Twelve years younger than Aaron."

"*You* took her home from the Sings. When she was young. And later. Still single. Still going to the Sings." Resolve stopped the tremble in my lips. "Violet told me."

"Sometimes, I did." He bit his lip. "Did she tell you; Aaron did too?"

I didn't answer.

"I don't think they meant for anything to happen. Aaron and Lily." He bent and clasped his knees. "But it did. And both of them have paid dearly for that sin."

"Aaron's alive." I glared at him. *"And so are you."*

Eyes focused on the ground, he shook his head. "It wasn't me. You'd like it to have been. But it wasn't." He rubbed the side of his nose, shrugged. "I would have liked it to have been me, but it was Aaron she favored."

I bent my head, raised my hands, and covered my eyes for a moment, listened to his words.

"Aaron wanted to tell you. Thought after all these years, you should know truth. Yet, he thought, on the other hand, it would be cruel to you, mean, to reveal their disloyalty. His and Lily's coupling. To you. It was like he felt he'd betrayed you. He came close to it once, telling you, but he didn't. Mostly when I wasn't there, he just tried to stay away from you. Can't you see, it wasn't Aaron I was trying to protect." He lifted his head. "It was you. I wanted you to hate me enough to stay away from Aaron."

"Why?"

"I thought it would break you if you knew."

I clenched my teeth. "Do I look broken?"

He grinned. "A little angry." He lifted his eyebrows. "Indignant?"

I ignored his arrogantly conclusive remarks. "He said he was with Lily when she died."

"Not *when,* but before," he corrected.

"Was he the reason," I swallowed, "she drowned?"

"I don't think so. Jacob Lapp found her. He saw her clothes and a water jar on the creekbank, so he figured she was taking a swim before dark, maybe later was going to take water out to the field hands. But he figured he'd better check to be sure."

"Probably wanted to see her naked," I said, frowning, "even knowing she would have on her underclothes."

"That, too." Schrock smiled. "Anyway, that's how she was found."

"Why did they say it was suicide?"

"The whole community knew she was unstable. Everybody was aware of her erratic behavior . . . ." He stopped. "That could have been enough."

"I don't think so," I said. "What else?"

"She was with child." His words were blunt and quickly said.

I drew in my breath. "No, she wasn't. She couldn't have been." I clenched my hands into tight fists. "And how could they know?"

"Word can travel fast in the Amish world." He looked hard at me. "You know that. One person makes a guess, verifies it, the tongue slips, everyone knows. Not unkindly intended, but told for Amish prayer and help for those most pained."

"The baby?" Eyes pleading, I looked back at him.

He said nothing.

"Aaron's?" I said softly.

"Aaron's."

"You're sure?" "Yes."

"A second child." A thought shot quickly through my mind. *They should have been mine.*

"Yes."

"Did anyone know it was Aaron's?"

"There were suspicions."

"I've talked with many of the Amish women. Questioned them about Lily. Her last days. Not one said anything about pregnancy. *Not one.*"

"They wouldn't, Cora. She's dead. Why smear her reputation further?"

"They buried her outside the cemetery."

"Yes."

"But they knew. They *knew.*" I leaned toward him. I didn't understand. "I asked. But they didn't tell me."

"Yeah, they knew." He shook his head. Smiled ruefully. "But, you're not true Amish, not anymore. In their minds, yes. In their hearts, not quite." He looked into my eyes. "And their hearts wouldn't betray Lily. Not to an outsider." He paused. "Almost an outsider."

"So that was her sin. Unsanctioned love. A baby conceived outside the boundaries of marriage." I bit my lip. Hard. "They should have told me."

Schrock shrugged. "Maybe."

"And why wasn't Aaron shunned? His was the greater sin . . . an older man damaging a young girl.

"She was twenty-one, Cora. Not so young." He picked up a twig, pulled its bark. "And no one absolutely *knows* either baby was Aaron's. Not even Violet."

"I hope not." I sighed, then barely able to let the words out, "Do you think he killed her?"

"No."

"He was there. Admitted he was there." I was pleading. "Maybe he pushed her. Maybe he pushed her and walked away. Didn't know she fell in the water. An accident. He wouldn't hurt her . . . I don't think he would hurt her." I swallowed, bit my lip. "Would he? *Would he?*"

"Do you really think Aaron would put his hands on her in anger? I probably would. Might. Regretfully, I might have done so. But not Aaron. No matter what."

"Do you think she drowned herself on purpose?" I leaned toward him, willed him to say,

"No."

He didn't. He sat stone-faced, unreadable, and finally, shook his head and spoke. "I don't know."

I looked down at my hands. Helpless. Not there to pull Lily from the water. Not there to put Annabelle in her arms. Not there to comfort her when the baby was gone, to wipe her tears, to tell her I would take her sorrow and make her better. Not there to help her say 'no' to Aaron. "We won't ever know, will we?" I said sadly.

"No, we won't." He stood. "Come on. It's time to go." He

walked to the edge of the clearing and parted the limbs for us to walk through.

I drove him back to his farm. There were no words spoken in the car. Before he got out, he looked at me for a long time, then he reached and touched my arm, patted it, and nodded. I nodded back.

He got out, and I drove away.

Chapter Fifty-Three

It was done. There would be no more answers for me.

Depleted, I drove the Amish roads I'd loved so much in the days I'd walked in white *kapp* and full, dark skirt with hands holding a child, my baby sisters, on either side of me.

Violet and Lily. So innocent and so happy. The sun shone clear and bright above me dropping glittering rays on changing leaves, throwing shadows of limbs slowly baring, making space for snow to gather and outline them with white. A changing time. A slash of lush, colorful fall making way for the cold and pristine spread of snow, over winter woods. Beautiful. Each season unique.

I passed the cemetery. I neither stopped nor looked. Lily wasn't there. Only bones lay in that hole. Next to the grave that held a plastic doll. Both of us, Mattie and me, had looked in the wrong place for comfort and reason. Neither were there. Hearts and memories were their graves, and the joy of remembrance their flowers. And I could choose the memories I wished to keep.

I stopped at the place I'd stood with the Baby Annabelle the night I gave her away and had looked down over lamplit Wander Lane, knowing when I'd reach there, I would give her up to a better life where there would be no sin painted forever over her mother's persona. And the grief, like then, overwhelmed me. I bent my head and sought God. I waited. And He came. And the forgiveness I had sought, but not accepted for so long, flowed over and into me. He knew. He knew and He forgave me. A quiet and deep wonderful joy settled within my soul. And I accepted.

Almighty God . . . Father, Son and Holy Spirit.

I lift my heart to You, my soul, my body. With gratefulness. With love. I've walked a tumultuous, uncertain path these past months in a sealed Amish world. Thank you for never leaving me during that time, for allowing the struggle through the disabling thoughts and happenings to renew the knowing of my need for You, and to acknowledge my strength without Yours is paltry and ineffective, but grows through seeking Your presence, heeding Your direction, and absorbing Your love.

Most precious God, I humbly accept Your forgiveness and offer myself to You.

In Jesus' name, Amen.

I went back to the motel and packed. I filled my car with all I needed. I took no Amish mementos.

Before I drove out of Wander Lane, I stopped at the village office building, walked around to the back of it, and opened the door to Sheriff Lowell Parker's rooms.

Tilly was at her desk.

"It's late. You should be home eating dinner with husband and kids," I said.

She looked up and smiled.

"There are days when Sheriff Parker has no clock."

"Is he in?" I asked.

"Yes." She tilted her head and frowned. "But probably grouchy," She shook her head.

"Very grouchy."

"I'll chance it." I smiled and went around her desk, touched her shoulder. "Thank you. You've been a friend."

She looked up, aware. "You're going, aren't you? Back up north."

I nodded, and she stood and hugged me. We shared teary eyes and a knowing our friendship was good.

"Write," she said.

"You, too."

One last, squeezing hug, and I turned, and walked down the hall to Lowell's office. I didn't knock. I went quietly through the door. He was sitting at his desk, unaware. I looked at him a long time, until, finally, he sensed my presence and looked up. "Cora."

"It's done," I said.

He heard it in my voice. I could tell. There was a knowing that flashed over his face.

"You're going home," he said.

"It's done," I repeated.

"You're sure?"

"I'm sure."

He said nothing. I couldn't read his face. It hinted disappointment, sadness. But I wasn't sure.

"I have to go. I just wanted to say thank you."

He grunted. "For what?"

I smiled. "I think you know."

He dropped his eyes to his desk, then looked up.

"You got enough answers?"

I nodded.

"And you're satisfied?"

"Yes," I whispered.

His eyes rose. He looked at me a long time. Said nothing.

I put my hand on the doorknob, made ready to go. Then I turned, looked at him. "When you retire, come look me up."

He grinned. "I just might do that."

Acclaim for Dottie Rexford's books:

Praise For
MAY SNOW

"a wonderful sense of the loneliness, the friendships, the memories and dreams, the dichotomy between an old body and an ever-young consciousness—all those things that are the mixed blessing of not dying young."

WilliamTapply
Author of the *Brady Coyne Mystery Series*

Praise For
SONGS IN THE NIGHT

". . . author's sensory realism makes an already solid structure amazing, ad THEN you mix in a beautiful writing voice."

Judge, *Writer's Digest*

Praise For
CORA POOLER

"Rexford captures the longings and emotions of those who seek deep and rich relationships, all the who doubt and seek answers and all who seek to be whole."

Dunkirk Observer

"Rexford is a gifted writer. Her descriptive abilities bring the reader fully into the sensory elements of a scene. This is a book readers will wish to retain on their bookshelves for it is filled with gorgeous writing,"

Writer's Digest